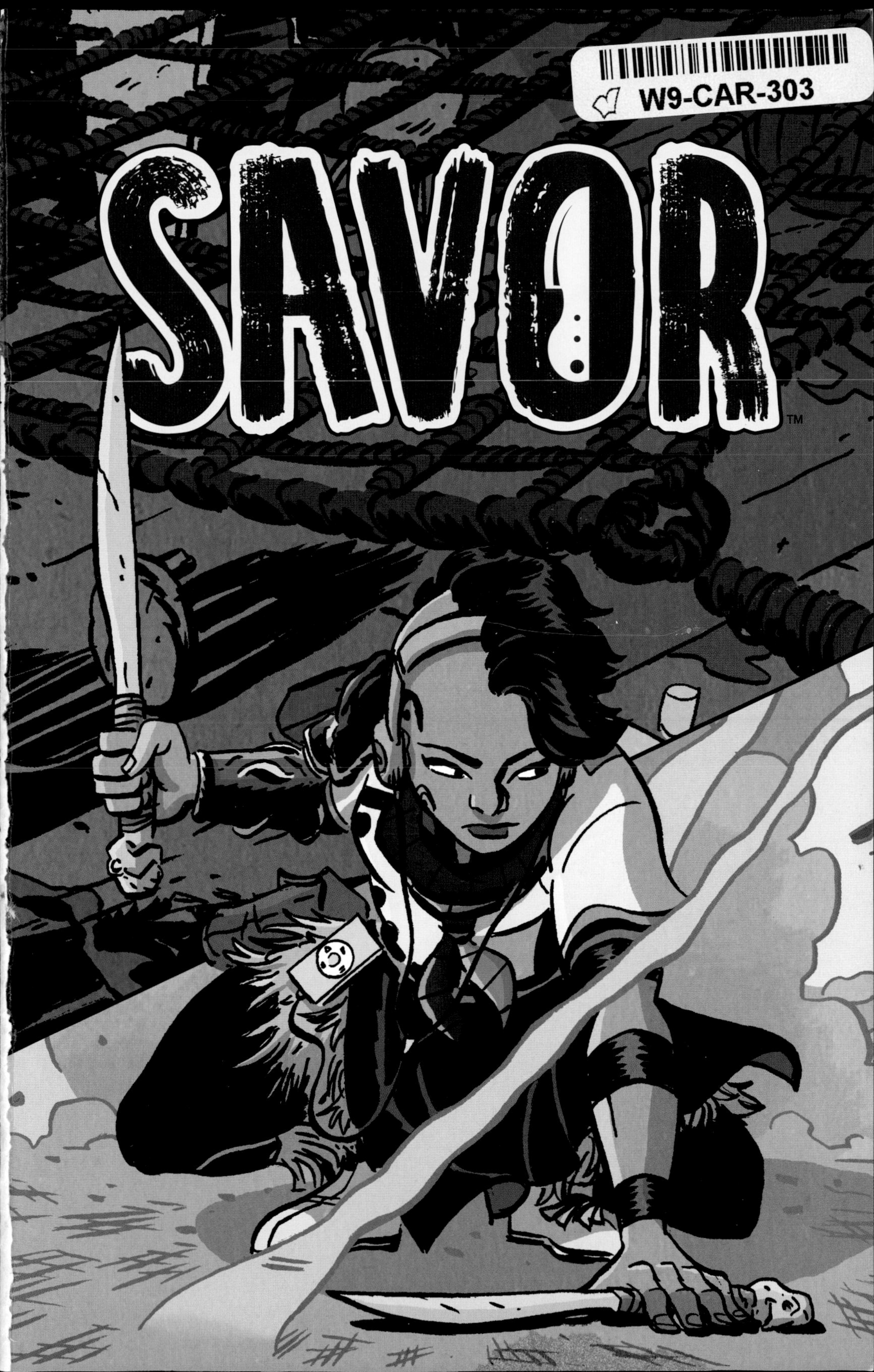
SAVOR™

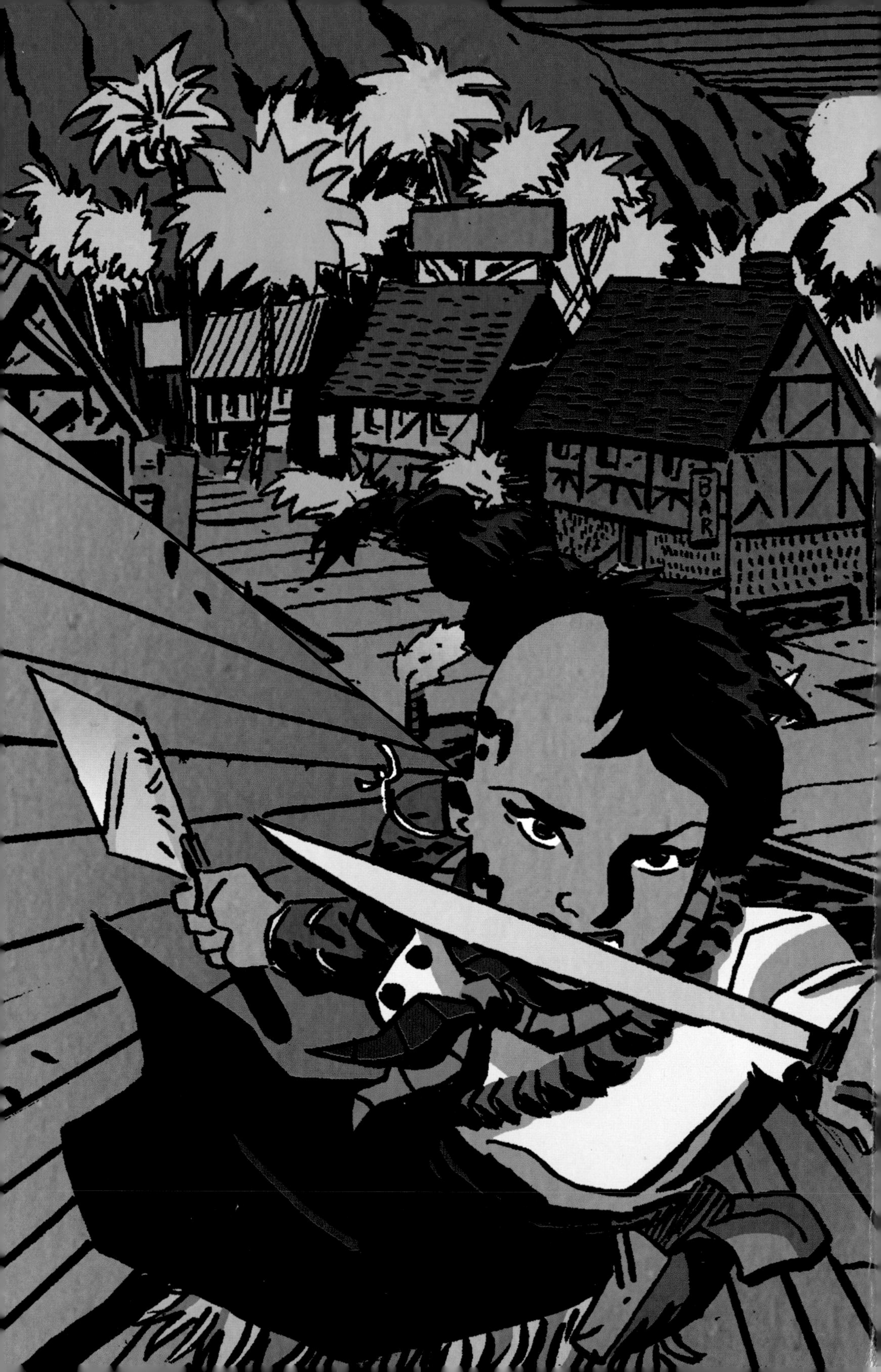
BAR

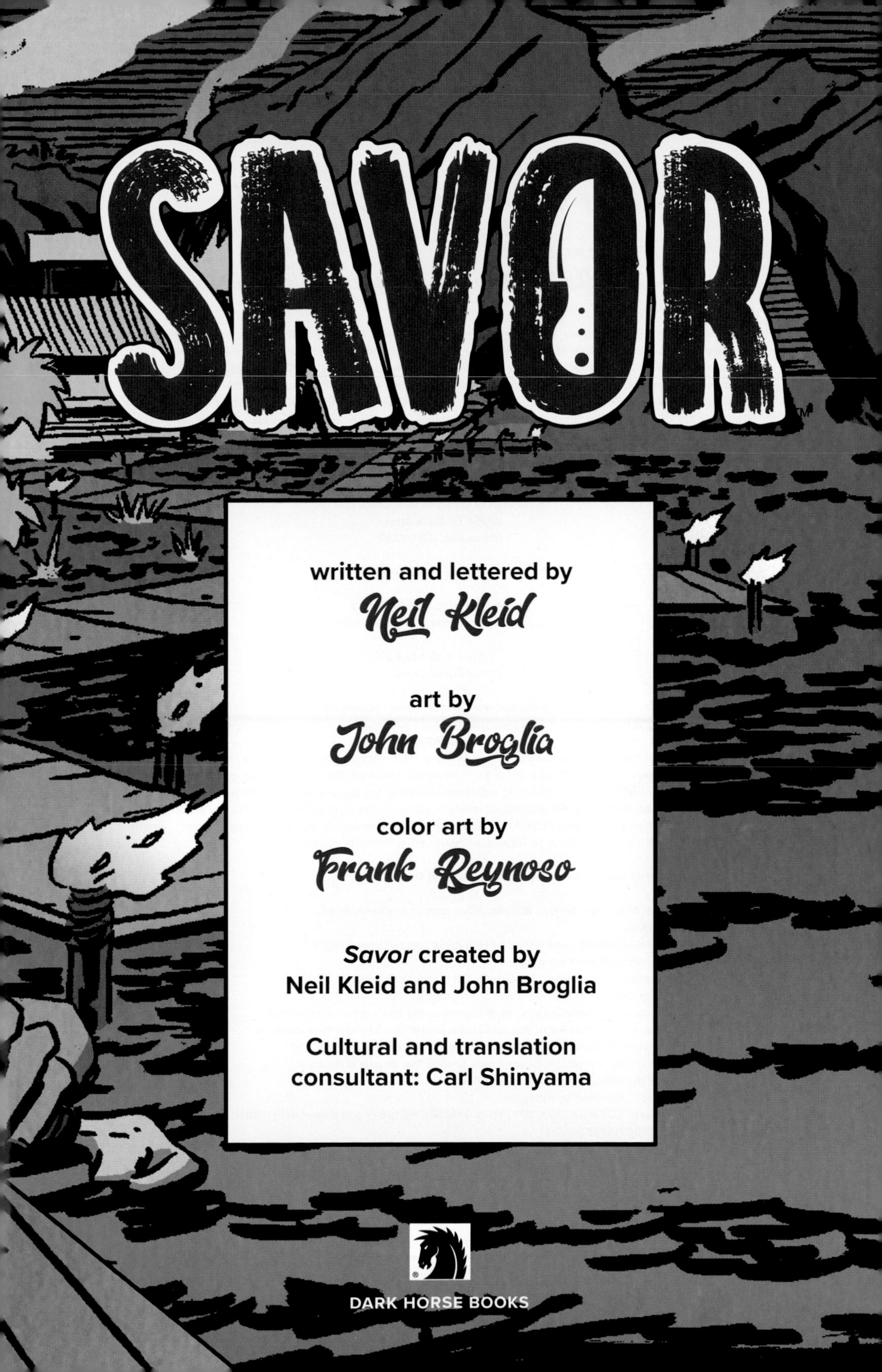

SAVOR™

written and lettered by
Neil Kleid

art by
John Broglia

color art by
Frank Reynoso

Savor created by
Neil Kleid and John Broglia

Cultural and translation
consultant: Carl Shinyama

DARK HORSE BOOKS

president and publisher
Mike Richardson

editor
Brett Israel

digital art technician
Josie Christensen

collection designer
Skyler Weissenfluh

Neil Hankerson Executive Vice President • **Tom Weddle** Chief Financial Officer • **Randy Stradley** Vice President of Publishing • **Nick McWhorter** Chief Business Development Officer • **Dale LaFountain** Chief Information Officer • **Matt Parkinson** Vice President of Marketing • **Vanessa Todd-Holmes** Vice President of Production and Scheduling • **Mark Bernardi** Vice President of Book Trade and Digital Sales • **Ken Lizzi** General Counsel • **Dave Marshall** Editor in Chief • **Davey Estrada** Editorial Director **Chris Warner** Senior Books Editor • **Cary Grazzini** Director of Specialty Projects • **Lia Ribacchi** Art Director • **Matt Dryer** Director of Digital Art and Prepress • **Michael Gombos** Senior Director of Licensed Publications • **Kari Yadro** Director of Custom Programs • **Kari Torson** Director of International Licensing • **Sean Brice** Director of Trade Sales

Published by Dark Horse Books
A division of Dark Horse Comics LLC
10956 SE Main Street
Milwaukie, OR 97222

First edition: January 2021

Ebook ISBN 978-1-50671-519-3
Trade paperback ISBN 978-1-50671-518-6

1 3 5 7 9 10 8 6 4 2
Printed in China

Comic Shop Locator Service: comicshoplocator.com

Library of Congress Cataloging-in-Publication Data

Names: Kleid, Neil, writer. | Broglia, John, artist. | Reynoso, Frank,
   colourist.
Title: Savor / written and letters by Neil Kleid ; art by John Broglia ;
   color art by Frank Reynoso.
Description: First edition. | Milwaukie, OR : Dark Horse Books, 2020. |
   "Savor created by Neil Kleid and John Broglia" | Audience: Ages 10+ |
   Summary: "Discovering a band of demon cooks has captured her island
   home, warrior chef Savor Batonnet must undertake her very first quest as
   a newly minted hero! But are being called a "hero" and a handful of
   skills all the ingredients Savor needs to face five deadly restaurants,
   build the ultimate knife, save both her parents and the woman she
   loves?"-- Provided by publisher.
Identifiers: LCCN 2020007277 | ISBN 9781506715186 (trade paperback) | ISBN
   9781506715193 (epub)
Subjects: LCSH: Graphic novels. | CYAC: Graphic novels. | Heroes--Fiction.
   | Cooks--Fiction. | Quests (Expeditions)--Fiction.
Classification: LCC PZ7.7.K598 Sav 2020 | DDC 741.5/973--dc23
LC record available at https://lccn.loc.gov/2020007277

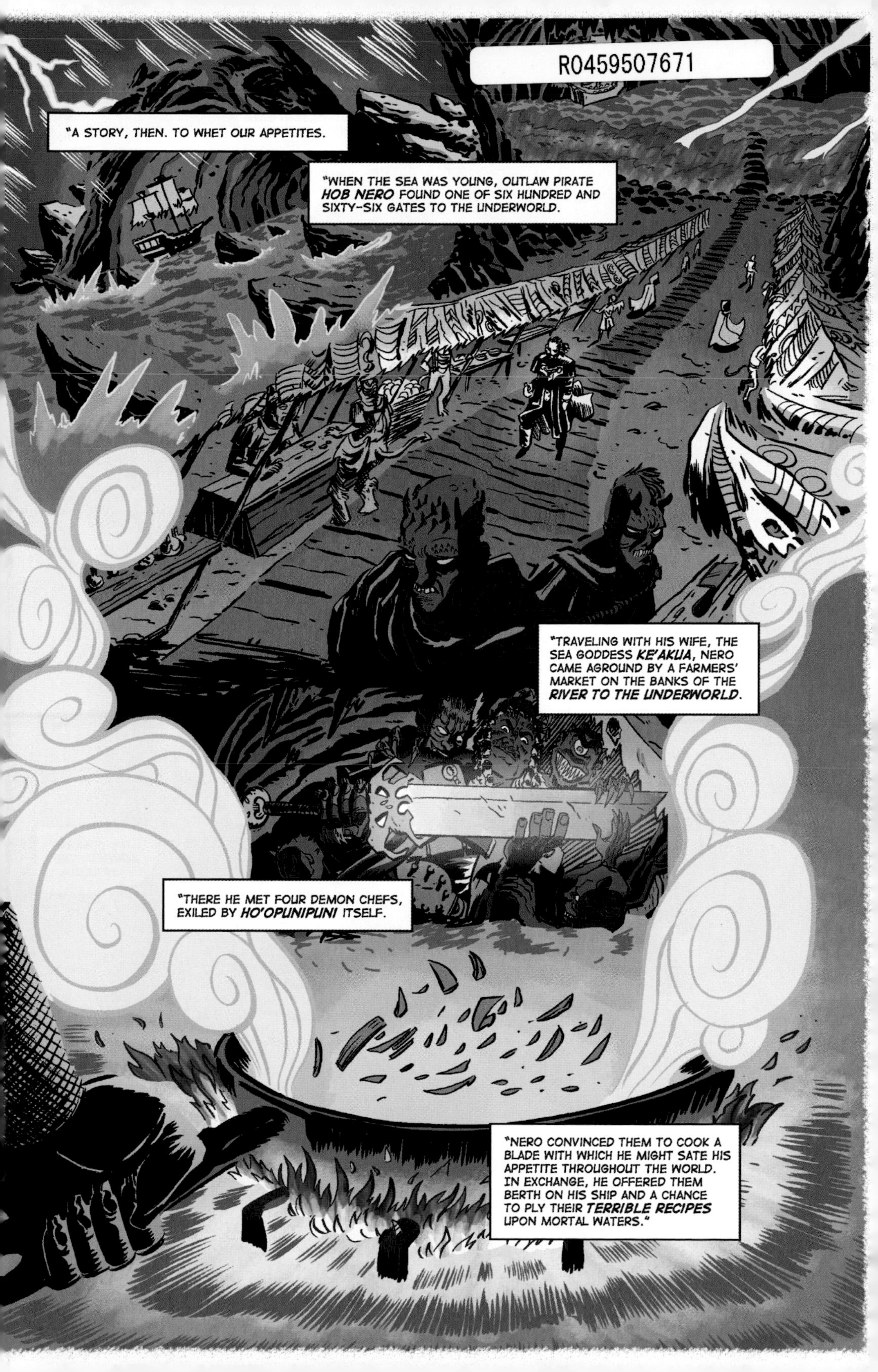
R0459507671
"A STORY, THEN. TO WHET OUR APPETITES.
"WHEN THE SEA WAS YOUNG, OUTLAW PIRATE HOB NERO FOUND ONE OF SIX HUNDRED AND SIXTY-SIX GATES TO THE UNDERWORLD.
"TRAVELING WITH HIS WIFE, THE SEA GODDESS KE'AKUA, NERO CAME AGROUND BY A FARMERS' MARKET ON THE BANKS OF THE RIVER TO THE UNDERWORLD.
"THERE HE MET FOUR DEMON CHEFS, EXILED BY HO'OPUNIPUNI ITSELF.
"NERO CONVINCED THEM TO COOK A BLADE WITH WHICH HE MIGHT SATE HIS APPETITE THROUGHOUT THE WORLD. IN EXCHANGE, HE OFFERED THEM BERTH ON HIS SHIP AND A CHANCE TO PLY THEIR TERRIBLE RECIPES UPON MORTAL WATERS."

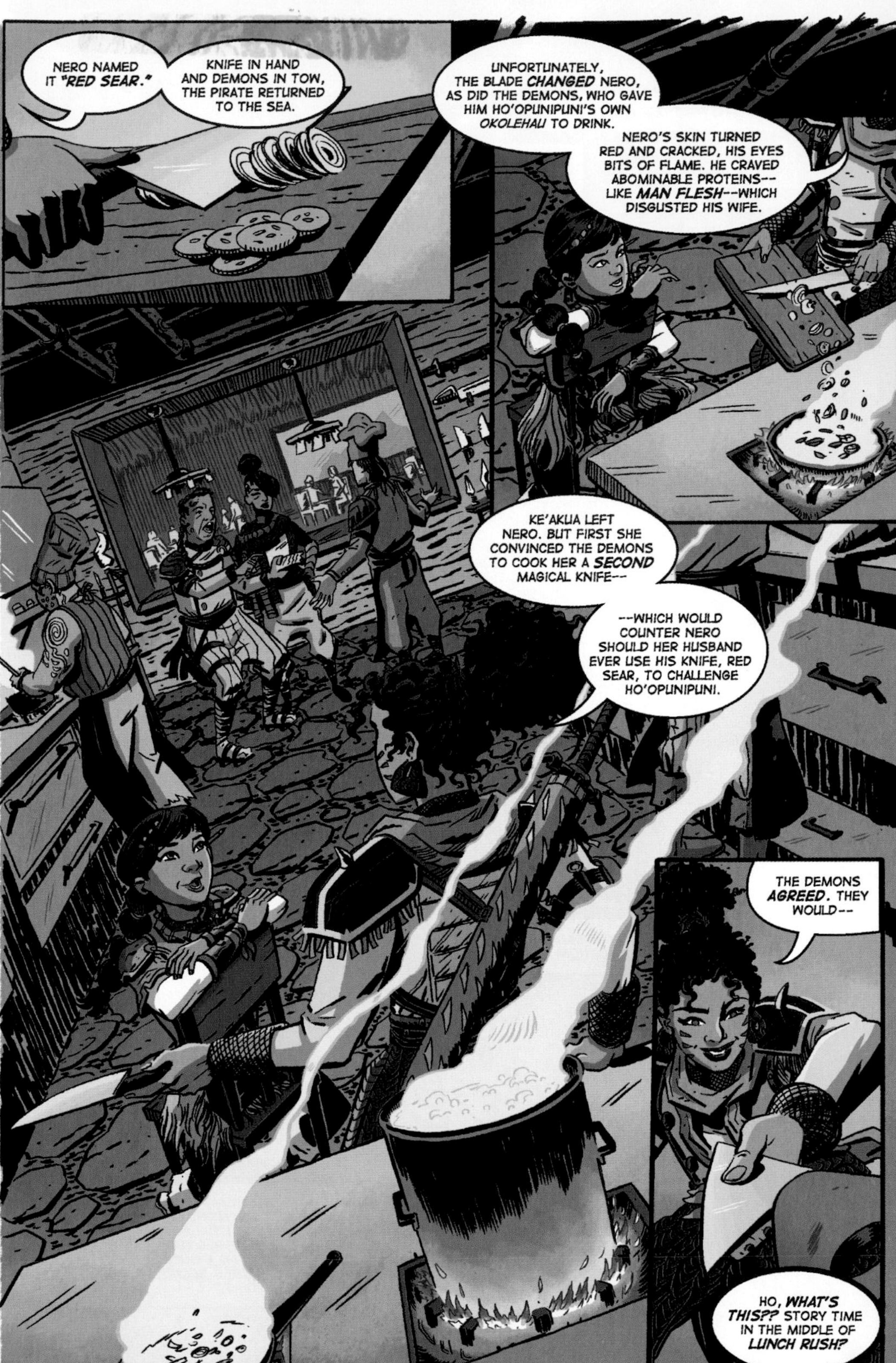
NERO NAMED IT "RED SEAR."
KNIFE IN HAND AND DEMONS IN TOW, THE PIRATE RETURNED TO THE SEA.
UNFORTUNATELY, THE BLADE CHANGED NERO, AS DID THE DEMONS, WHO GAVE HIM HO'OPUNIPUNI'S OWN OKOLEHAU TO DRINK.
NERO'S SKIN TURNED RED AND CRACKED, HIS EYES BITS OF FLAME. HE CRAVED ABOMINABLE PROTEINS--LIKE MAN FLESH--WHICH DISGUSTED HIS WIFE.
KE'AKUA LEFT NERO. BUT FIRST SHE CONVINCED THE DEMONS TO COOK HER A SECOND MAGICAL KNIFE--
--WHICH WOULD COUNTER NERO SHOULD HER HUSBAND EVER USE HIS KNIFE, RED SEAR, TO CHALLENGE HO'OPUNIPUNI.
THE DEMONS AGREED. THEY WOULD--
HO, WHAT'S THIS?? STORY TIME IN THE MIDDLE OF LUNCH RUSH?

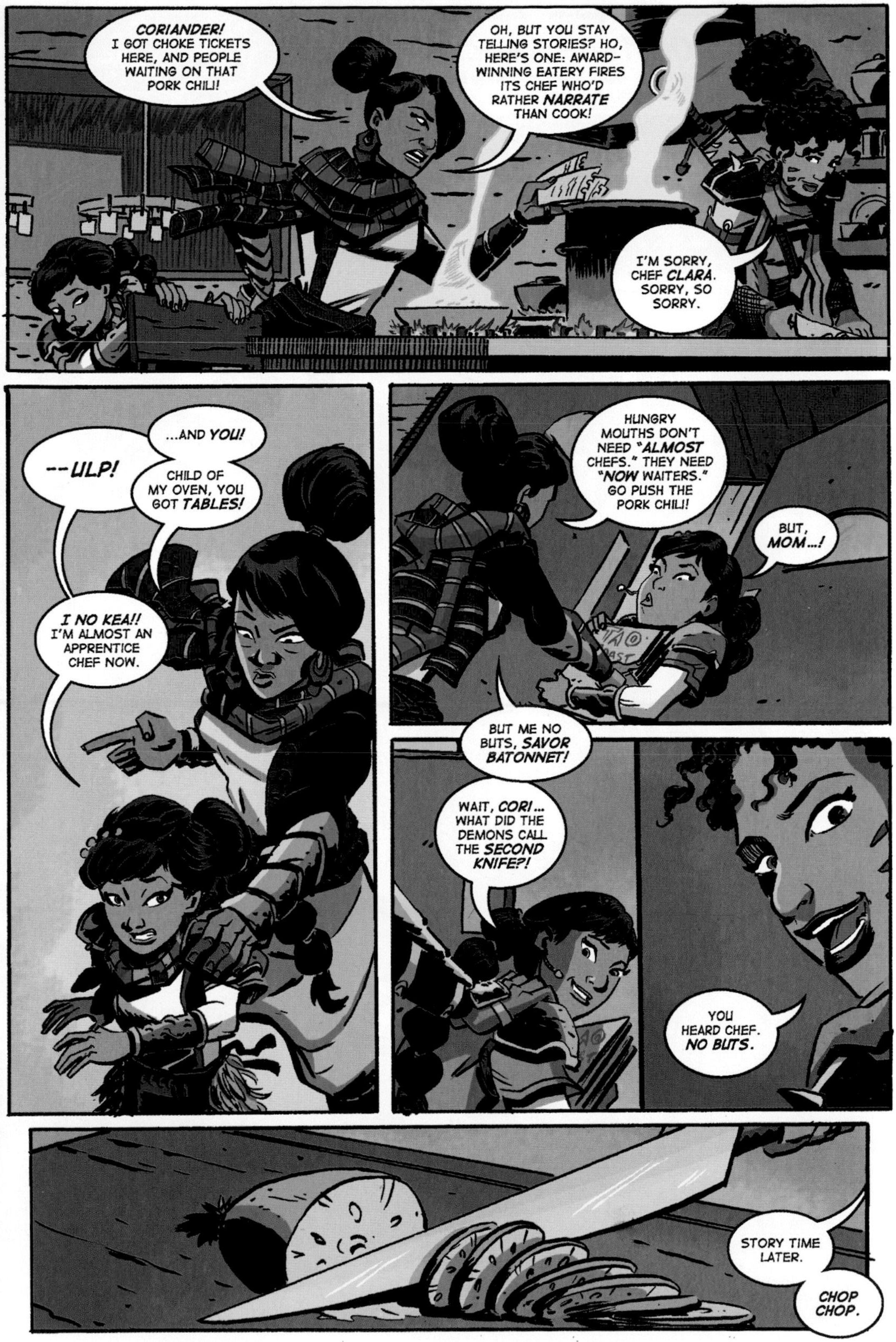
CORIANDER! I GOT CHOKE TICKETS HERE, AND PEOPLE WAITING ON THAT PORK CHILI!
OH, BUT YOU STAY TELLING STORIES? HO, HERE'S ONE: AWARD-WINNING EATERY FIRES ITS CHEF WHO'D RATHER NARRATE THAN COOK!
I'M SORRY, CHEF CLARA. SORRY, SO SORRY.
...AND YOU!
CHILD OF MY OVEN, YOU GOT TABLES!
--ULP!
I NO KEA!! I'M ALMOST AN APPRENTICE CHEF NOW.
HUNGRY MOUTHS DON'T NEED "ALMOST CHEFS." THEY NEED "NOW WAITERS." GO PUSH THE PORK CHILI!
BUT, MOM...!
BUT ME NO BUTS, SAVOR BATONNET!
WAIT, CORI... WHAT DID THE DEMONS CALL THE SECOND KNIFE?!
YOU HEARD CHEF. NO BUTS.
STORY TIME LATER.
CHOP CHOP.

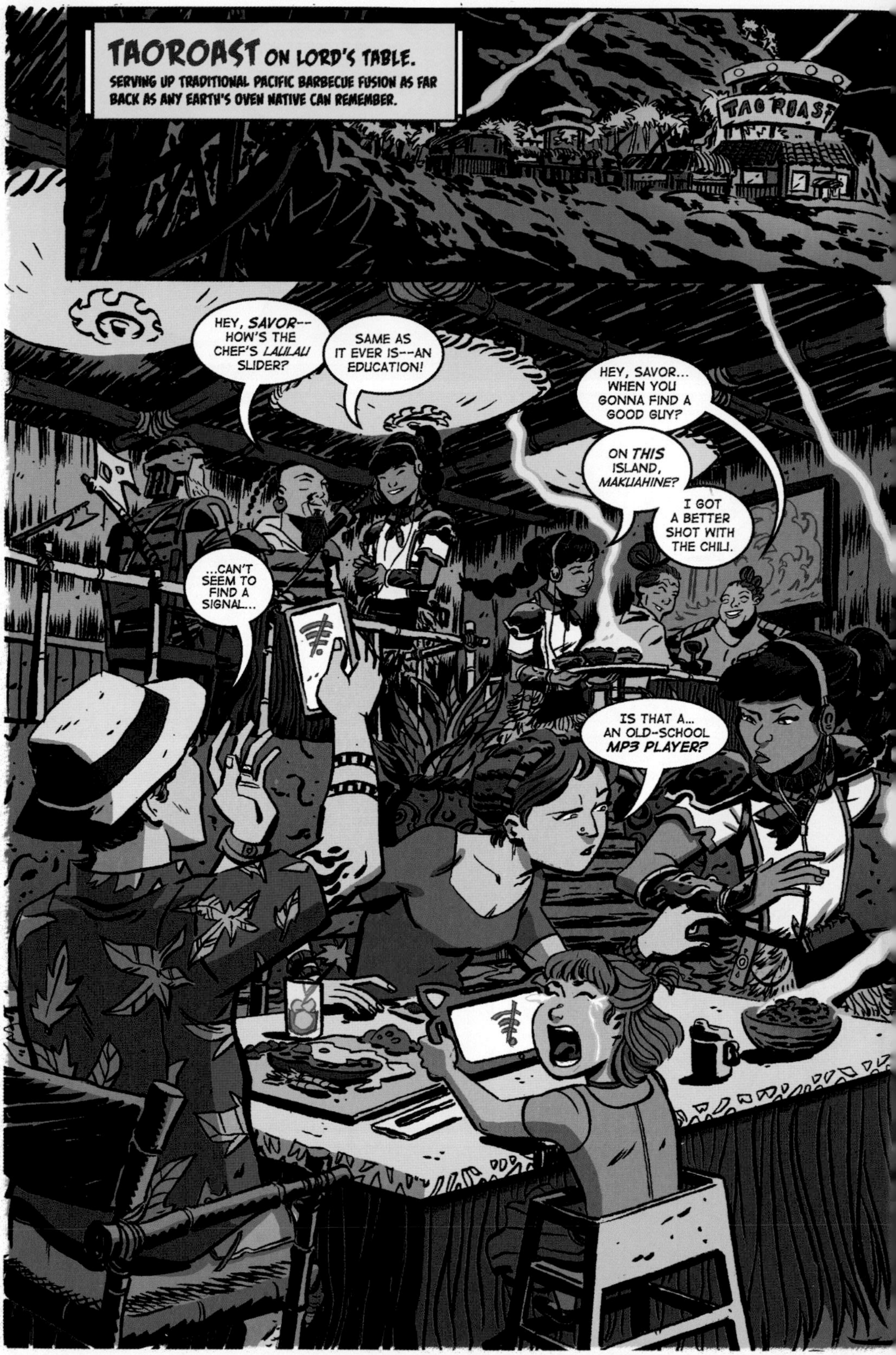
TAOROAST ON LORD'S TABLE.
SERVING UP TRADITIONAL PACIFIC BARBECUE FUSION AS FAR BACK AS ANY EARTH'S OVEN NATIVE CAN REMEMBER.
TAO ROAST
HEY, SAVOR-- HOW'S THE CHEF'S LAULAU SLIDER?
SAME AS IT EVER IS--AN EDUCATION!
HEY, SAVOR... WHEN YOU GONNA FIND A GOOD GUY?
ON THIS ISLAND, MAKUAHINE?
I GOT A BETTER SHOT WITH THE CHILI.
...CAN'T SEEM TO FIND A SIGNAL...
IS THAT A... AN OLD-SCHOOL MP3 PLAYER?

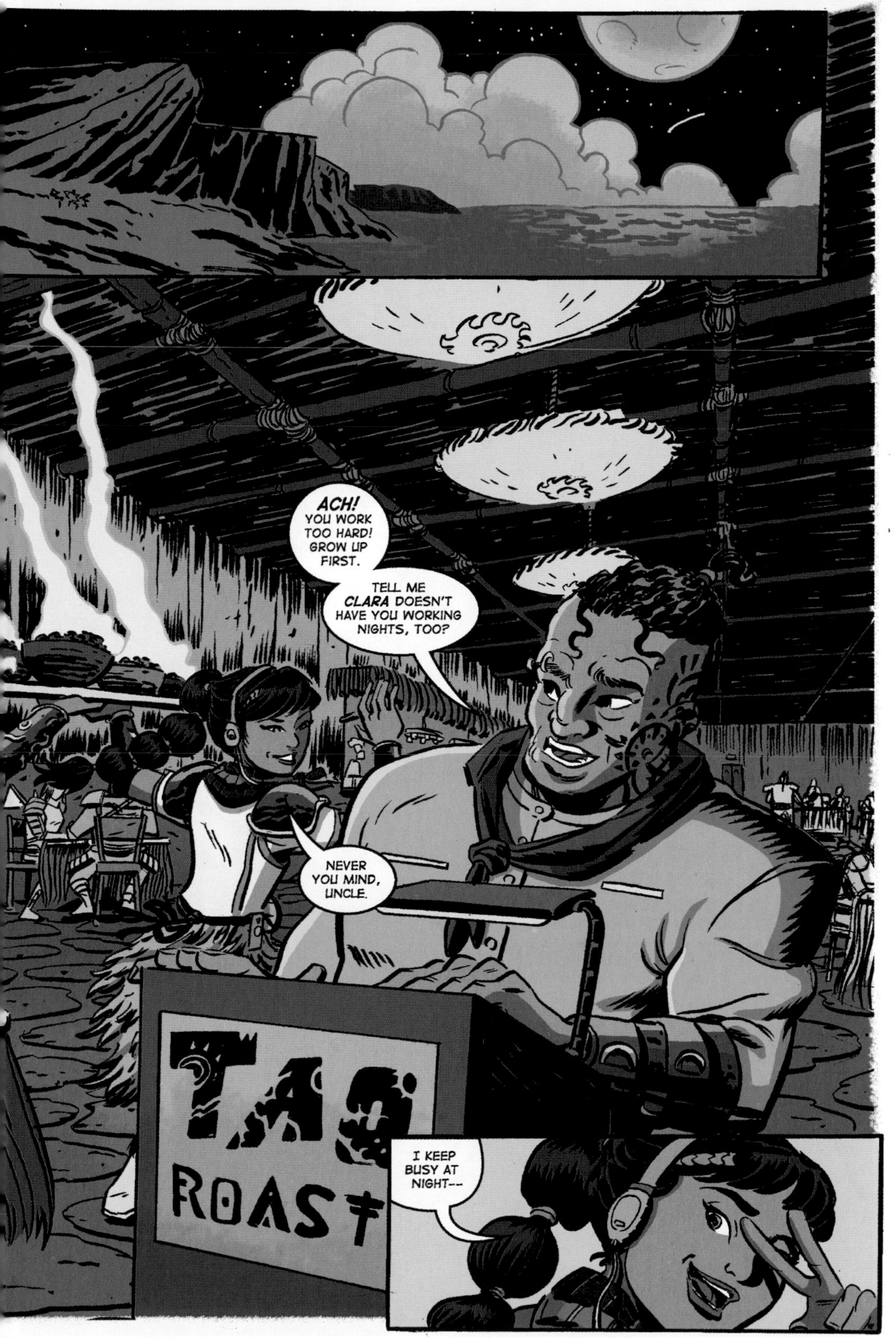
ACH! YOU WORK TOO HARD! GROW UP FIRST.
TELL ME CLARA DOESN'T HAVE YOU WORKING NIGHTS, TOO?
NEVER YOU MIND, UNCLE.
ROAST
I KEEP BUSY AT NIGHT--

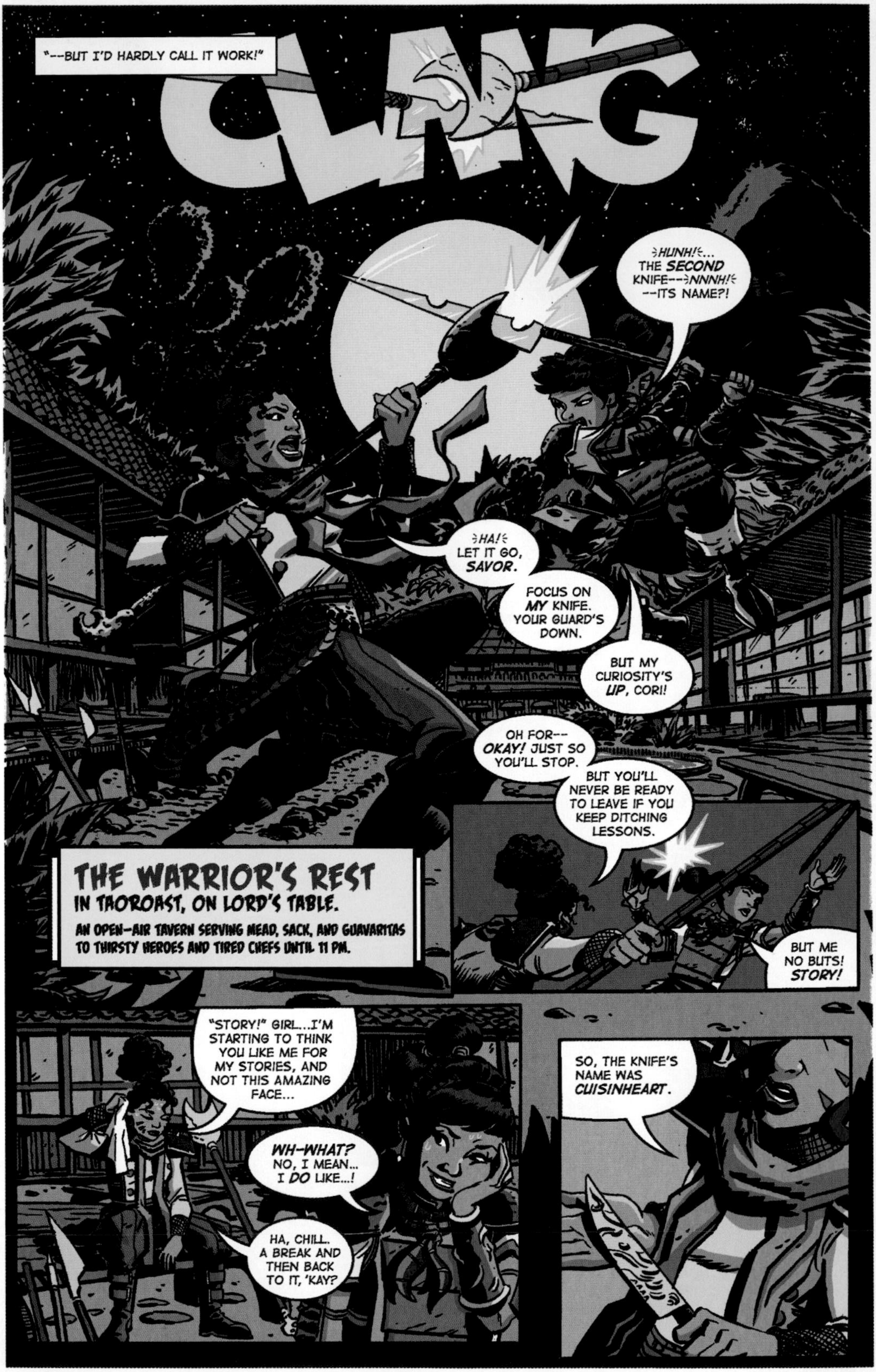
"--BUT I'D HARDLY CALL IT WORK!"
CLANG
HUNH!... THE SECOND KNIFE--NNNH! --ITS NAME?!
HA! LET IT GO, SAVOR.
FOCUS ON MY KNIFE. YOUR GUARD'S DOWN.
BUT MY CURIOSITY'S UP, CORI!
OH FOR-- OKAY! JUST SO YOU'LL STOP.
BUT YOU'LL NEVER BE READY TO LEAVE IF YOU KEEP DITCHING LESSONS.
THE WARRIOR'S REST
IN TAOROAST, ON LORD'S TABLE.
AN OPEN-AIR TAVERN SERVING MEAD, SACK, AND GUAVARITAS TO THIRSTY HEROES AND TIRED CHEFS UNTIL 11 PM.
BUT ME NO BUTS! STORY!
"STORY!" GIRL...I'M STARTING TO THINK YOU LIKE ME FOR MY STORIES, AND NOT THIS AMAZING FACE...
WH-WHAT? NO, I MEAN... I DO LIKE...!
HA, CHILL. A BREAK AND THEN BACK TO IT, 'KAY?
SO, THE KNIFE'S NAME WAS CUISINHEART.

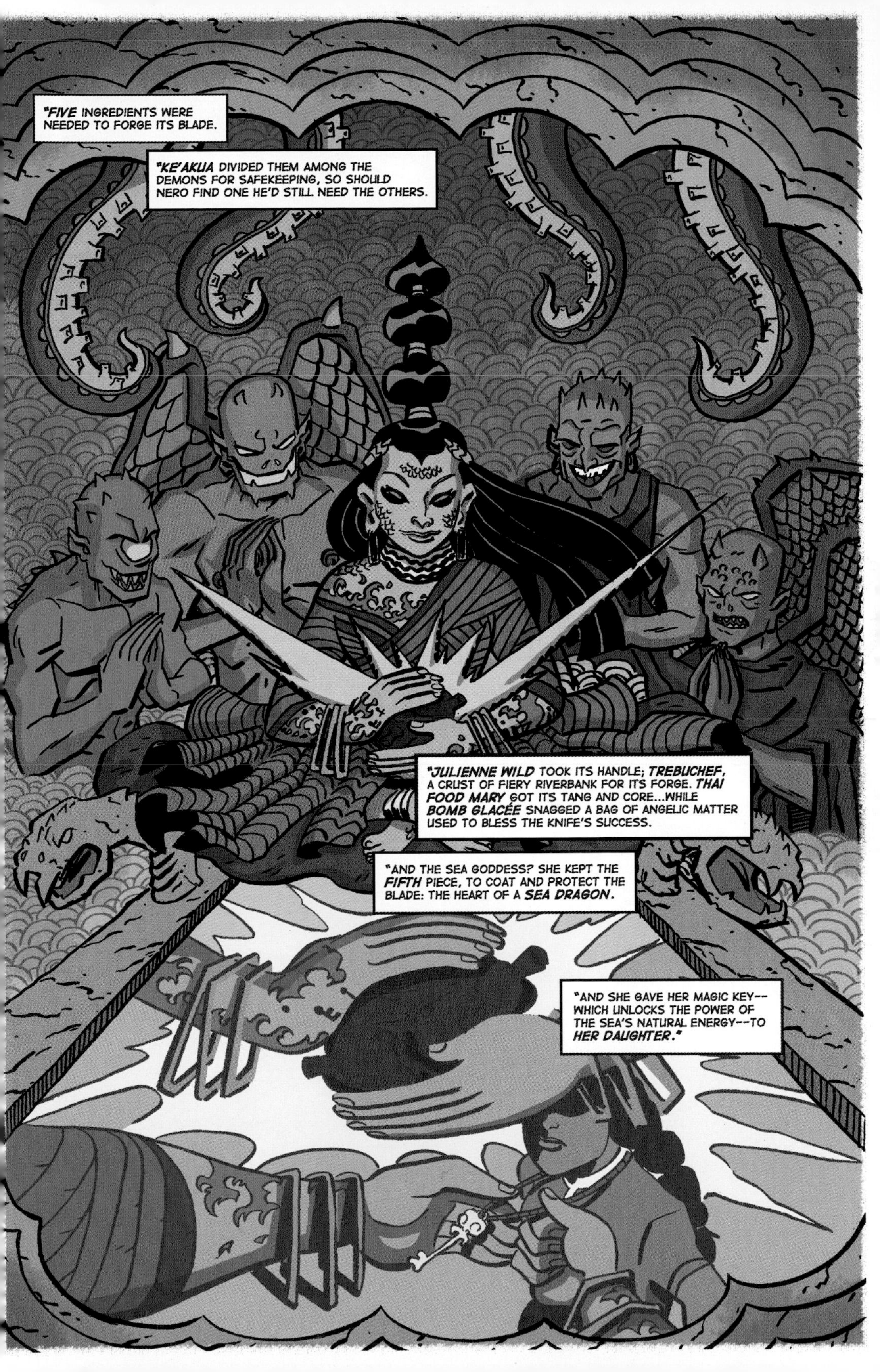
"FIVE INGREDIENTS WERE NEEDED TO FORGE ITS BLADE.
"KE'AKUA DIVIDED THEM AMONG THE DEMONS FOR SAFEKEEPING, SO SHOULD NERO FIND ONE HE'D STILL NEED THE OTHERS.
"JULIENNE WILD TOOK ITS HANDLE; TREBUCHEF, A CRUST OF FIERY RIVERBANK FOR ITS FORGE. THAI FOOD MARY GOT ITS TANG AND CORE...WHILE BOMB GLACÉE SNAGGED A BAG OF ANGELIC MATTER USED TO BLESS THE KNIFE'S SUCCESS.
"AND THE SEA GODDESS? SHE KEPT THE FIFTH PIECE, TO COAT AND PROTECT THE BLADE: THE HEART OF A SEA DRAGON.
"AND SHE GAVE HER MAGIC KEY--WHICH UNLOCKS THE POWER OF THE SEA'S NATURAL ENERGY--TO HER DAUGHTER."

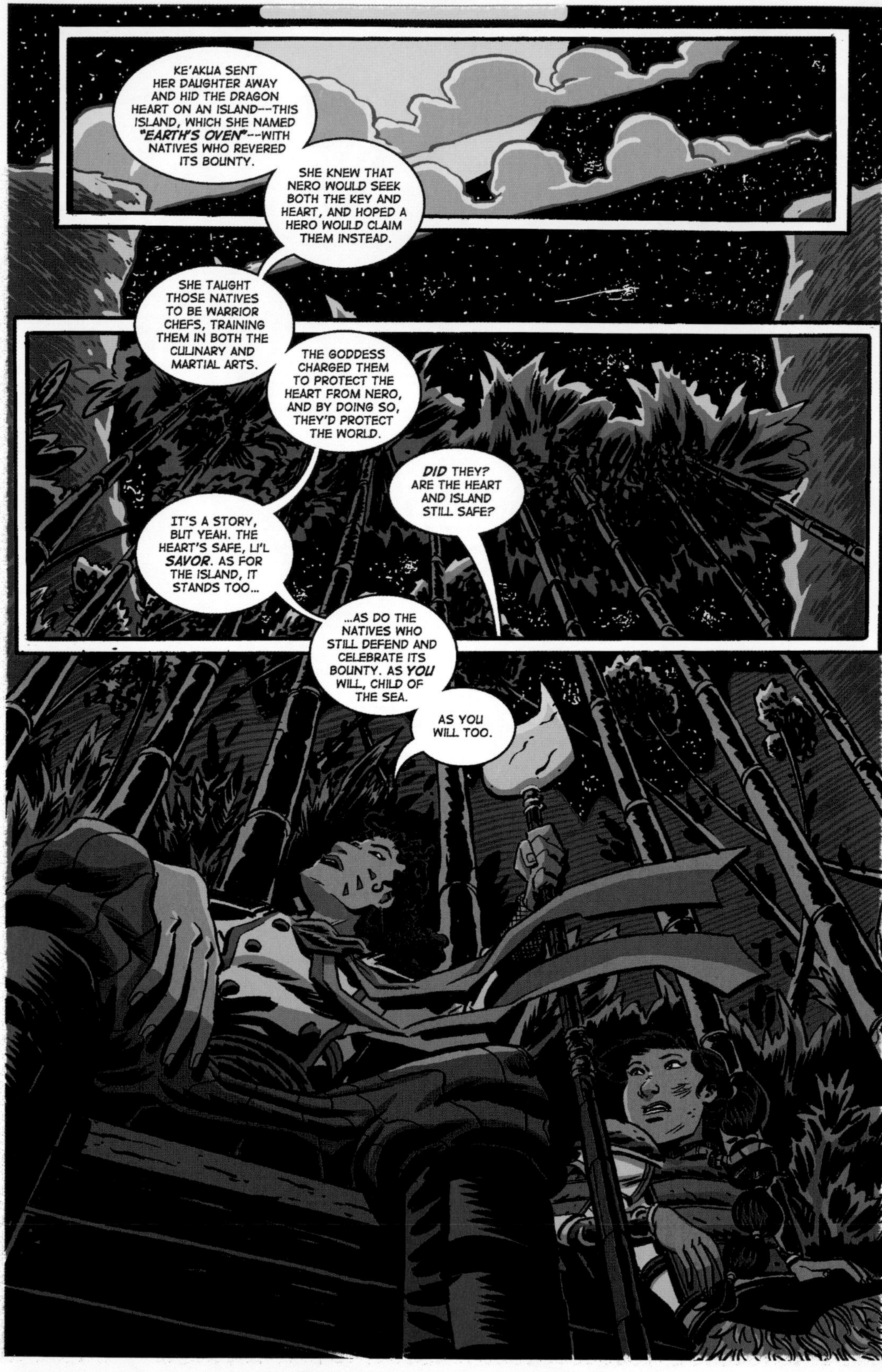
KE'AKUA SENT HER DAUGHTER AWAY AND HID THE DRAGON HEART ON AN ISLAND--THIS ISLAND, WHICH SHE NAMED *"EARTH'S OVEN"*--WITH NATIVES WHO REVERED ITS BOUNTY.
SHE KNEW THAT NERO WOULD SEEK BOTH THE KEY AND HEART, AND HOPED A HERO WOULD CLAIM THEM INSTEAD.
SHE TAUGHT THOSE NATIVES TO BE WARRIOR CHEFS, TRAINING THEM IN BOTH THE CULINARY AND MARTIAL ARTS.
THE GODDESS CHARGED THEM TO PROTECT THE HEART FROM NERO, AND BY DOING SO, THEY'D PROTECT THE WORLD.
DID THEY? ARE THE HEART AND ISLAND STILL SAFE?
IT'S A STORY, BUT YEAH. THE HEART'S SAFE, LI'L **SAVOR**. AS FOR THE ISLAND, IT STANDS TOO...
...AS DO THE NATIVES WHO STILL DEFEND AND CELEBRATE ITS BOUNTY. AS *YOU* WILL, CHILD OF THE SEA.
AS YOU WILL TOO.

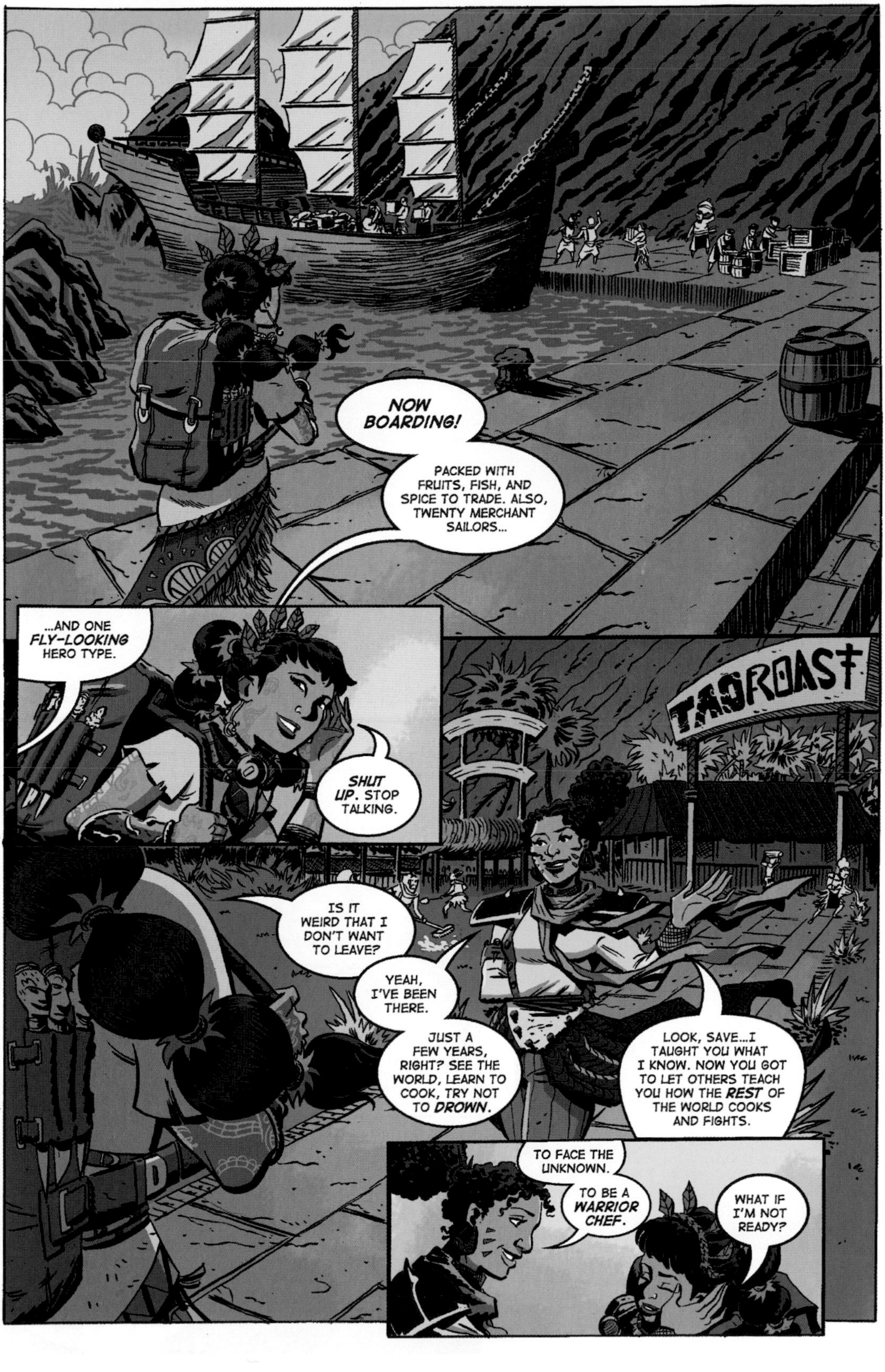
NOW BOARDING!
PACKED WITH FRUITS, FISH, AND SPICE TO TRADE. ALSO, TWENTY MERCHANT SAILORS...
...AND ONE FLY-LOOKING HERO TYPE.
SHUT UP. STOP TALKING.
TAOROAST
IS IT WEIRD THAT I DON'T WANT TO LEAVE?
YEAH, I'VE BEEN THERE.
JUST A FEW YEARS, RIGHT? SEE THE WORLD, LEARN TO COOK, TRY NOT TO DROWN.
LOOK, SAVE...I TAUGHT YOU WHAT I KNOW. NOW YOU GOT TO LET OTHERS TEACH YOU HOW THE REST OF THE WORLD COOKS AND FIGHTS.
TO FACE THE UNKNOWN.
TO BE A WARRIOR CHEF.
WHAT IF I'M NOT READY?

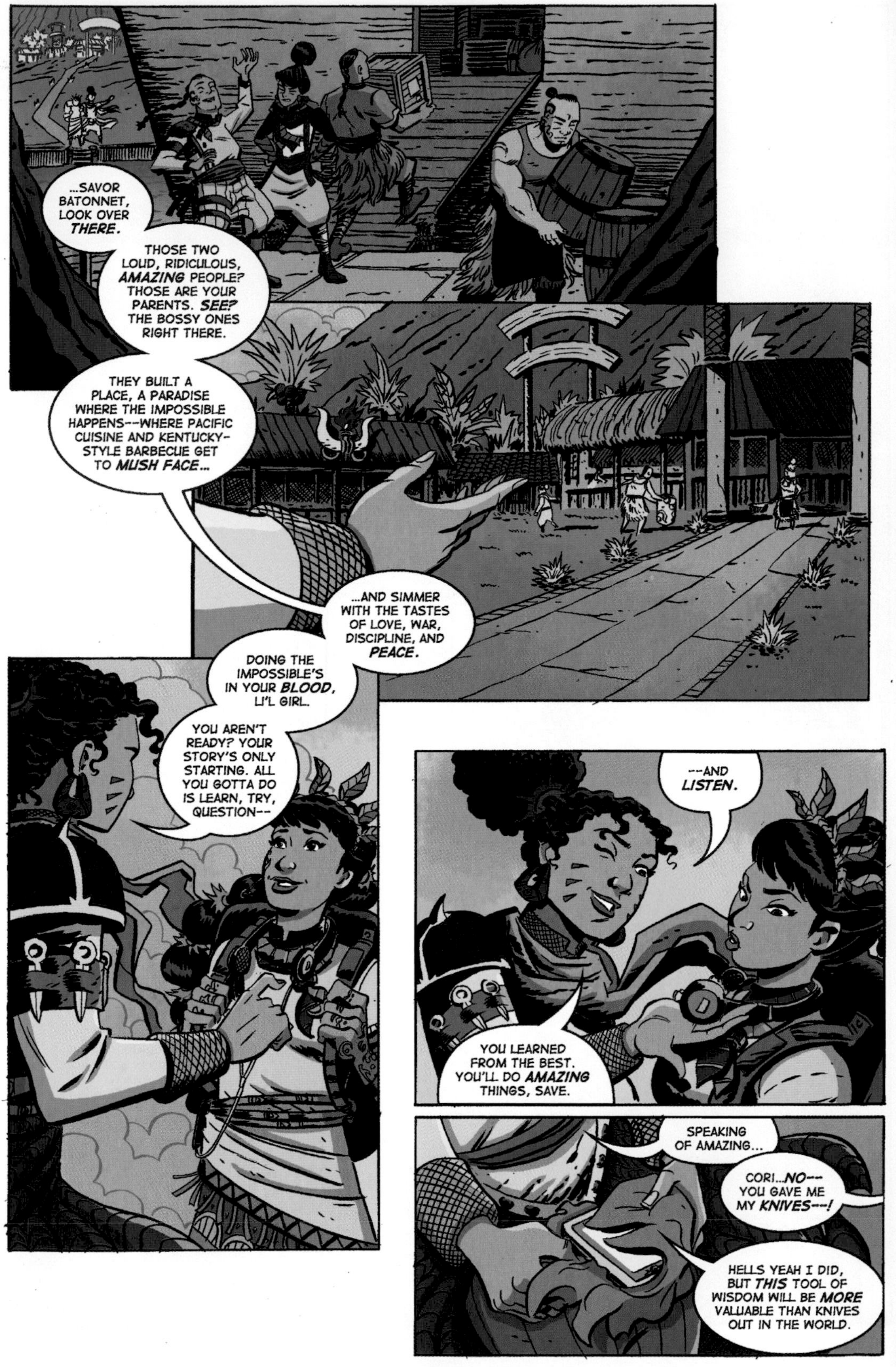
...SAVOR BATONNET, LOOK OVER THERE.
THOSE TWO LOUD, RIDICULOUS, AMAZING PEOPLE? THOSE ARE YOUR PARENTS. SEE? THE BOSSY ONES RIGHT THERE.
THEY BUILT A PLACE, A PARADISE WHERE THE IMPOSSIBLE HAPPENS--WHERE PACIFIC CUISINE AND KENTUCKY-STYLE BARBECUE GET TO MUSH FACE...
...AND SIMMER WITH THE TASTES OF LOVE, WAR, DISCIPLINE, AND PEACE.
DOING THE IMPOSSIBLE'S IN YOUR BLOOD, LI'L GIRL.
YOU AREN'T READY? YOUR STORY'S ONLY STARTING. ALL YOU GOTTA DO IS LEARN, TRY, QUESTION--
--AND LISTEN.
YOU LEARNED FROM THE BEST. YOU'LL DO AMAZING THINGS, SAVE.
SPEAKING OF AMAZING...
CORI...NO--- YOU GAVE ME MY KNIVES---!
HELLS YEAH I DID, BUT THIS TOOL OF WISDOM WILL BE MORE VALUABLE THAN KNIVES OUT IN THE WORLD.

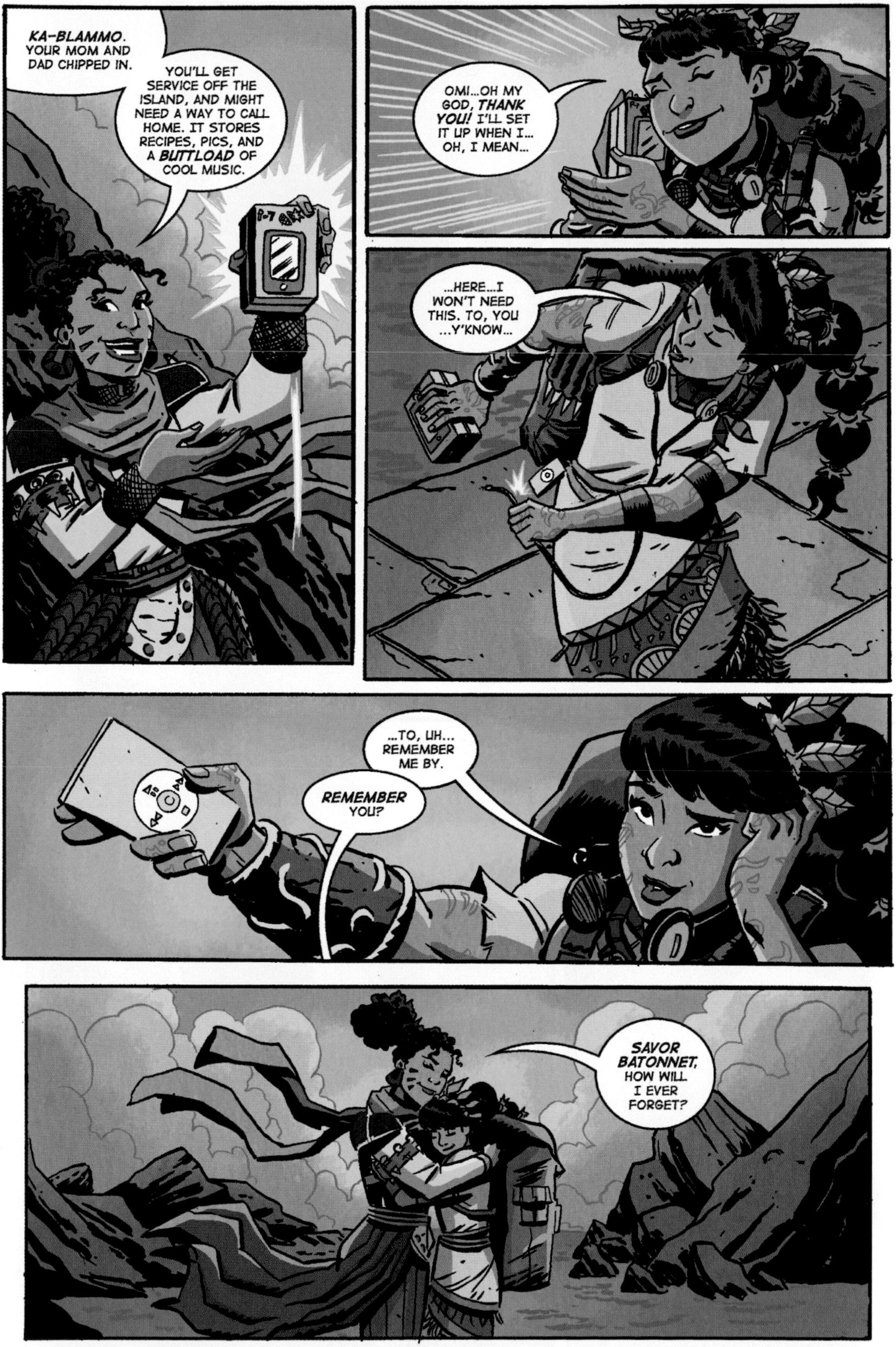
KA-BLAMMO. YOUR MOM AND DAD CHIPPED IN.
YOU'LL GET SERVICE OFF THE ISLAND, AND MIGHT NEED A WAY TO CALL HOME. IT STORES RECIPES, PICS, AND A BUTTLOAD OF COOL MUSIC.
OMI...OH MY GOD, THANK YOU! I'LL SET IT UP WHEN I... OH, I MEAN...
...HERE...I WON'T NEED THIS. TO, YOU ...Y'KNOW...
...TO, UH... REMEMBER ME BY.
REMEMBER YOU?
SAVOR BATONNET, HOW WILL I EVER FORGET?

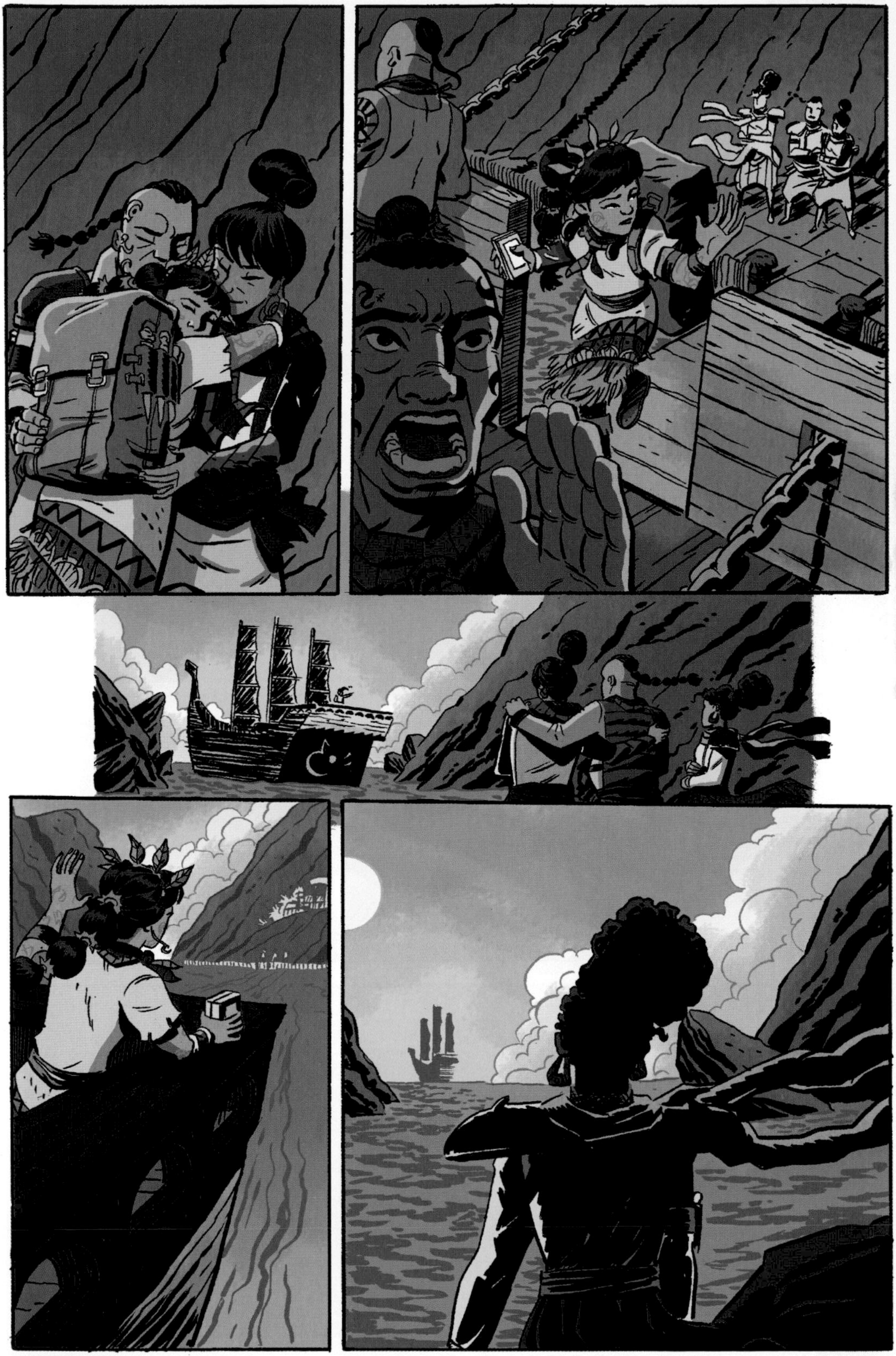

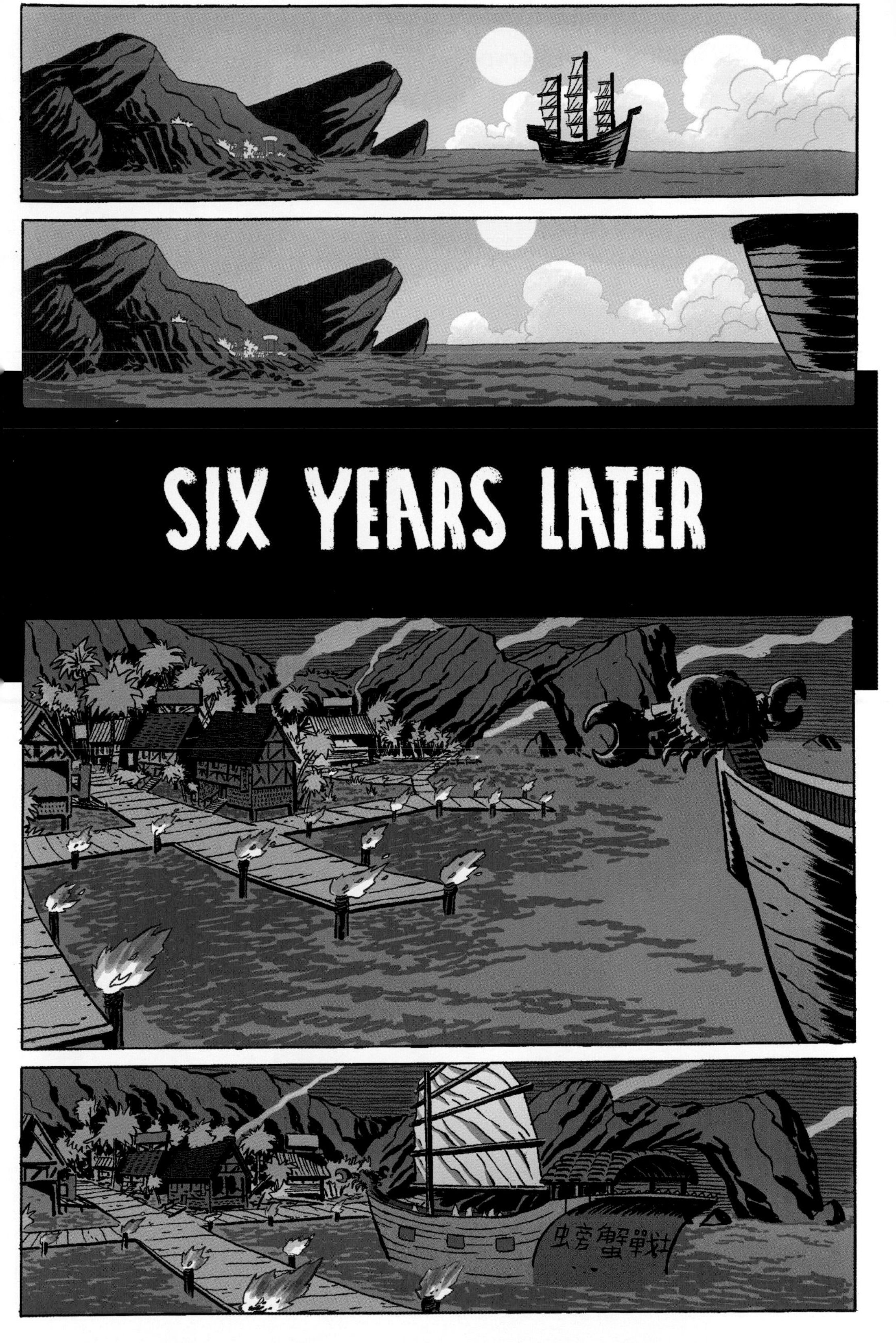
SIX YEARS LATER
虫旁蟹戰士

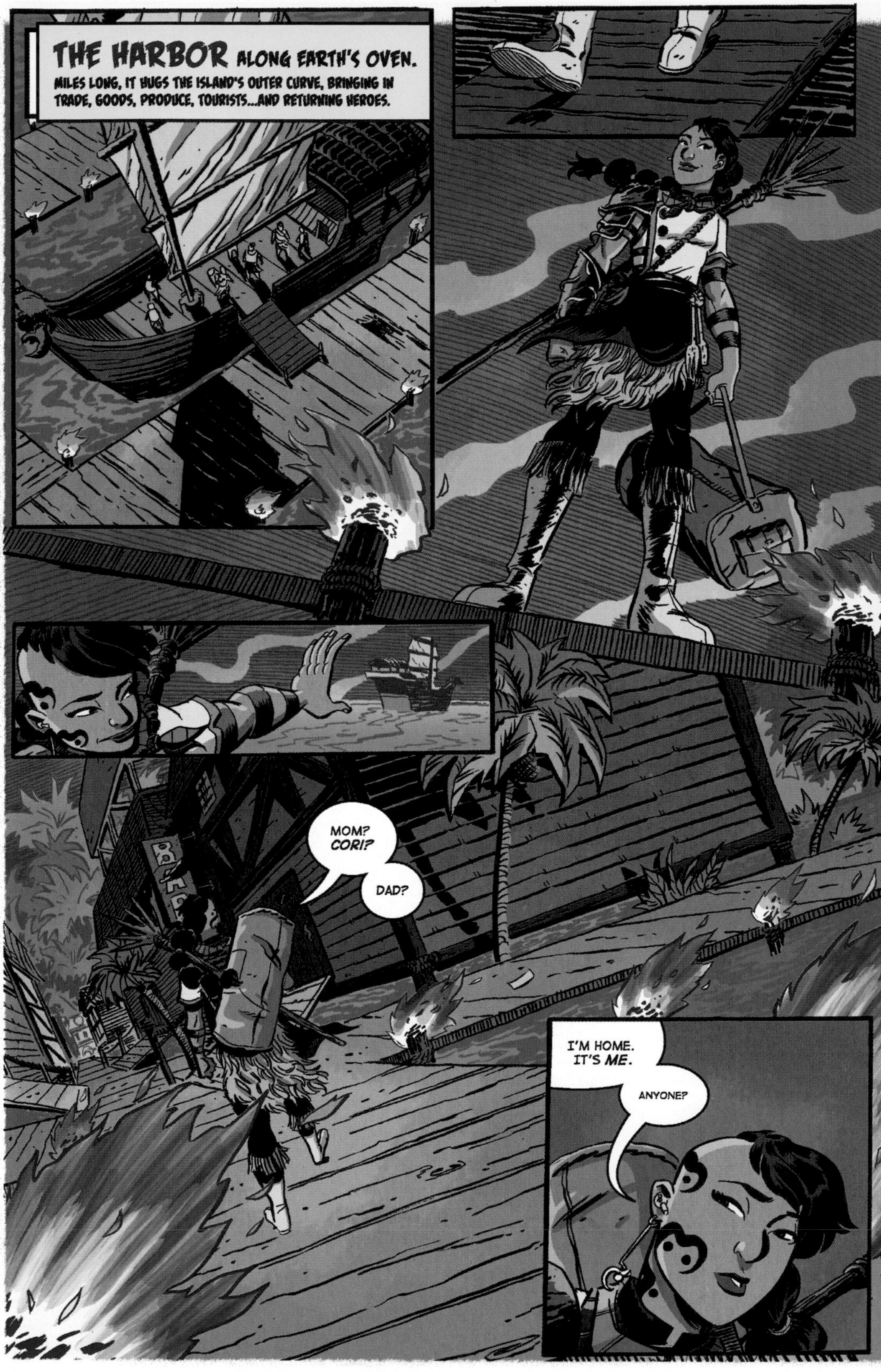
THE HARBOR ALONG EARTH'S OVEN.
MILES LONG, IT HUGS THE ISLAND'S OUTER CURVE, BRINGING IN TRADE, GOODS, PRODUCE, TOURISTS...AND RETURNING HEROES.
MOM? CORI?
DAD?
I'M HOME. IT'S ME.
ANYONE?

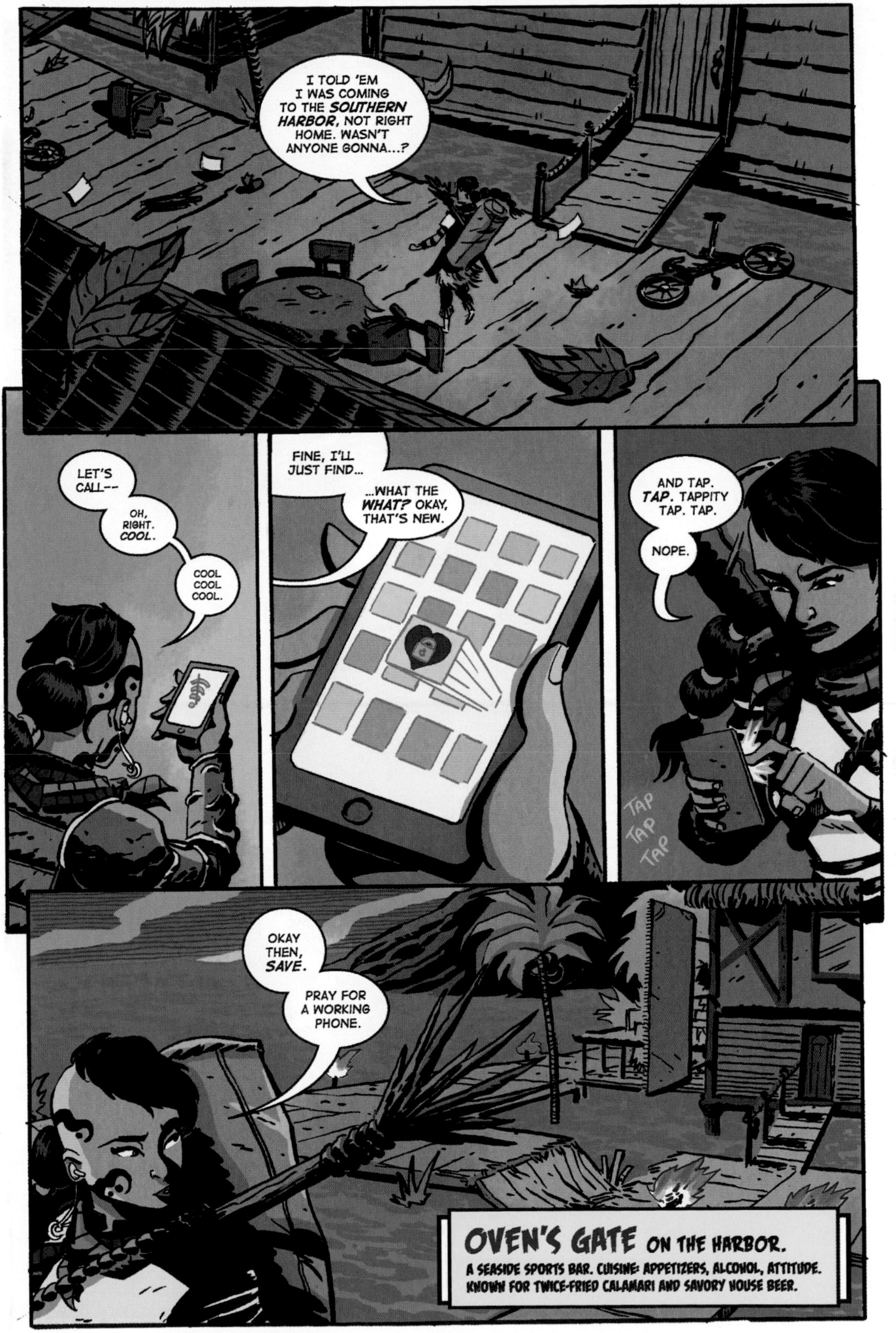
I TOLD 'EM I WAS COMING TO THE SOUTHERN HARBOR, NOT RIGHT HOME. WASN'T ANYONE GONNA...?
LET'S CALL--
OH, RIGHT. COOL.
COOL COOL COOL.
FINE, I'LL JUST FIND...
...WHAT THE WHAT? OKAY, THAT'S NEW.
AND TAP. TAP. TAPPITY TAP. TAP.
NOPE.
TAP TAP TAP
OKAY THEN, SAVE.
PRAY FOR A WORKING PHONE.
OVEN'S GATE ON THE HARBOR.
A SEASIDE SPORTS BAR. CUISINE: APPETIZERS, ALCOHOL, ATTITUDE. KNOWN FOR TWICE-FRIED CALAMARI AND SAVORY HOUSE BEER.

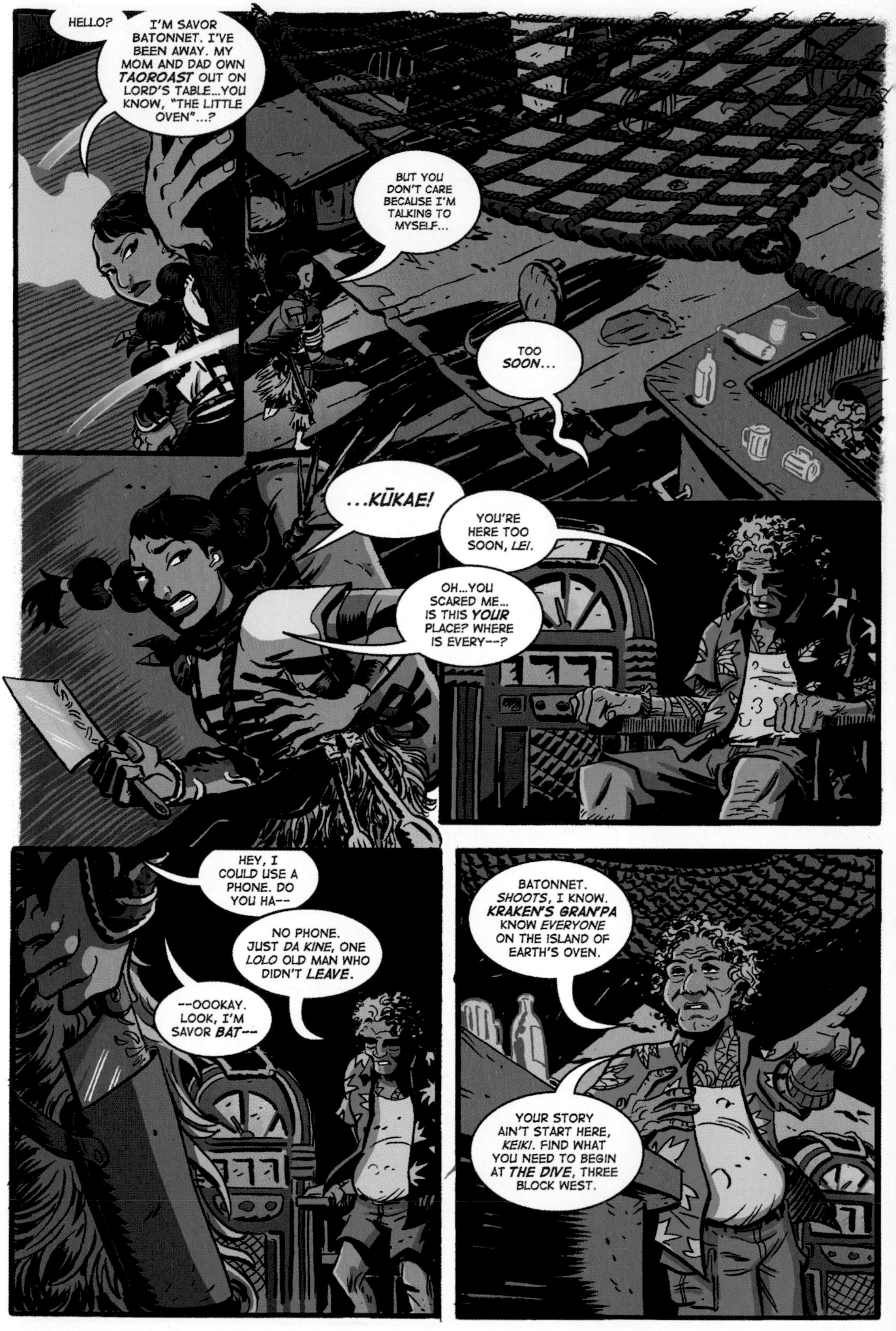

HELLO?
I'M SAVOR BATONNET. I'VE BEEN AWAY. MY MOM AND DAD OWN TAOROAST OUT ON LORD'S TABLE...YOU KNOW, "THE LITTLE OVEN"...?
BUT YOU DON'T CARE BECAUSE I'M TALKING TO MYSELF...
TOO SOON...
...KŪKAE!
YOU'RE HERE TOO SOON, LEI.
OH...YOU SCARED ME... IS THIS YOUR PLACE? WHERE IS EVERY--?
HEY, I COULD USE A PHONE. DO YOU HA--
NO PHONE. JUST DA KINE, ONE LOLO OLD MAN WHO DIDN'T LEAVE.
--OOOKAY. LOOK, I'M SAVOR BAT---
BATONNET. SHOOTS, I KNOW. KRAKEN'S GRAN'PA KNOW EVERYONE ON THE ISLAND OF EARTH'S OVEN.
YOUR STORY AIN'T START HERE, KEIKI. FIND WHAT YOU NEED TO BEGIN AT THE DIVE, THREE BLOCK WEST.

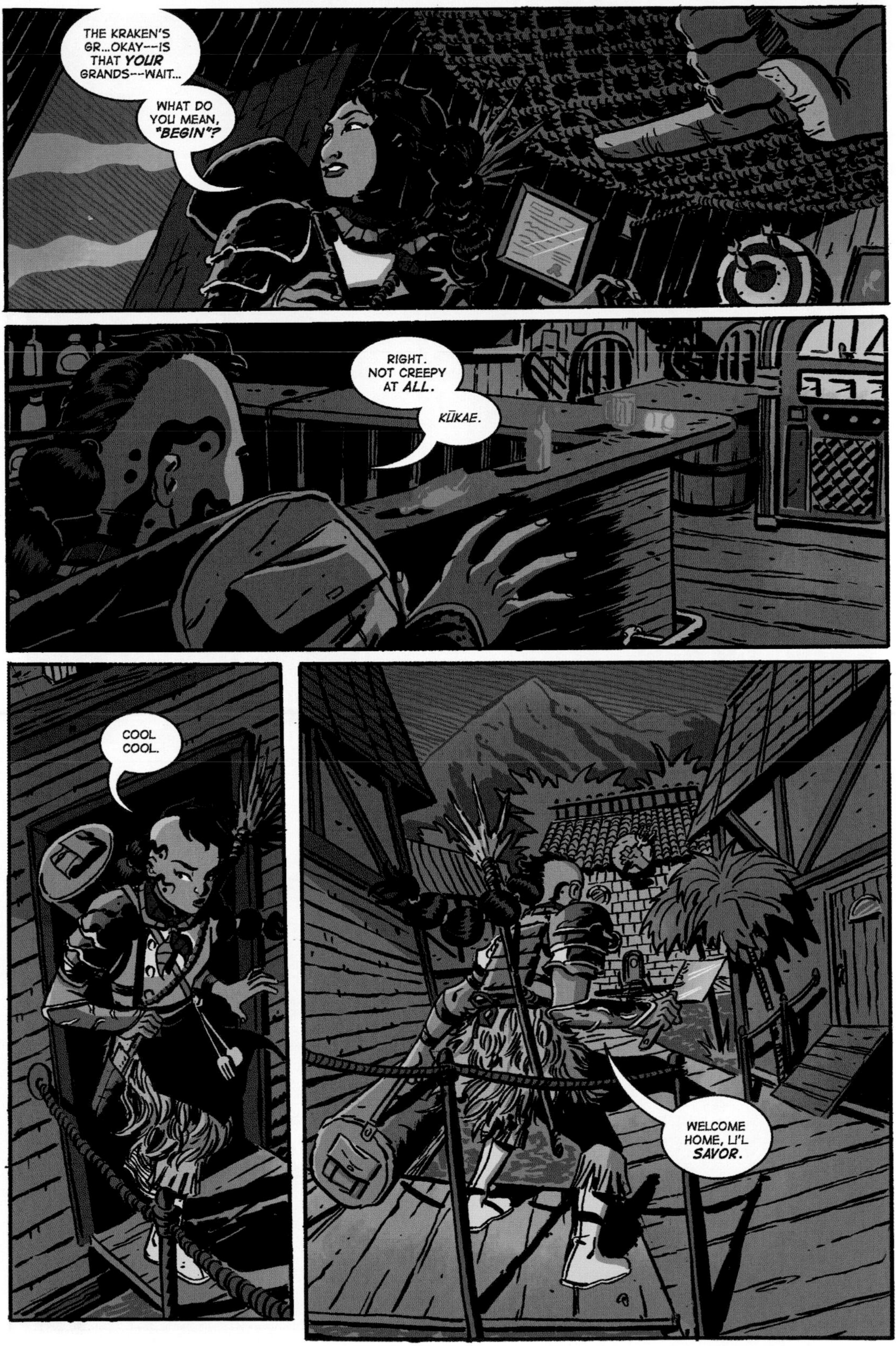
THE KRAKEN'S GR...OKAY--IS THAT YOUR GRANDS--WAIT...
WHAT DO YOU MEAN, "BEGIN"?
RIGHT. NOT CREEPY AT ALL.
KŪKAE.
COOL COOL.
WELCOME HOME, LI'L SAVOR.

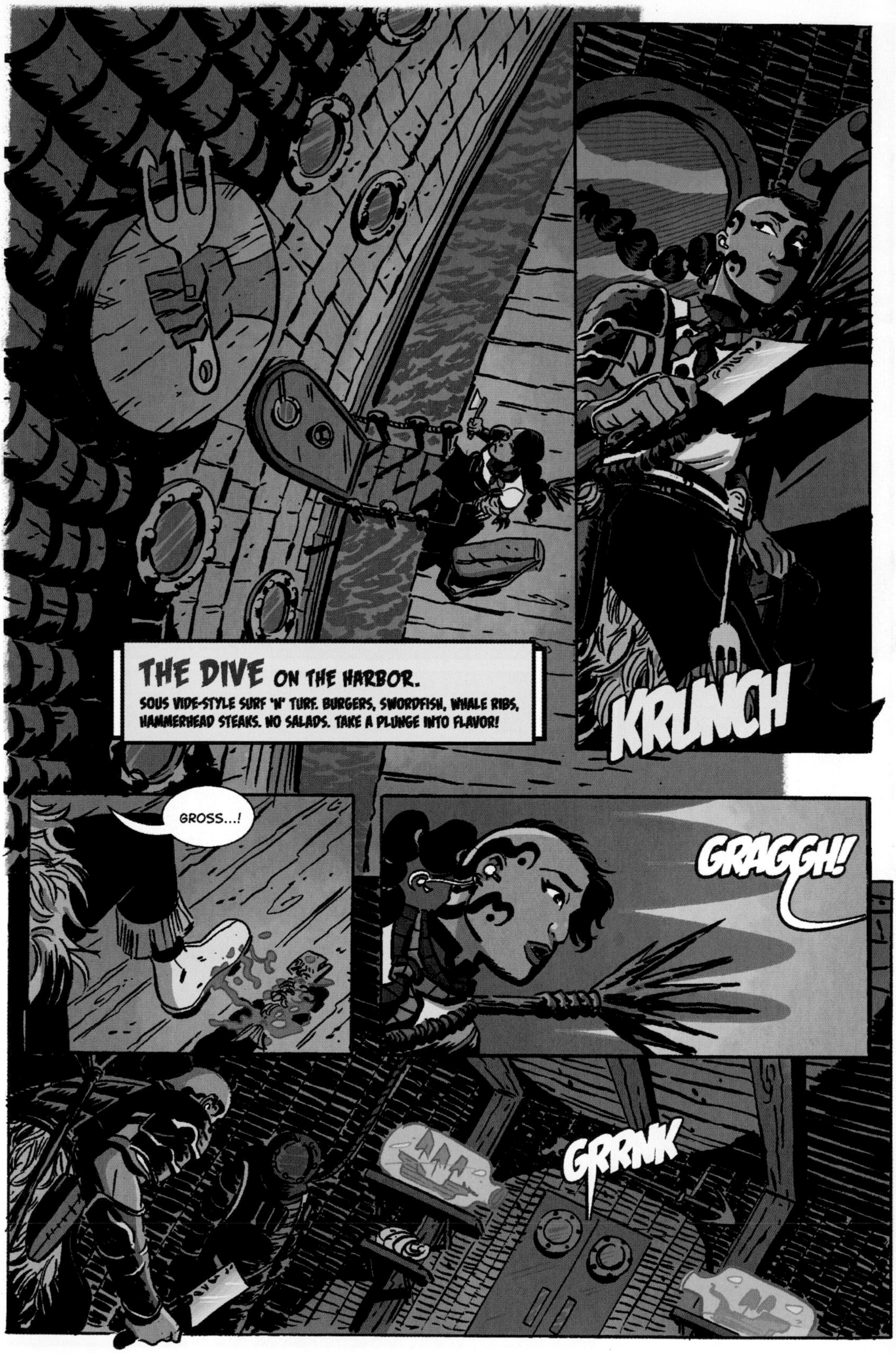
THE DIVE ON THE HARBOR.
SOUS VIDE-STYLE SURF 'N' TURF. BURGERS, SWORDFISH, WHALE RIBS, HAMMERHEAD STEAKS. NO SALADS. TAKE A PLUNGE INTO FLAVOR!
KRUNCH
GROSS...!
GRAGGH!
GRRNK

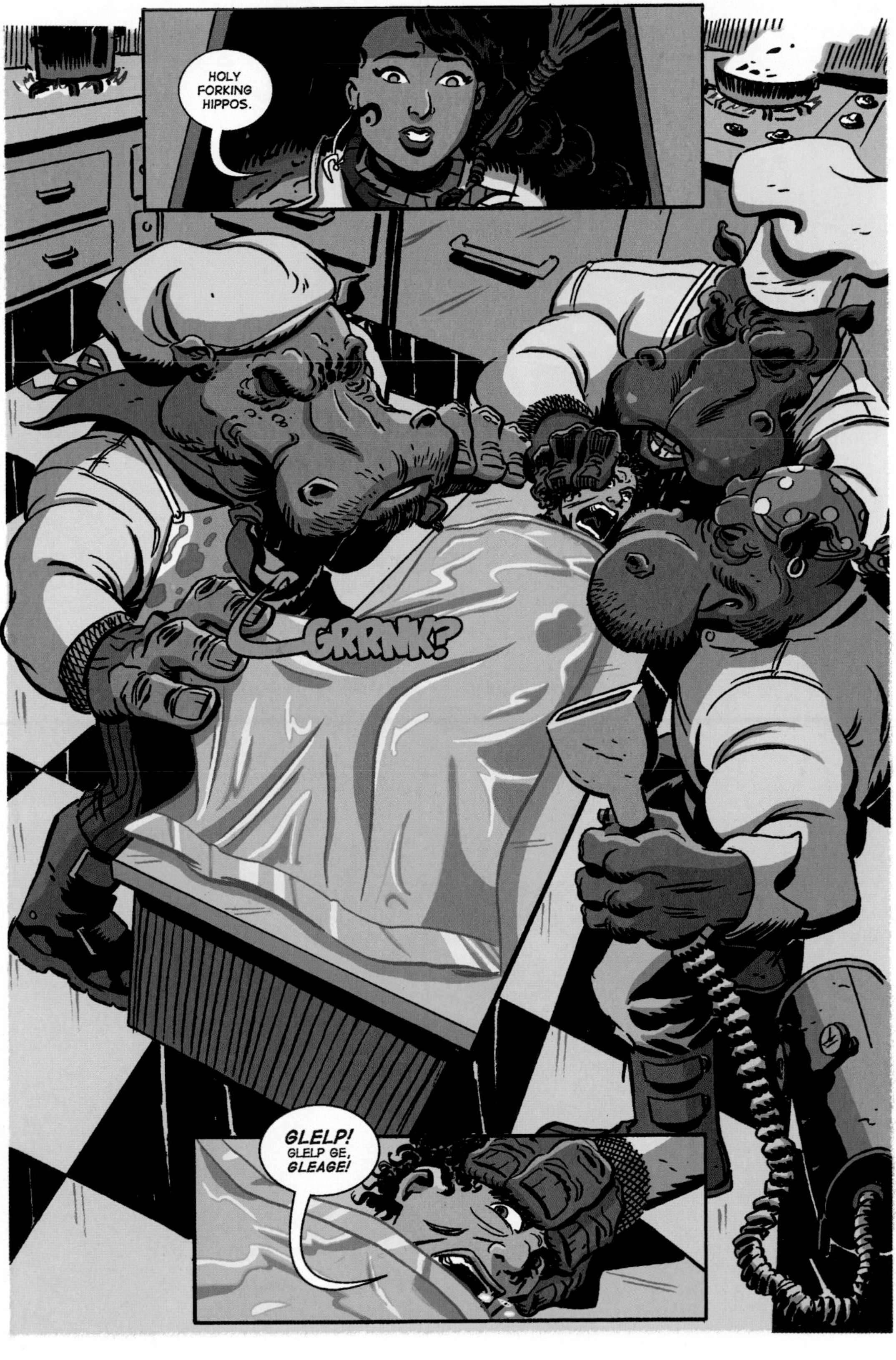
HOLY FORKING HIPPOS.
GRRNK?
GLELP! GLELP GE, GLEAGE!

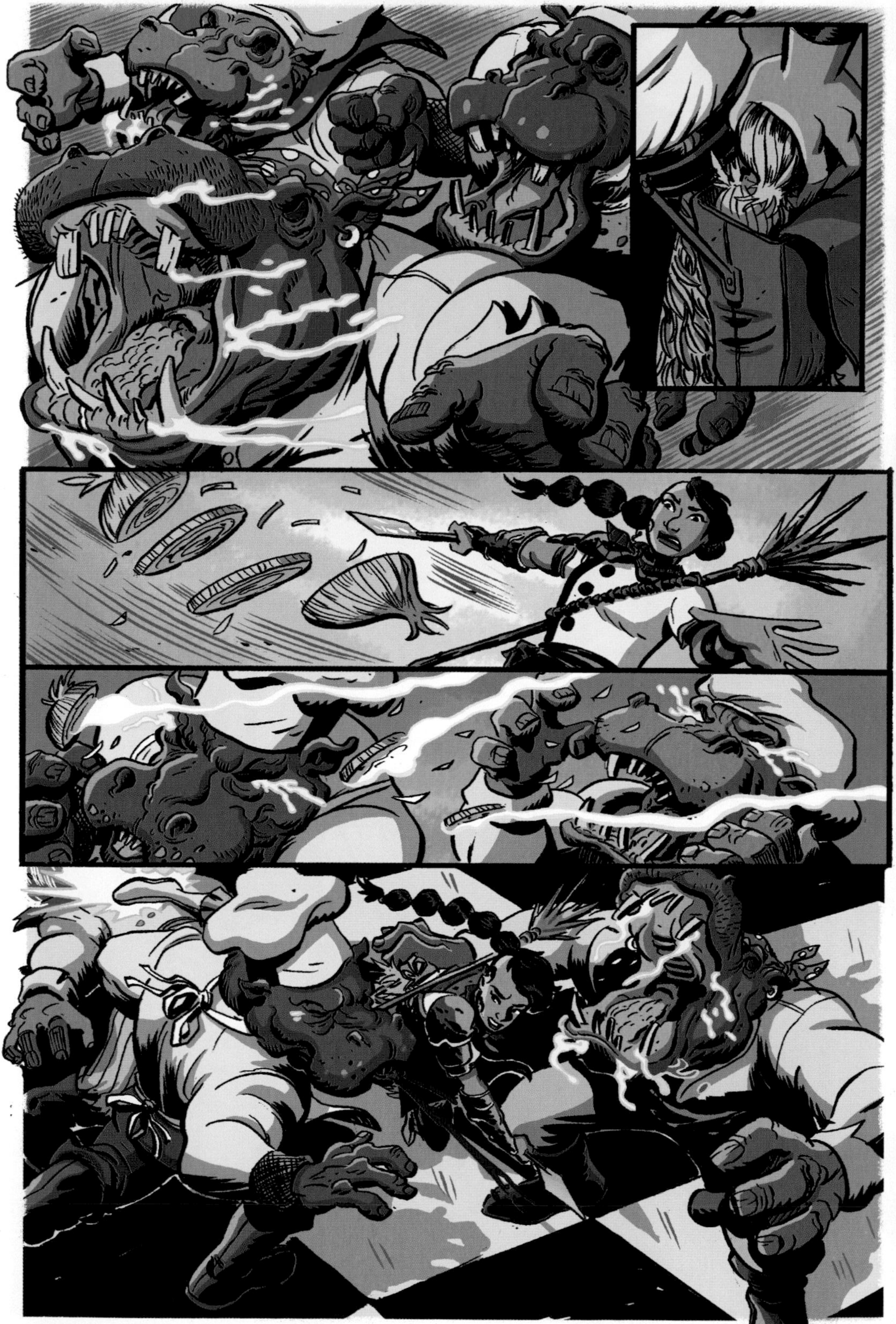

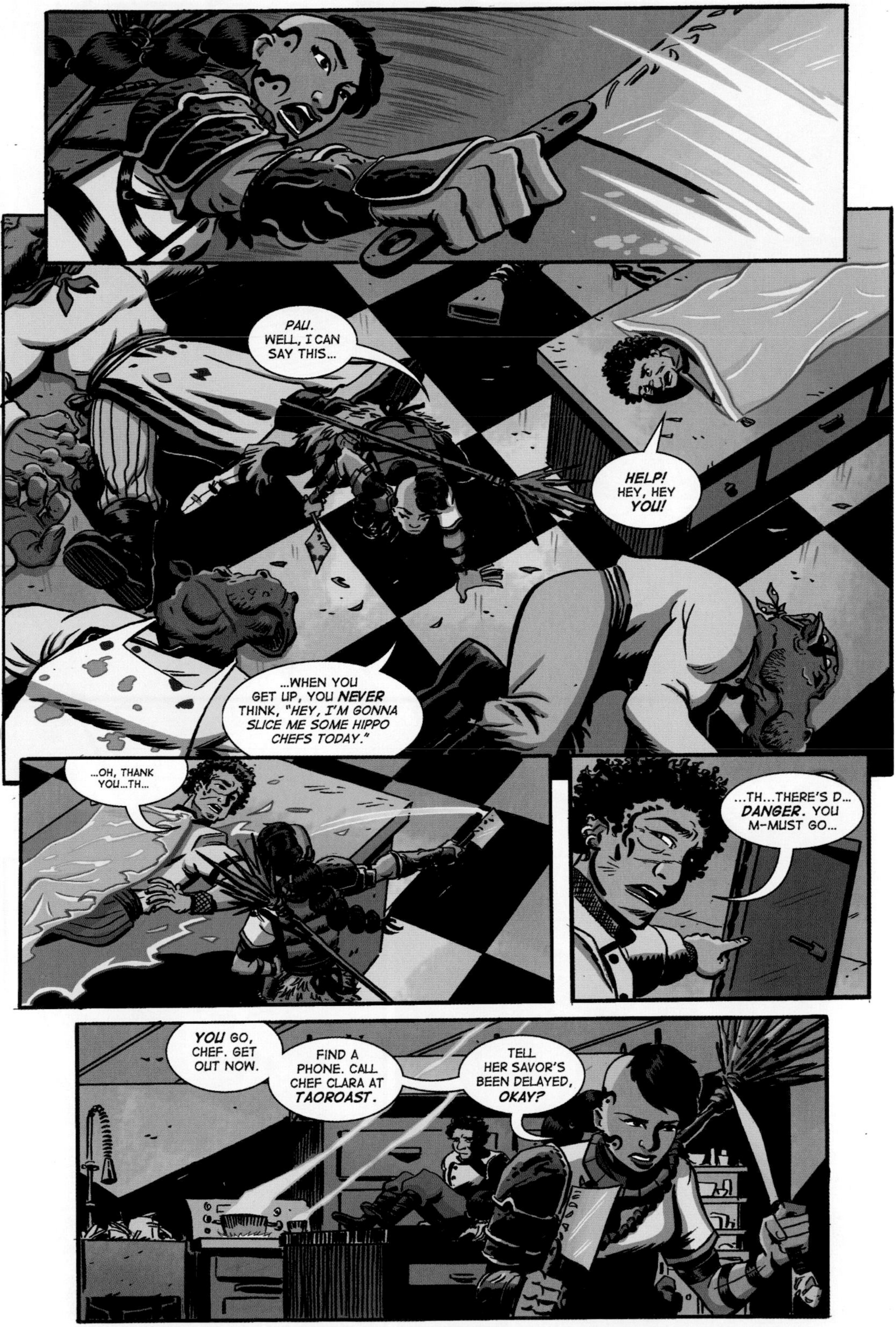

PAU.
WELL, I CAN
SAY THIS...
HELP!
HEY, HEY
YOU!
...WHEN YOU
GET UP, YOU NEVER
THINK, "HEY, I'M GONNA
SLICE ME SOME HIPPO
CHEFS TODAY."
...OH, THANK
YOU...TH...
...TH...THERE'S D...
DANGER. YOU
M-MUST GO...
YOU GO,
CHEF. GET
OUT NOW.
FIND A
PHONE. CALL
CHEF CLARA AT
TAOROAST.
TELL
HER SAVOR'S
BEEN DELAYED,
OKAY?

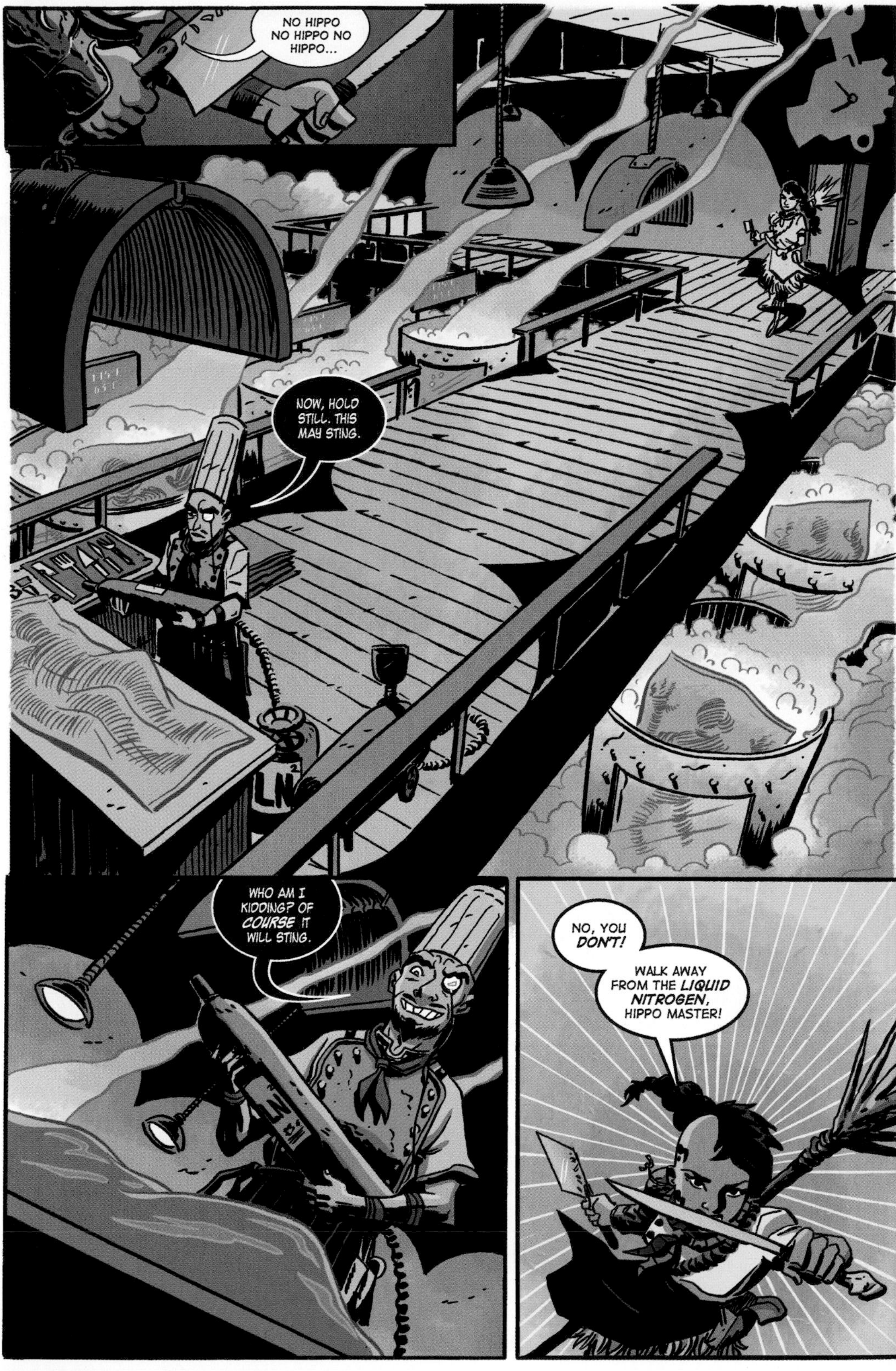
NO HIPPO NO HIPPO NO HIPPO...
NOW, HOLD STILL. THIS MAY STING.
WHO AM I KIDDING? OF COURSE IT WILL STING.
NO, YOU DON'T!
WALK AWAY FROM THE LIQUID NITROGEN, HIPPO MASTER!

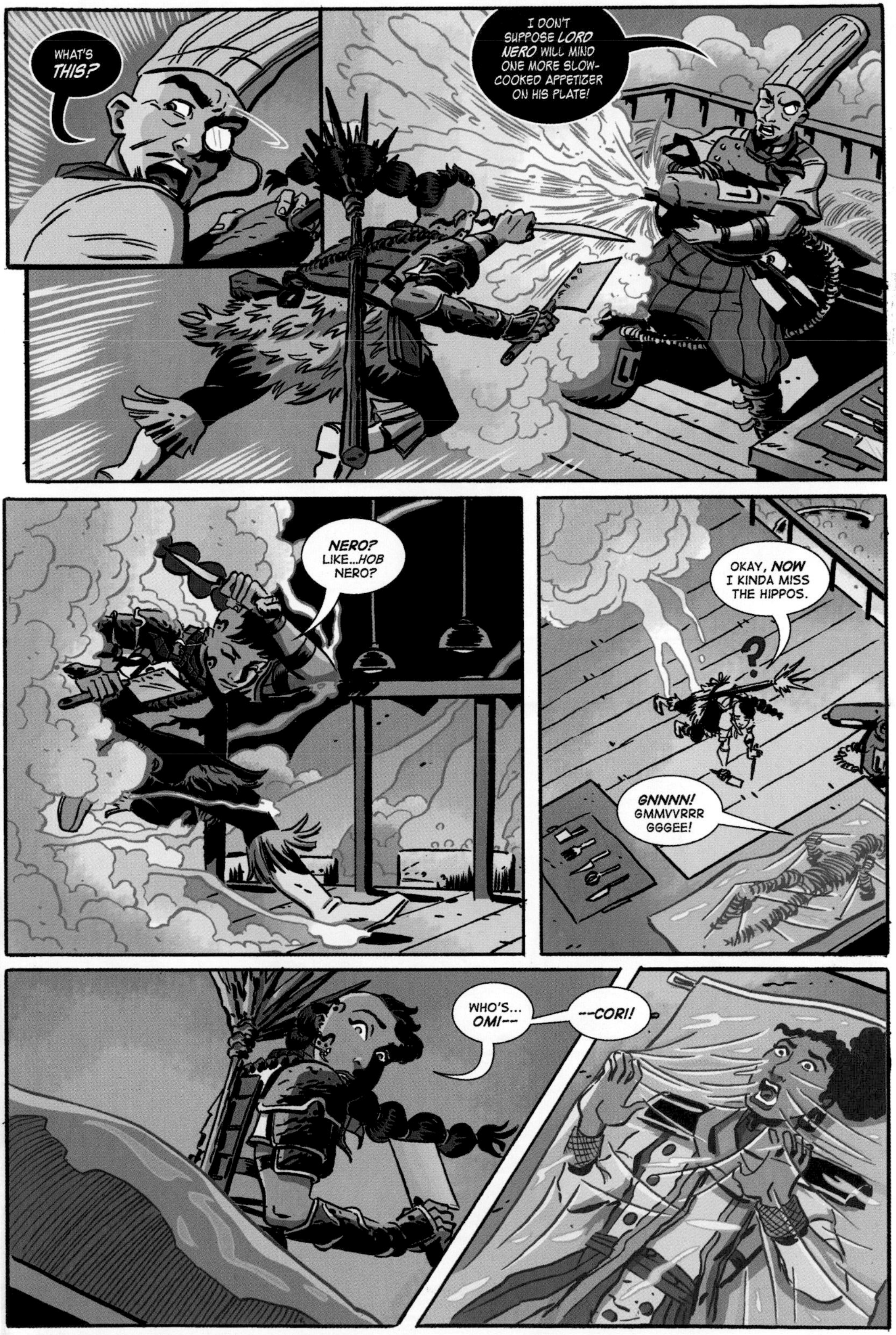
WHAT'S THIS?
I DON'T SUPPOSE LORD NERO WILL MIND ONE MORE SLOW-COOKED APPETIZER ON HIS PLATE!
NERO? LIKE...HOB NERO?
OKAY, NOW I KINDA MISS THE HIPPOS.
GNNNN! GMMVVRRR GGGEE!
WHO'S... OMI--
--CORI!

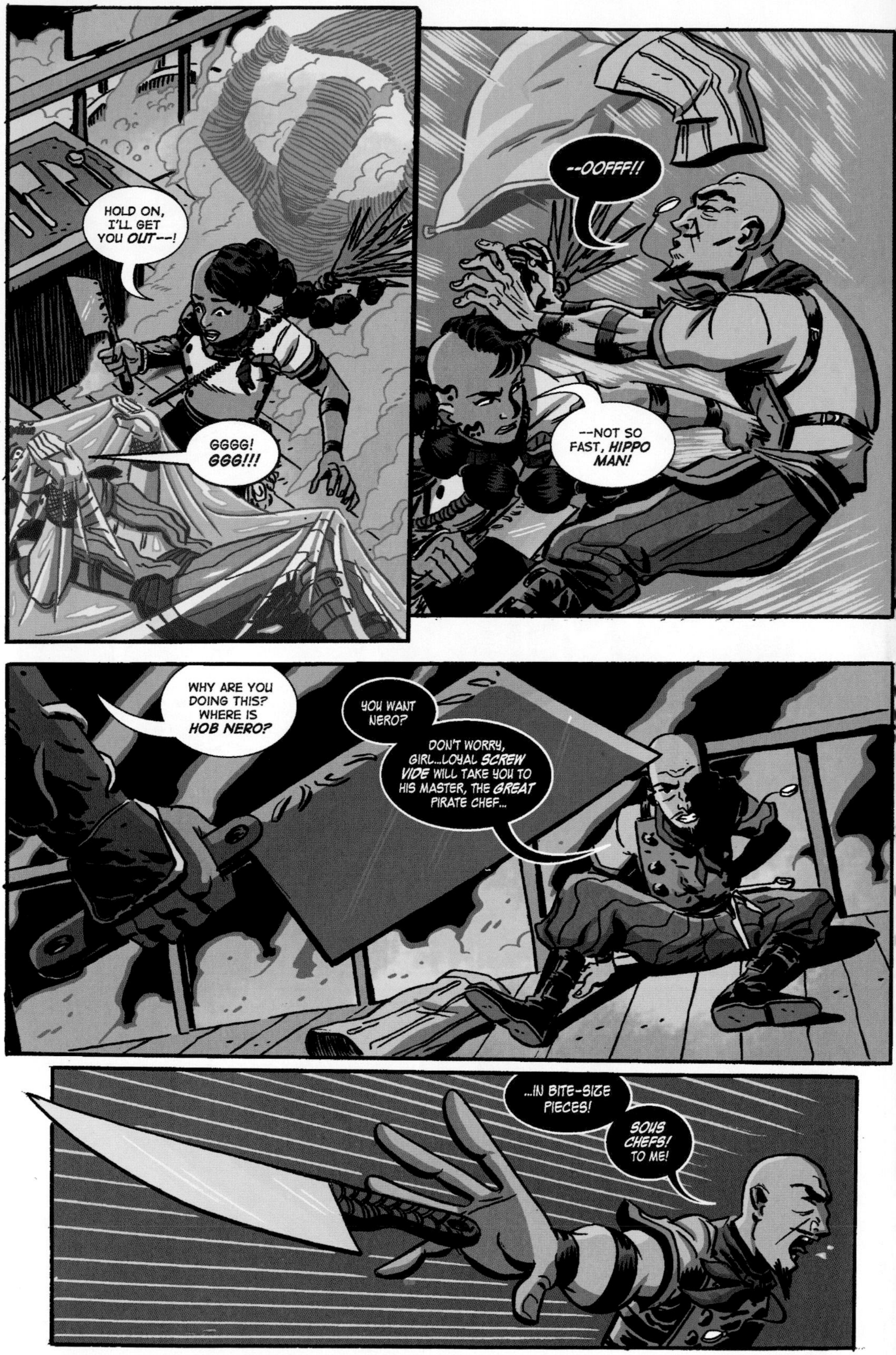
HOLD ON, I'LL GET YOU OUT--!
GGGG! GGG!!!
--OOFFF!!
--NOT SO FAST, HIPPO MAN!
WHY ARE YOU DOING THIS? WHERE IS HOB NERO?
YOU WANT NERO?
DON'T WORRY, GIRL...LOYAL SCREW VIDE WILL TAKE YOU TO HIS MASTER, THE GREAT PIRATE CHEF...
...IN BITE-SIZE PIECES!
SOUS CHEFS! TO ME!

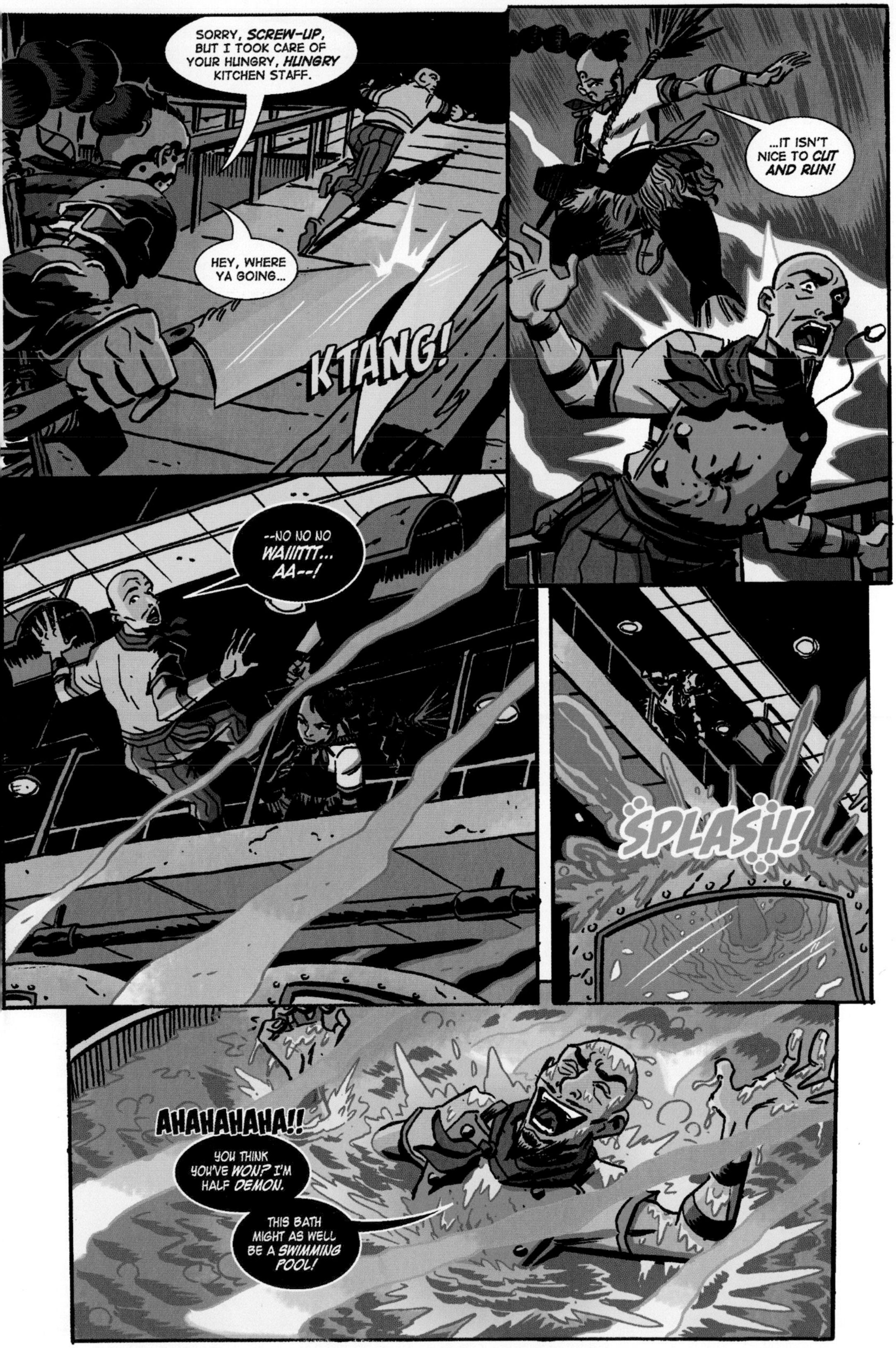
SORRY, SCREW-UP, BUT I TOOK CARE OF YOUR HUNGRY, HUNGRY KITCHEN STAFF.
HEY, WHERE YA GOING...
KTANG!
...IT ISN'T NICE TO CUT AND RUN!
--NO NO NO WAIIITTT... AA--!
SPLASH!
AHAHAHAHA!!
YOU THINK YOU'VE WON? I'M HALF DEMON.
THIS BATH MIGHT AS WELL BE A SWIMMING POOL!

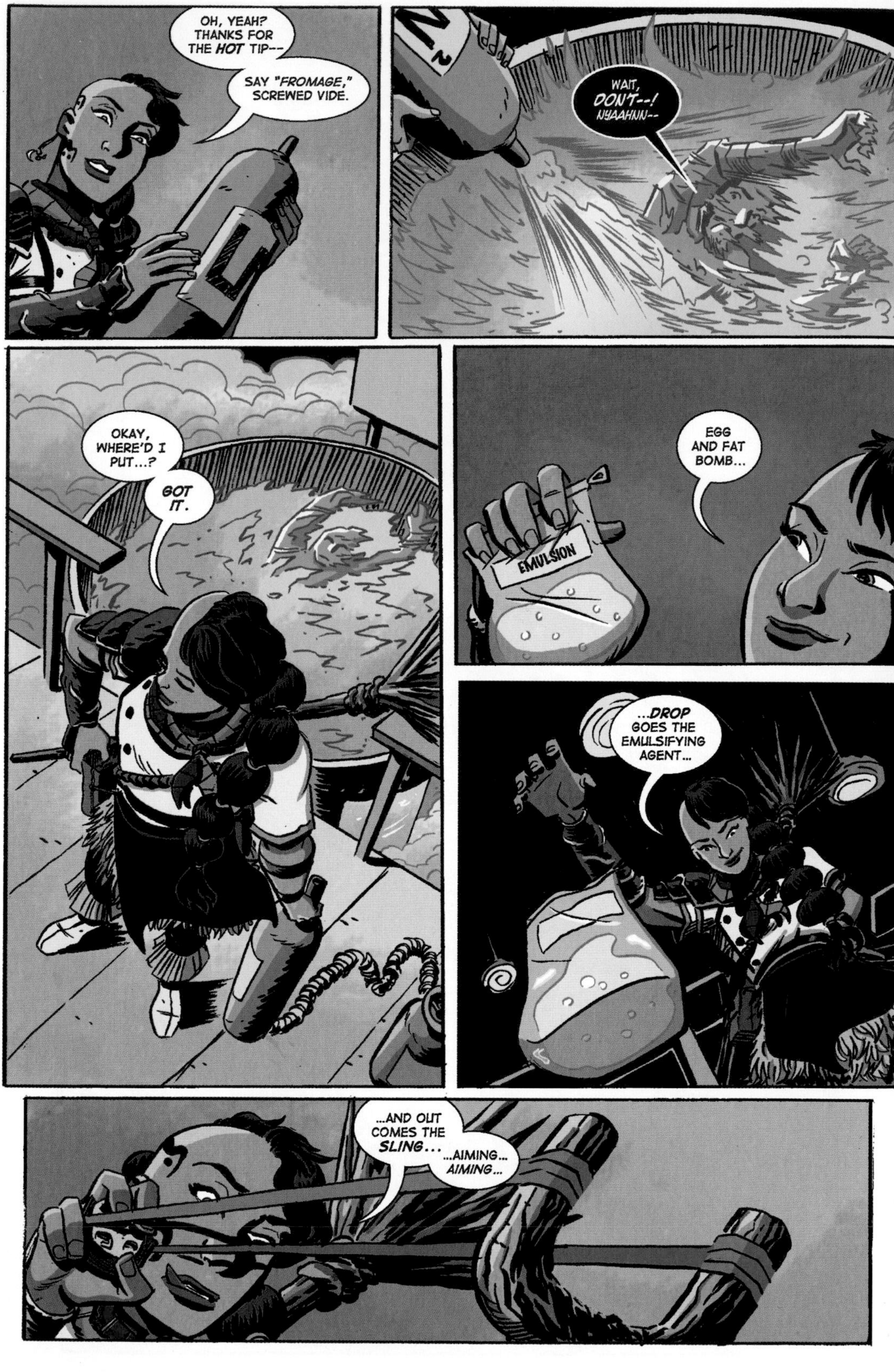
OH, YEAH? THANKS FOR THE *HOT* TIP--
SAY "*FROMAGE*," SCREWED VIDE.
WAIT, *DON'T--!* *NYAAHNN--*
OKAY, WHERE'D I PUT...?
GOT IT.
EGG AND FAT BOMB...
EMULSION
...*DROP* GOES THE EMULSIFYING AGENT...
...AND OUT COMES THE *SLING*...
...AIMING... *AIMING*...

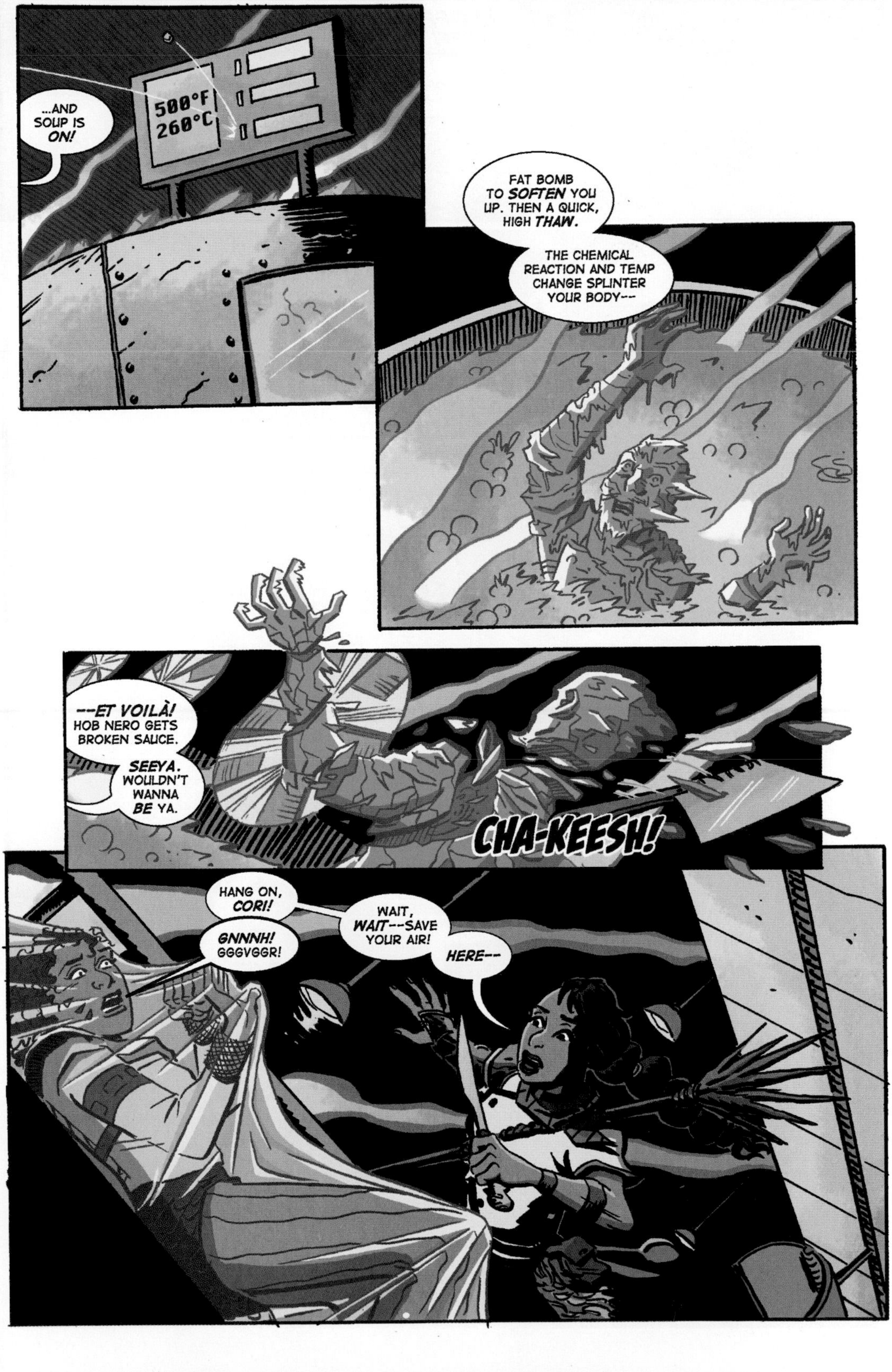
500°F
260°C
...AND SOUP IS ON!
FAT BOMB TO SOFTEN YOU UP. THEN A QUICK, HIGH THAW.
THE CHEMICAL REACTION AND TEMP CHANGE SPLINTER YOUR BODY--
--ET VOILÀ! HOB NERO GETS BROKEN SAUCE.
SEEYA. WOULDN'T WANNA BE YA.
CHA-KEESH!
HANG ON, CORI!
GNNNH! GGGVGGR!
WAIT, WAIT--SAVE YOUR AIR!
HERE--

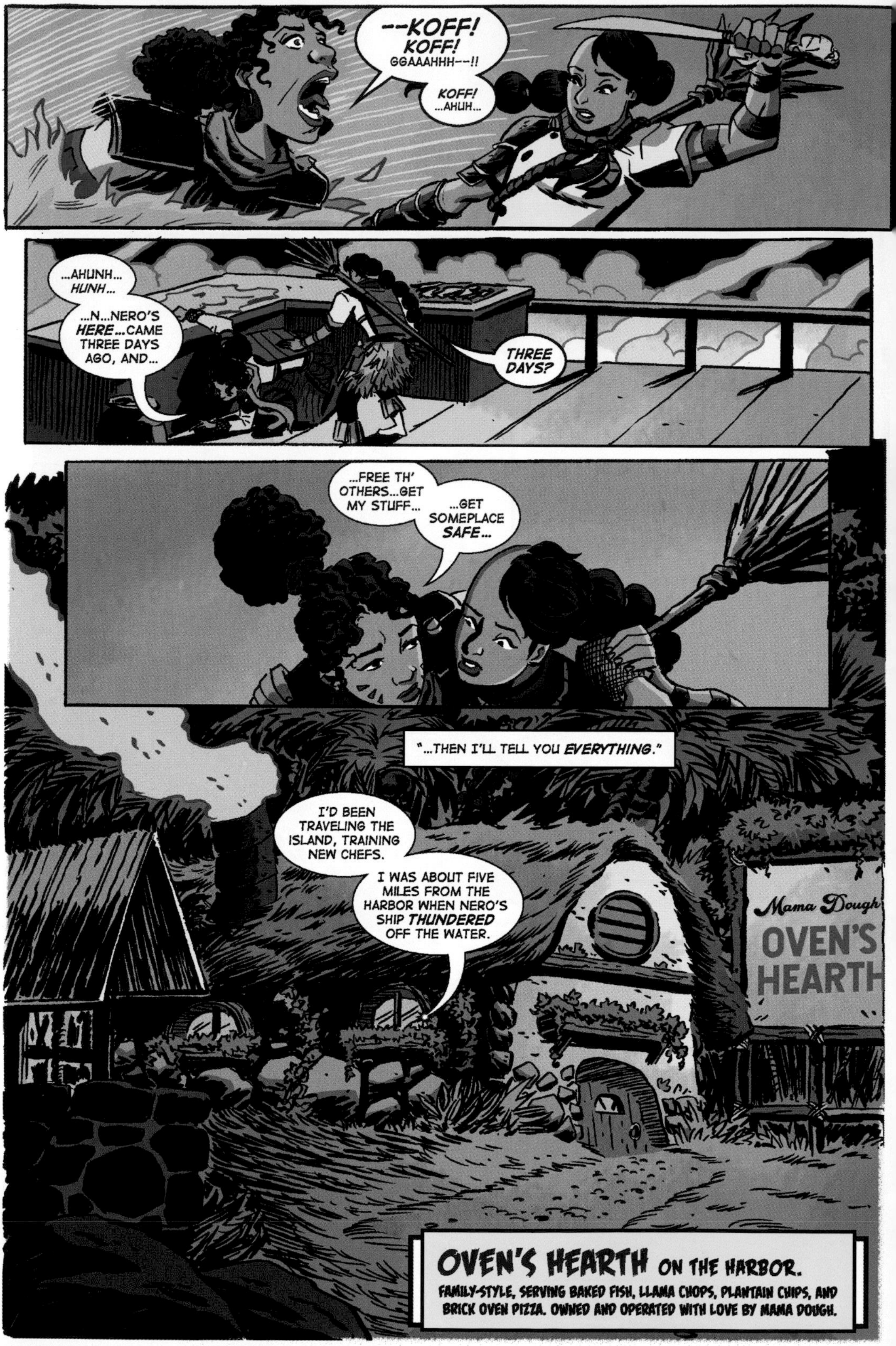
--KOFF! KOFF! GGAAAHHH--!!
KOFF! ...AHUH...
...AHUNH... HUNH...
...N...NERO'S HERE...CAME THREE DAYS AGO, AND...
THREE DAYS?
...FREE TH' OTHERS...GET MY STUFF...
...GET SOMEPLACE SAFE...
"...THEN I'LL TELL YOU EVERYTHING."
I'D BEEN TRAVELING THE ISLAND, TRAINING NEW CHEFS.
I WAS ABOUT FIVE MILES FROM THE HARBOR WHEN NERO'S SHIP THUNDERED OFF THE WATER.
Mama Dough's
OVEN'S HEARTH
OVEN'S HEARTH ON THE HARBOR.
FAMILY-STYLE, SERVING BAKED FISH, LLAMA CHOPS, PLANTAIN CHIPS, AND BRICK OVEN PIZZA. OWNED AND OPERATED WITH LOVE BY MAMA DOUGH.

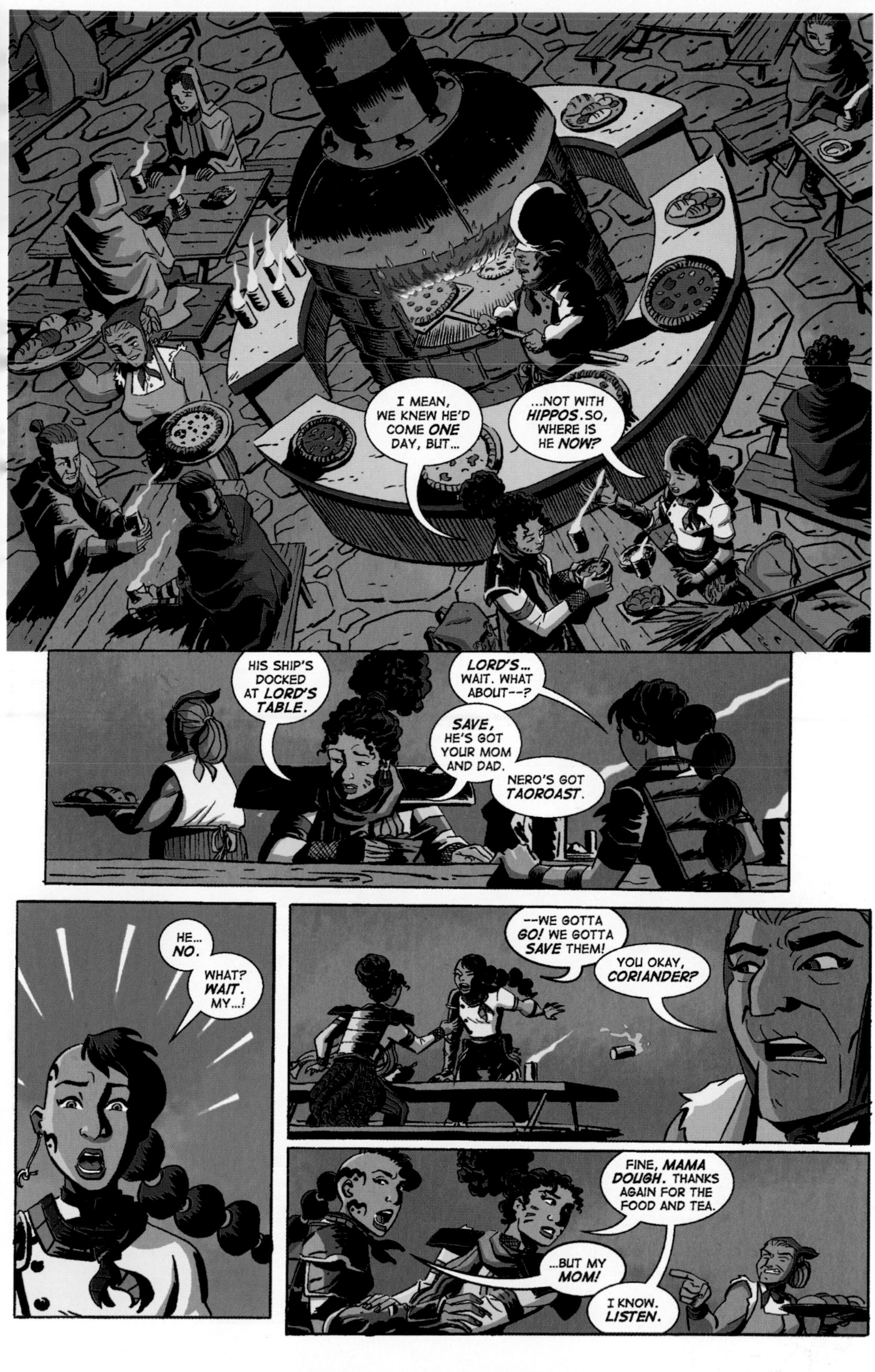
I MEAN, WE KNEW HE'D COME ONE DAY, BUT...
...NOT WITH HIPPOS. SO, WHERE IS HE NOW?
HIS SHIP'S DOCKED AT LORD'S TABLE.
LORD'S... WAIT. WHAT ABOUT--?
SAVE, HE'S GOT YOUR MOM AND DAD.
NERO'S GOT TAOROAST.
HE... NO.
WHAT? WAIT. MY...!
--WE GOTTA GO! WE GOTTA SAVE THEM!
YOU OKAY, CORIANDER?
FINE, MAMA DOUGH. THANKS AGAIN FOR THE FOOD AND TEA.
...BUT MY MOM!
I KNOW. LISTEN.

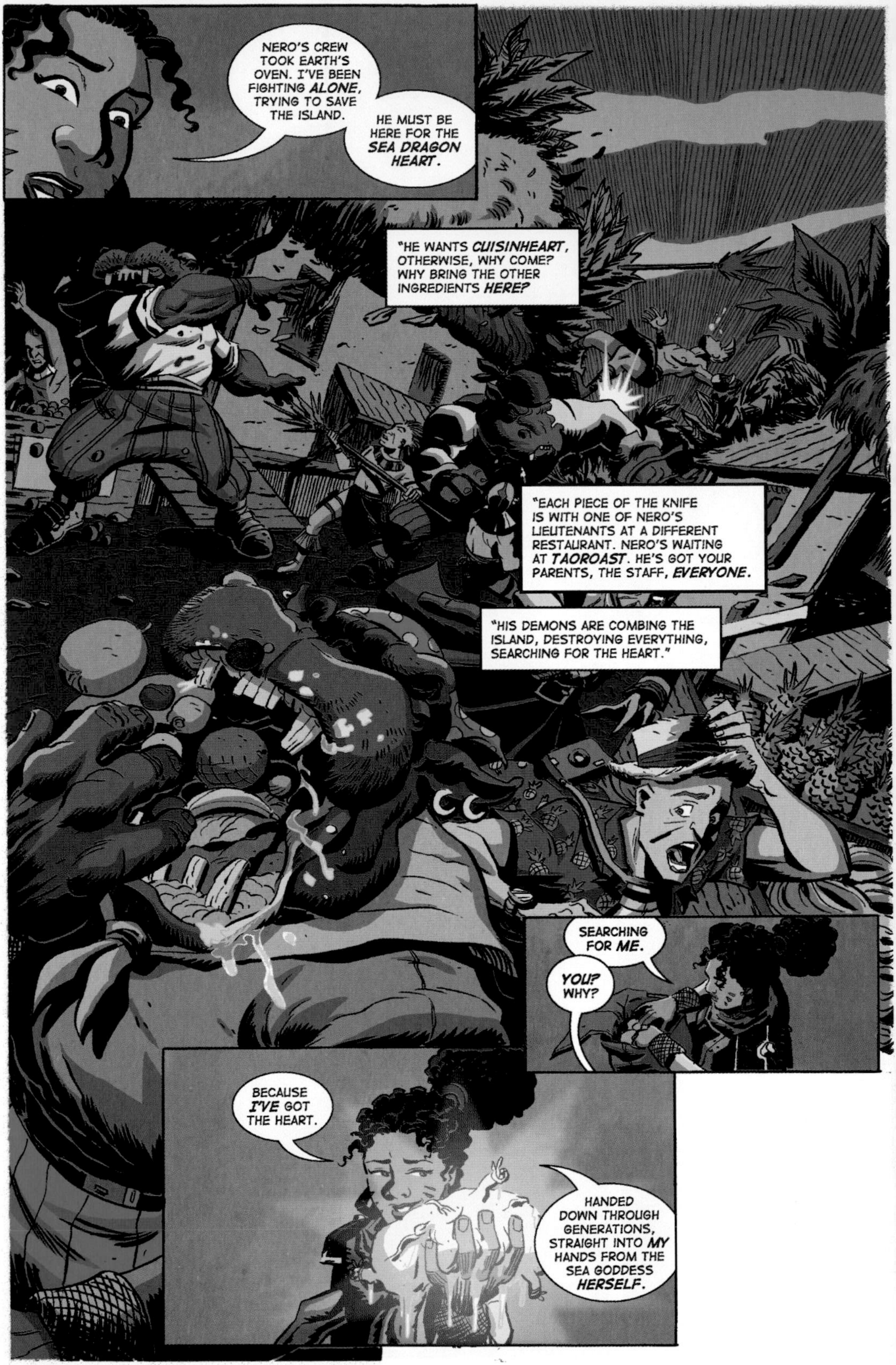
NERO'S CREW TOOK EARTH'S OVEN. I'VE BEEN FIGHTING ALONE, TRYING TO SAVE THE ISLAND.
HE MUST BE HERE FOR THE SEA DRAGON HEART.
"HE WANTS CUISINHEART, OTHERWISE, WHY COME? WHY BRING THE OTHER INGREDIENTS HERE?
"EACH PIECE OF THE KNIFE IS WITH ONE OF NERO'S LIEUTENANTS AT A DIFFERENT RESTAURANT. NERO'S WAITING AT TAOROAST. HE'S GOT YOUR PARENTS, THE STAFF, EVERYONE.
"HIS DEMONS ARE COMBING THE ISLAND, DESTROYING EVERYTHING, SEARCHING FOR THE HEART."
SEARCHING FOR ME.
YOU? WHY?
BECAUSE I'VE GOT THE HEART.
HANDED DOWN THROUGH GENERATIONS, STRAIGHT INTO MY HANDS FROM THE SEA GODDESS HERSELF.

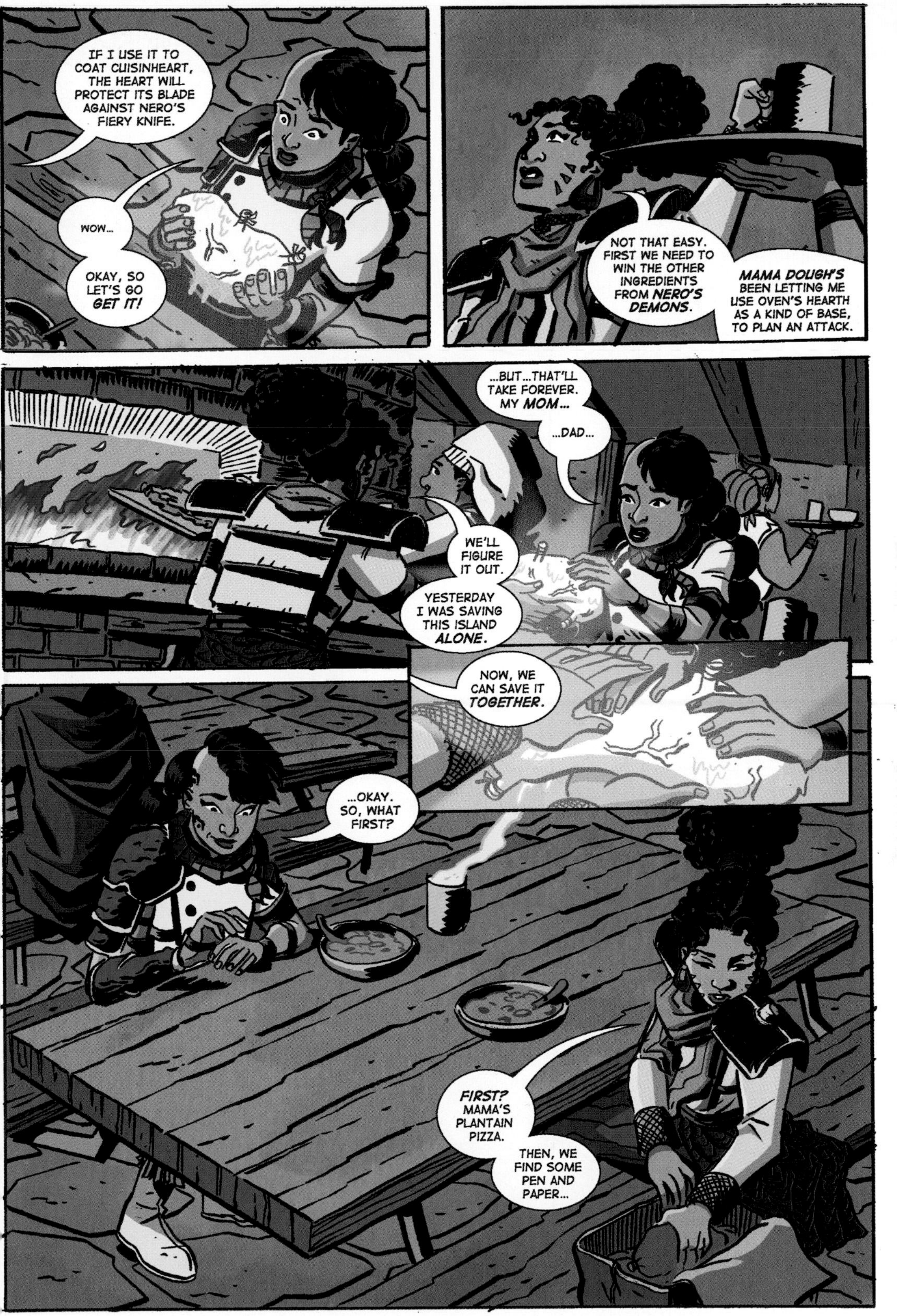
IF I USE IT TO COAT CUISINHEART, THE HEART WILL PROTECT ITS BLADE AGAINST NERO'S FIERY KNIFE.
WOW...
OKAY, SO LET'S GO *GET IT!*
NOT THAT EASY. FIRST WE NEED TO WIN THE OTHER INGREDIENTS FROM *NERO'S DEMONS*.
MAMA DOUGH'S BEEN LETTING ME USE OVEN'S HEARTH AS A KIND OF BASE, TO PLAN AN ATTACK.
...BUT...THAT'LL TAKE FOREVER. MY *MOM*...
...DAD...
WE'LL FIGURE IT OUT.
YESTERDAY I WAS SAVING THIS ISLAND *ALONE*.
NOW, WE CAN SAVE IT *TOGETHER*.
...OKAY. SO, WHAT FIRST?
FIRST? MAMA'S PLANTAIN PIZZA.
THEN, WE FIND SOME PEN AND PAPER...

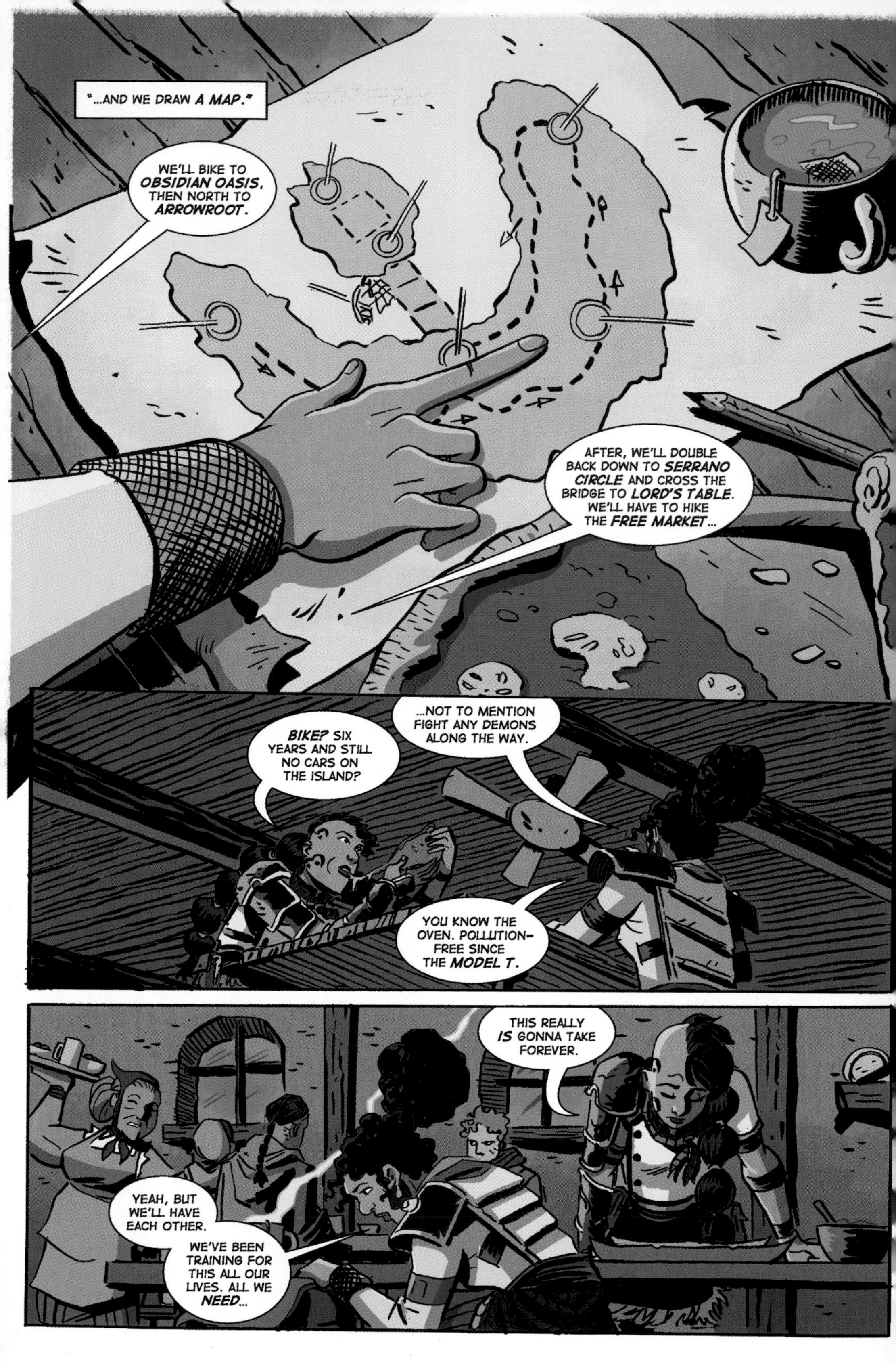
"...AND WE DRAW *A MAP*."
WE'LL BIKE TO *OBSIDIAN OASIS*, THEN NORTH TO *ARROWROOT*.
AFTER, WE'LL DOUBLE BACK DOWN TO *SERRANO CIRCLE* AND CROSS THE BRIDGE TO *LORD'S TABLE*. WE'LL HAVE TO HIKE THE *FREE MARKET*...
BIKE? SIX YEARS AND STILL NO CARS ON THE ISLAND?
...NOT TO MENTION FIGHT ANY DEMONS ALONG THE WAY.
YOU KNOW THE OVEN. POLLUTION-FREE SINCE THE *MODEL T*.
THIS REALLY *IS* GONNA TAKE FOREVER.
YEAH, BUT WE'LL HAVE EACH OTHER.
WE'VE BEEN TRAINING FOR THIS ALL OUR LIVES. ALL WE *NEED*...

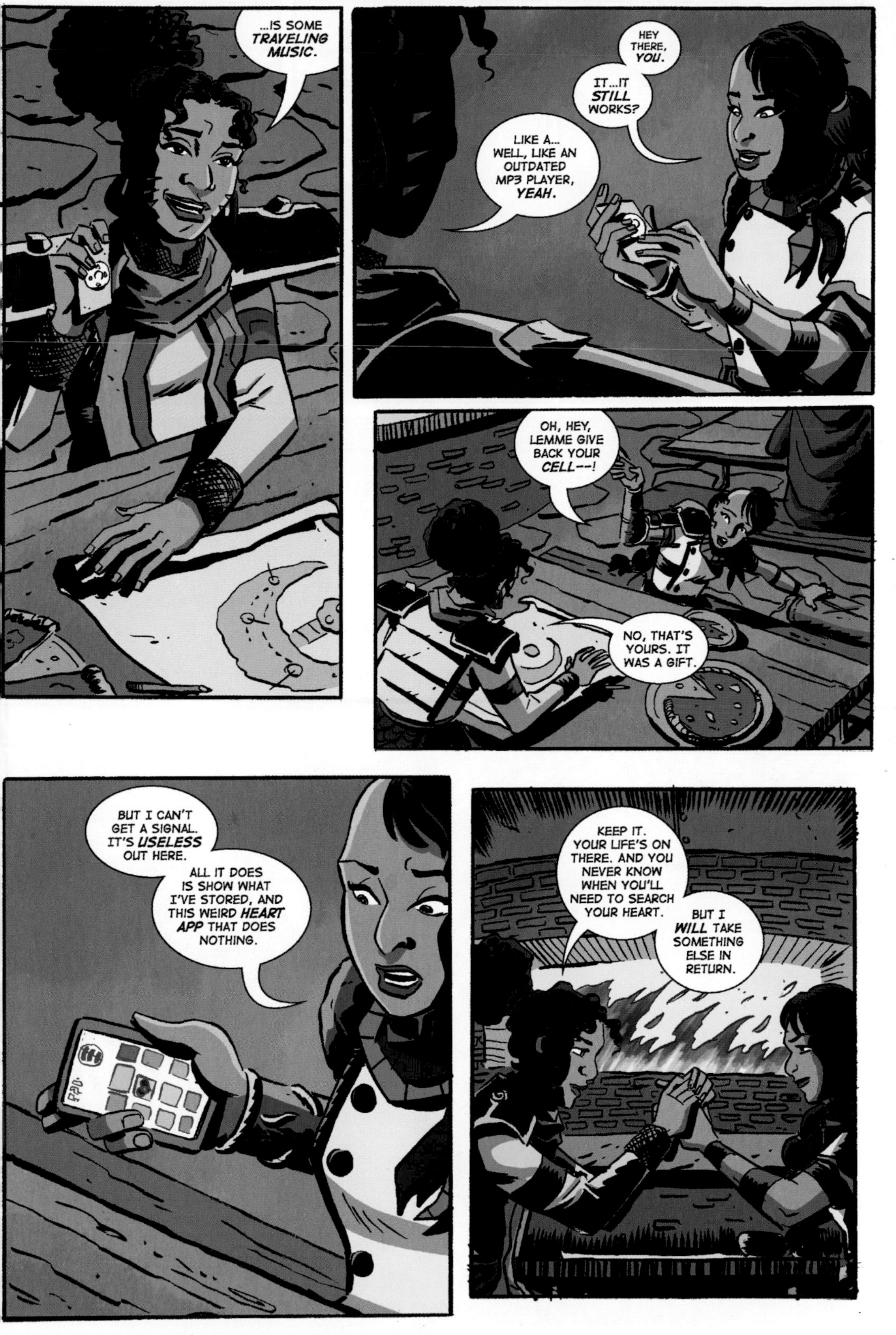

...IS SOME TRAVELING MUSIC.
HEY THERE, YOU.
IT...IT STILL WORKS?
LIKE A... WELL, LIKE AN OUTDATED MP3 PLAYER, YEAH.
OH, HEY, LEMME GIVE BACK YOUR CELL--!
NO, THAT'S YOURS. IT WAS A GIFT.
BUT I CAN'T GET A SIGNAL. IT'S USELESS OUT HERE.
ALL IT DOES IS SHOW WHAT I'VE STORED, AND THIS WEIRD HEART APP THAT DOES NOTHING.
KEEP IT. YOUR LIFE'S ON THERE. AND YOU NEVER KNOW WHEN YOU'LL NEED TO SEARCH YOUR HEART.
BUT I WILL TAKE SOMETHING ELSE IN RETURN.

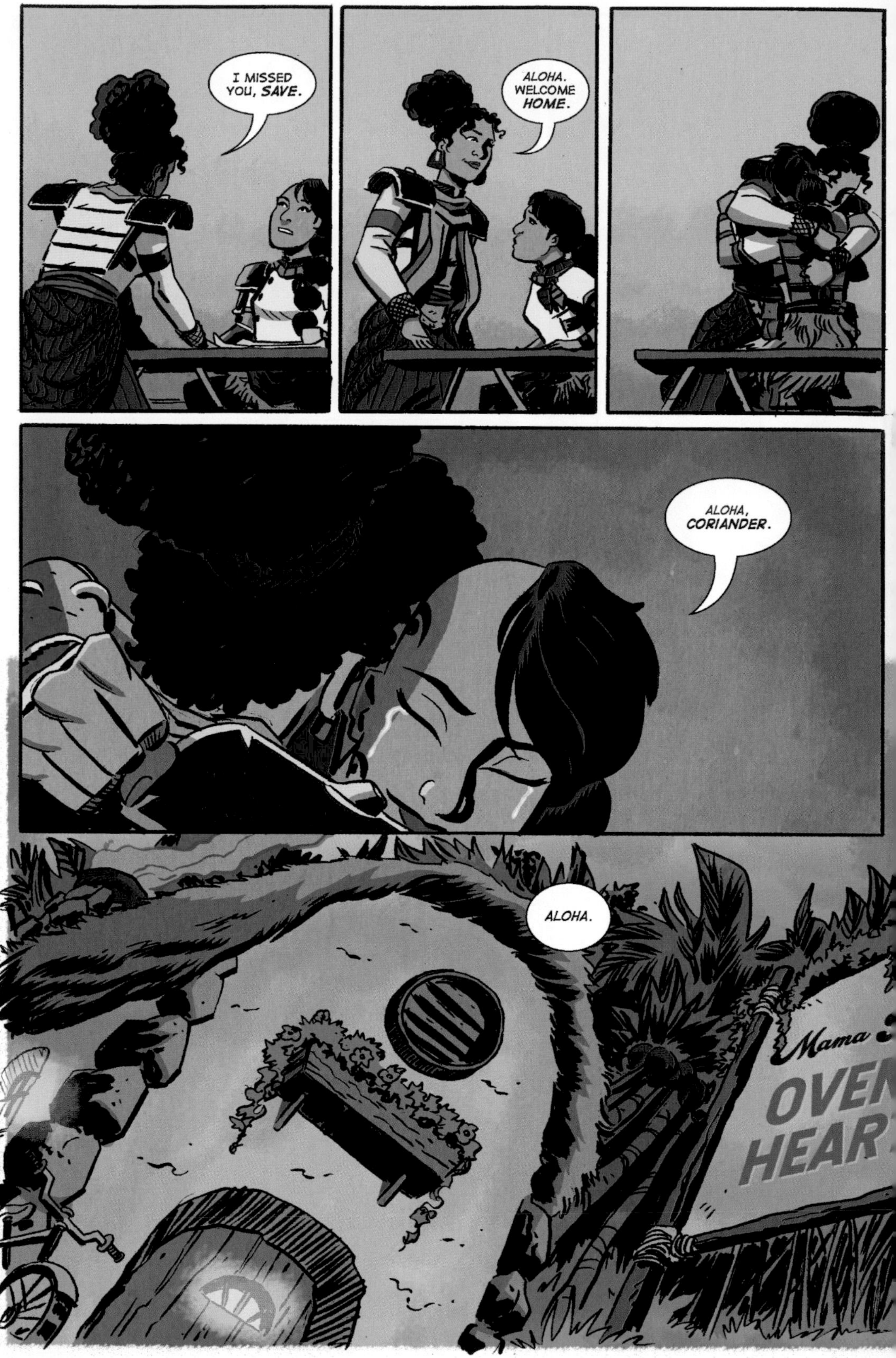
I MISSED YOU, SAVE.
ALOHA. WELCOME HOME.
ALOHA, CORIANDER.
ALOHA.
Mama

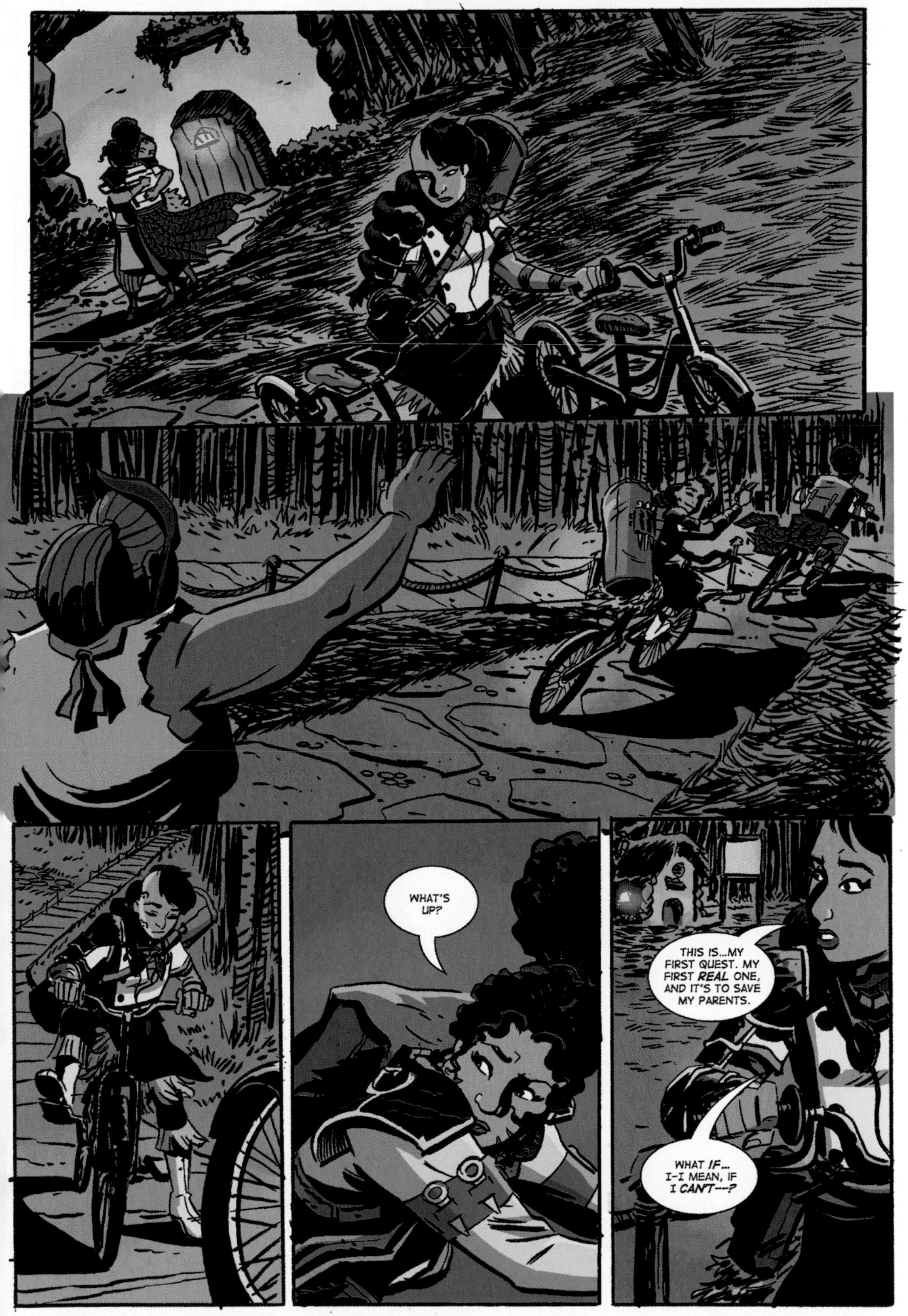
WHAT'S UP?
THIS IS...MY FIRST QUEST. MY FIRST REAL ONE, AND IT'S TO SAVE MY PARENTS.
WHAT IF... I-I MEAN, IF I CAN'T--?

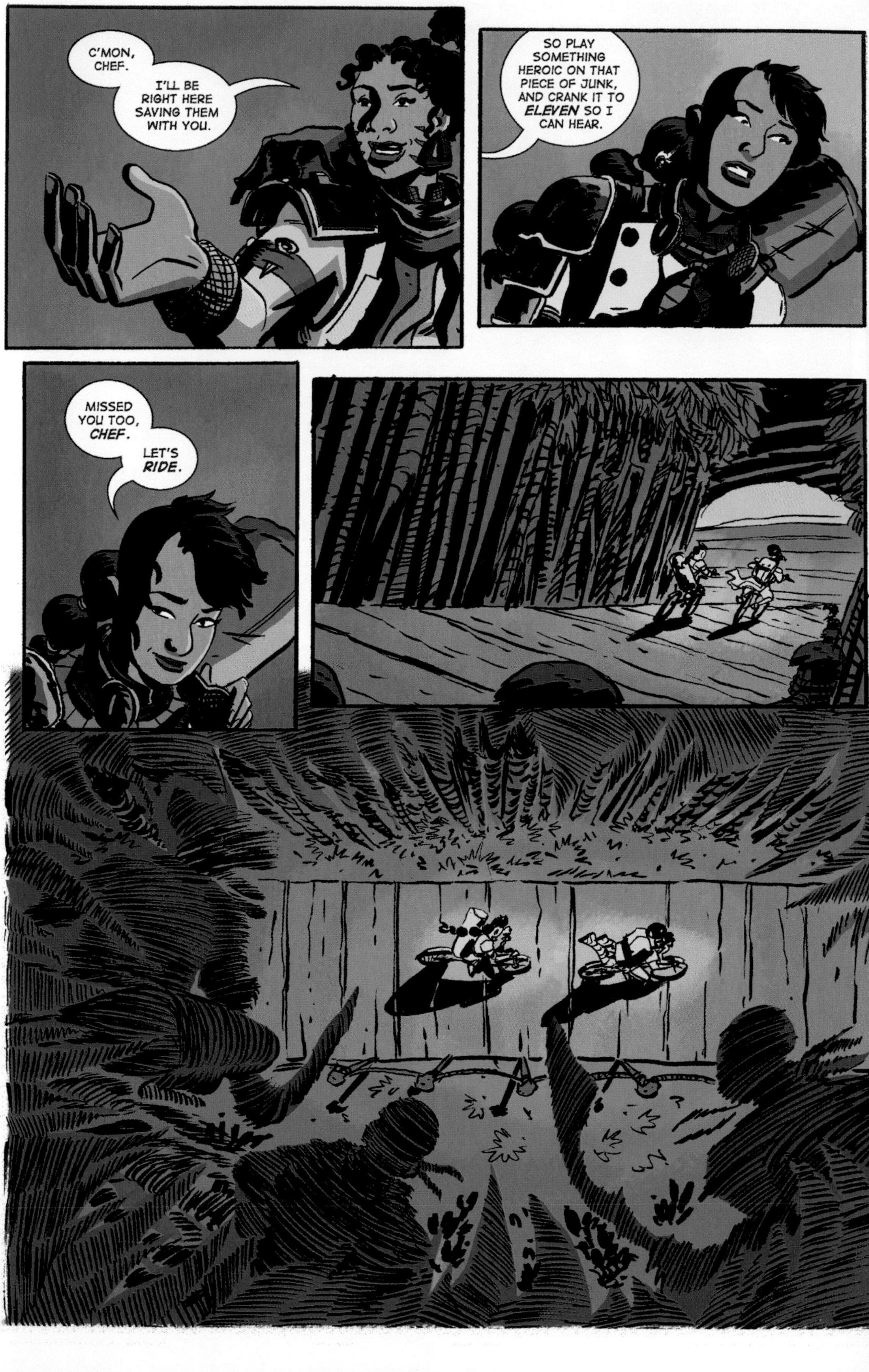
C'MON, CHEF.
I'LL BE RIGHT HERE SAVING THEM WITH YOU.
SO PLAY SOMETHING HEROIC ON THAT PIECE OF JUNK, AND CRANK IT TO ELEVEN SO I CAN HEAR.
MISSED YOU TOO, CHEF.
LET'S RIDE.

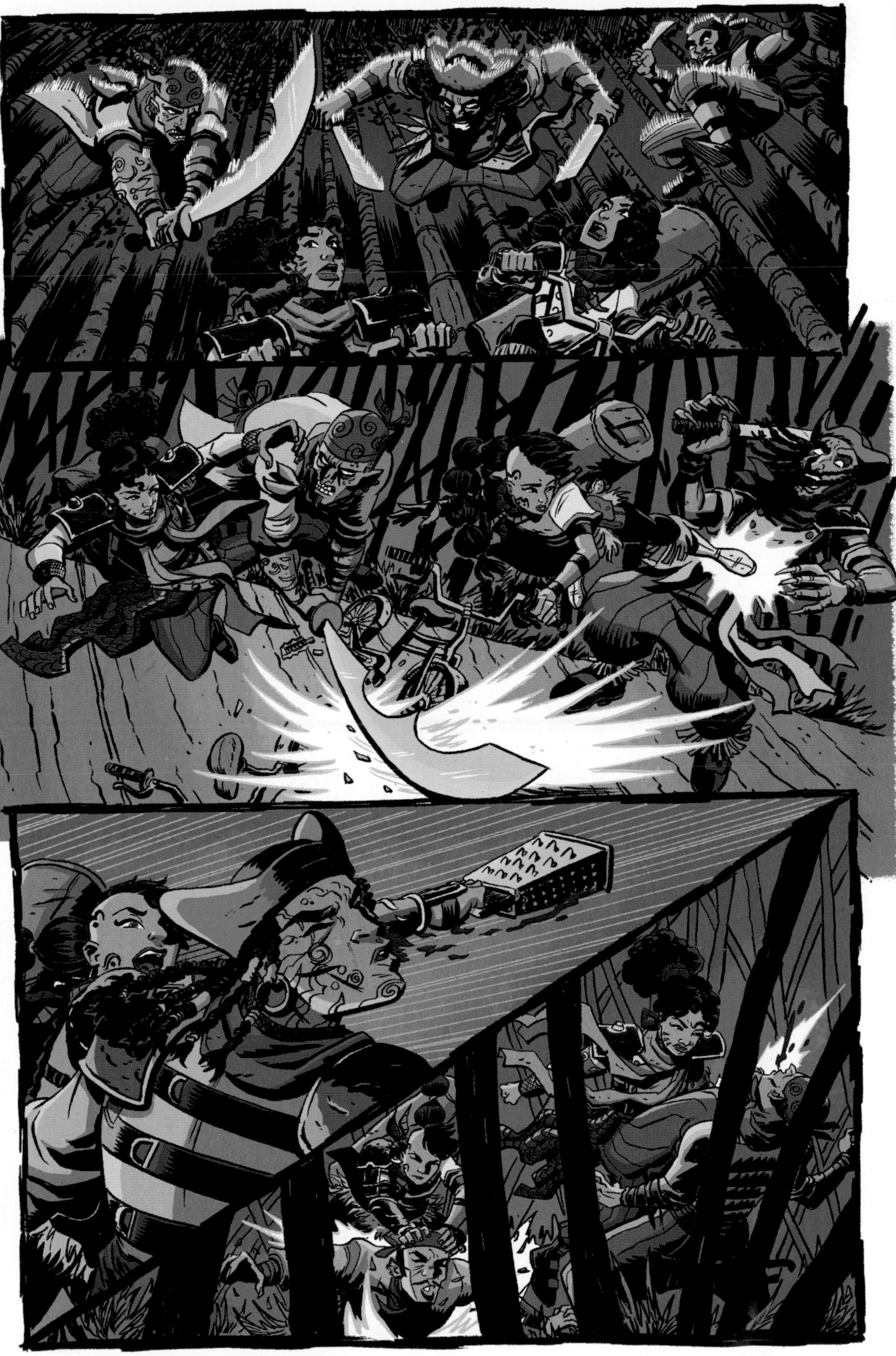

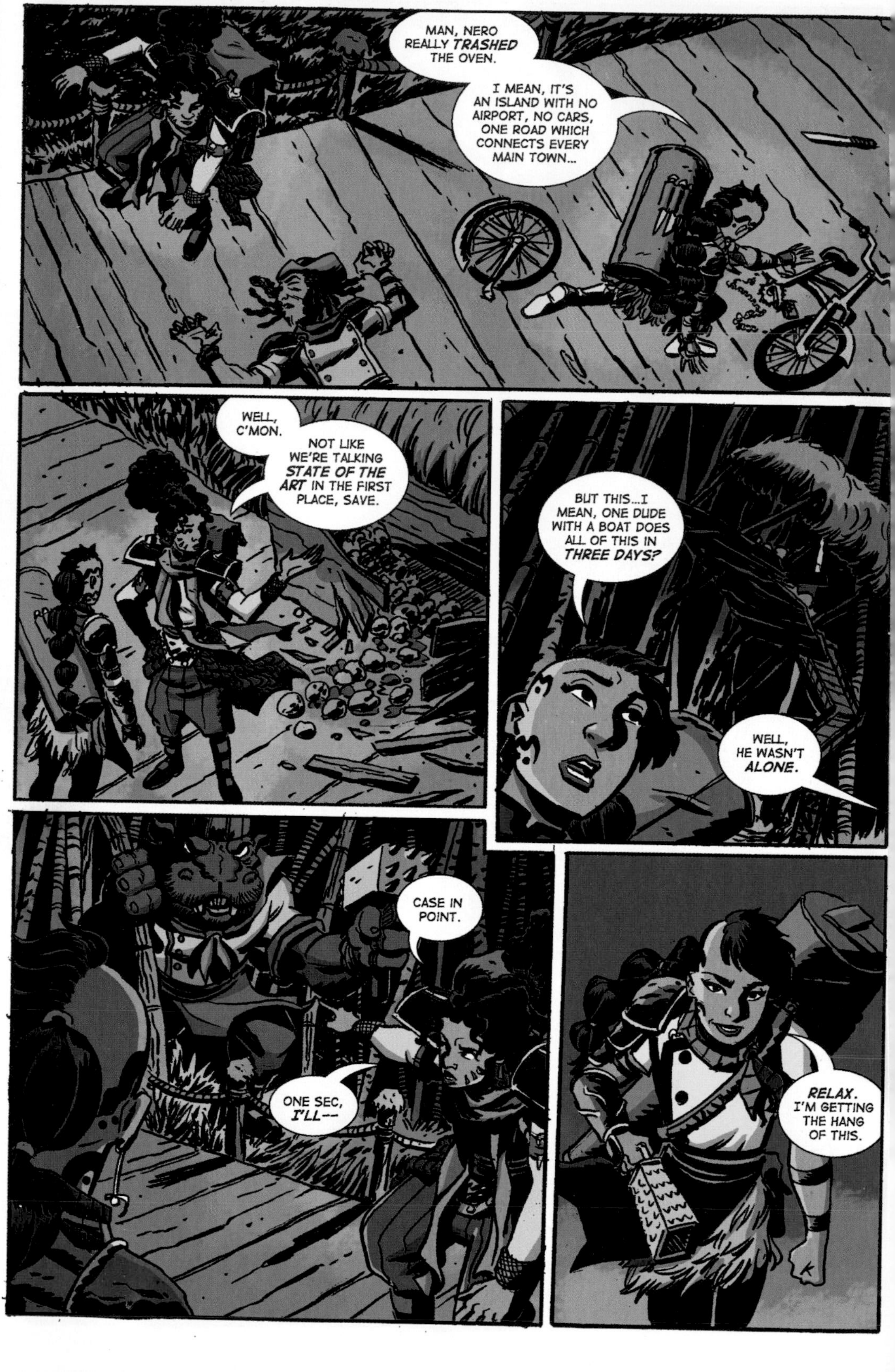
MAN, NERO REALLY *TRASHED* THE OVEN.
I MEAN, IT'S AN ISLAND WITH NO AIRPORT, NO CARS, ONE ROAD WHICH CONNECTS EVERY MAIN TOWN...
WELL, C'MON.
NOT LIKE WE'RE TALKING ***STATE OF THE ART*** IN THE FIRST PLACE, SAVE.
BUT THIS...I MEAN, ONE DUDE WITH A BOAT DOES ALL OF THIS IN ***THREE DAYS?***
WELL, HE WASN'T ***ALONE***.
CASE IN POINT.
ONE SEC, ***I'LL***--
RELAX. I'M GETTING THE HANG OF THIS.

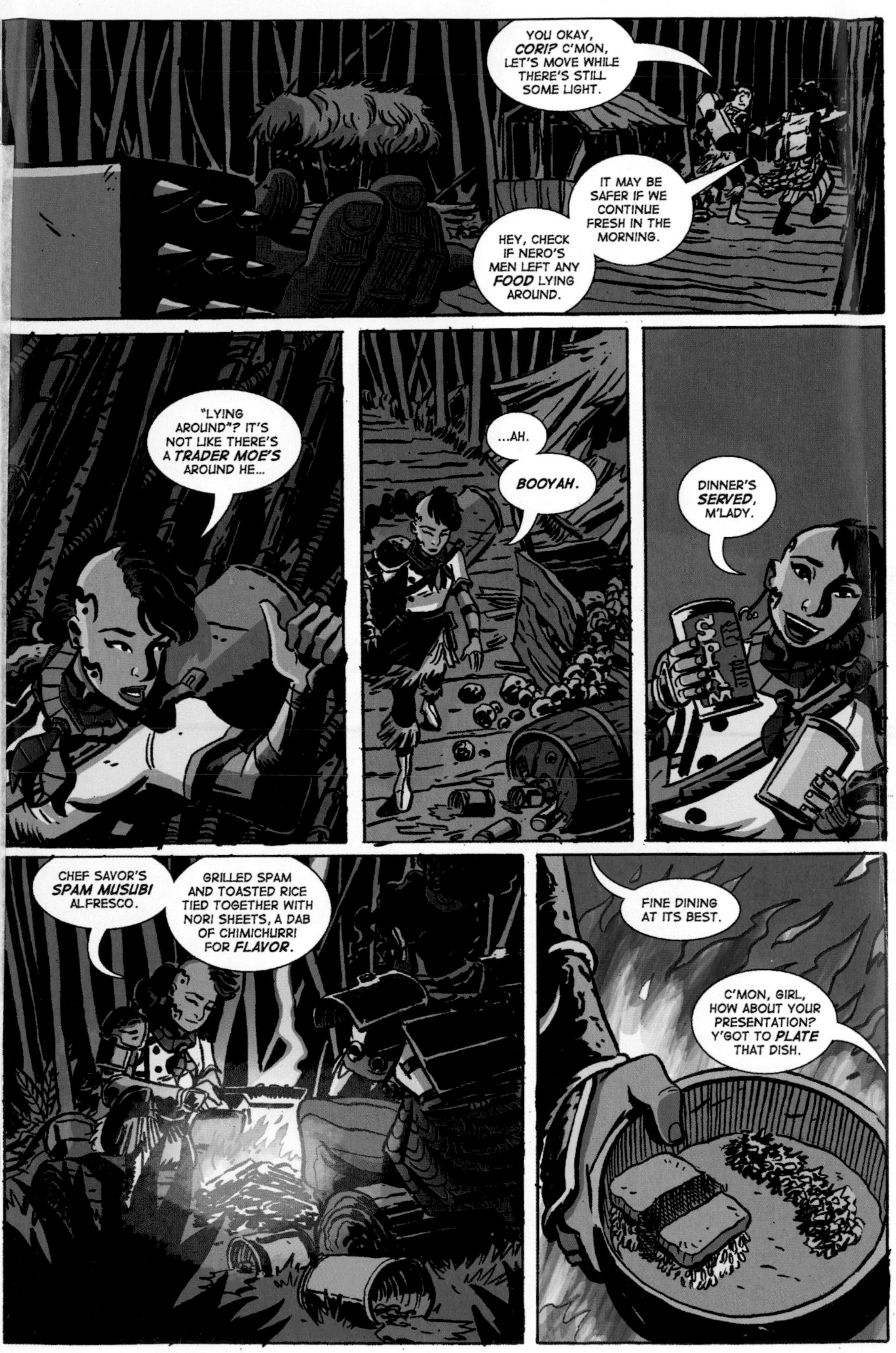
YOU OKAY, CORI? C'MON, LET'S MOVE WHILE THERE'S STILL SOME LIGHT.
IT MAY BE SAFER IF WE CONTINUE FRESH IN THE MORNING.
HEY, CHECK IF NERO'S MEN LEFT ANY FOOD LYING AROUND.
"LYING AROUND"? IT'S NOT LIKE THERE'S A TRADER MOE'S AROUND HE...
...AH.
BOOYAH.
DINNER'S SERVED, M'LADY.
CHEF SAVOR'S SPAM MUSUBI ALFRESCO.
GRILLED SPAM AND TOASTED RICE TIED TOGETHER WITH NORI SHEETS, A DAB OF CHIMICHURRI FOR FLAVOR.
FINE DINING AT ITS BEST.
C'MON, GIRL, HOW ABOUT YOUR PRESENTATION? Y'GOT TO PLATE THAT DISH.

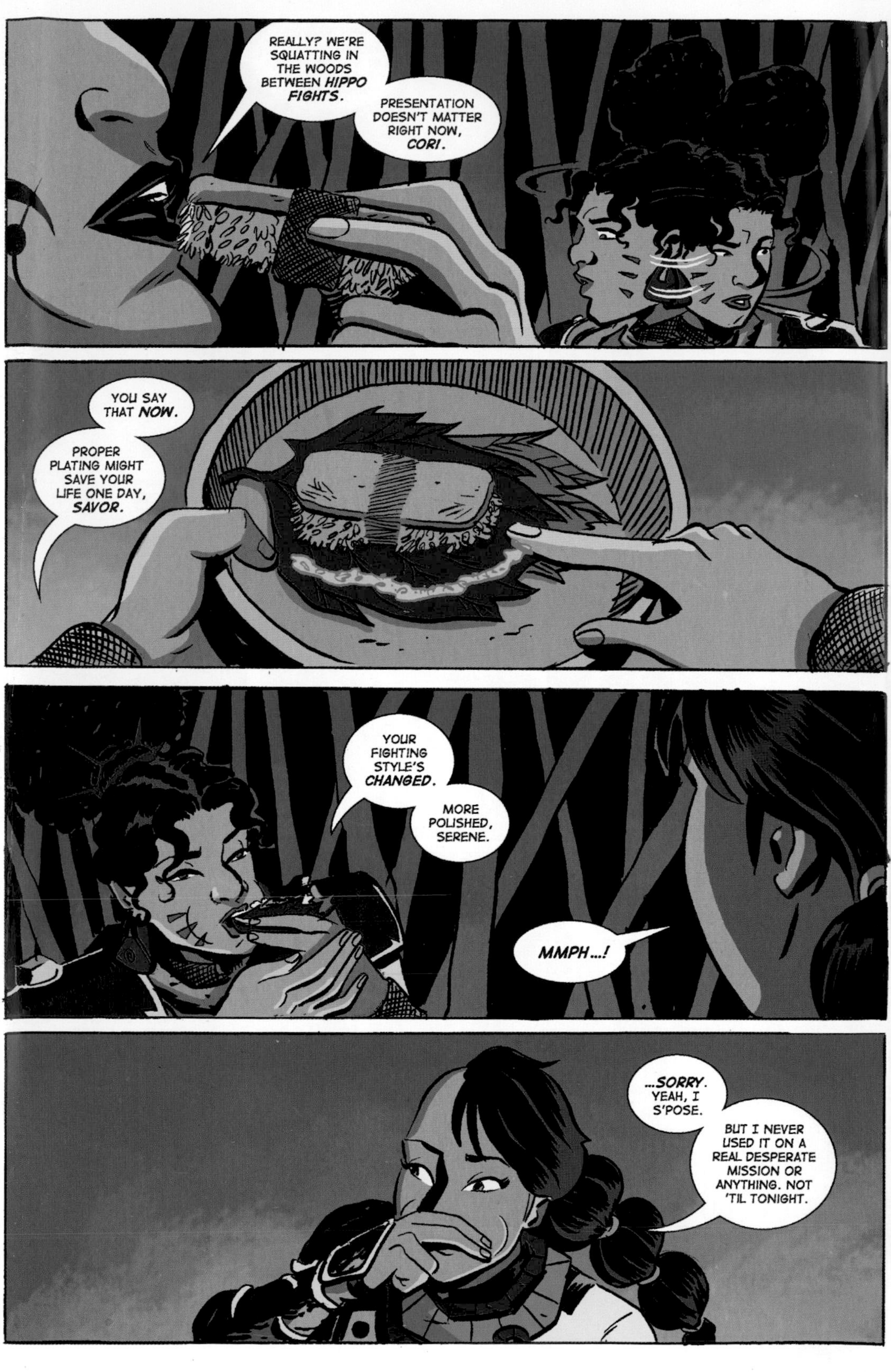
REALLY? WE'RE SQUATTING IN THE WOODS BETWEEN HIPPO FIGHTS.
PRESENTATION DOESN'T MATTER RIGHT NOW, CORI.
YOU SAY THAT NOW.
PROPER PLATING MIGHT SAVE YOUR LIFE ONE DAY, SAVOR.
YOUR FIGHTING STYLE'S CHANGED.
MORE POLISHED, SERENE.
MMPH...!
...SORRY. YEAH, I S'POSE.
BUT I NEVER USED IT ON A REAL DESPERATE MISSION OR ANYTHING. NOT 'TIL TONIGHT.

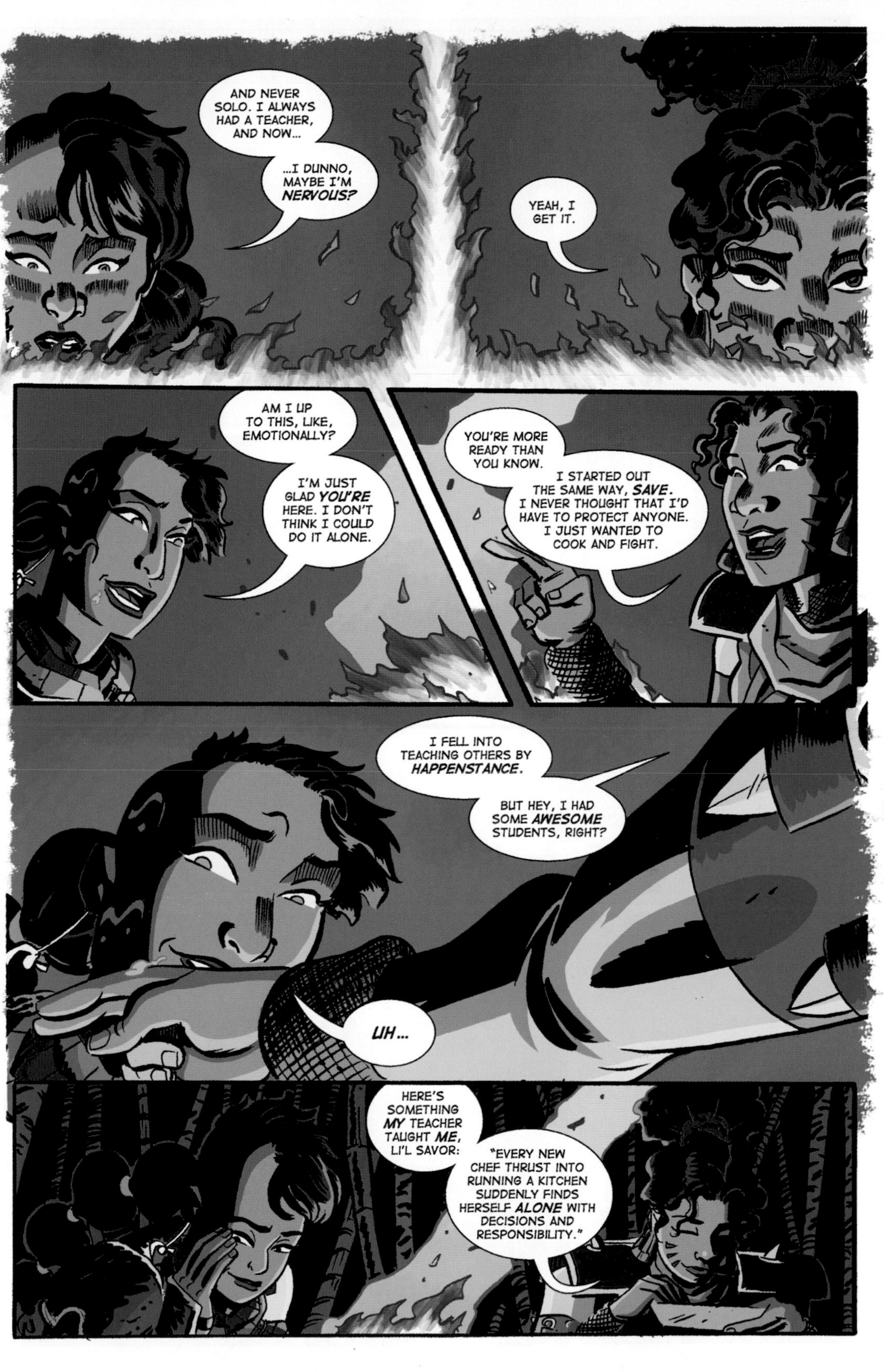
AND NEVER SOLO. I ALWAYS HAD A TEACHER, AND NOW...
...I DUNNO, MAYBE I'M NERVOUS?
YEAH, I GET IT.
AM I UP TO THIS, LIKE, EMOTIONALLY?
I'M JUST GLAD YOU'RE HERE. I DON'T THINK I COULD DO IT ALONE.
YOU'RE MORE READY THAN YOU KNOW.
I STARTED OUT THE SAME WAY, SAVE. I NEVER THOUGHT THAT I'D HAVE TO PROTECT ANYONE. I JUST WANTED TO COOK AND FIGHT.
I FELL INTO TEACHING OTHERS BY HAPPENSTANCE.
BUT HEY, I HAD SOME AWESOME STUDENTS, RIGHT?
UH...
HERE'S SOMETHING MY TEACHER TAUGHT ME, LI'L SAVOR:
"EVERY NEW CHEF THRUST INTO RUNNING A KITCHEN SUDDENLY FINDS HERSELF ALONE WITH DECISIONS AND RESPONSIBILITY."

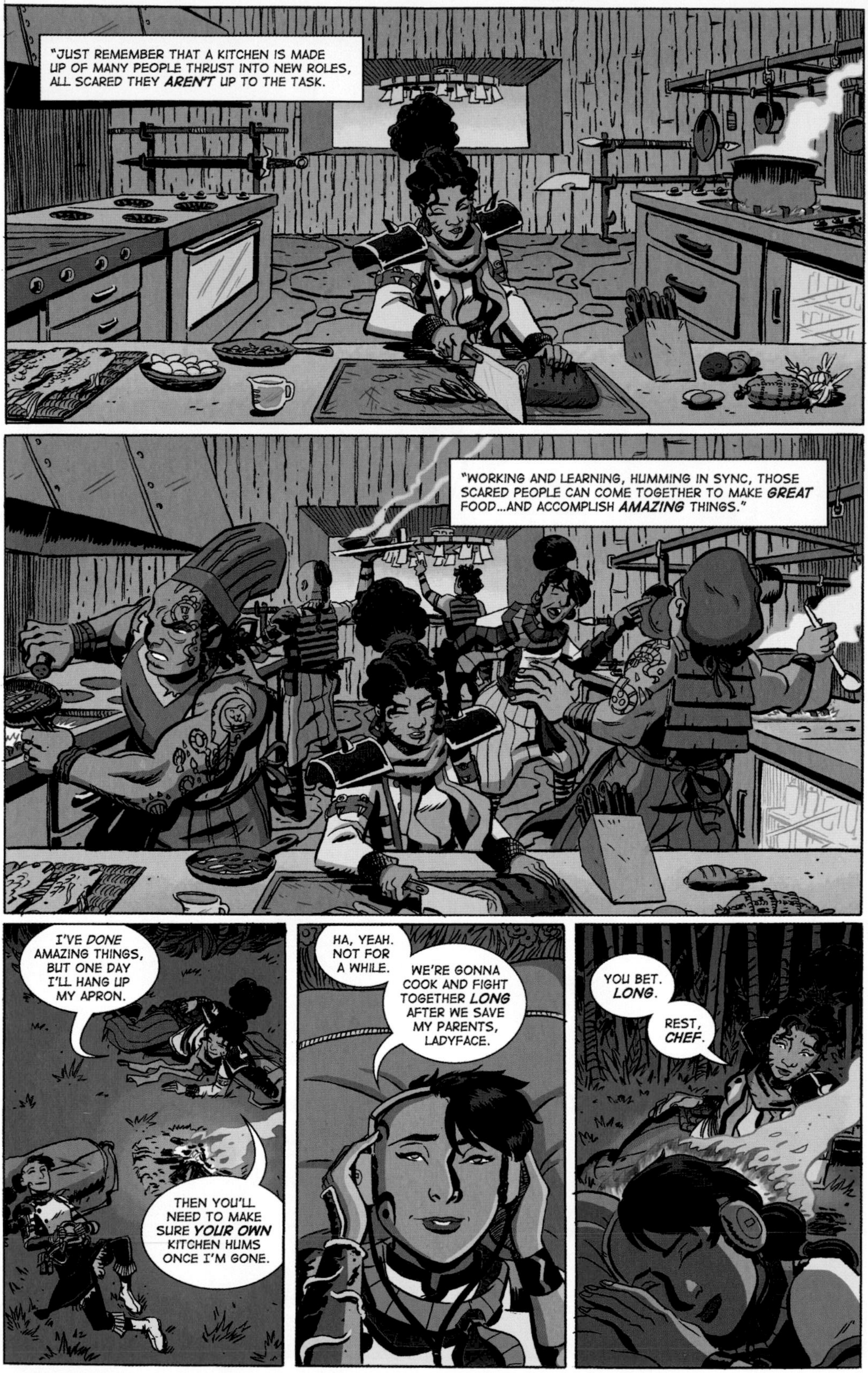
"JUST REMEMBER THAT A KITCHEN IS MADE UP OF MANY PEOPLE THRUST INTO NEW ROLES, ALL SCARED THEY AREN'T UP TO THE TASK.
"WORKING AND LEARNING, HUMMING IN SYNC, THOSE SCARED PEOPLE CAN COME TOGETHER TO MAKE GREAT FOOD...AND ACCOMPLISH AMAZING THINGS."
I'VE DONE AMAZING THINGS, BUT ONE DAY I'LL HANG UP MY APRON.
THEN YOU'LL NEED TO MAKE SURE YOUR OWN KITCHEN HUMS ONCE I'M GONE.
HA, YEAH. NOT FOR A WHILE.
WE'RE GONNA COOK AND FIGHT TOGETHER LONG AFTER WE SAVE MY PARENTS, LADYFACE.
YOU BET. LONG.
REST, CHEF.

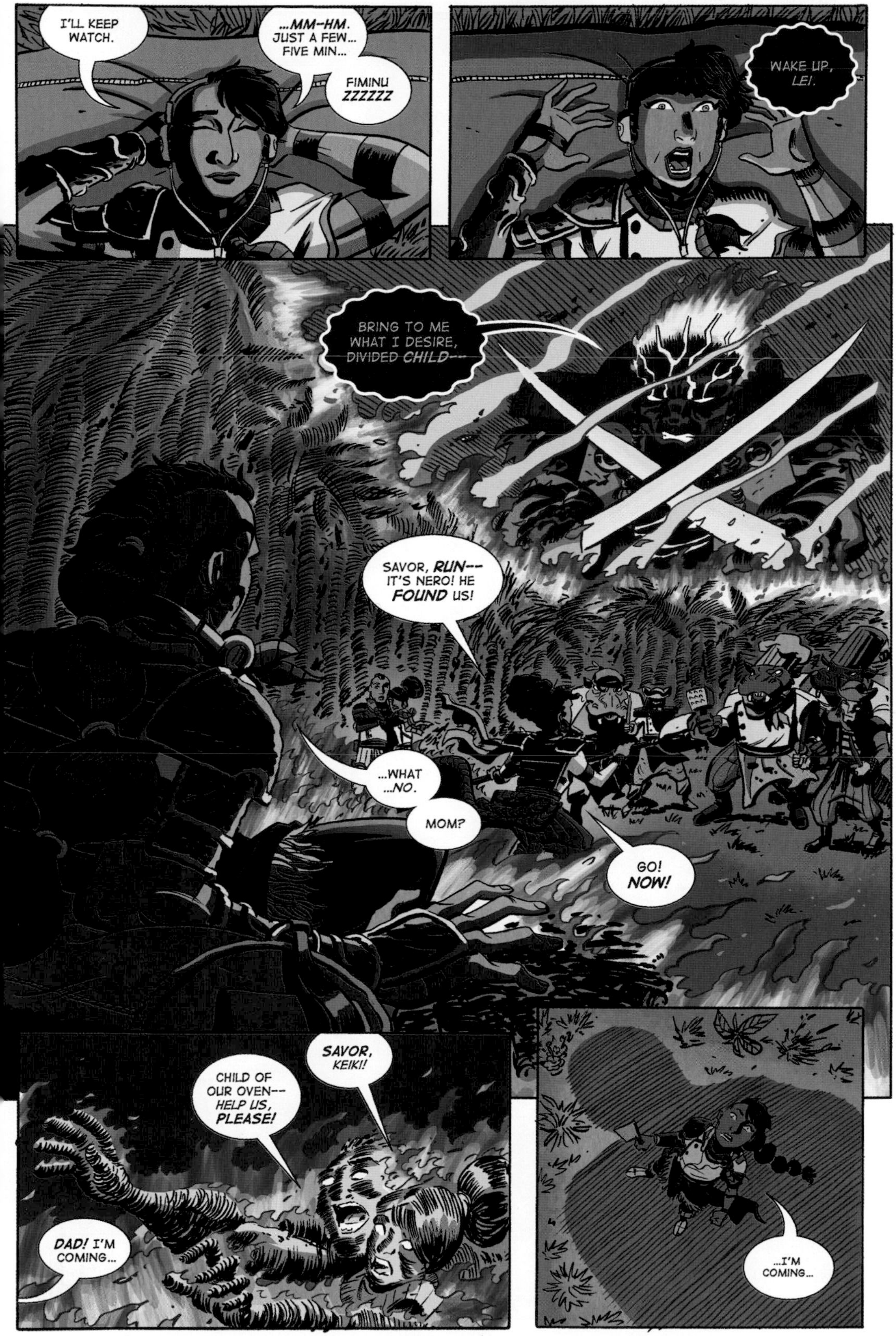

I'LL KEEP WATCH.
...MM-HM. JUST A FEW... FIVE MIN...
FIMINU ZZZZZZ
WAKE UP, LEI.
BRING TO ME WHAT I DESIRE, DIVIDED CHILD--
SAVOR, RUN-- IT'S NERO! HE FOUND US!
...WHAT ...NO.
MOM?
GO! NOW!
SAVOR, KEIKI!
CHILD OF OUR OVEN-- HELP US, PLEASE!
DAD! I'M COMING...
...I'M COMING...

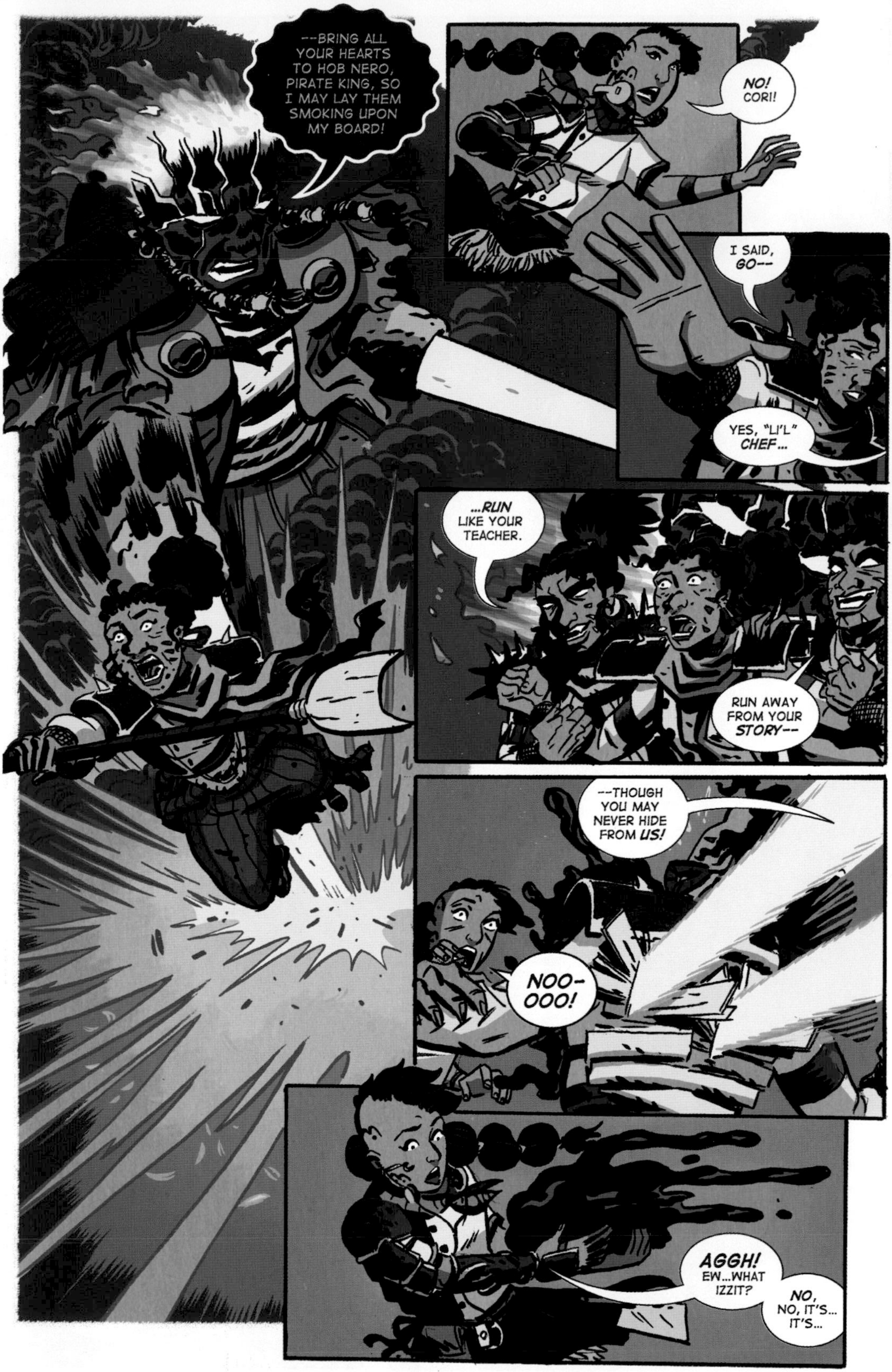
--BRING ALL YOUR HEARTS TO HOB NERO, PIRATE KING, SO I MAY LAY THEM SMOKING UPON MY BOARD!
NO! CORI!
I SAID, GO--
YES, "LI'L" CHEF...
...RUN LIKE YOUR TEACHER.
RUN AWAY FROM YOUR STORY--
--THOUGH YOU MAY NEVER HIDE FROM US!
NOO-OOO!
AGGH! EW...WHAT IZZIT?
NO, NO, IT'S... IT'S...

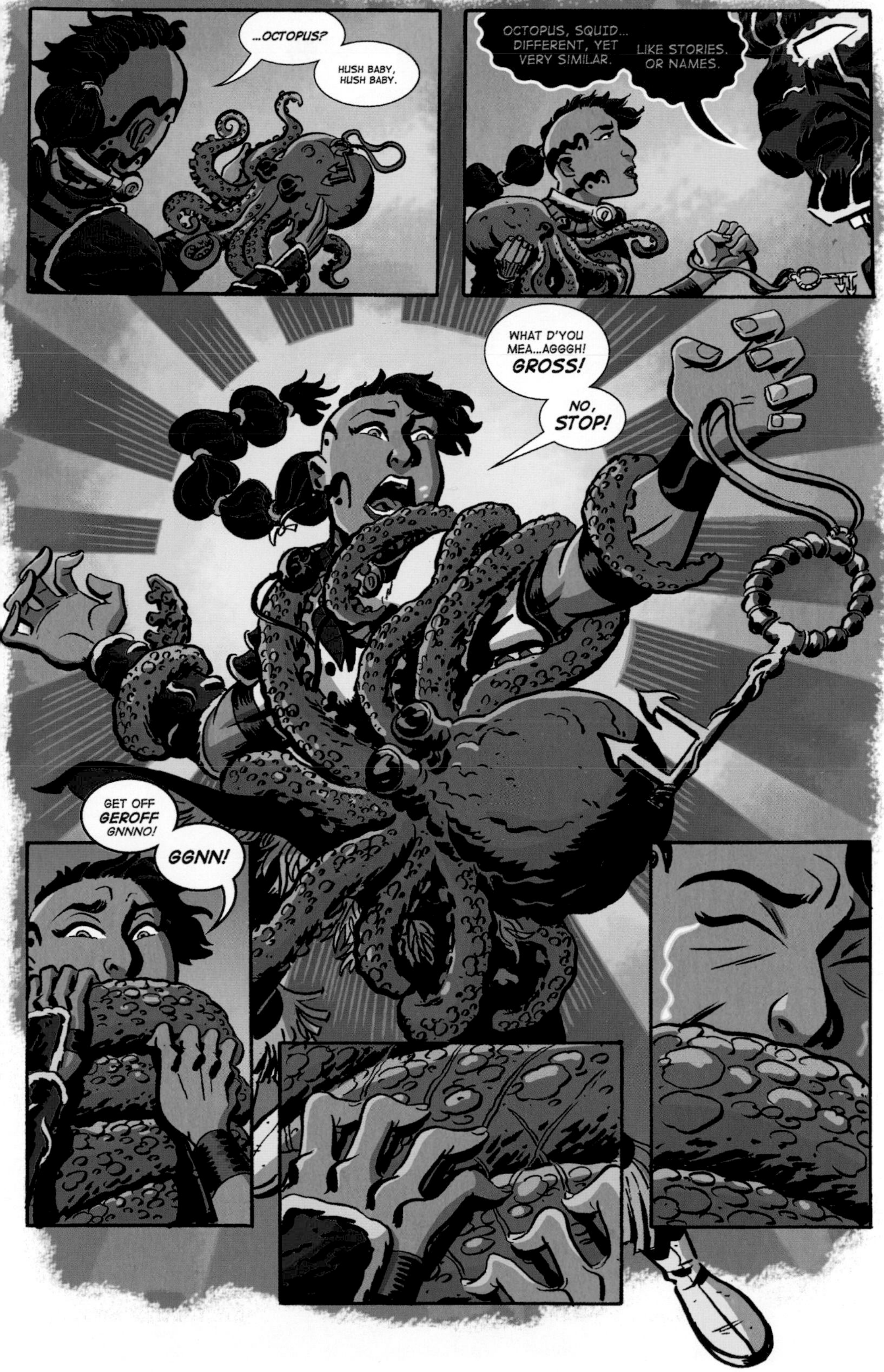
...OCTOPUS?
HUSH BABY, HUSH BABY.
OCTOPUS, SQUID... DIFFERENT, YET VERY SIMILAR.
LIKE STORIES. OR NAMES.
WHAT D'YOU MEA...AGGGH! GROSS!
NO, STOP!
GET OFF GEROFF GNNNO!
GGNN!

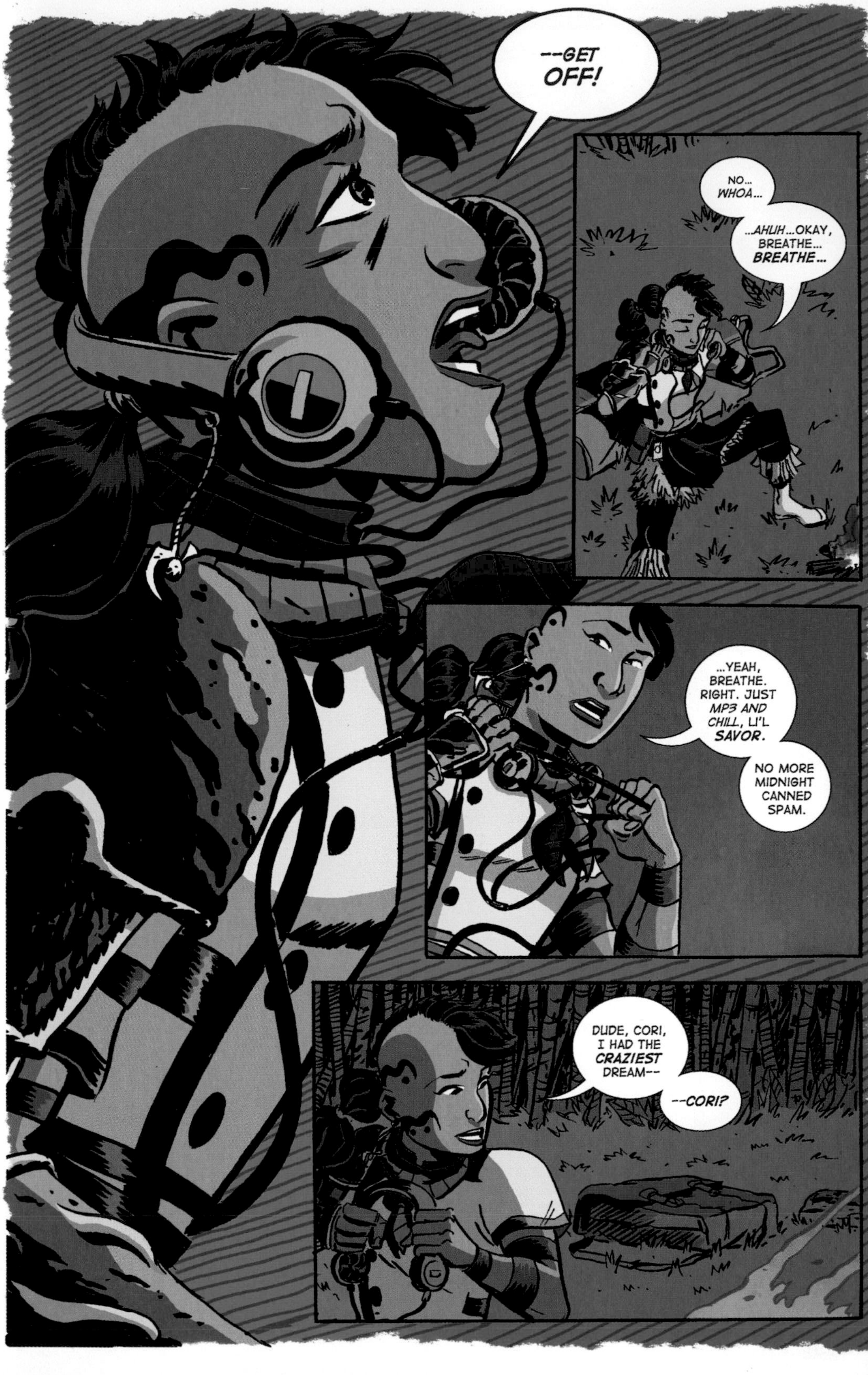
--GET OFF!
NO... WHOA...
...AHUH...OKAY, BREATHE... BREATHE...
...YEAH, BREATHE. RIGHT. JUST MP3 AND CHILL, LI'L SAVOR.
NO MORE MIDNIGHT CANNED SPAM.
DUDE, CORI, I HAD THE CRAZIEST DREAM--
--CORI?

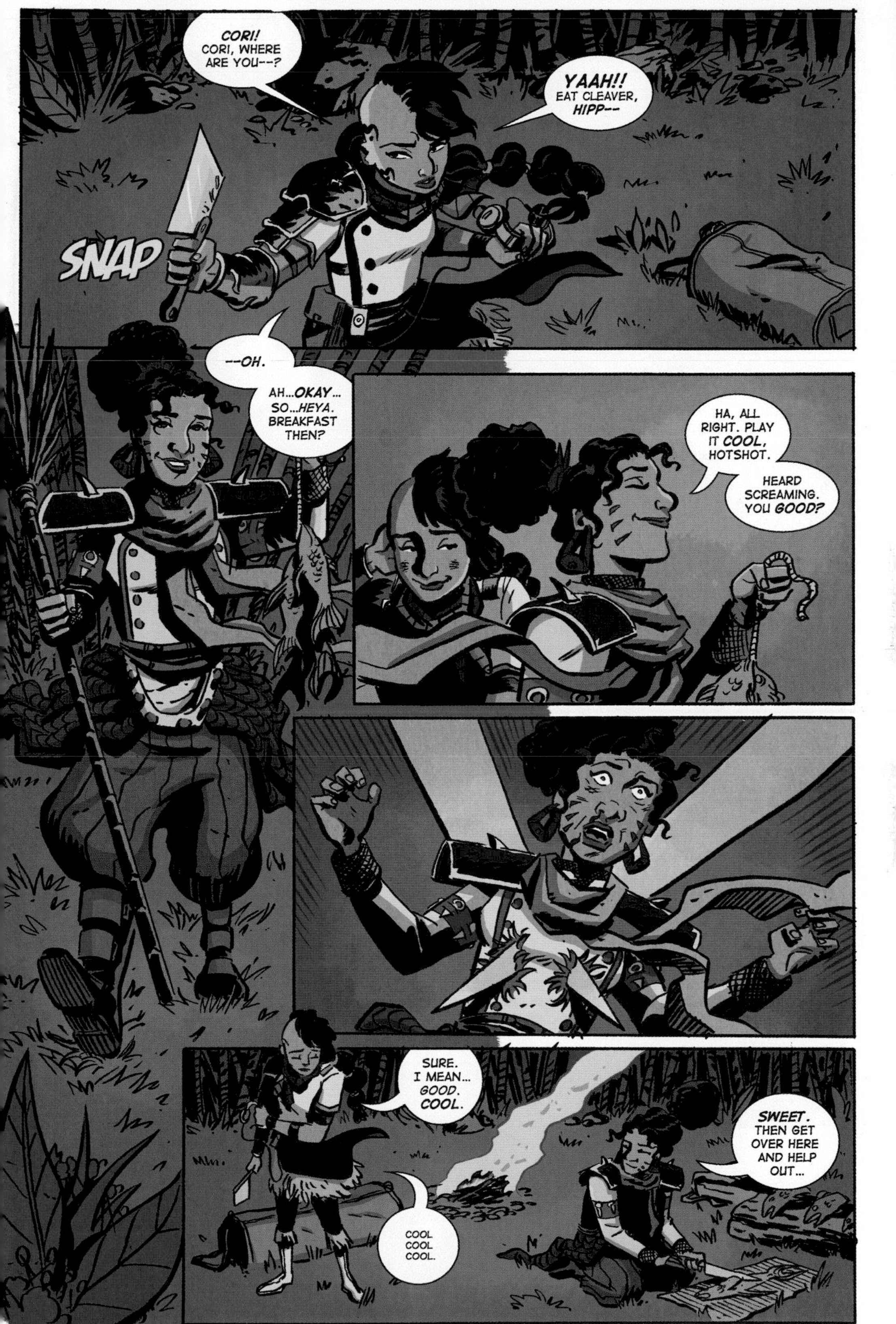
CORI! CORI, WHERE ARE YOU--?
YAAH!! EAT CLEAVER, HIPP--
SNAP
--OH.
AH...OKAY... SO...HEYA. BREAKFAST THEN?
HA, ALL RIGHT. PLAY IT COOL, HOTSHOT.
HEARD SCREAMING. YOU GOOD?
SURE. I MEAN... GOOD. COOL.
COOL COOL COOL.
SWEET. THEN GET OVER HERE AND HELP OUT...

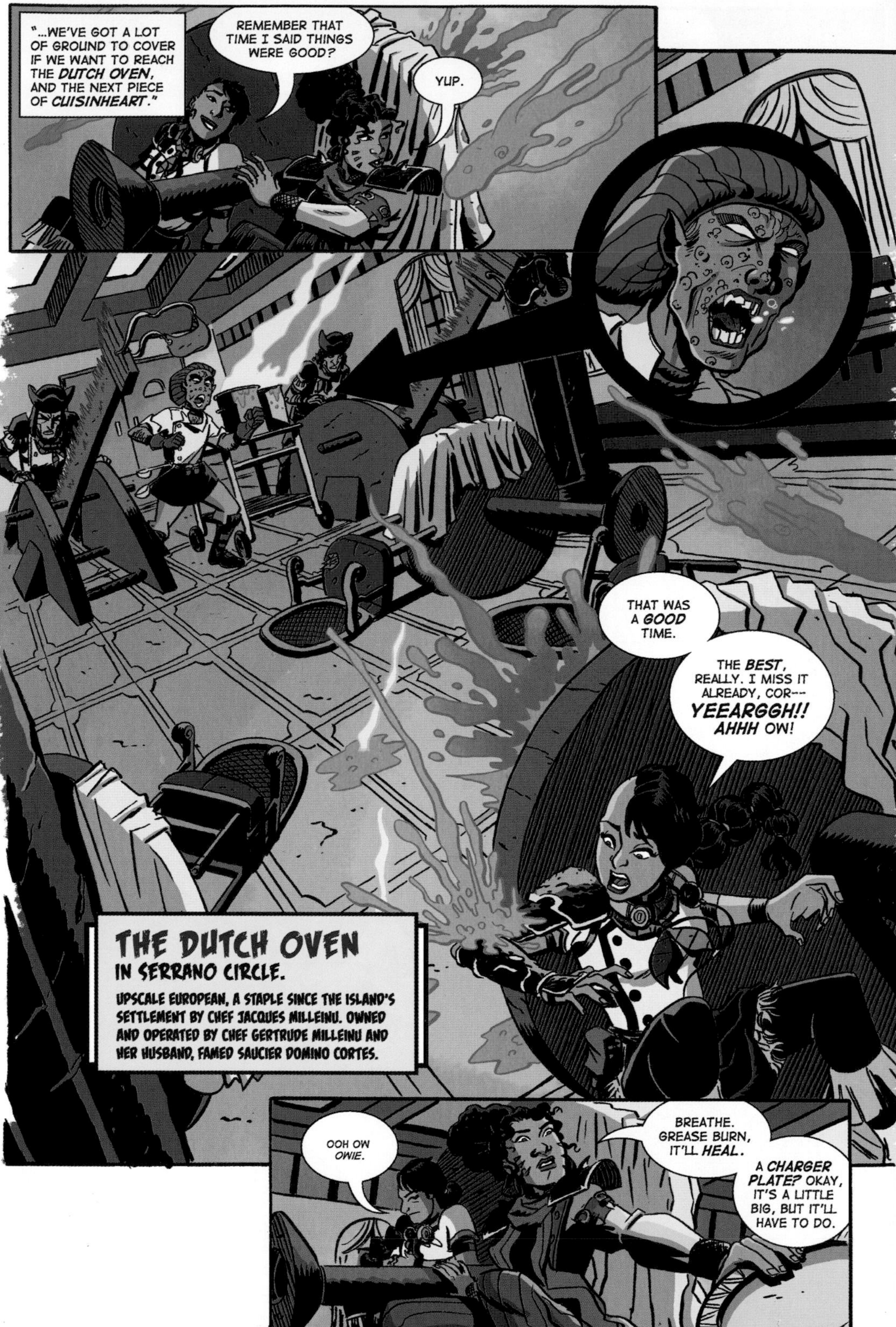
"...WE'VE GOT A LOT OF GROUND TO COVER IF WE WANT TO REACH THE *DUTCH OVEN*, AND THE NEXT PIECE OF *CUISINHEART*."
REMEMBER THAT TIME I SAID THINGS WERE GOOD?
YUP.
THAT WAS A *GOOD* TIME.
THE *BEST*, REALLY. I MISS IT ALREADY, COR-- **YEEARGGH!! AHHH** OW!
THE DUTCH OVEN
IN SERRANO CIRCLE.
UPSCALE EUROPEAN, A STAPLE SINCE THE ISLAND'S SETTLEMENT BY CHEF JACQUES MILLEINU. OWNED AND OPERATED BY CHEF GERTRUDE MILLEINU AND HER HUSBAND, FAMED SAUCIER DOMINO CORTES.
OOH OW *OWIE*.
BREATHE. GREASE BURN, IT'LL *HEAL*.
A *CHARGER PLATE?* OKAY, IT'S A LITTLE BIG, BUT IT'LL HAVE TO DO.

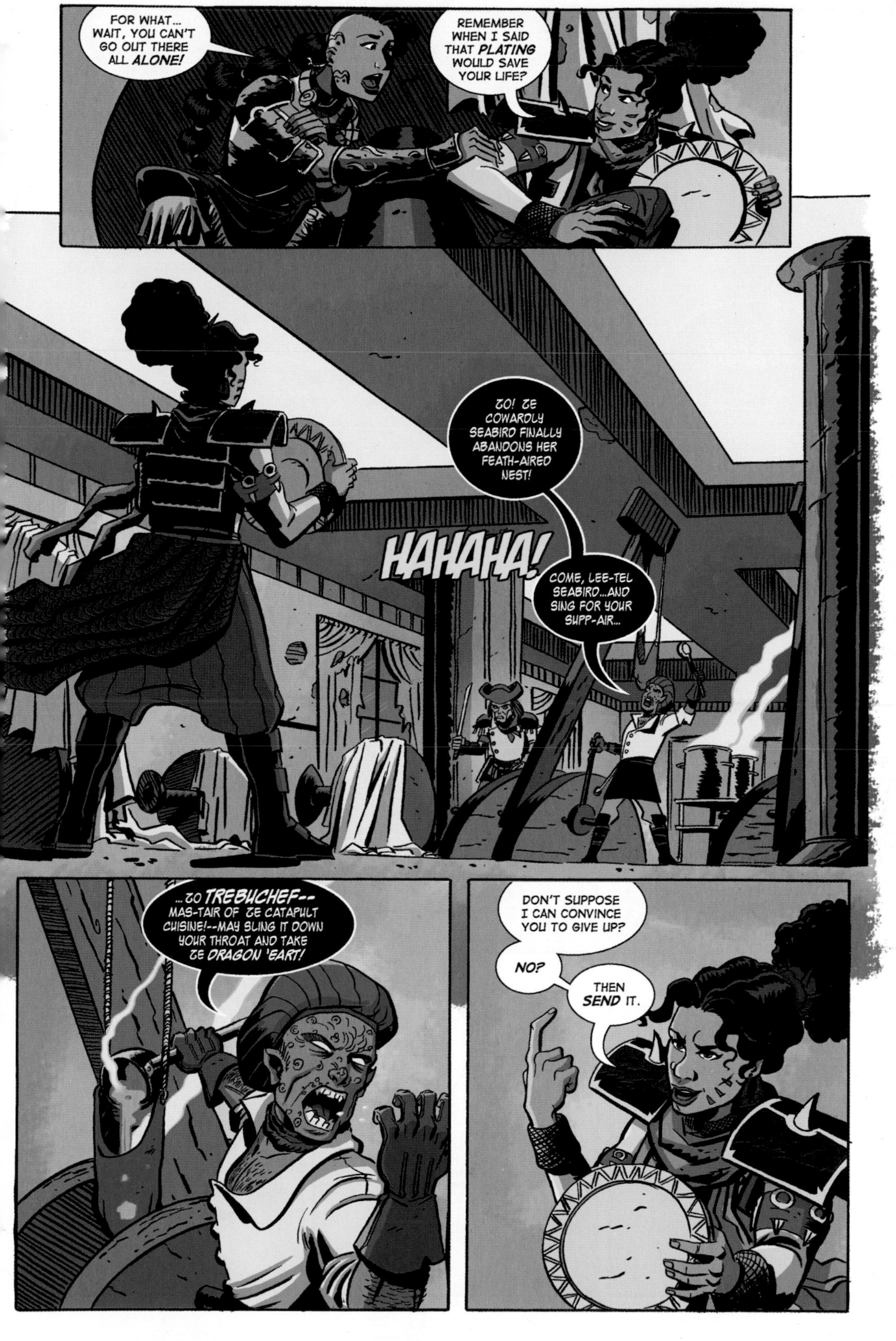
FOR WHAT... WAIT, YOU CAN'T GO OUT THERE ALL *ALONE!*
REMEMBER WHEN I SAID THAT *PLATING* WOULD SAVE YOUR LIFE?
ƵO! ƵE COWARDLY SEABIRD FINALLY ABANDONS HER FEATH-AIRED NEST!
HAHAHA!
COME, LEE-TEL SEABIRD...AND SING FOR YOUR SUPP-AIR...
...ƵO *TREBUCHEF*--MAS-TAIR OF ƵE CATAPULT CUISINE!--MAY SLING IT DOWN YOUR THROAT AND TAKE ƵE *DRAGON 'EART!*
DON'T SUPPOSE I CAN CONVINCE YOU TO GIVE UP?
NO?
THEN *SEND* IT.

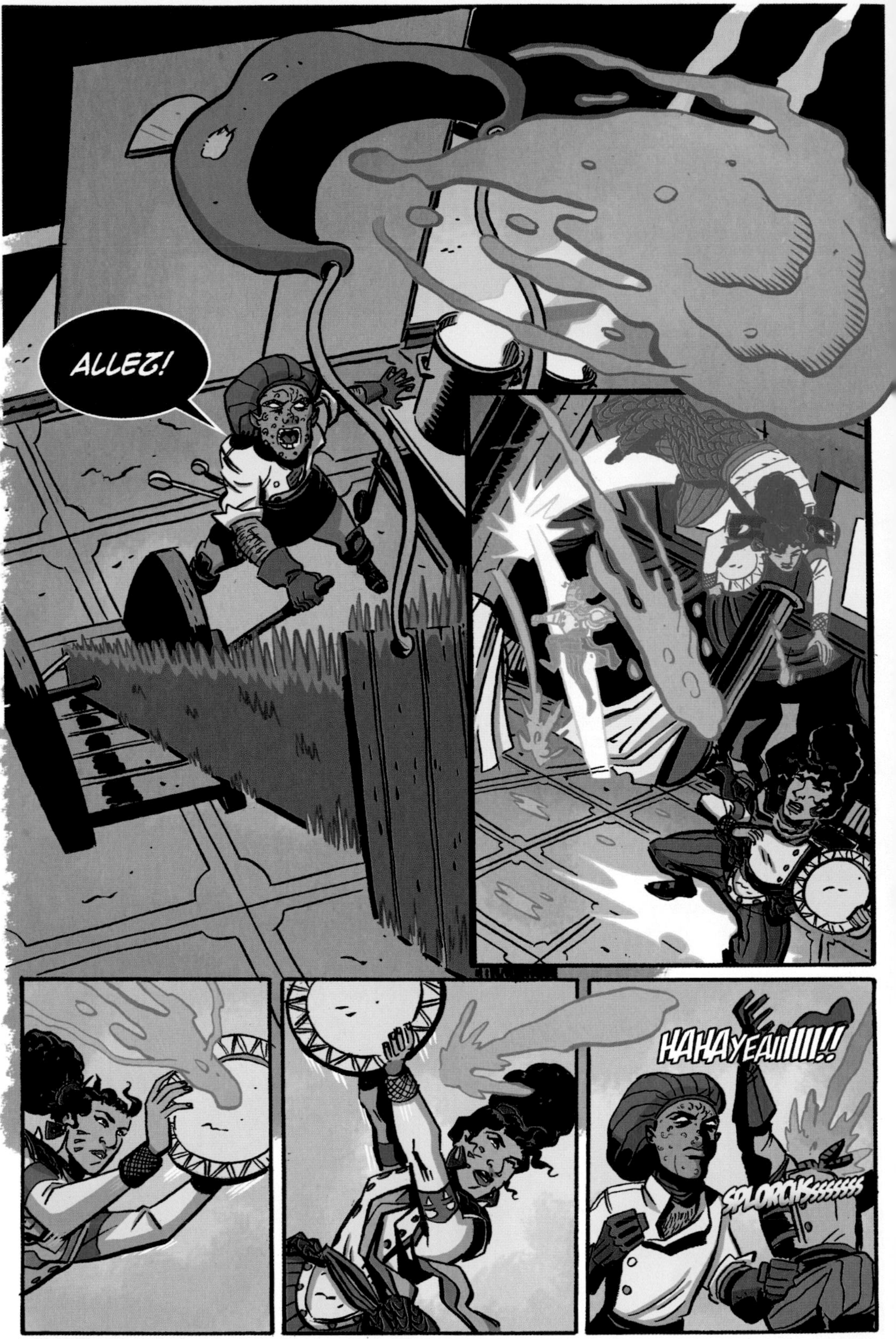
ALLEZ!
HAHAYEAIIIIII!!
SPLORCHSSSSSSSS

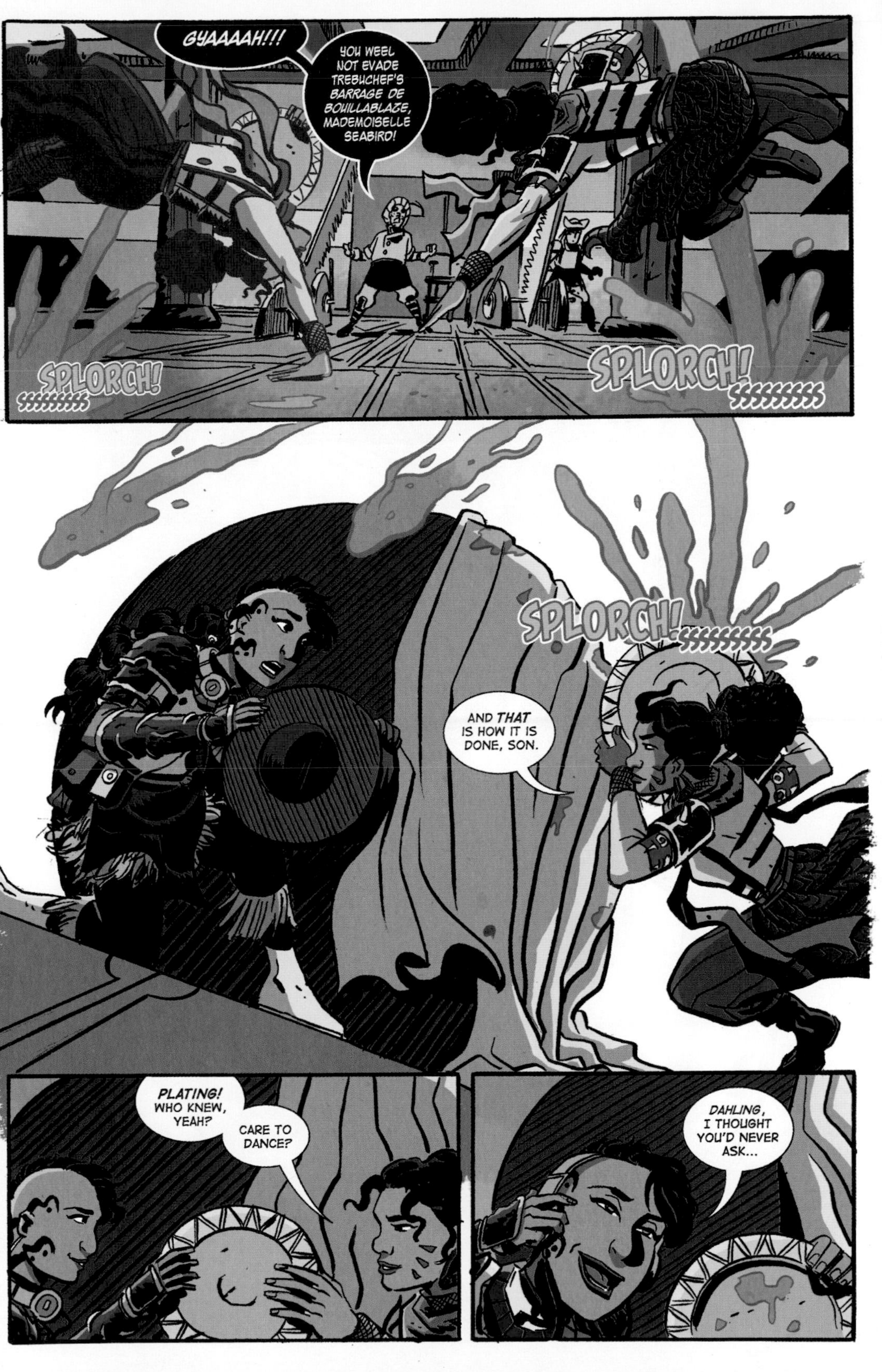
GYAAAAH!!!
YOU WEEL NOT EVADE TREBUCHEF'S BARRAGE DE BOUILLABLAZE, MADEMOISELLE SEABIRD!
SPLORCH! SSSSSSSSS
SPLORCH! SSSSSSSSS
SPLORCH! SSSSSSSSS
AND THAT IS HOW IT IS DONE, SON.
PLATING! WHO KNEW, YEAH?
CARE TO DANCE?
DAHLING, I THOUGHT YOU'D NEVER ASK...

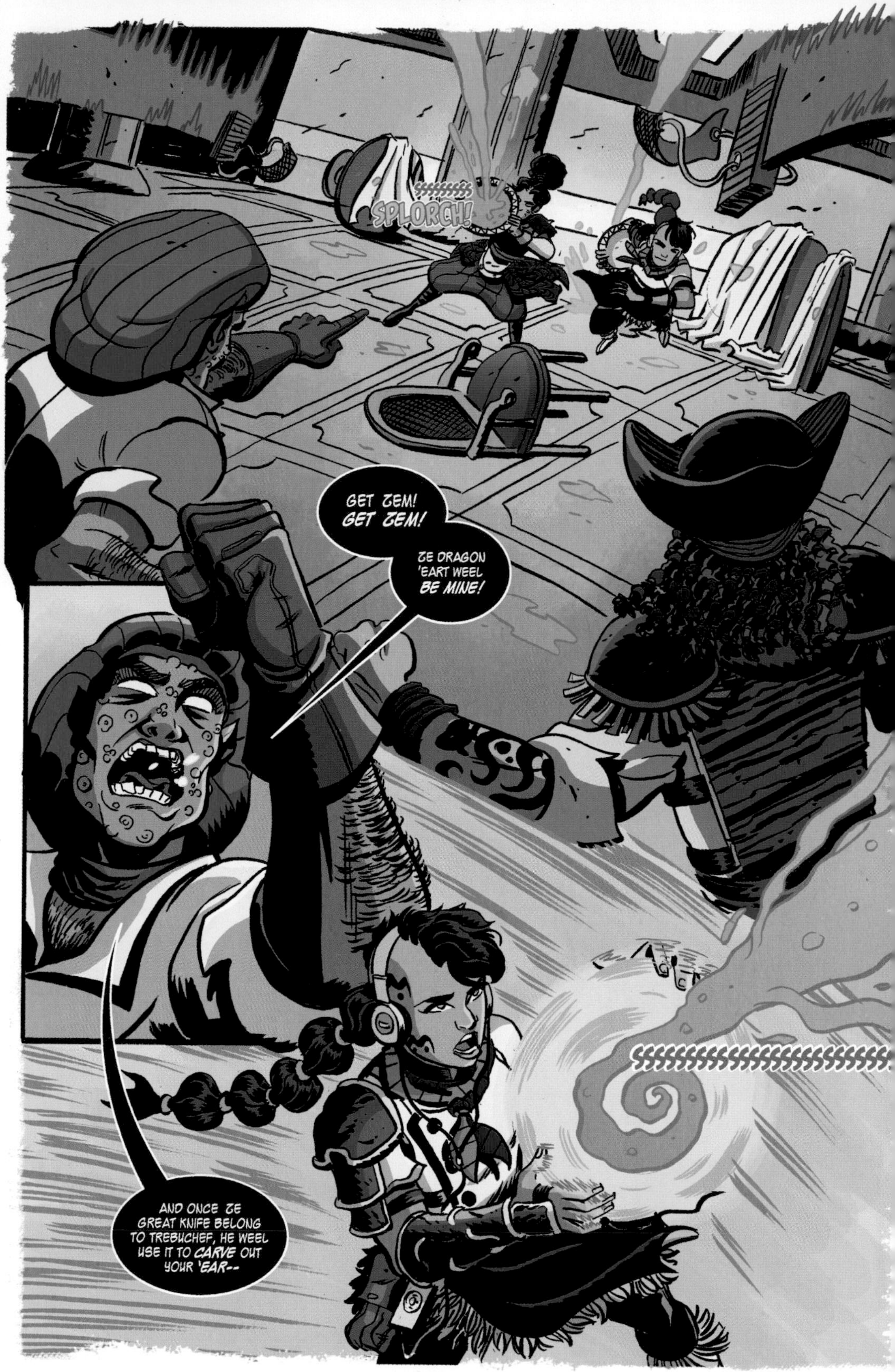
SSSSSSSSS
SPLORCH!
GET ZEM! GET ZEM!
ZE DRAGON 'EART WEEL BE MINE!
AND ONCE ZE GREAT KNIFE BELONG TO TREBUCHEF, HE WEEL USE IT TO CARVE OUT YOUR 'EAR--
SSSSSSSSSSSSSSSSSSSSSSS

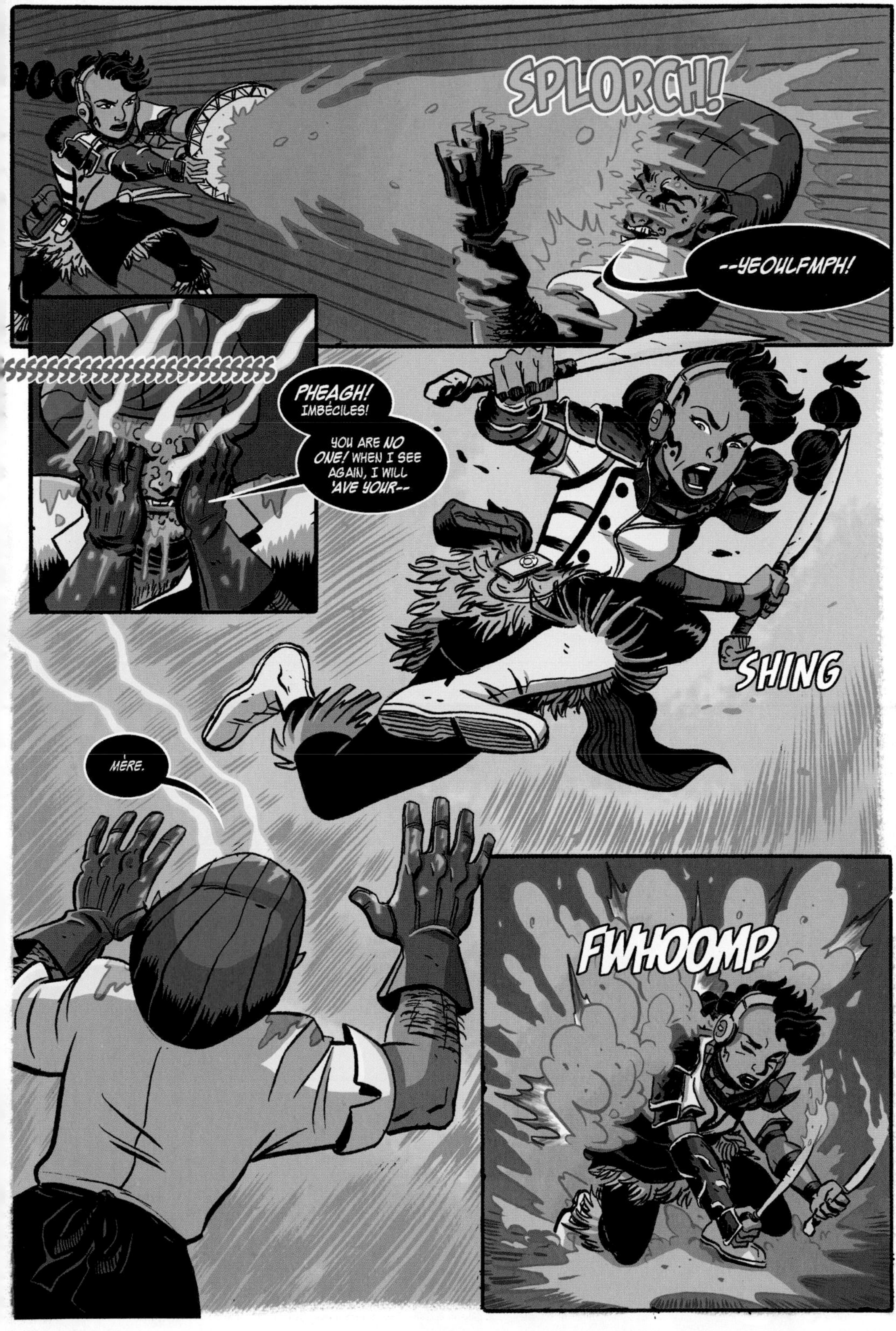
SPLORCH!
--YEOULFMPH!
PHEAGH! IMBÉCILES!
YOU ARE NO ONE! WHEN I SEE AGAIN, I WILL 'AVE YOUR--
SHING
MÈRE.
FWHOOMP

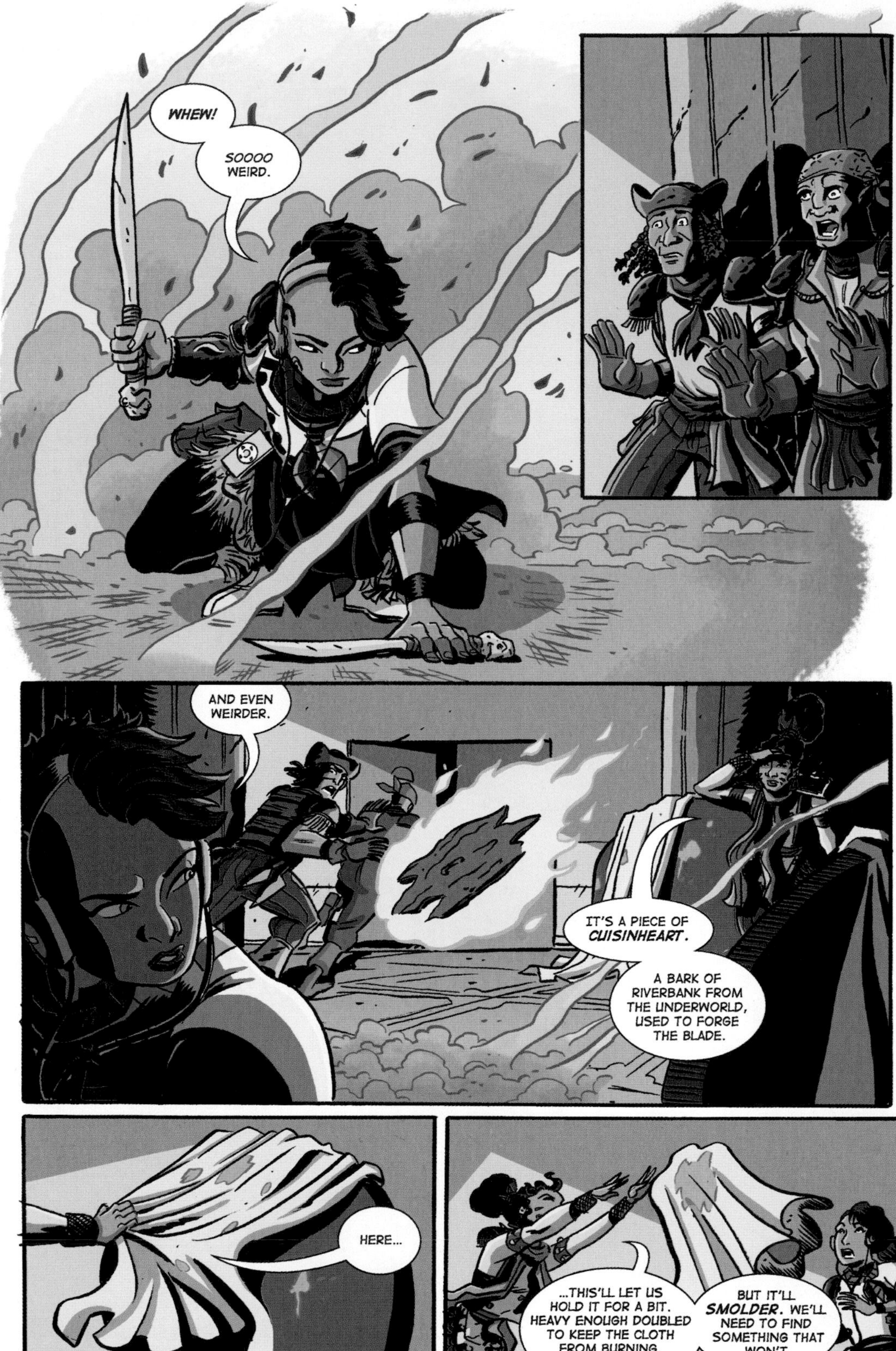
WHEW!
SOOOO WEIRD.
AND EVEN WEIRDER.
IT'S A PIECE OF CUISINHEART.
A BARK OF RIVERBANK FROM THE UNDERWORLD, USED TO FORGE THE BLADE.
HERE...
...THIS'LL LET US HOLD IT FOR A BIT. HEAVY ENOUGH DOUBLED TO KEEP THE CLOTH FROM BURNING.
BUT IT'LL SMOLDER. WE'LL NEED TO FIND SOMETHING THAT WON'T.

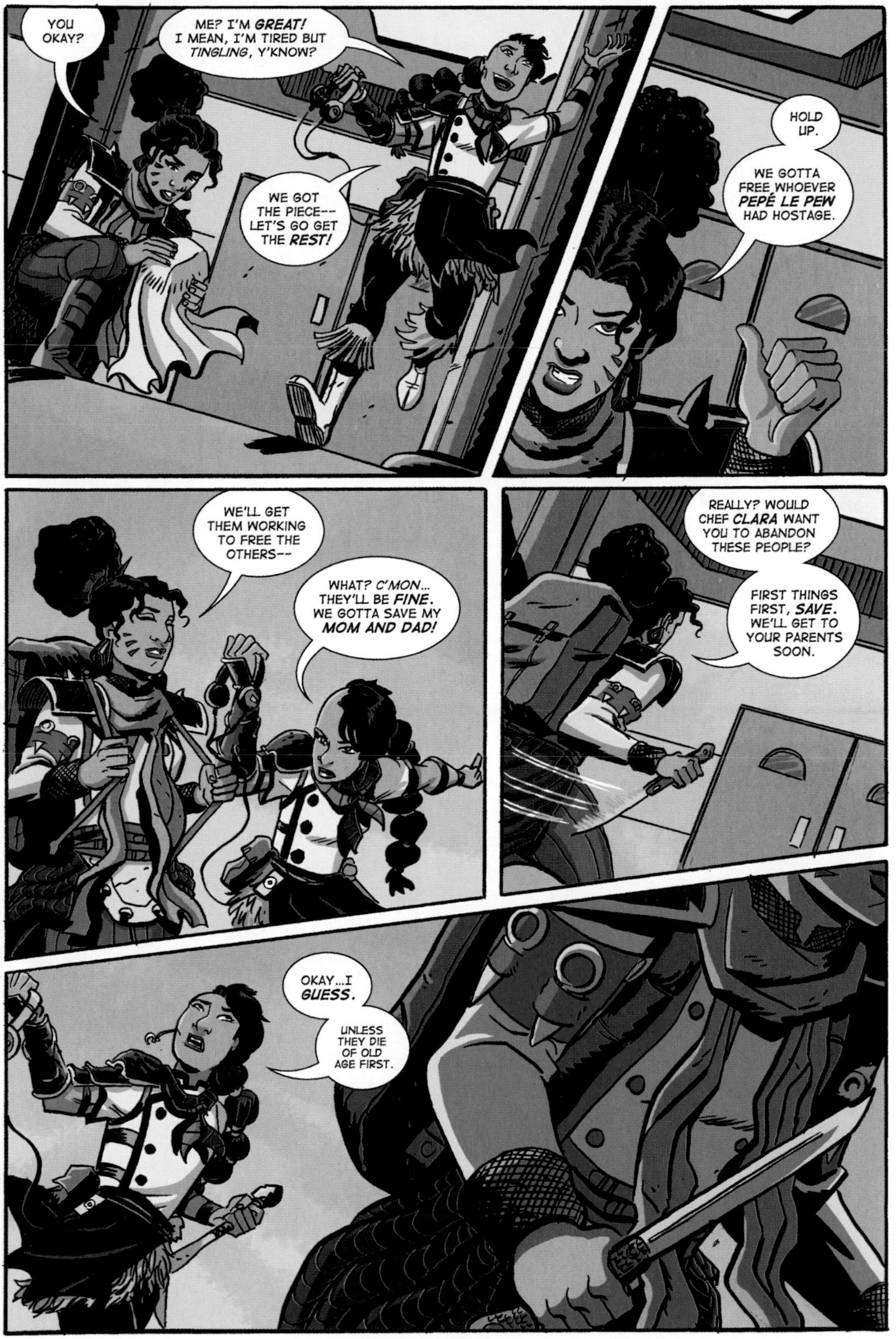
YOU OKAY?
ME? I'M *GREAT!* I MEAN, I'M TIRED BUT *TINGLING*, Y'KNOW?
WE GOT THE PIECE--LET'S GO GET THE *REST!*
HOLD UP.
WE GOTTA FREE WHOEVER *PEPÉ LE PEW* HAD HOSTAGE.
WE'LL GET THEM WORKING TO FREE THE OTHERS--
WHAT? *C'MON*... THEY'LL BE *FINE*. WE GOTTA SAVE MY *MOM AND DAD!*
REALLY? WOULD CHEF *CLARA* WANT YOU TO ABANDON THESE PEOPLE?
FIRST THINGS FIRST, *SAVE*. WE'LL GET TO YOUR PARENTS SOON.
OKAY...I *GUESS*.
UNLESS THEY DIE OF OLD AGE FIRST.

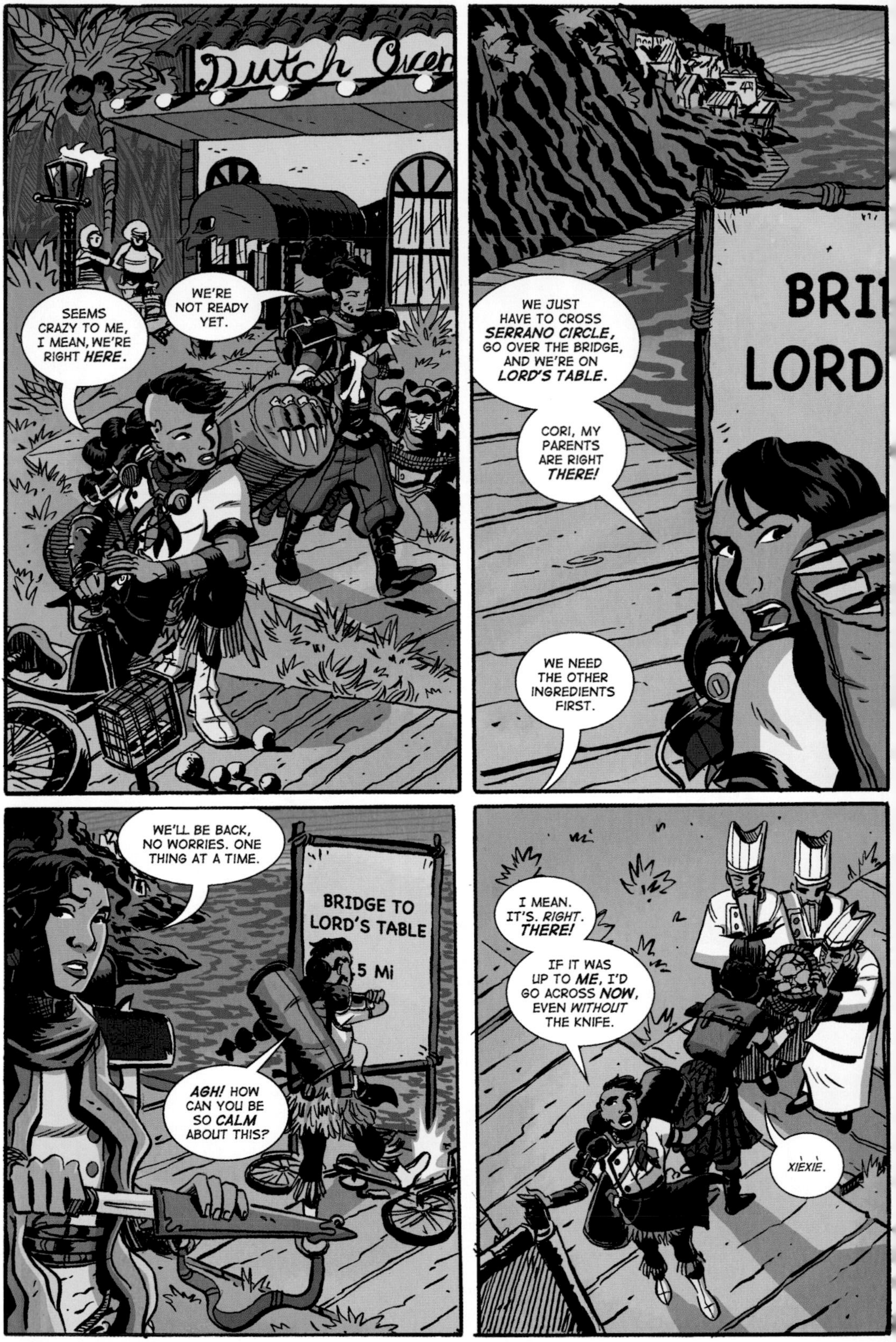
Dutch Oven
SEEMS CRAZY TO ME, I MEAN, WE'RE RIGHT HERE.
WE'RE NOT READY YET.
WE JUST HAVE TO CROSS SERRANO CIRCLE, GO OVER THE BRIDGE, AND WE'RE ON LORD'S TABLE.
CORI, MY PARENTS ARE RIGHT THERE!
WE NEED THE OTHER INGREDIENTS FIRST.
WE'LL BE BACK, NO WORRIES. ONE THING AT A TIME.
BRIDGE TO LORD'S TABLE
AGH! HOW CAN YOU BE SO CALM ABOUT THIS?
I MEAN. IT'S. RIGHT. THERE!
IF IT WAS UP TO ME, I'D GO ACROSS NOW, EVEN WITHOUT THE KNIFE.
XIEXIE.

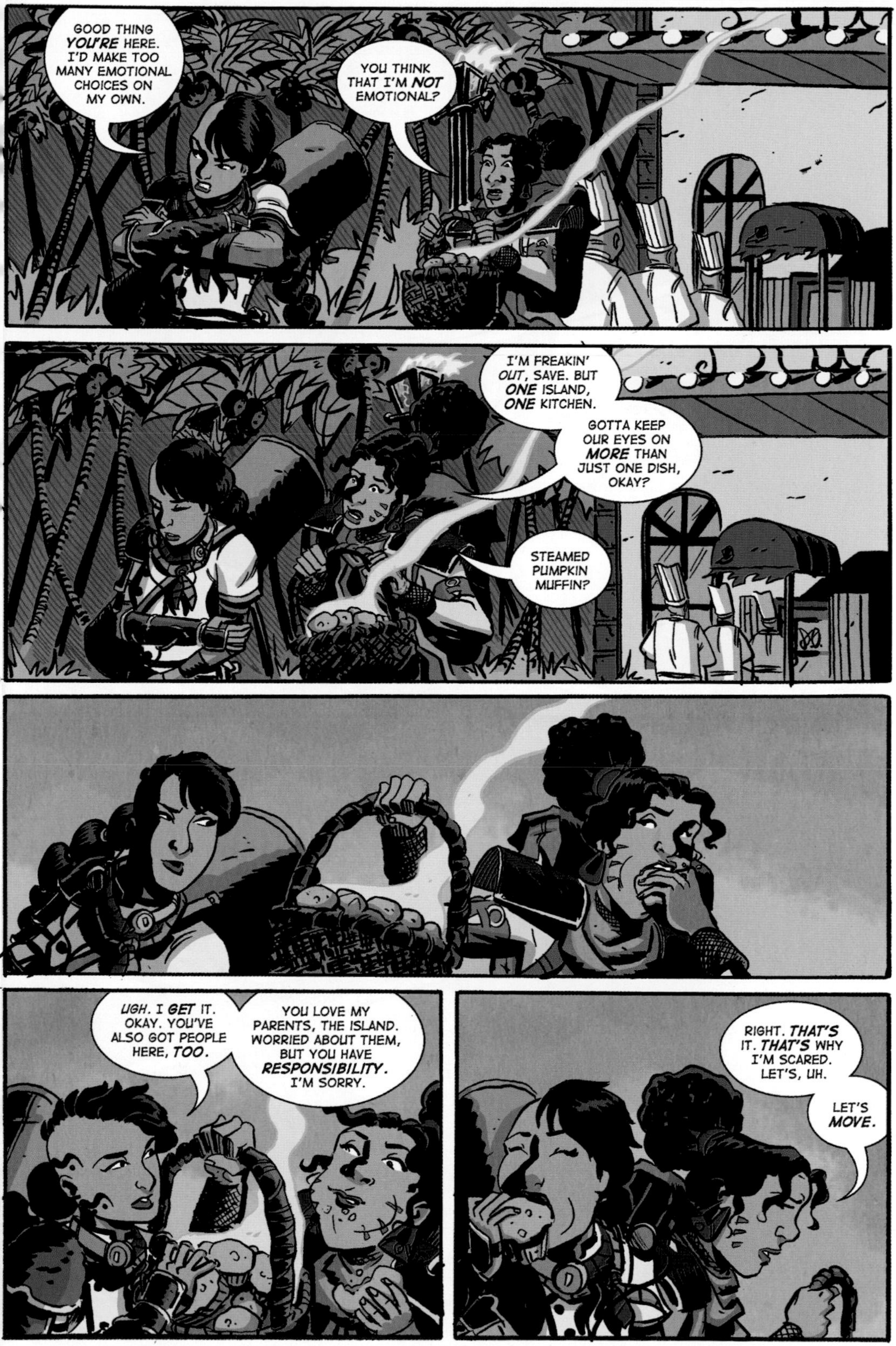
GOOD THING *YOU'RE* HERE. I'D MAKE TOO MANY EMOTIONAL CHOICES ON MY OWN.
YOU THINK THAT I'M *NOT* EMOTIONAL?
I'M FREAKIN' *OUT*, SAVE. BUT *ONE* ISLAND, *ONE* KITCHEN.
GOTTA KEEP OUR EYES ON *MORE* THAN JUST ONE DISH, OKAY?
STEAMED PUMPKIN MUFFIN?
UGH. I *GET* IT. OKAY. YOU'VE ALSO GOT PEOPLE HERE, *TOO*.
YOU LOVE MY PARENTS, THE ISLAND. WORRIED ABOUT THEM, BUT YOU HAVE *RESPONSIBILITY*. I'M SORRY.
RIGHT. *THAT'S* IT. *THAT'S* WHY I'M SCARED. LET'S, UH.
LET'S *MOVE*.

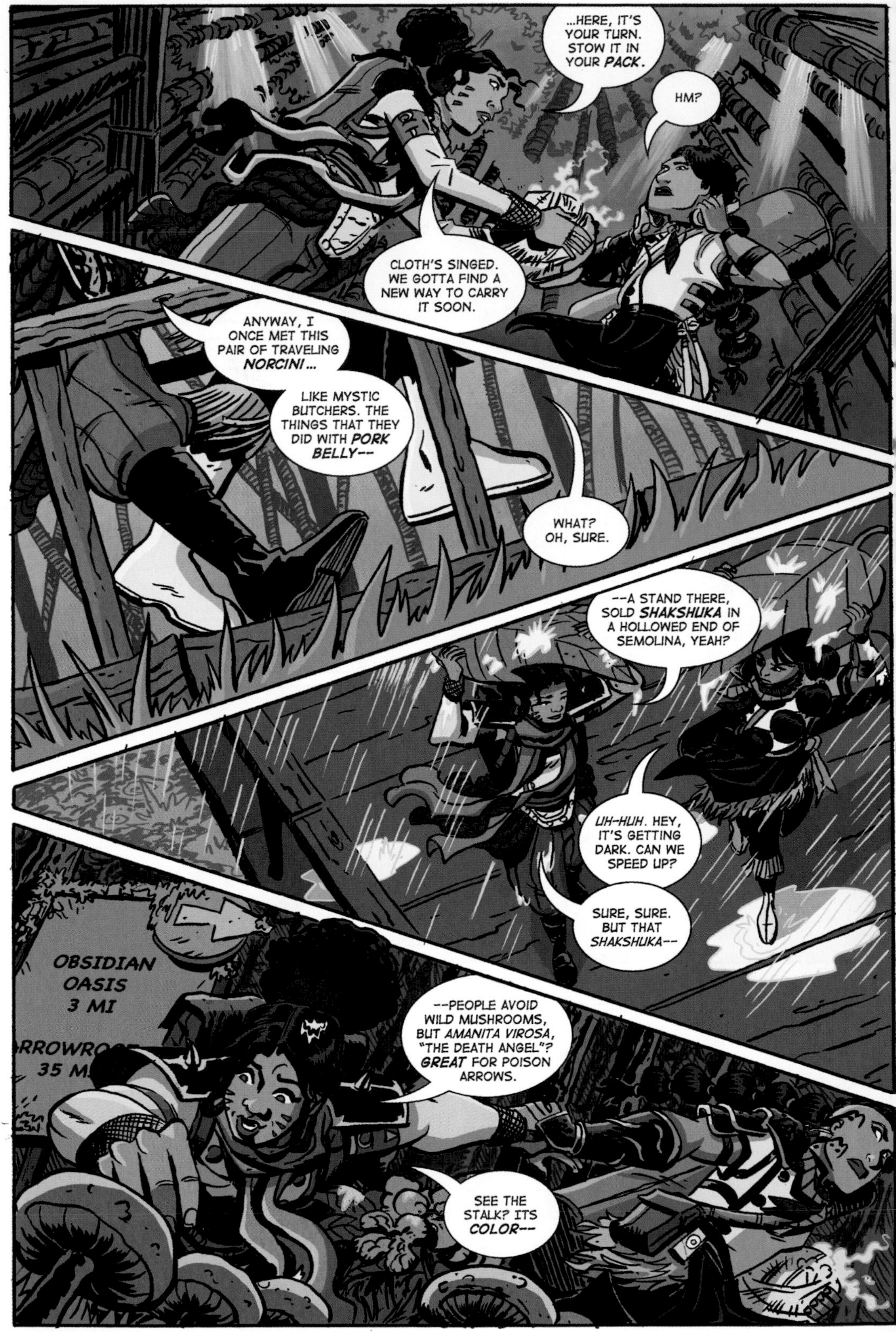

...HERE, IT'S YOUR TURN. STOW IT IN YOUR PACK.
HM?
CLOTH'S SINGED. WE GOTTA FIND A NEW WAY TO CARRY IT SOON.
ANYWAY, I ONCE MET THIS PAIR OF TRAVELING NORCINI...
LIKE MYSTIC BUTCHERS. THE THINGS THAT THEY DID WITH PORK BELLY--
WHAT? OH, SURE.
--A STAND THERE, SOLD SHAKSHUKA IN A HOLLOWED END OF SEMOLINA, YEAH?
UH-HUH. HEY, IT'S GETTING DARK. CAN WE SPEED UP?
SURE, SURE. BUT THAT SHAKSHUKA--
OBSIDIAN OASIS 3 MI
--PEOPLE AVOID WILD MUSHROOMS, BUT AMANITA VIROSA, "THE DEATH ANGEL"? GREAT FOR POISON ARROWS.
SEE THE STALK? ITS COLOR--

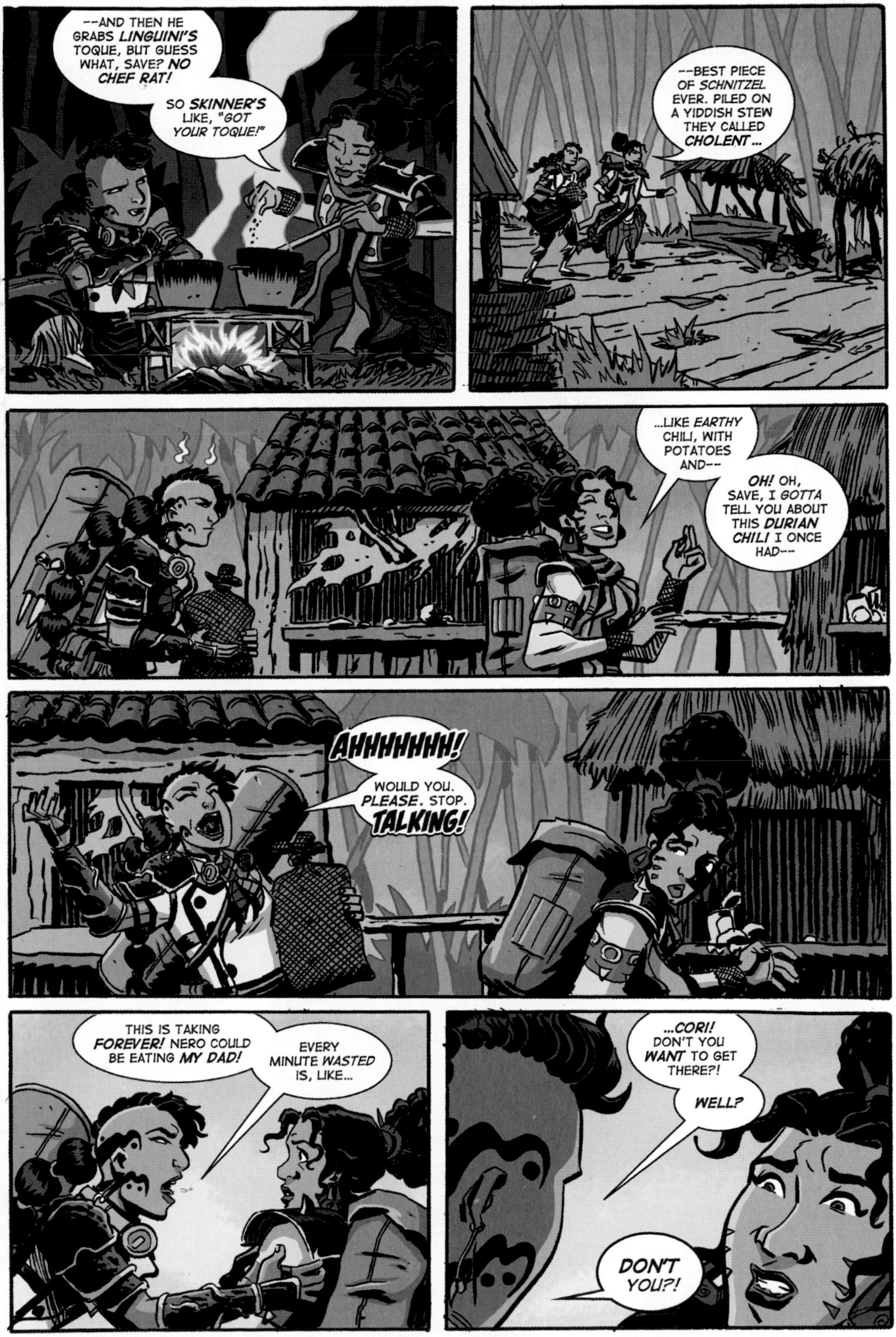
--AND THEN HE GRABS LINGUINI'S TOQUE, BUT GUESS WHAT, SAVE? NO CHEF RAT!
SO SKINNER'S LIKE, "GOT YOUR TOQUE!"
--BEST PIECE OF SCHNITZEL EVER. PILED ON A YIDDISH STEW THEY CALLED CHOLENT...
...LIKE EARTHY CHILI, WITH POTATOES AND--
OH! OH, SAVE, I GOTTA TELL YOU ABOUT THIS DURIAN CHILI I ONCE HAD--
AHHHHHHH!
WOULD YOU. PLEASE. STOP. TALKING!
THIS IS TAKING FOREVER! NERO COULD BE EATING MY DAD!
EVERY MINUTE WASTED IS, LIKE...
...CORI! DON'T YOU WANT TO GET THERE?!
WELL?
DON'T YOU?!

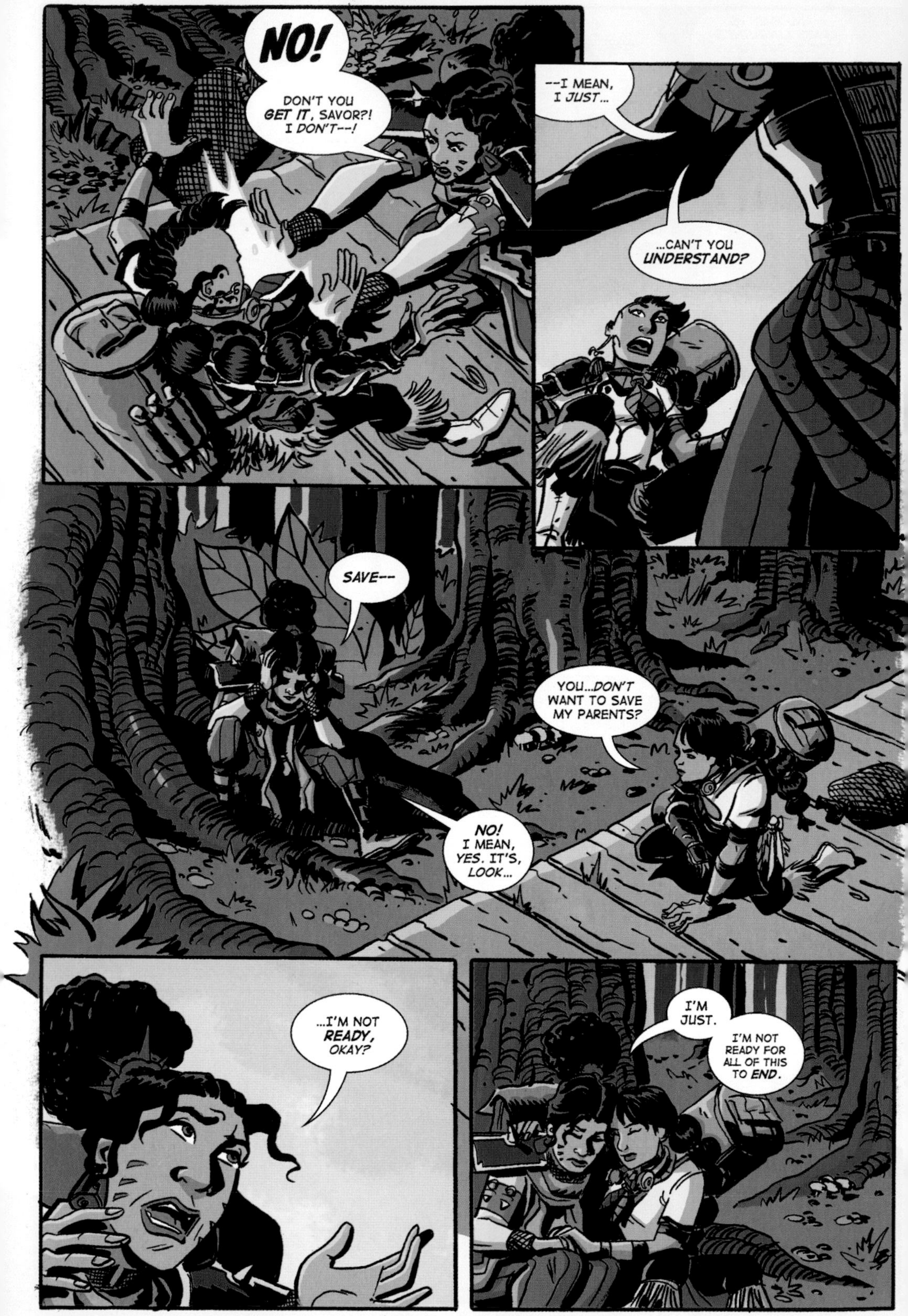
NO!
DON'T YOU GET IT, SAVOR?! I DON'T--!
--I MEAN, I JUST...
...CAN'T YOU UNDERSTAND?
SAVE---
YOU...DON'T WANT TO SAVE MY PARENTS?
NO! I MEAN, YES. IT'S, LOOK...
...I'M NOT READY, OKAY?
I'M JUST.
I'M NOT READY FOR ALL OF THIS TO END.

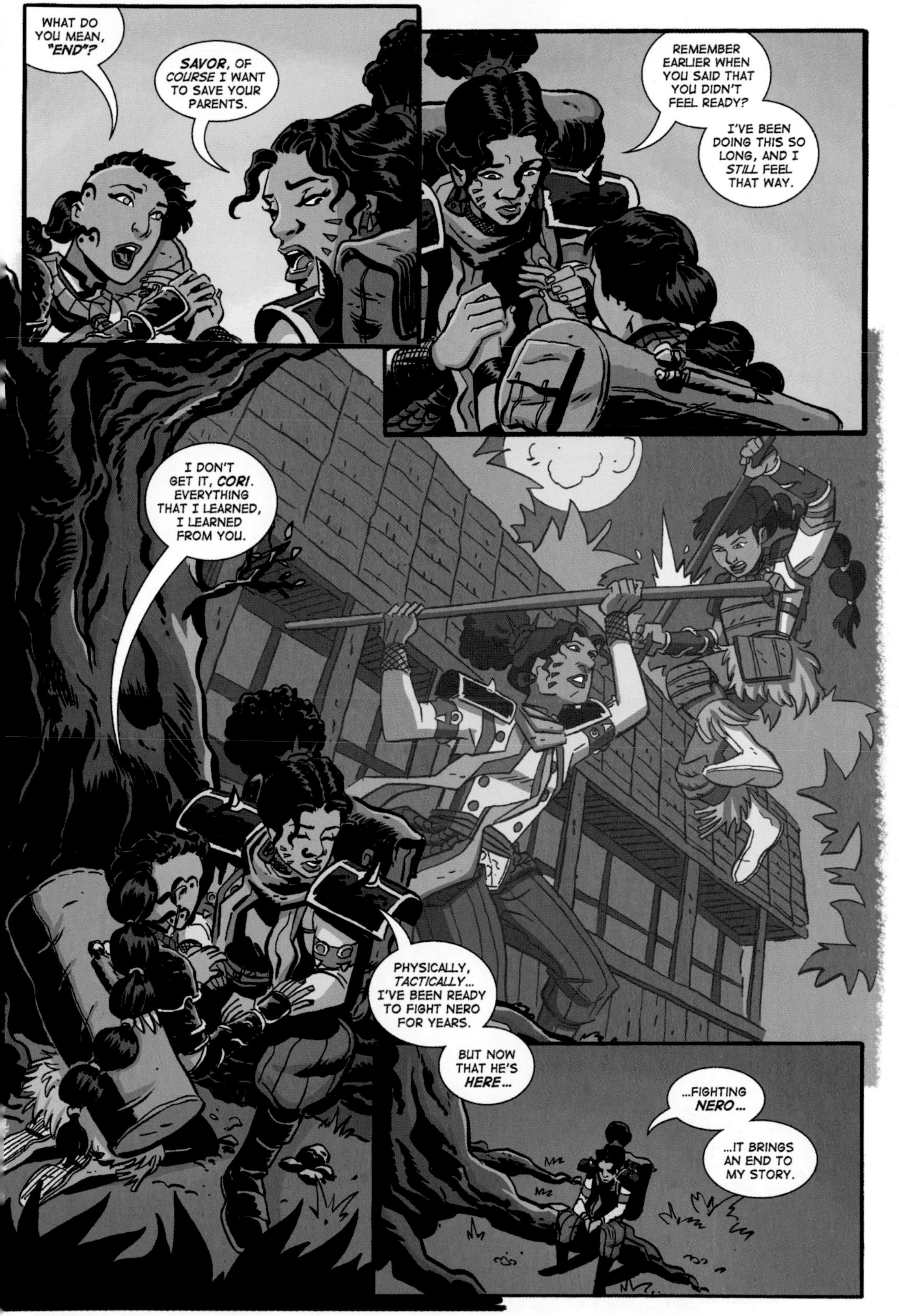
WHAT DO YOU MEAN, "END"?
SAVOR, OF COURSE I WANT TO SAVE YOUR PARENTS.
REMEMBER EARLIER WHEN YOU SAID THAT YOU DIDN'T FEEL READY?
I'VE BEEN DOING THIS SO LONG, AND I STILL FEEL THAT WAY.
I DON'T GET IT, CORI. EVERYTHING THAT I LEARNED, I LEARNED FROM YOU.
PHYSICALLY, TACTICALLY... I'VE BEEN READY TO FIGHT NERO FOR YEARS.
BUT NOW THAT HE'S HERE...
...FIGHTING NERO...
...IT BRINGS AN END TO MY STORY.

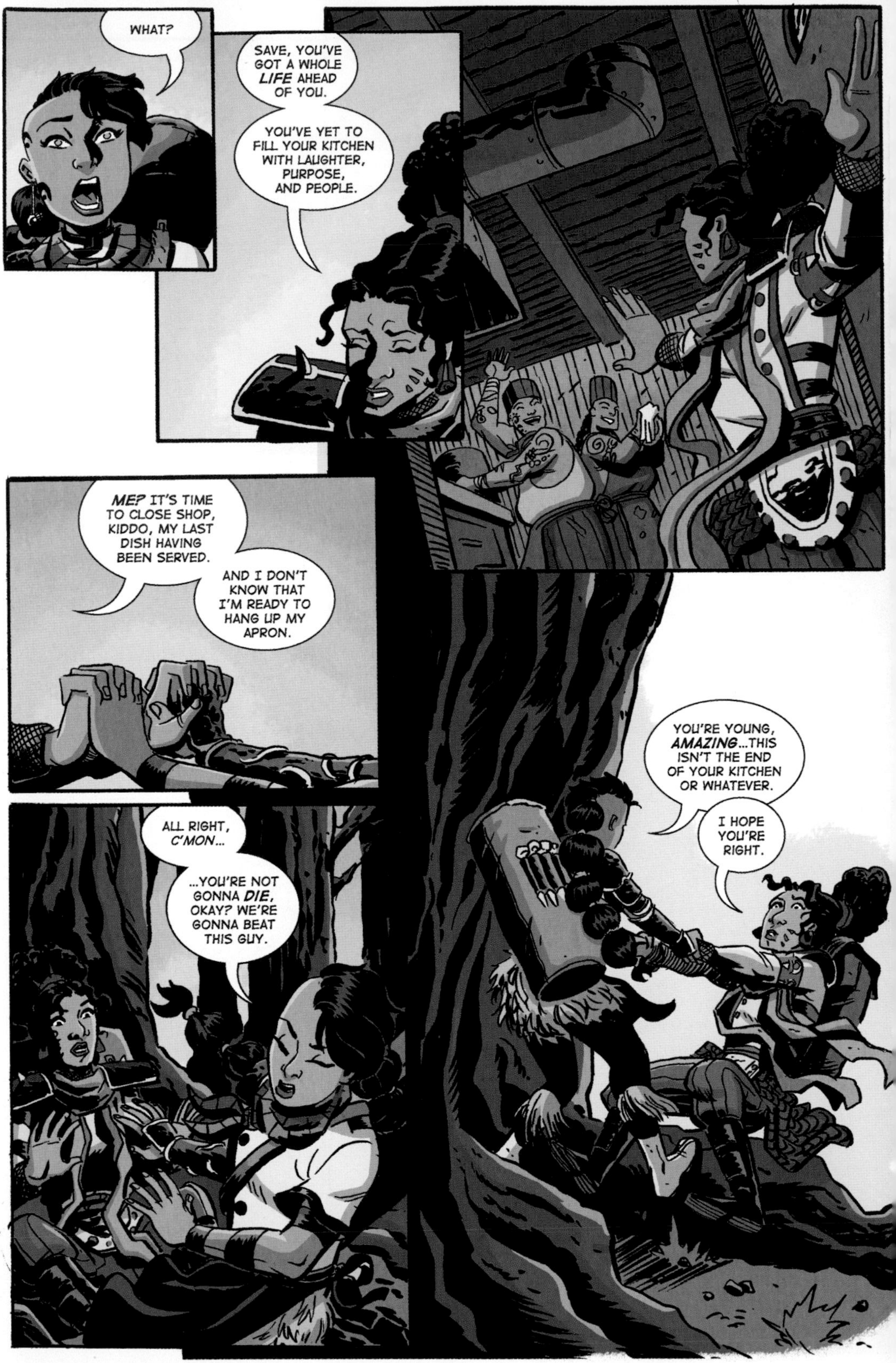
WHAT?
SAVE, YOU'VE GOT A WHOLE LIFE AHEAD OF YOU.
YOU'VE YET TO FILL YOUR KITCHEN WITH LAUGHTER, PURPOSE, AND PEOPLE.
ME? IT'S TIME TO CLOSE SHOP, KIDDO, MY LAST DISH HAVING BEEN SERVED.
AND I DON'T KNOW THAT I'M READY TO HANG UP MY APRON.
ALL RIGHT, C'MON...
...YOU'RE NOT GONNA DIE, OKAY? WE'RE GONNA BEAT THIS GUY.
YOU'RE YOUNG, AMAZING...THIS ISN'T THE END OF YOUR KITCHEN OR WHATEVER.
I HOPE YOU'RE RIGHT.

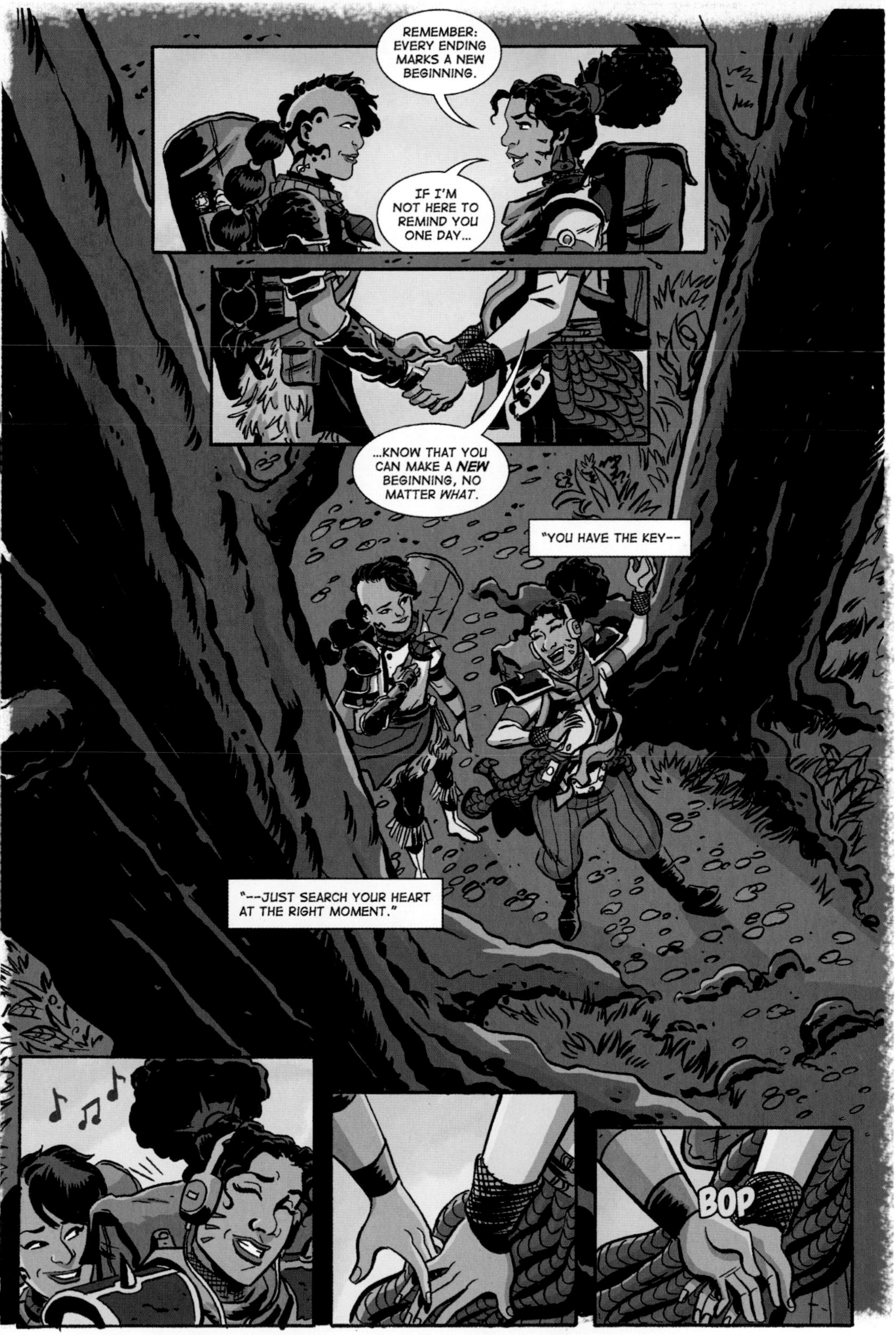
REMEMBER: EVERY ENDING MARKS A NEW BEGINNING.
IF I'M NOT HERE TO REMIND YOU ONE DAY...
...KNOW THAT YOU CAN MAKE A *NEW* BEGINNING, NO MATTER *WHAT*.
"YOU HAVE THE KEY--
"--JUST SEARCH YOUR HEART AT THE RIGHT MOMENT."
BOP

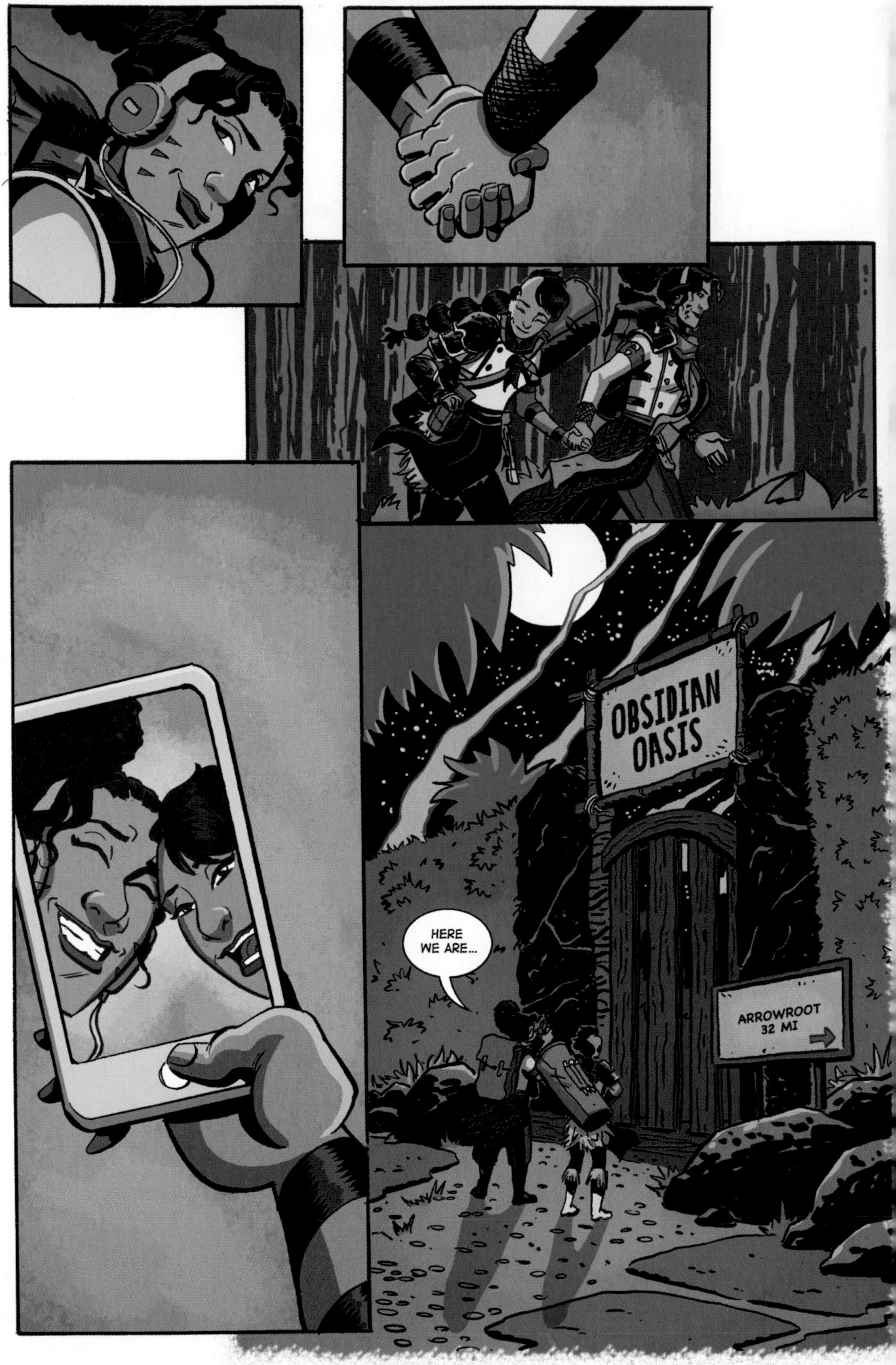
OBSIDIAN OASIS
HERE WE ARE...
ARROWROOT 32 MI

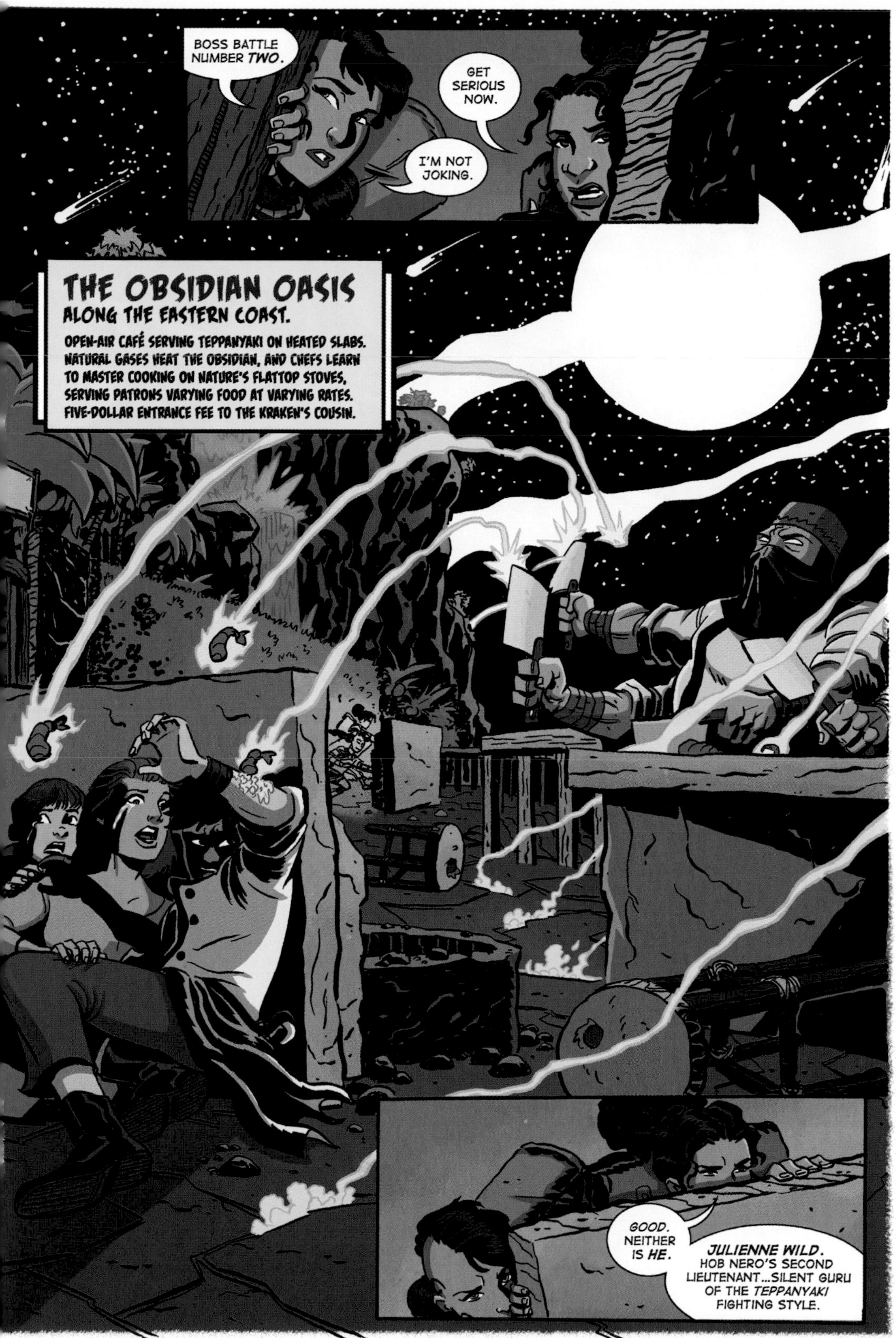
BOSS BATTLE NUMBER TWO.
GET SERIOUS NOW.
I'M NOT JOKING.
THE OBSIDIAN OASIS
ALONG THE EASTERN COAST.
OPEN-AIR CAFÉ SERVING TEPPANYAKI ON HEATED SLABS. NATURAL GASES HEAT THE OBSIDIAN, AND CHEFS LEARN TO MASTER COOKING ON NATURE'S FLATTOP STOVES, SERVING PATRONS VARYING FOOD AT VARYING RATES. FIVE-DOLLAR ENTRANCE FEE TO THE KRAKEN'S COUSIN.
GOOD. NEITHER IS HE.
JULIENNE WILD. HOB NERO'S SECOND LIEUTENANT...SILENT GURU OF THE TEPPANYAKI FIGHTING STYLE.

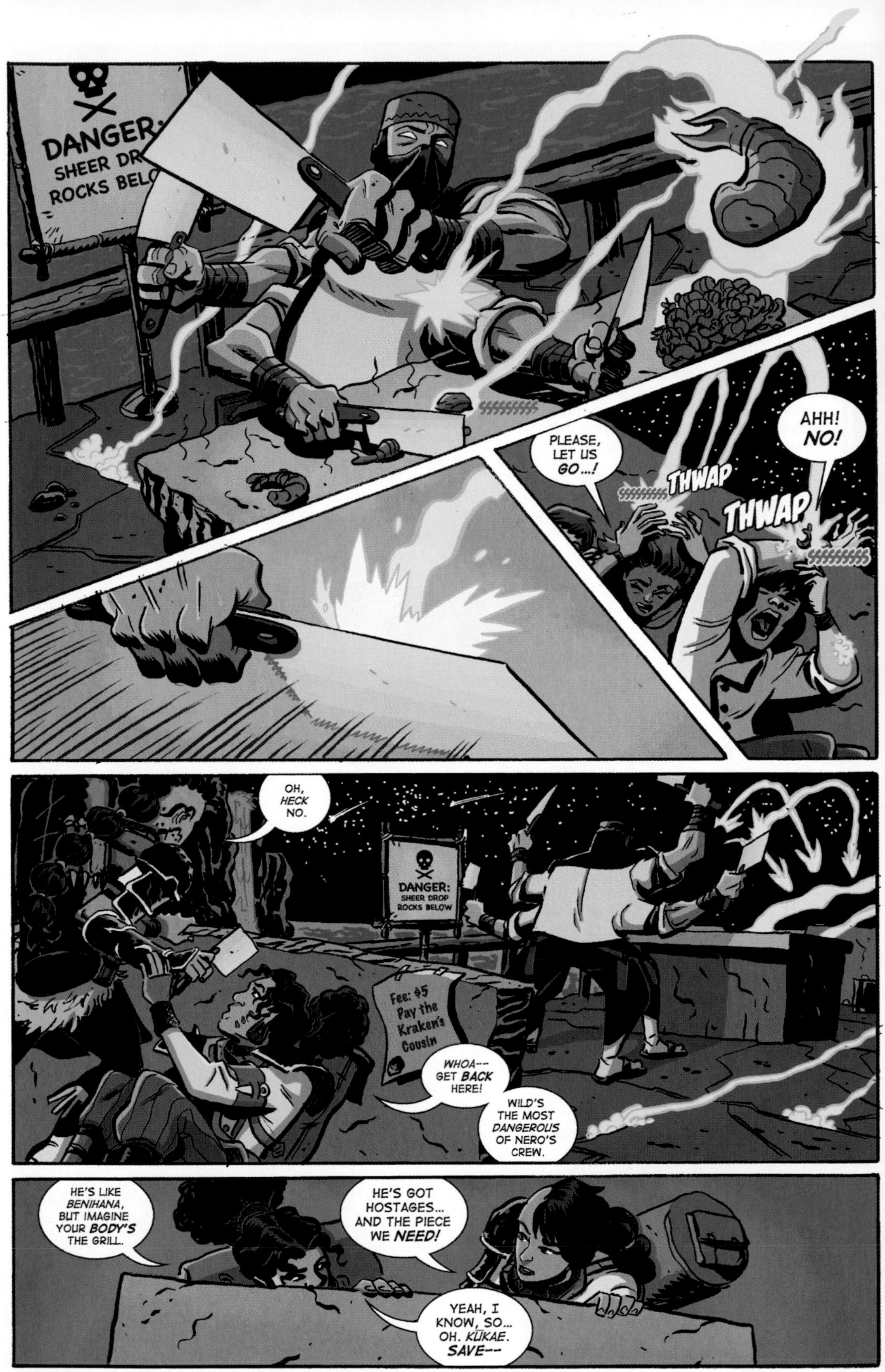
DANGER:
SHEER DR
ROCKS BELO
PLEASE, LET US GO...!
THWAP
THWAP
AHH! NO!
OH, HECK NO.
DANGER:
SHEER DROP
ROCKS BELOW
Fee: $5
Pay the Kraken's Cousin
WHOA--- GET BACK HERE!
WILD'S THE MOST DANGEROUS OF NERO'S CREW.
HE'S LIKE BENIHANA, BUT IMAGINE YOUR BODY'S THE GRILL.
HE'S GOT HOSTAGES... AND THE PIECE WE NEED!
YEAH, I KNOW, SO... OH. KŪKAE. SAVE---

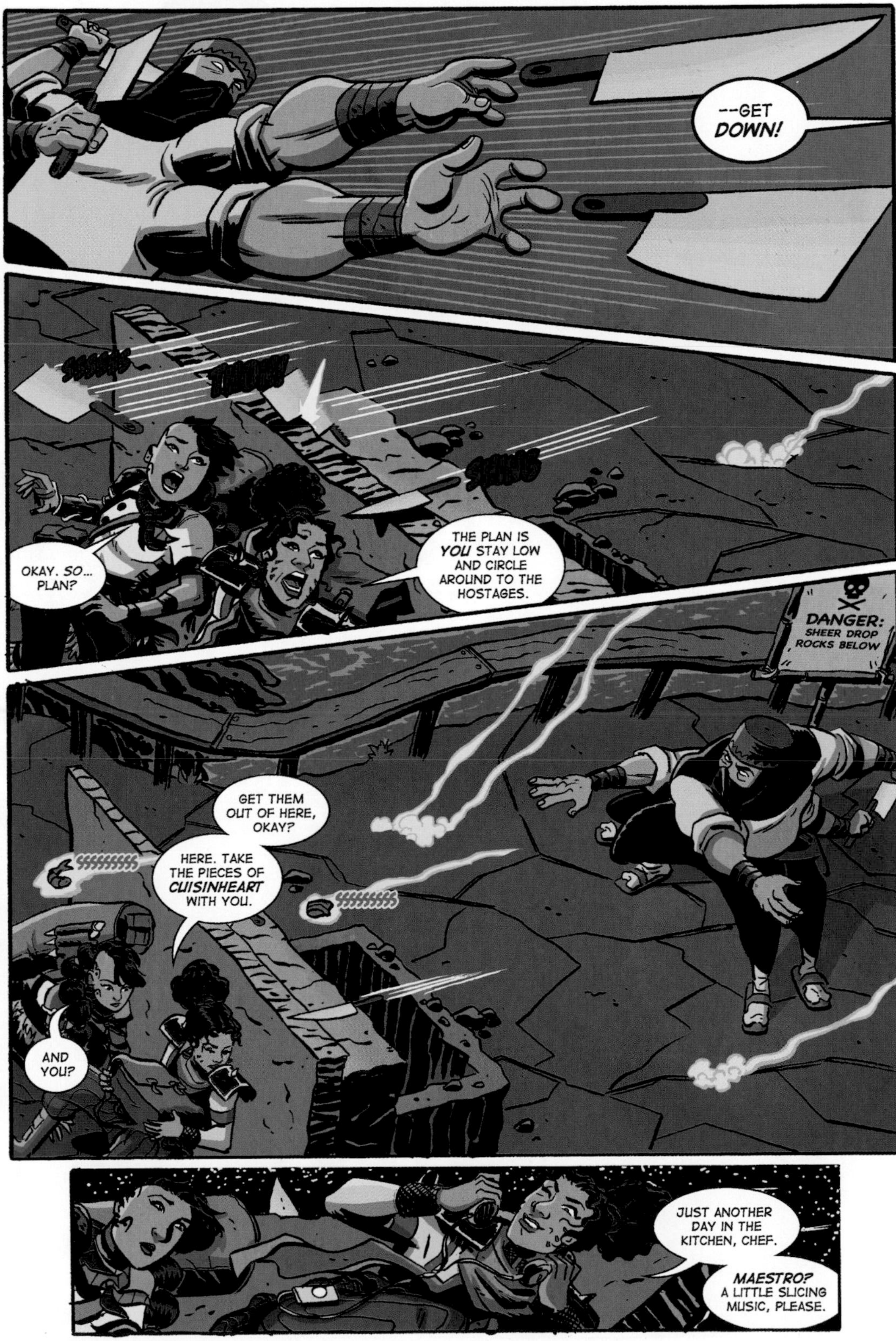
--GET DOWN!
OKAY. SO... PLAN?
THE PLAN IS YOU STAY LOW AND CIRCLE AROUND TO THE HOSTAGES.
DANGER: SHEER DROP ROCKS BELOW
GET THEM OUT OF HERE, OKAY?
HERE. TAKE THE PIECES OF CUISINHEART WITH YOU.
AND YOU?
JUST ANOTHER DAY IN THE KITCHEN, CHEF.
MAESTRO? A LITTLE SLICING MUSIC, PLEASE.

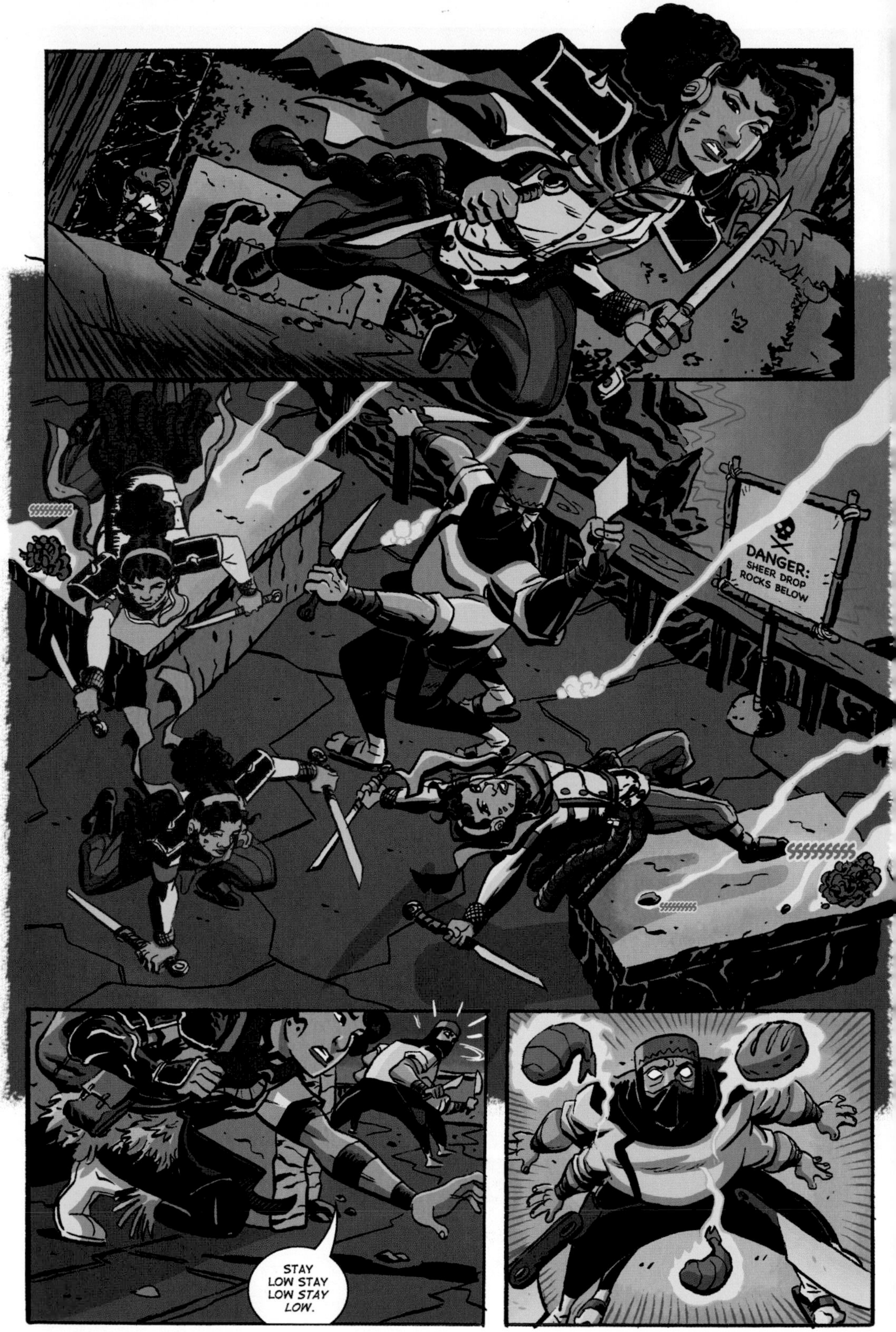
DANGER:
SHEER DROP
ROCKS BELOW
STAY LOW STAY LOW STAY LOW.

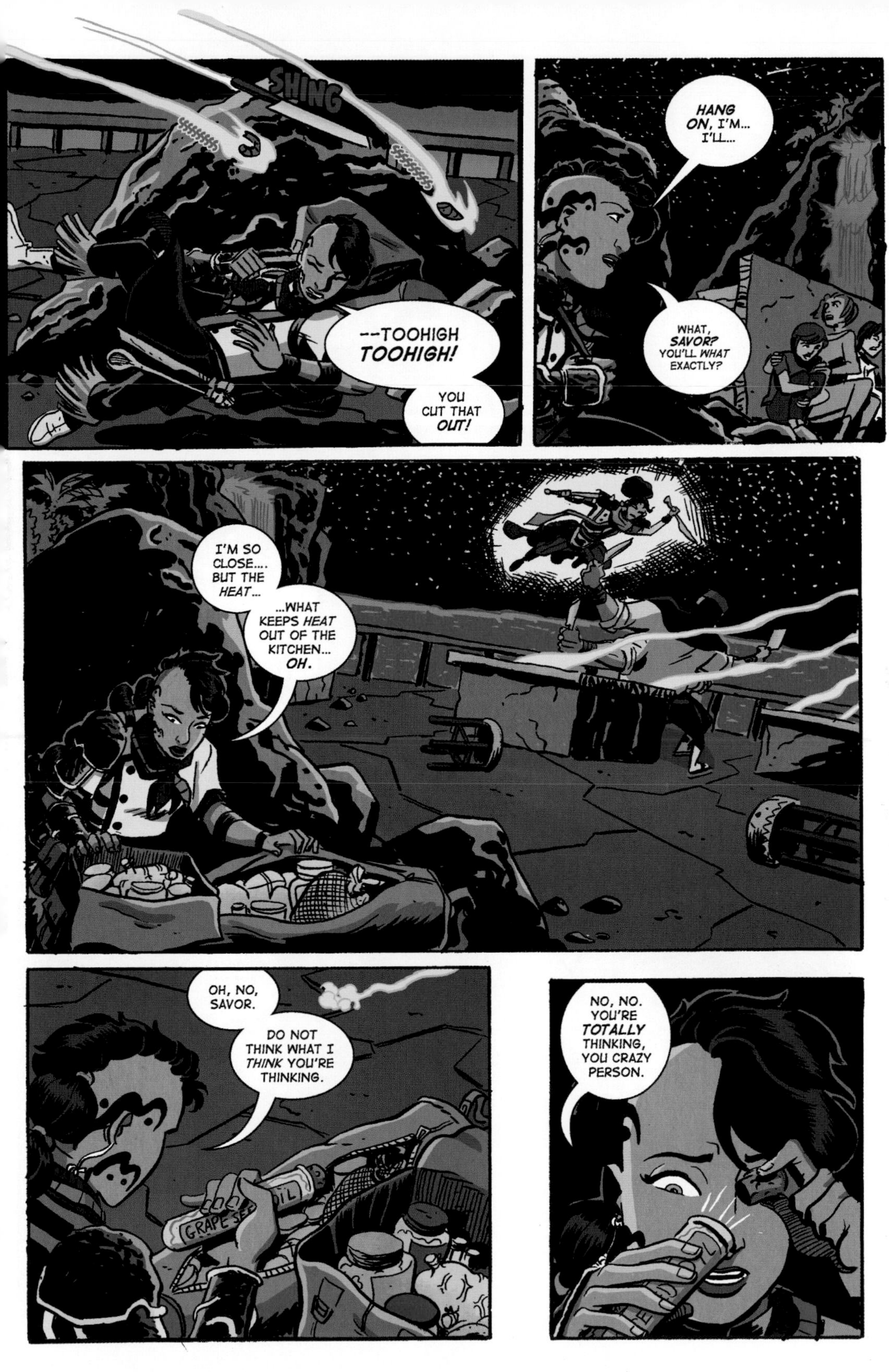
SHING
--TOOHIGH TOOHIGH!
YOU CUT THAT OUT!
HANG ON, I'M... I'LL...
WHAT, SAVOR? YOU'LL WHAT EXACTLY?
I'M SO CLOSE.... BUT THE HEAT...
...WHAT KEEPS HEAT OUT OF THE KITCHEN... OH.
OH, NO, SAVOR.
DO NOT THINK WHAT I THINK YOU'RE THINKING.
GRAPESEED OIL
NO, NO. YOU'RE TOTALLY THINKING, YOU CRAZY PERSON.

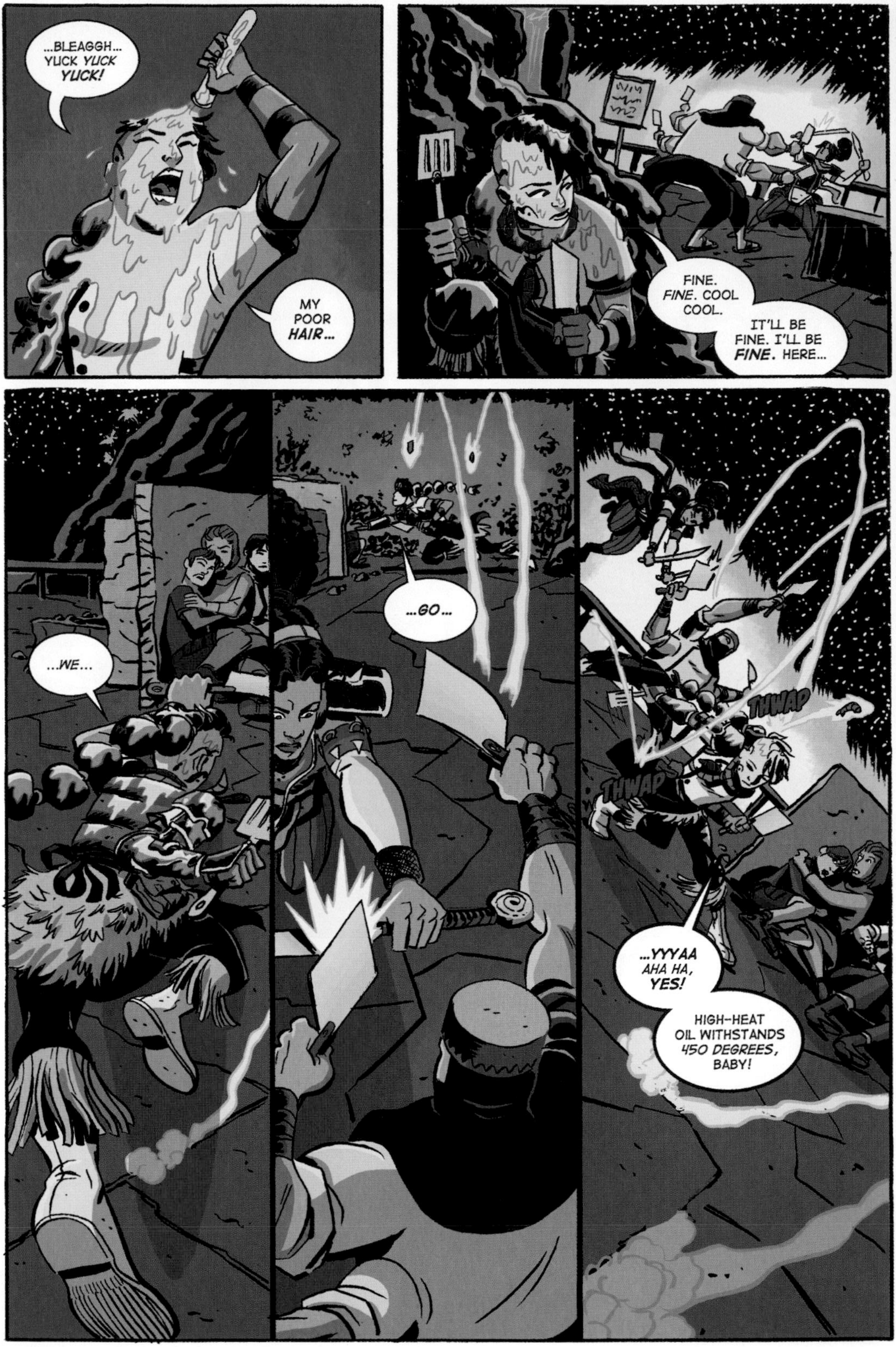
...BLEAGGH... YUCK YUCK YUCK!
MY POOR HAIR...
FINE. FINE. COOL COOL.
IT'LL BE FINE. I'LL BE FINE. HERE...
...WE...
...GO...
THWAP
THWAP
...YYYAA AHA HA, YES!
HIGH-HEAT OIL WITHSTANDS 450 DEGREES, BABY!

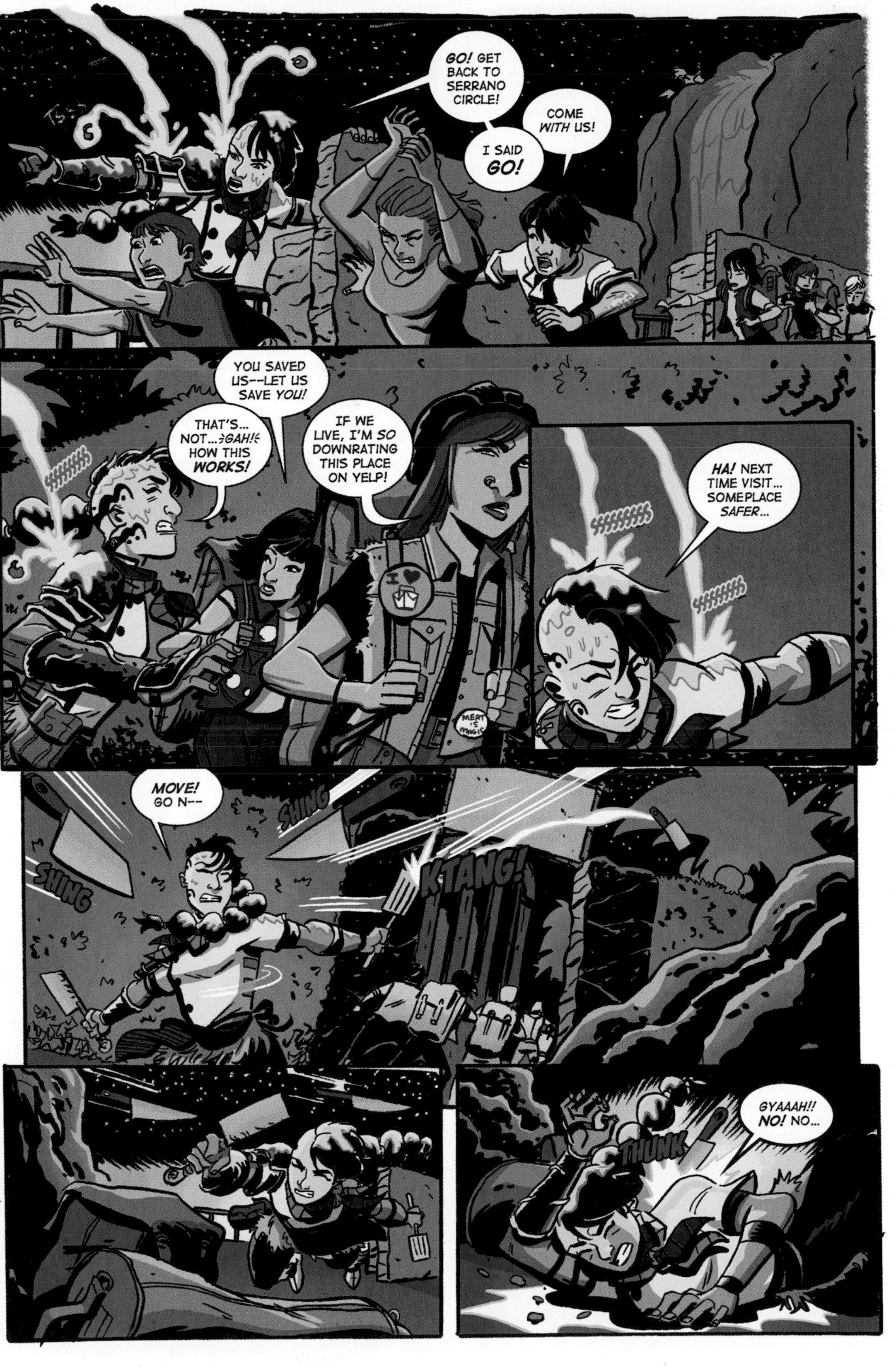
TSSS
GO! GET BACK TO SERRANO CIRCLE!
COME WITH US!
I SAID GO!
YOU SAVED US--LET US SAVE YOU!
THAT'S... NOT...GAH! HOW THIS WORKS!
IF WE LIVE, I'M SO DOWNRATING THIS PLACE ON YELP!
SSSSSSSSS
HA! NEXT TIME VISIT... SOMEPLACE SAFER...
MOVE! GO N--
SHING
SHING
KTANG!
THUNK
GYAAAH!! NO! NO...

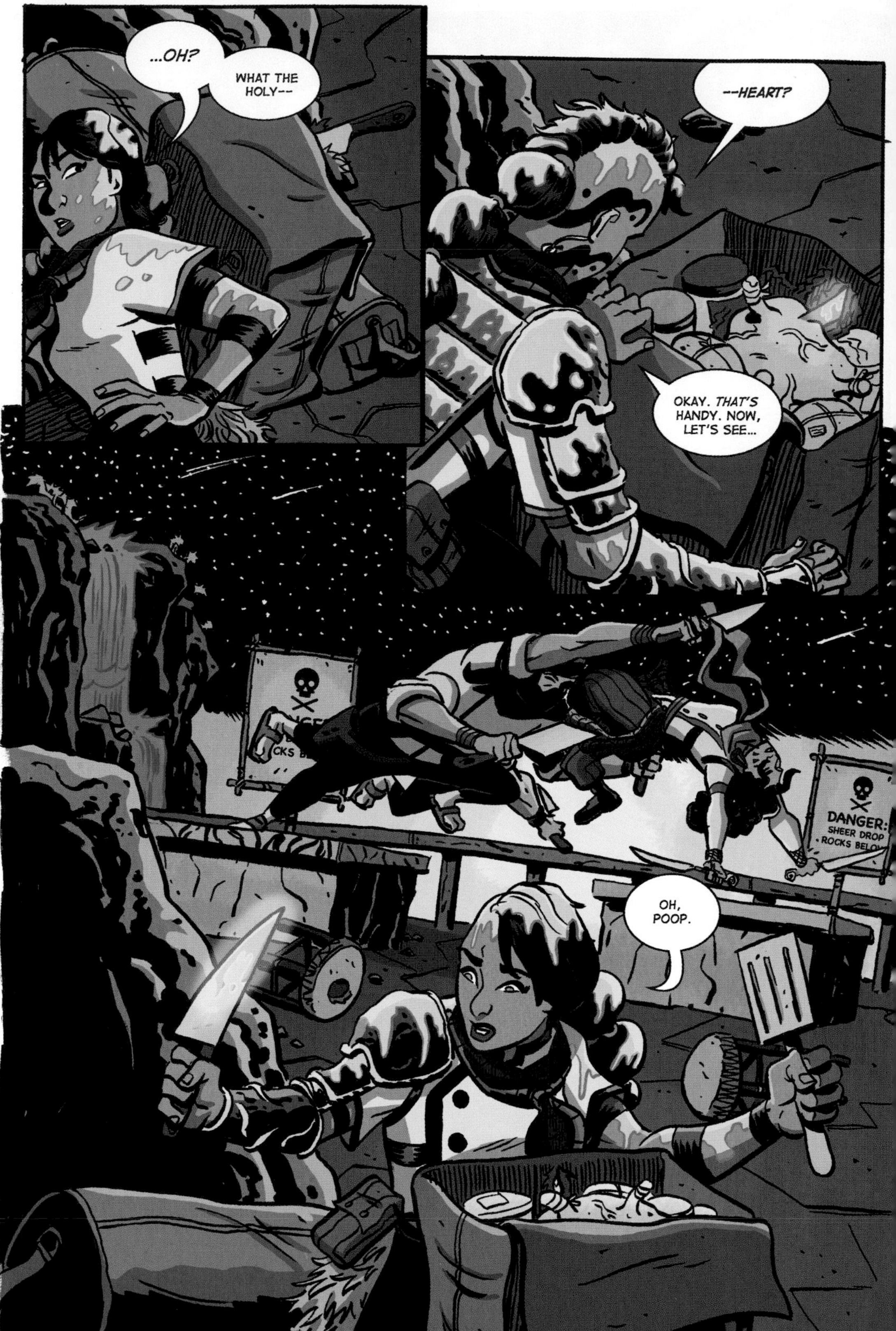
...OH?
WHAT THE HOLY--
--HEART?
OKAY. THAT'S HANDY. NOW, LET'S SEE...
DANGER: SHEER DROP ROCKS BELOW
OH, POOP.

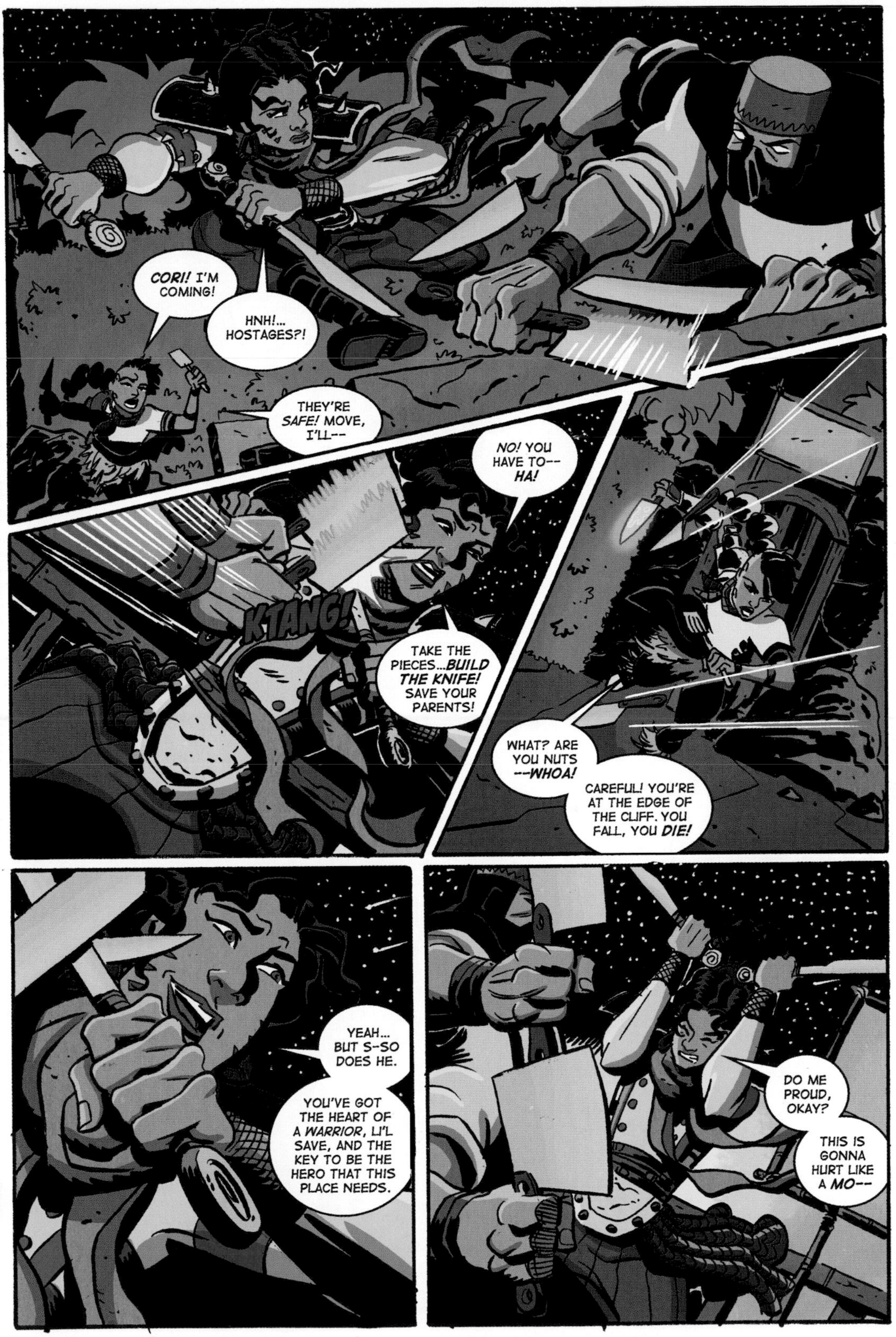
CORI! I'M COMING!
HNH!... HOSTAGES?!
THEY'RE SAFE! MOVE, I'LL--
NO! YOU HAVE TO-- HA!
KTANG!
TAKE THE PIECES...BUILD THE KNIFE! SAVE YOUR PARENTS!
WHAT? ARE YOU NUTS --WHOA!
CAREFUL! YOU'RE AT THE EDGE OF THE CLIFF. YOU FALL, YOU DIE!
YEAH... BUT S-SO DOES HE.
YOU'VE GOT THE HEART OF A WARRIOR, LI'L SAVE, AND THE KEY TO BE THE HERO THAT THIS PLACE NEEDS.
DO ME PROUD, OKAY?
THIS IS GONNA HURT LIKE A MO--

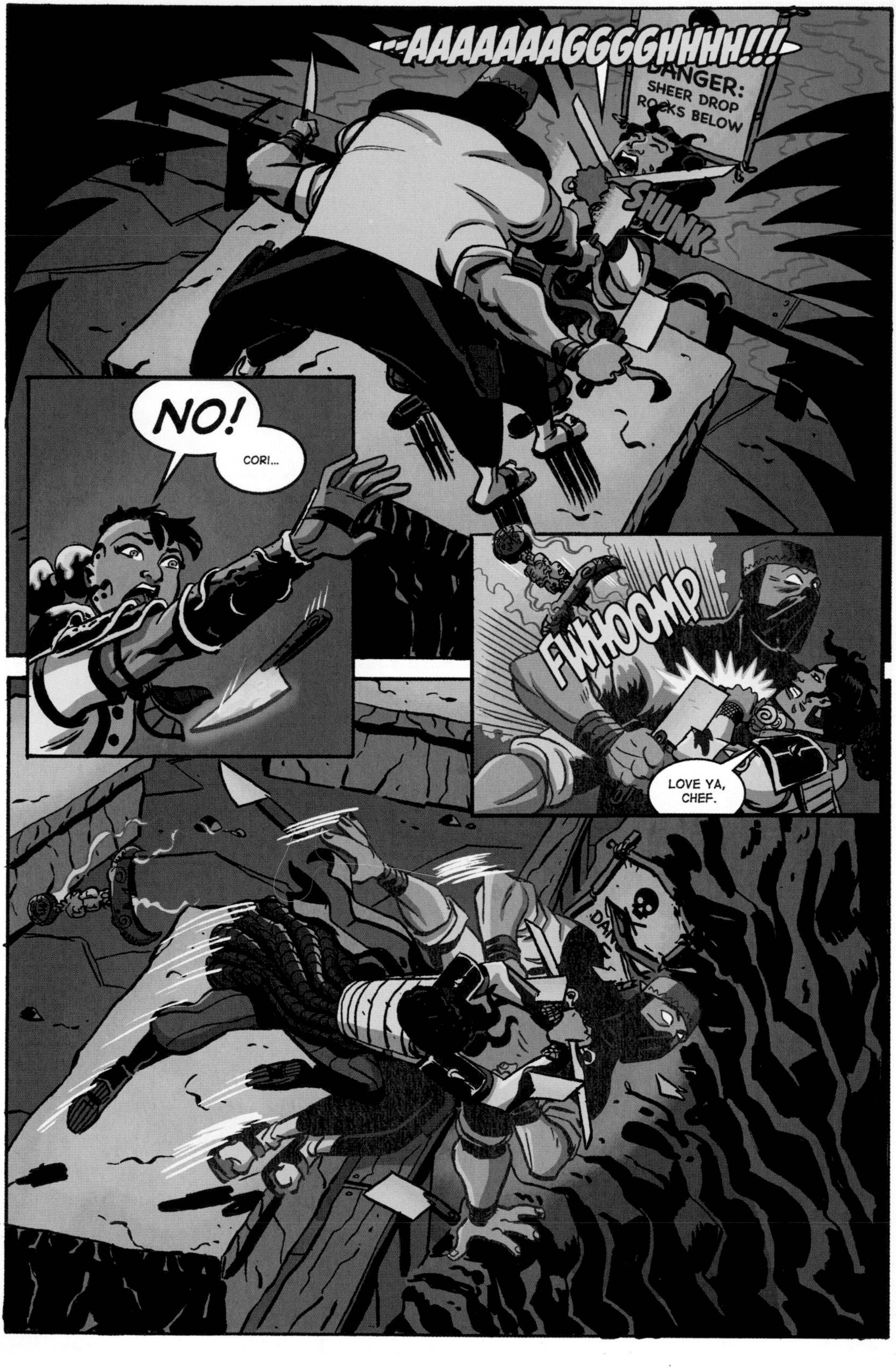
--AAAAAAAGGGGHHHH!!!
DANGER: SHEER DROP ROCKS BELOW
SHUNK
NO!
CORI...
FWHOOMP
LOVE YA, CHEF.

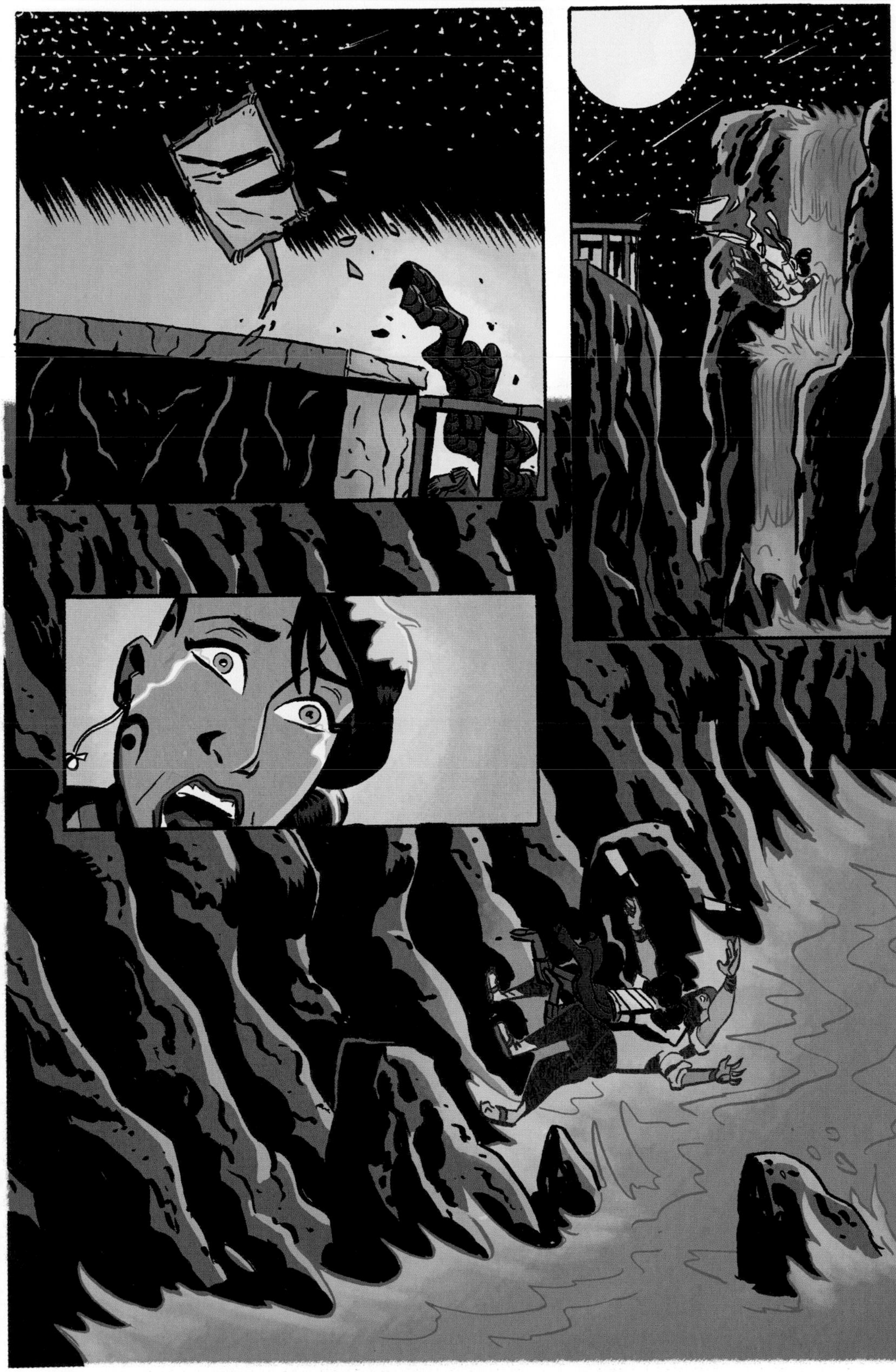

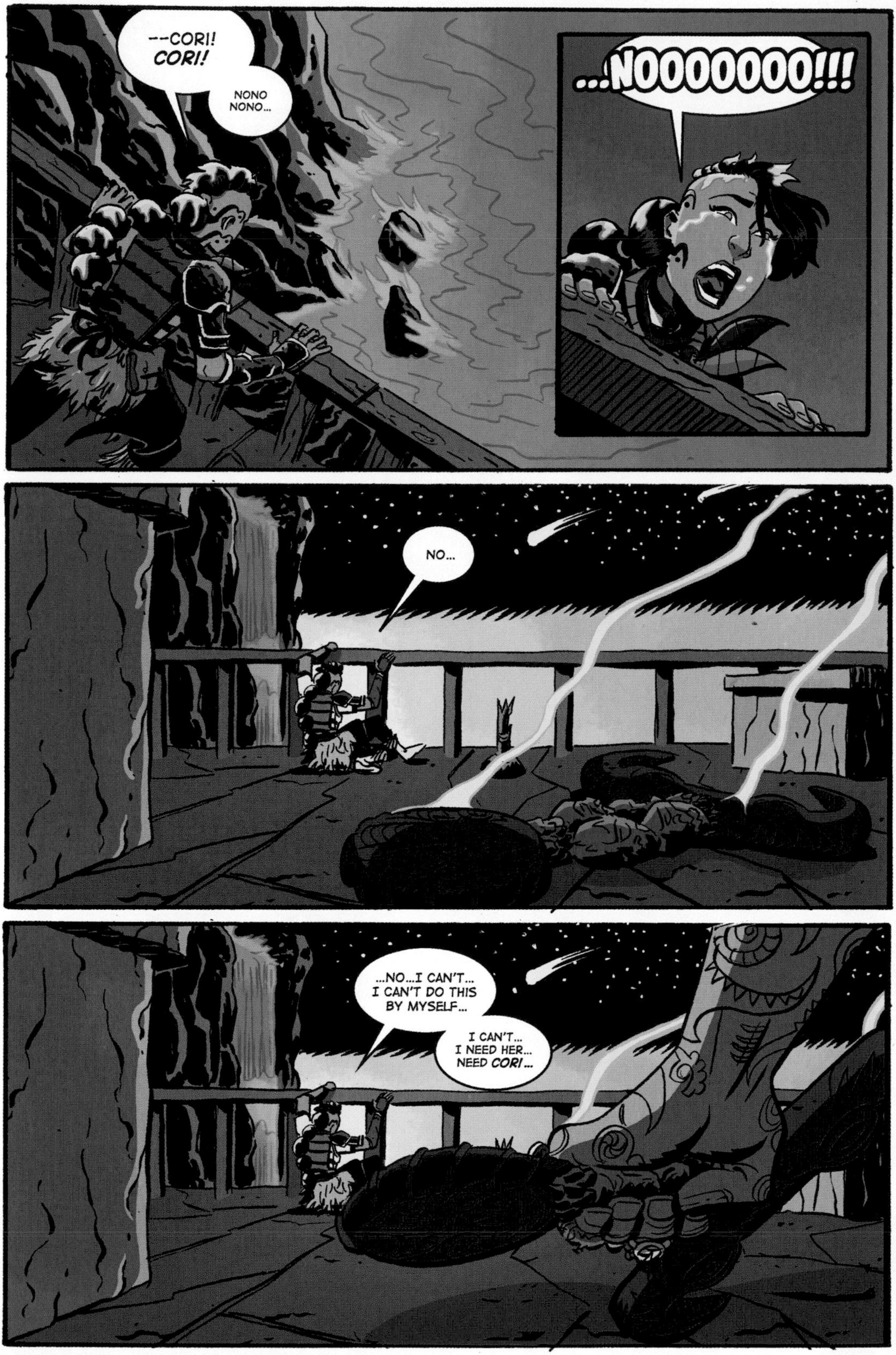
--CORI!
CORI!
NONO
NONO...
...NOOOOOOO!!!
NO...
...NO...I CAN'T...
I CAN'T DO THIS
BY MYSELF...
I CAN'T...
I NEED HER...
NEED CORI...

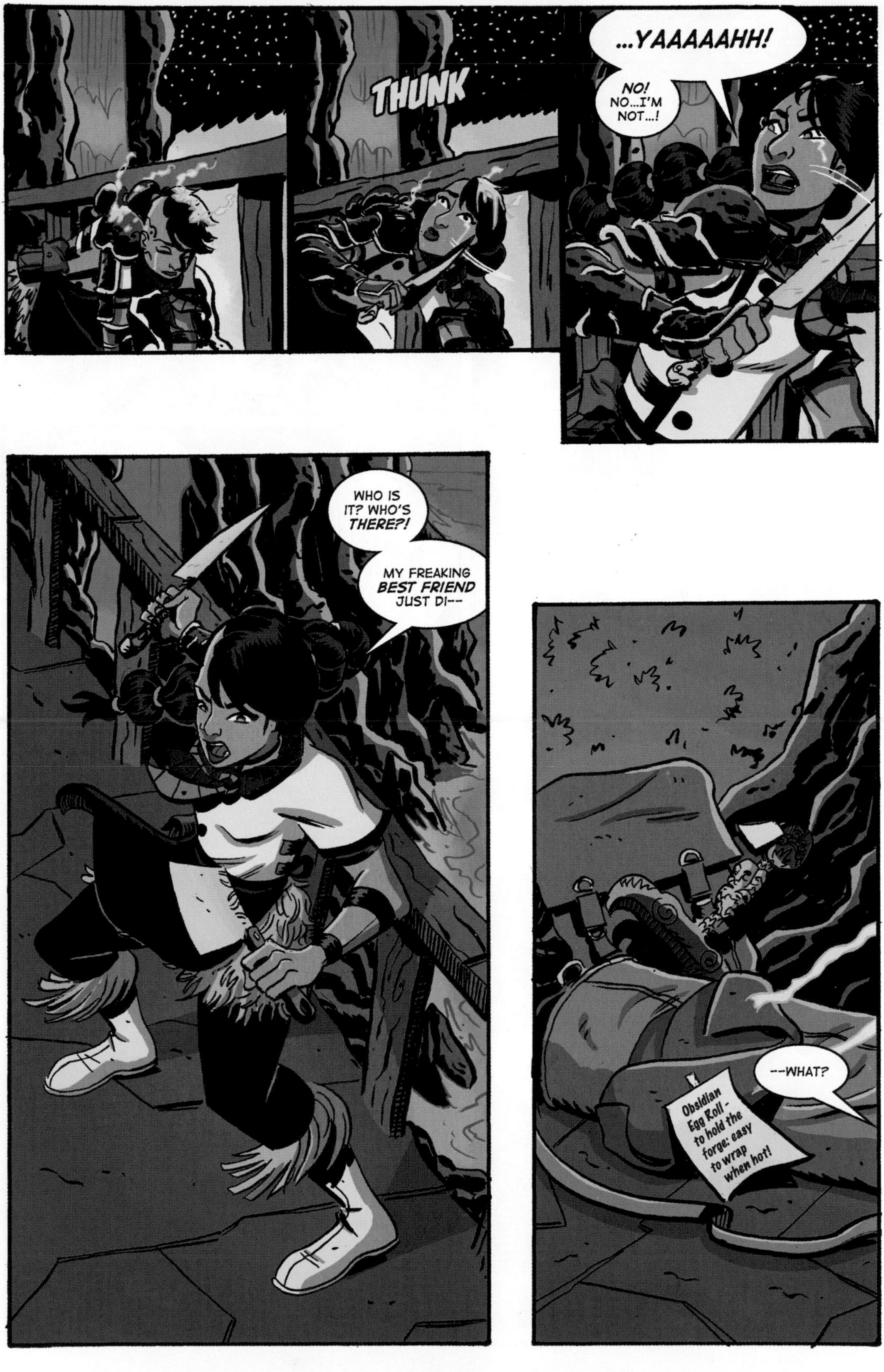
THUNK
...YAAAAAHH!
NO! NO...I'M NOT...!
WHO IS IT? WHO'S THERE?!
MY FREAKING BEST FRIEND JUST DI--
Obsidian Egg Roll - to hold the forge: easy to wrap when hot!
--WHAT?

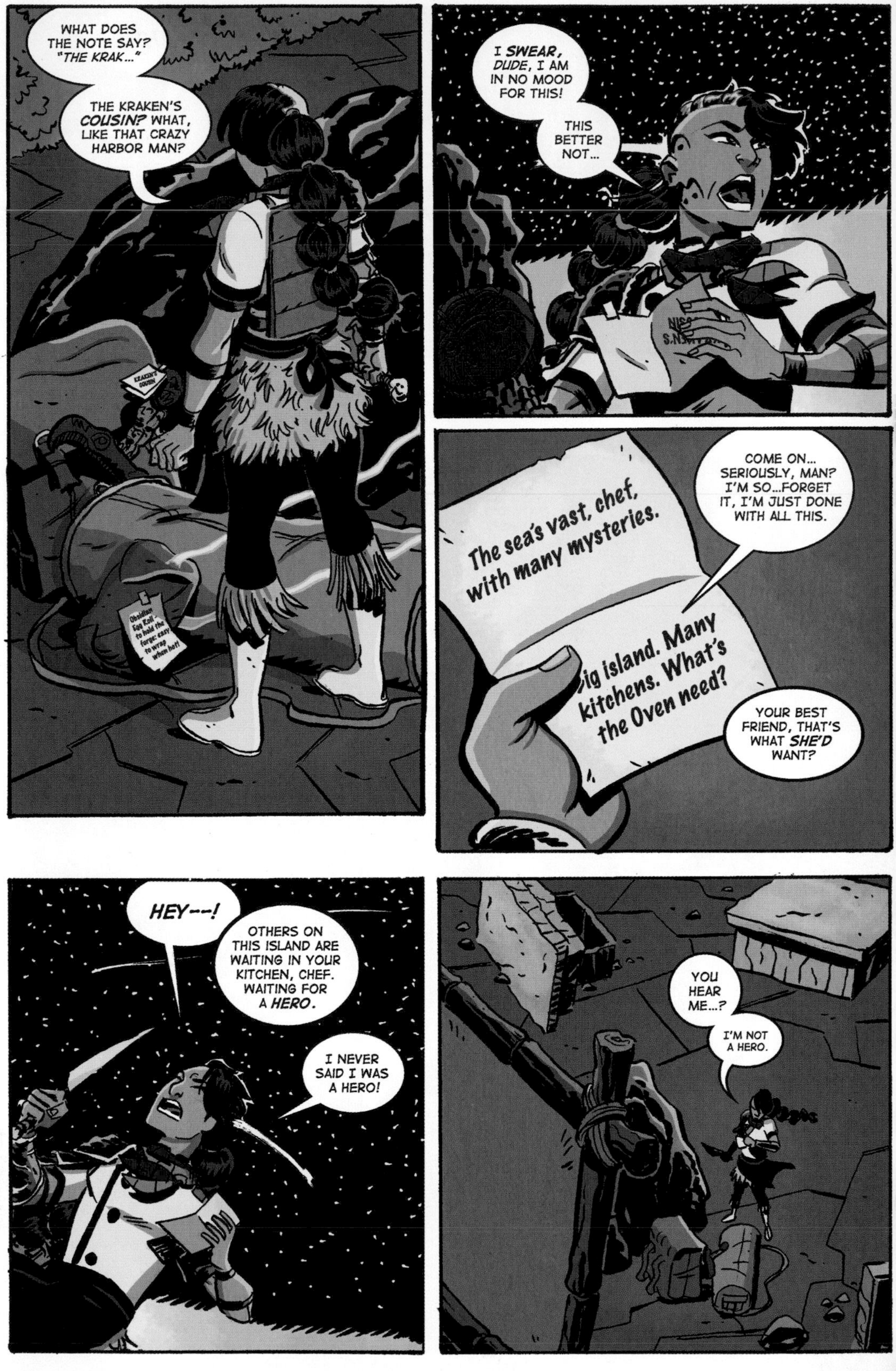
WHAT DOES THE NOTE SAY? "THE KRAK..."
THE KRAKEN'S COUSIN? WHAT, LIKE THAT CRAZY HARBOR MAN?
KRAKEN'S COUSIN
Obsidian Egg Roll - to hold the forge: easy to wrap when hot!
I SWEAR, DUDE, I AM IN NO MOOD FOR THIS!
THIS BETTER NOT...
The sea's vast, chef, with many mysteries.
Big island. Many kitchens. What's the Oven need?
COME ON... SERIOUSLY, MAN? I'M SO...FORGET IT, I'M JUST DONE WITH ALL THIS.
YOUR BEST FRIEND, THAT'S WHAT SHE'D WANT?
HEY--!
OTHERS ON THIS ISLAND ARE WAITING IN YOUR KITCHEN, CHEF. WAITING FOR A HERO.
I NEVER SAID I WAS A HERO!
YOU HEAR ME...?
I'M NOT A HERO.

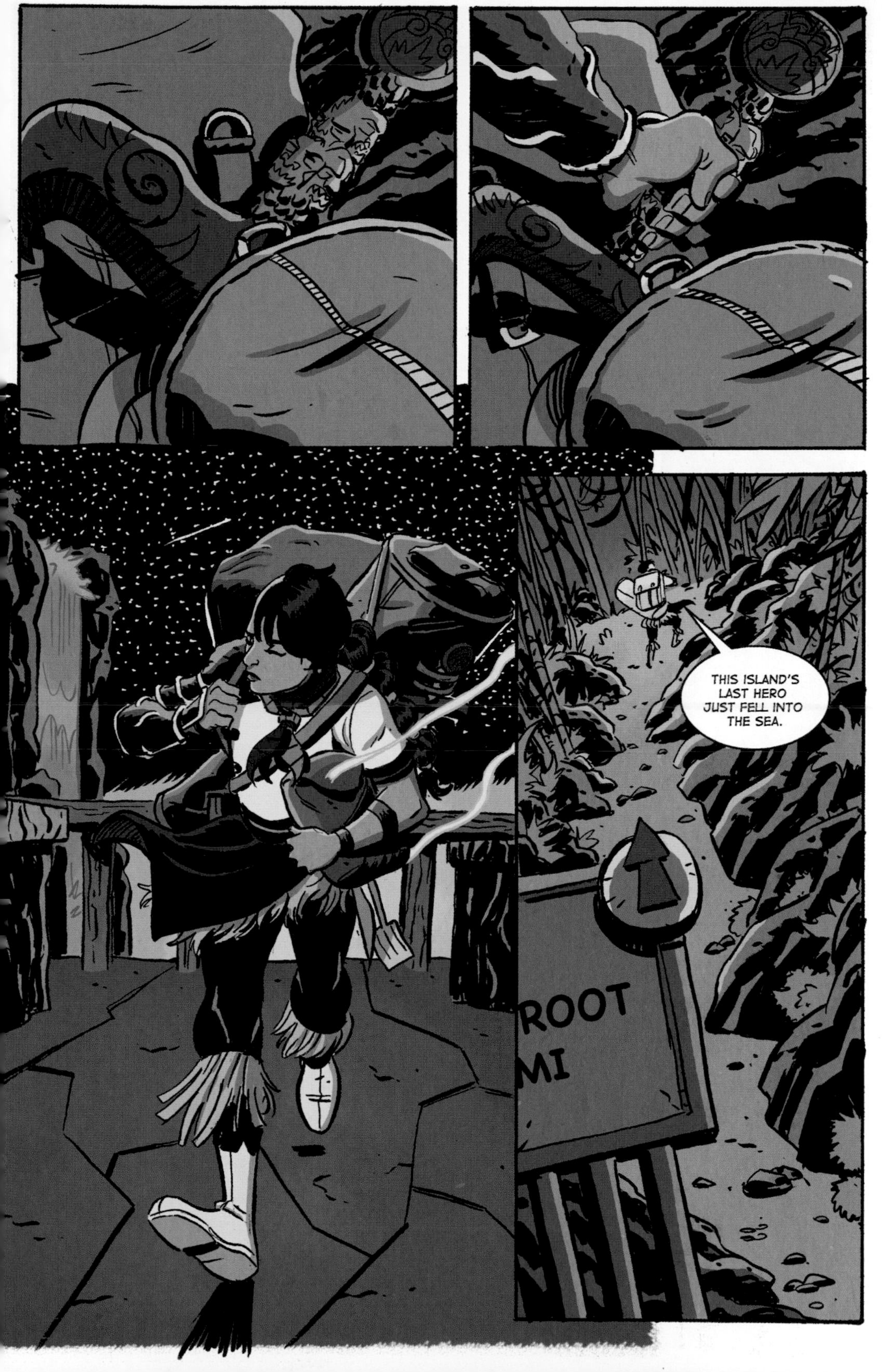
THIS ISLAND'S LAST HERO JUST FELL INTO THE SEA.
ROOT
MI

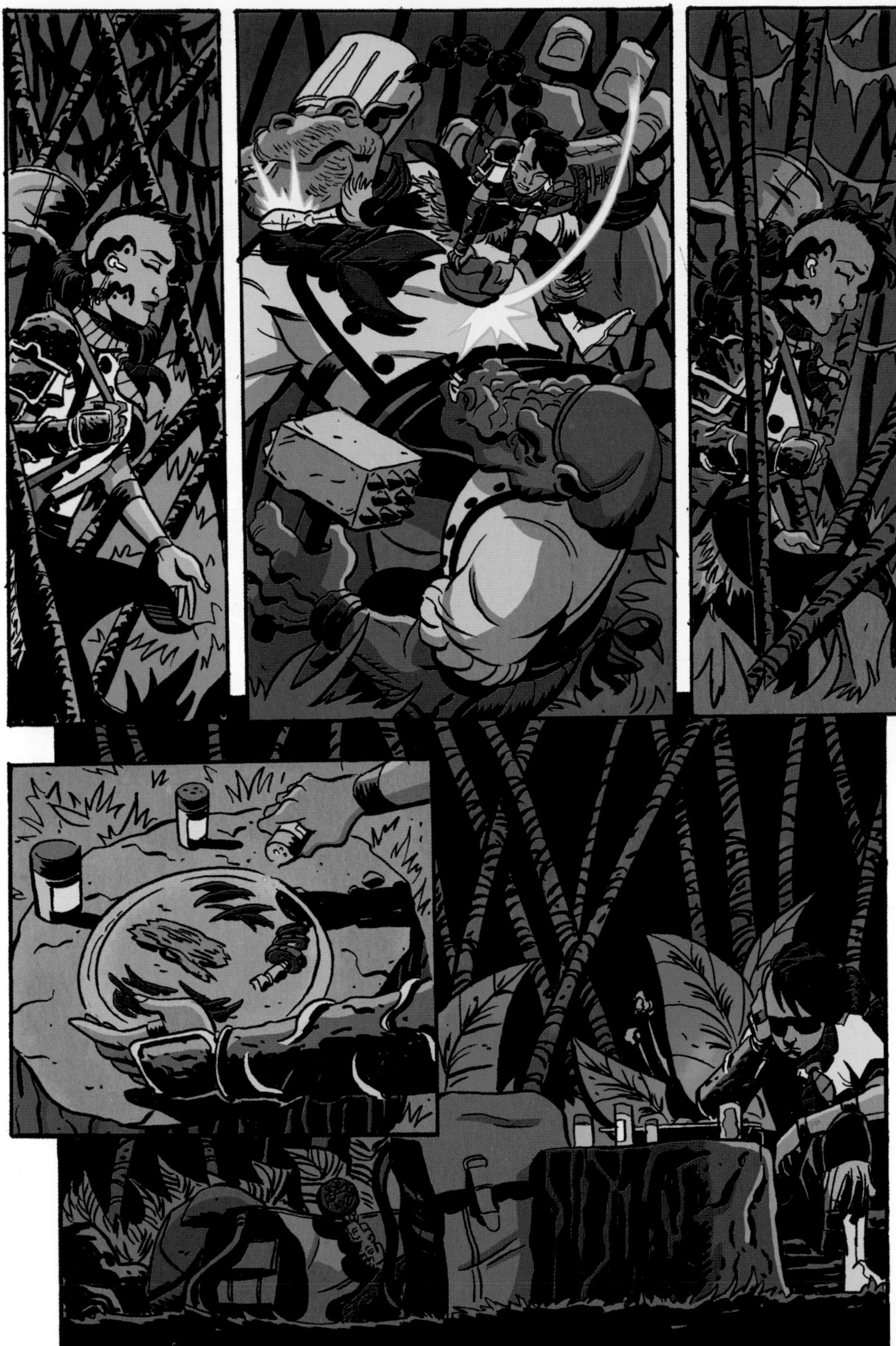

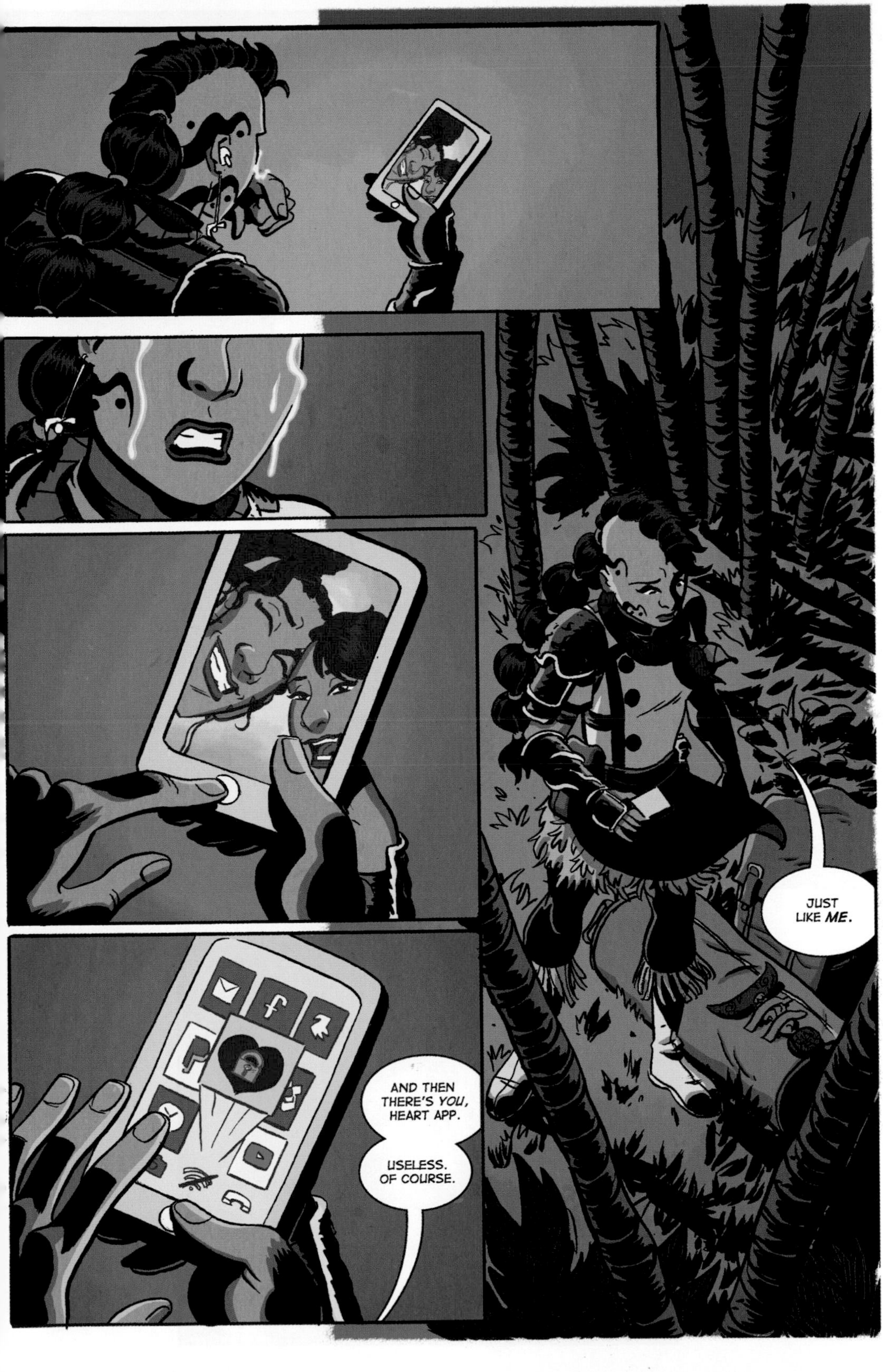
AND THEN THERE'S *YOU*, HEART APP.
USELESS. OF COURSE.
JUST LIKE ***ME***.

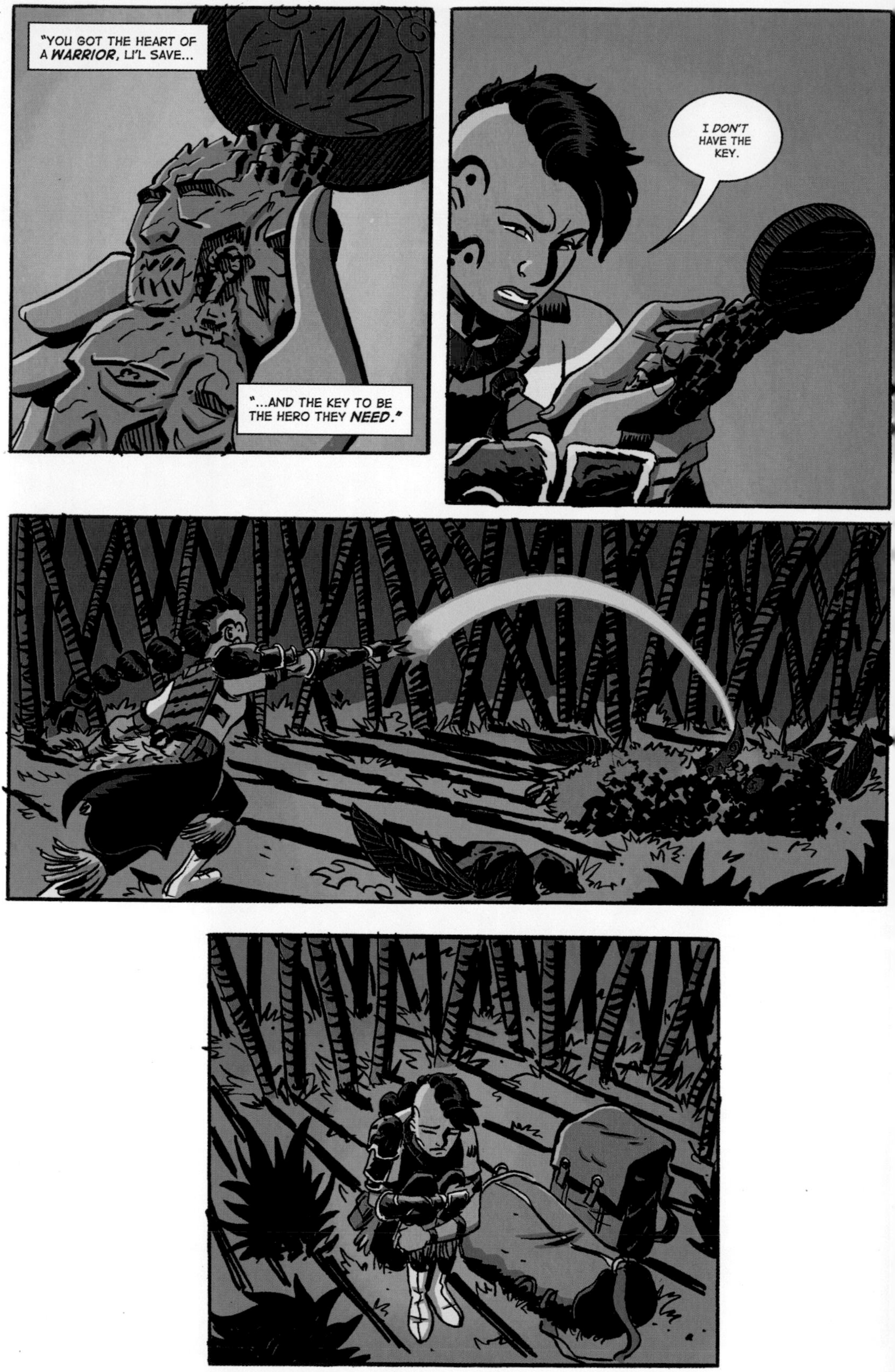
"YOU GOT THE HEART OF A WARRIOR, LI'L SAVE...
"...AND THE KEY TO BE THE HERO THEY NEED."
I DON'T HAVE THE KEY.

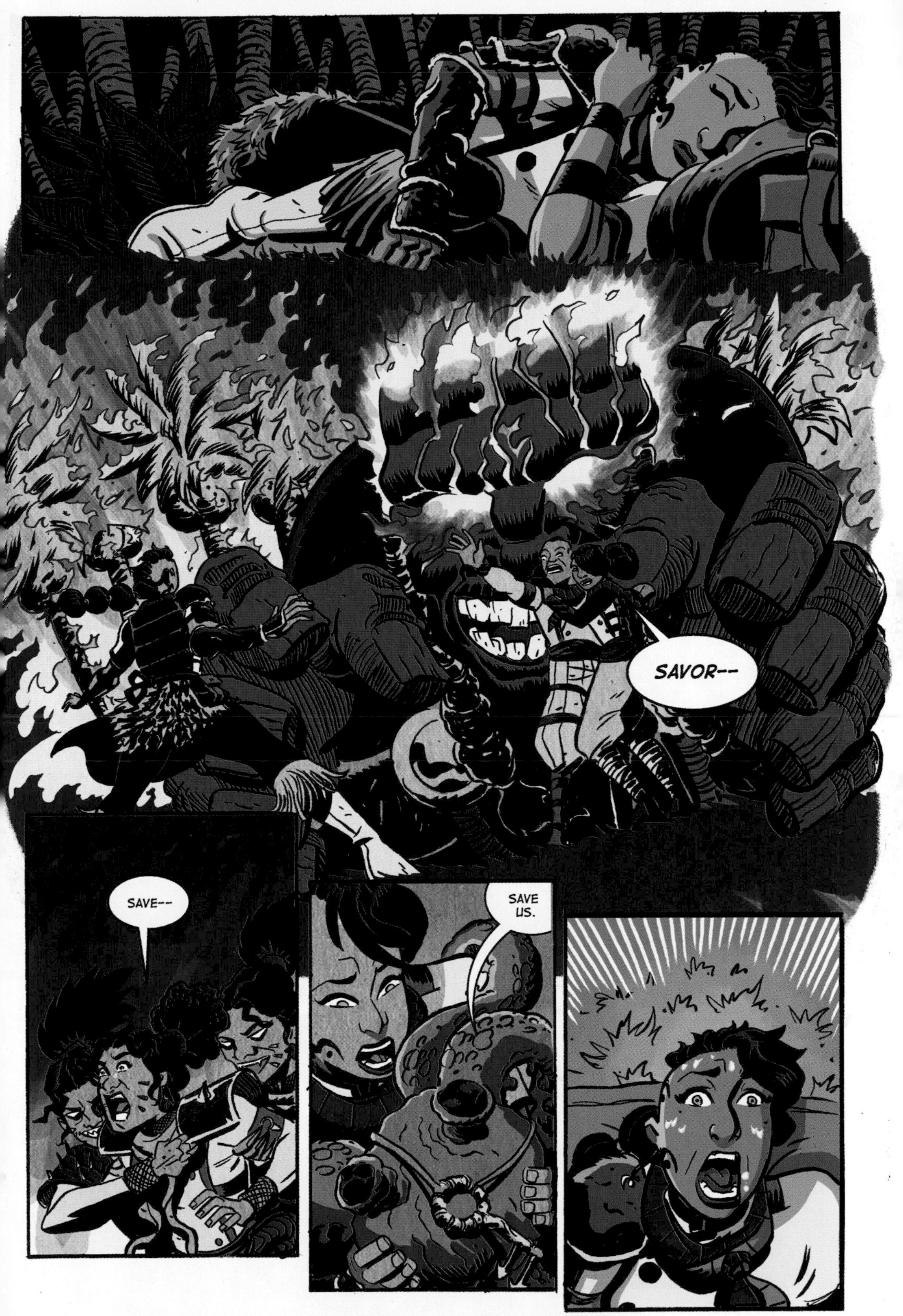
SAVOR--
SAVE--
SAVE US.

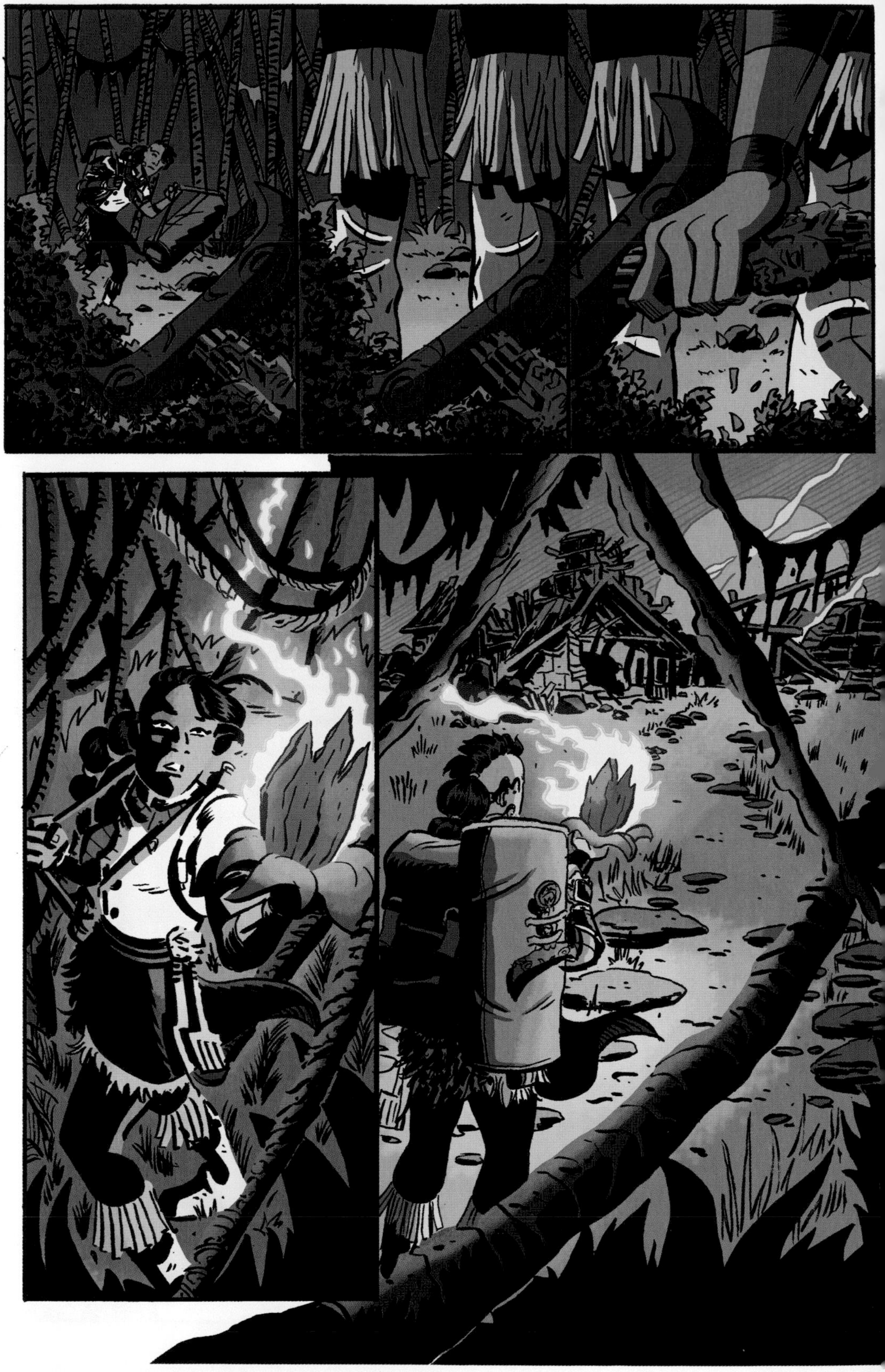

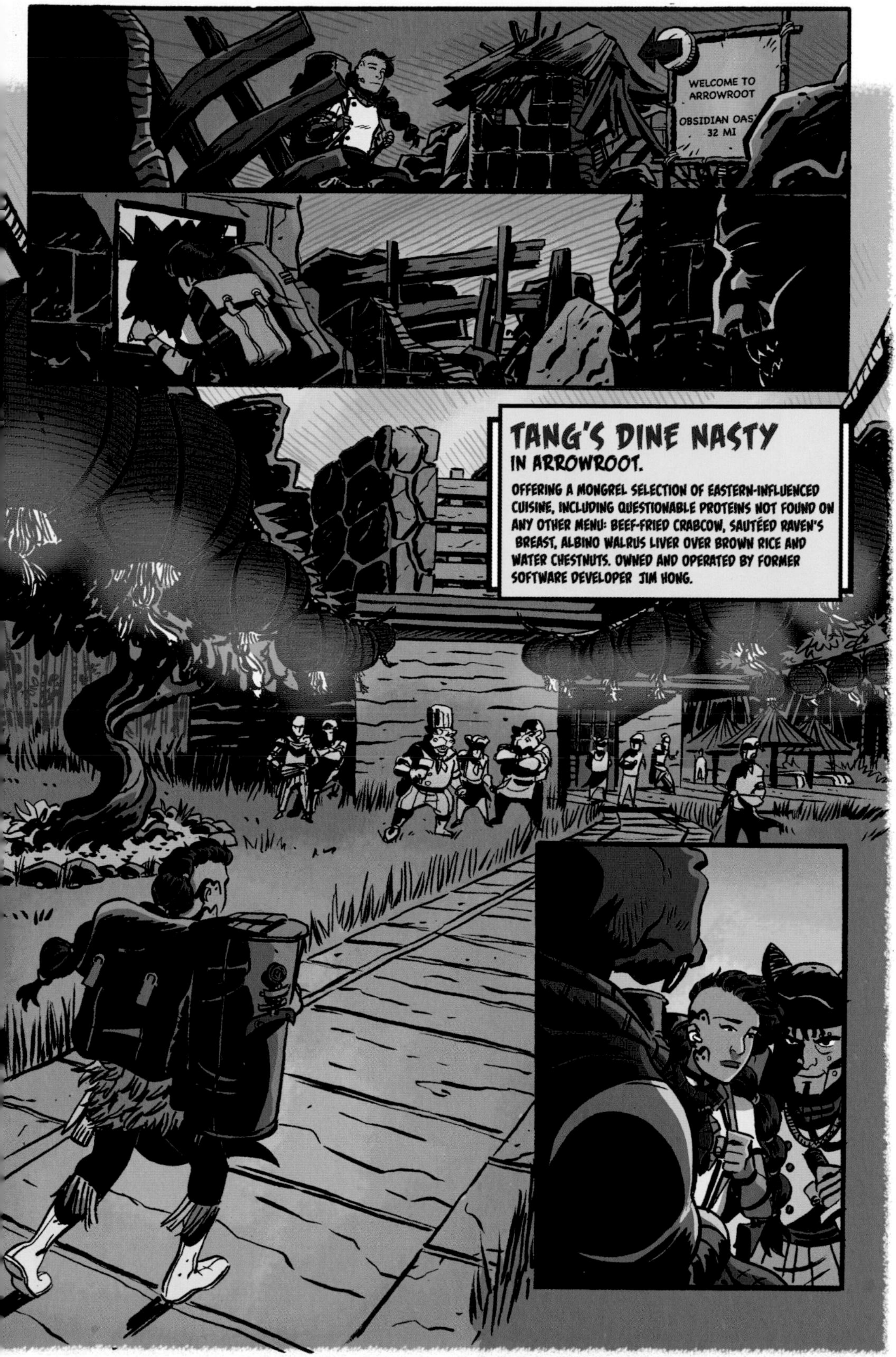
WELCOME TO ARROWROOT
OBSIDIAN OASIS 32 MI
TANG'S DINE NASTY IN ARROWROOT.
OFFERING A MONGREL SELECTION OF EASTERN-INFLUENCED CUISINE, INCLUDING QUESTIONABLE PROTEINS NOT FOUND ON ANY OTHER MENU: BEEF-FRIED CRABCOW, SAUTÉED RAVEN'S BREAST, ALBINO WALRUS LIVER OVER BROWN RICE AND WATER CHESTNUTS. OWNED AND OPERATED BY FORMER SOFTWARE DEVELOPER JIM HONG.

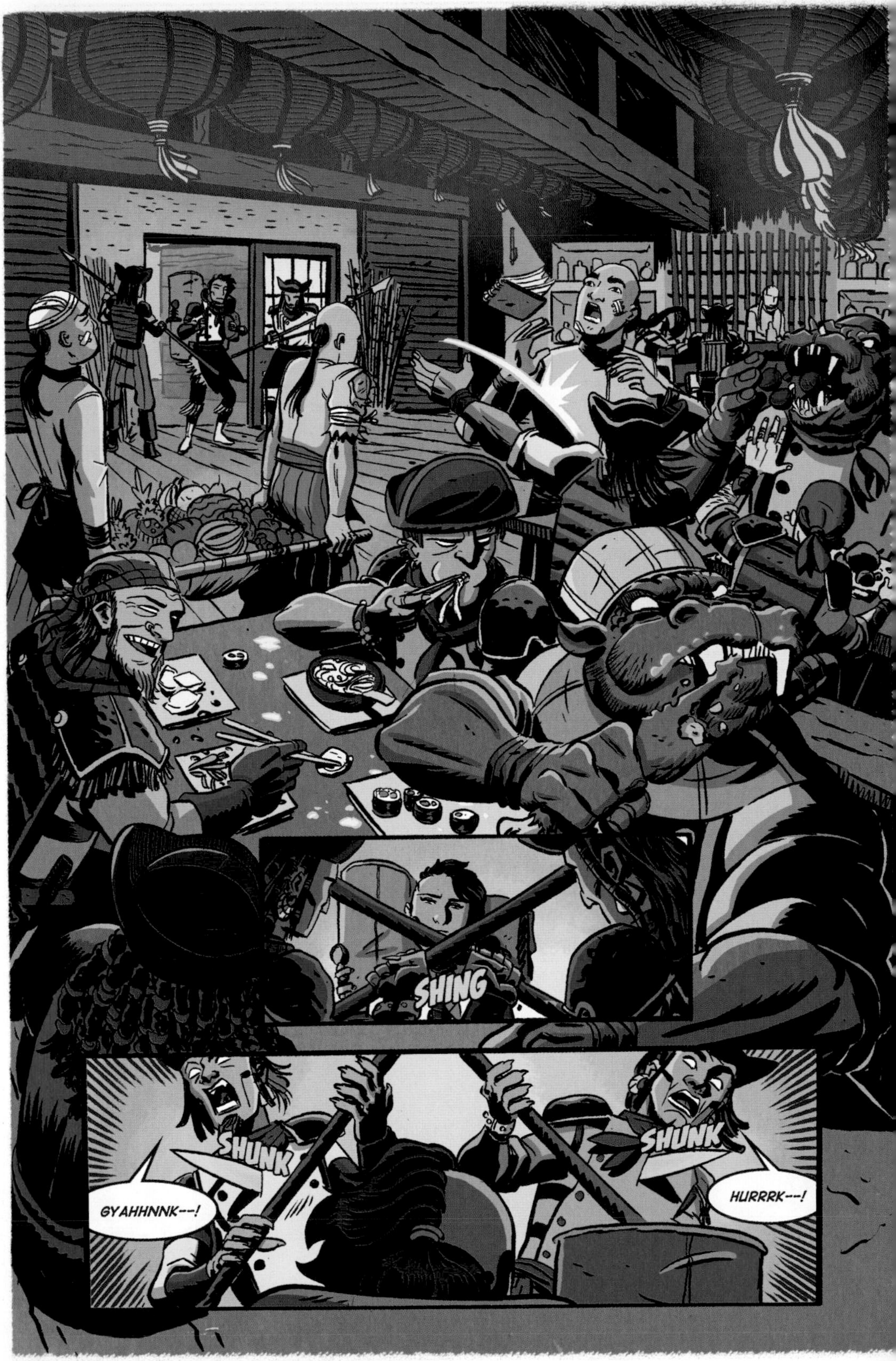
SHING
SHUNK
GYAHHNNK--!
SHUNK
HURRRK--!

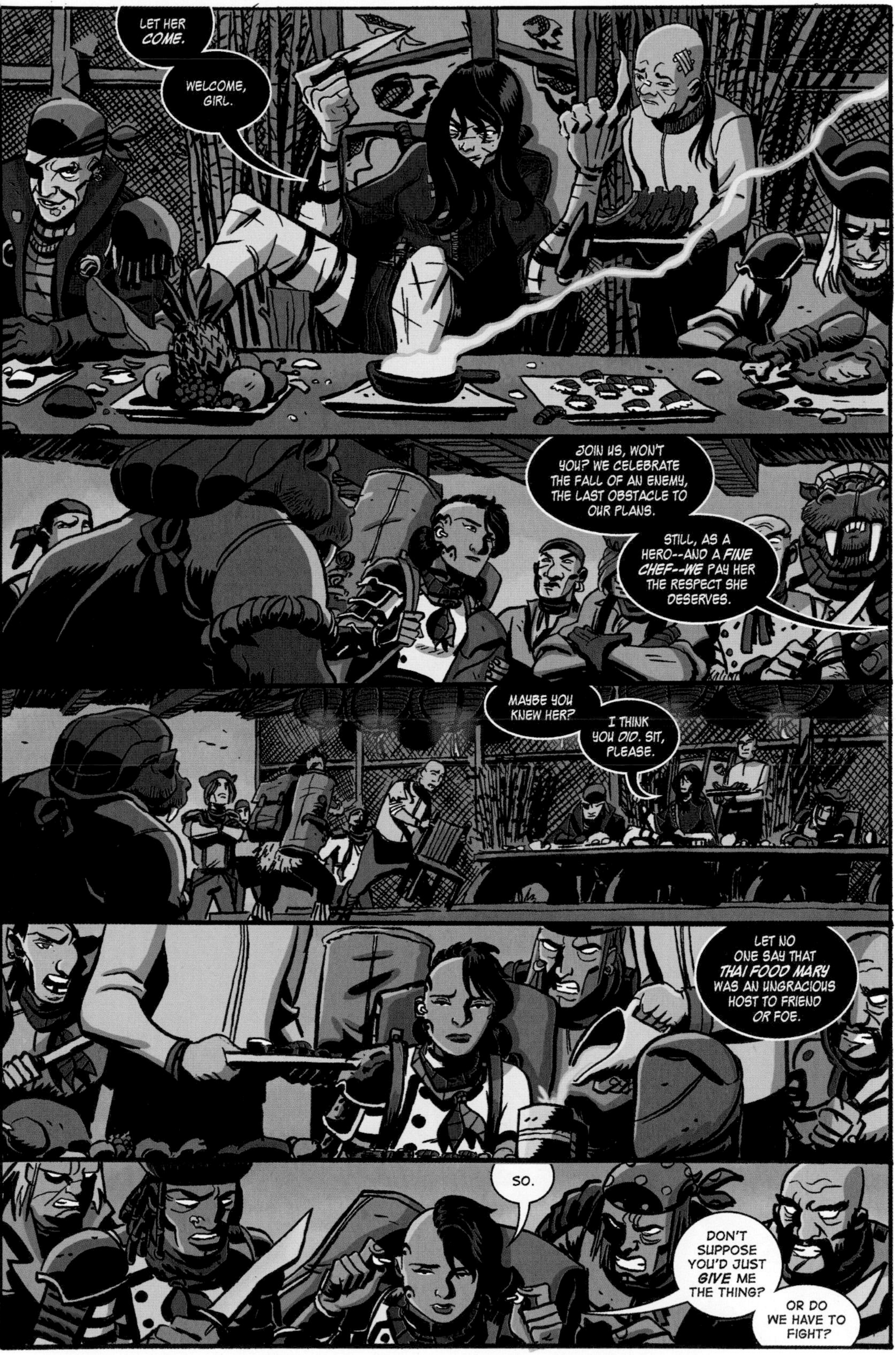
LET HER COME.
WELCOME, GIRL.
JOIN US, WON'T YOU? WE CELEBRATE THE FALL OF AN ENEMY, THE LAST OBSTACLE TO OUR PLANS.
STILL, AS A HERO--AND A FINE CHEF--WE PAY HER THE RESPECT SHE DESERVES.
MAYBE YOU KNEW HER?
I THINK YOU DID. SIT, PLEASE.
LET NO ONE SAY THAT THAI FOOD MARY WAS AN UNGRACIOUS HOST TO FRIEND OR FOE.
SO.
DON'T SUPPOSE YOU'D JUST GIVE ME THE THING?
OR DO WE HAVE TO FIGHT?

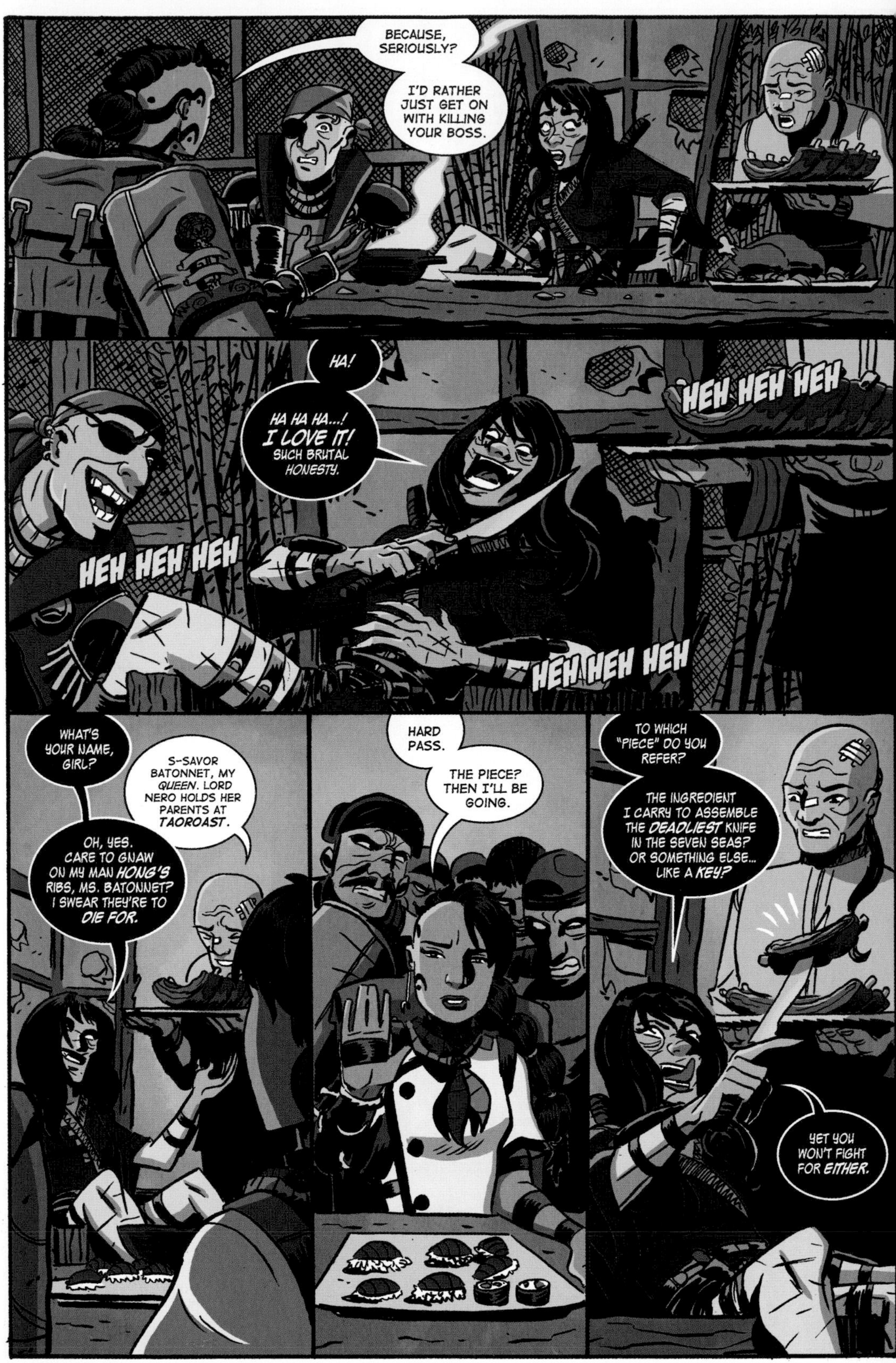
BECAUSE, SERIOUSLY?
I'D RATHER JUST GET ON WITH KILLING YOUR BOSS.
HA!
HA HA HA...! I LOVE IT! SUCH BRUTAL HONESTY.
HEH HEH HEH
HEH HEH HEH
HEH HEH HEH
WHAT'S YOUR NAME, GIRL?
S-SAVOR BATONNET, MY QUEEN. LORD NERO HOLDS HER PARENTS AT TAOROAST.
OH, YES. CARE TO GNAW ON MY MAN HONG'S RIBS, MS. BATONNET? I SWEAR THEY'RE TO DIE FOR.
HARD PASS.
THE PIECE? THEN I'LL BE GOING.
TO WHICH "PIECE" DO YOU REFER?
THE INGREDIENT I CARRY TO ASSEMBLE THE DEADLIEST KNIFE IN THE SEVEN SEAS? OR SOMETHING ELSE... LIKE A KEY?
YET YOU WON'T FIGHT FOR EITHER.

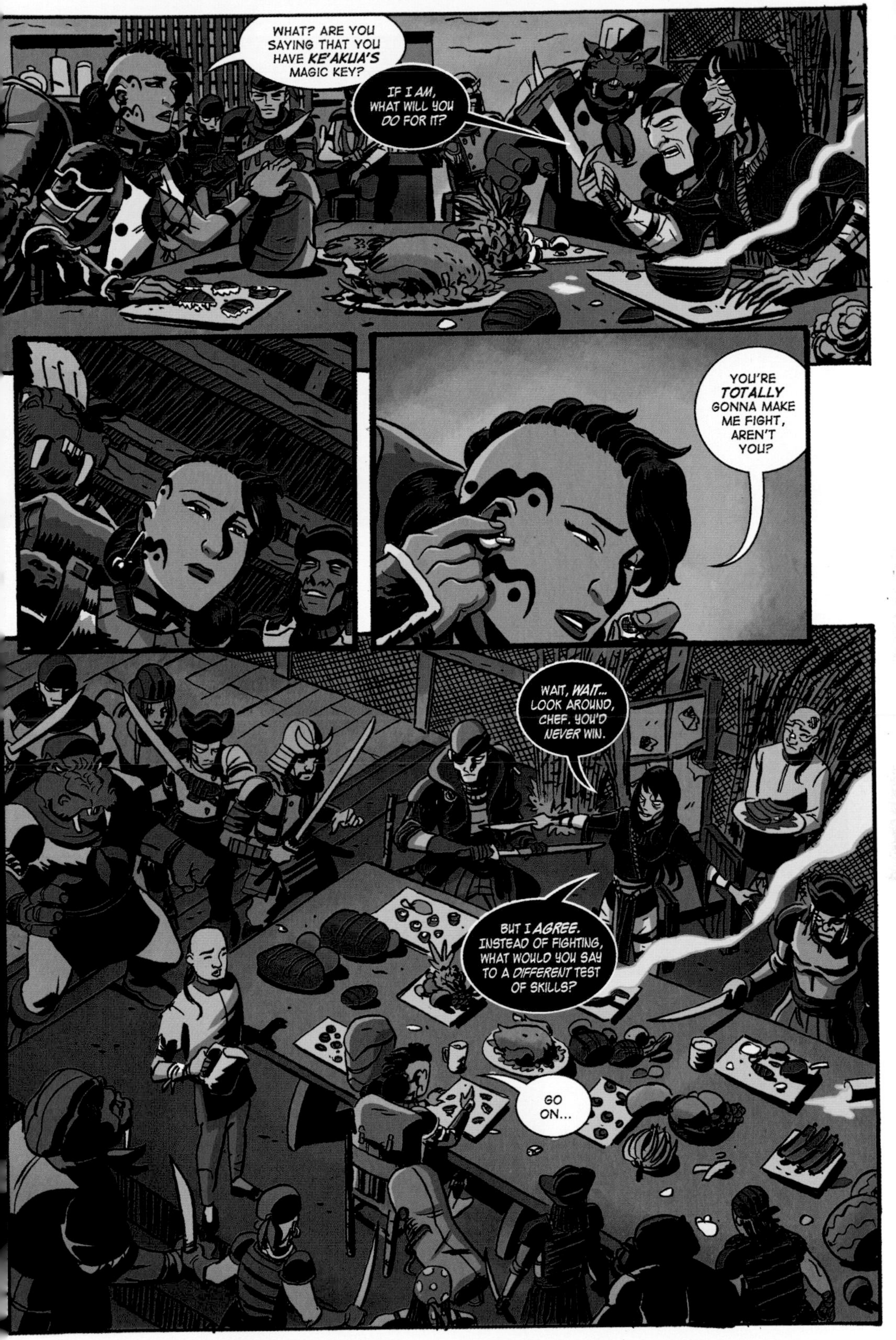
WHAT? ARE YOU SAYING THAT YOU HAVE *KE'AKUA'S* MAGIC KEY?
IF I *AM*, WHAT WILL YOU *DO* FOR IT?
YOU'RE ***TOTALLY*** GONNA MAKE ME FIGHT, AREN'T YOU?
WAIT, ***WAIT...*** LOOK AROUND, CHEF. YOU'D *NEVER* WIN.
BUT I *AGREE.* INSTEAD OF FIGHTING, WHAT WOULD YOU SAY TO A *DIFFERENT* TEST OF SKILLS?
GO ON...

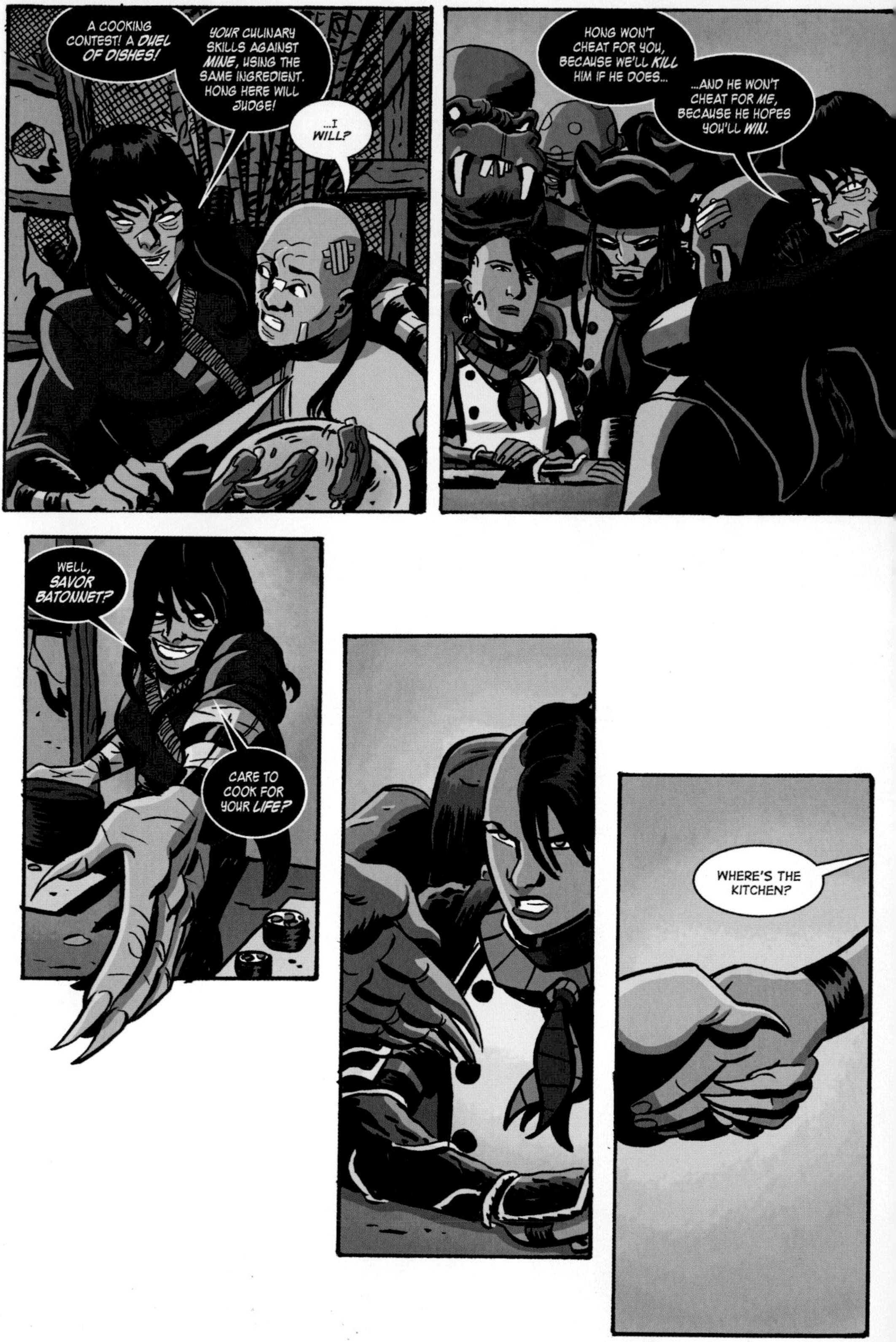

A COOKING CONTEST! A DUEL OF DISHES!
YOUR CULINARY SKILLS AGAINST MINE, USING THE SAME INGREDIENT. HONG HERE WILL JUDGE!
...I WILL?
HONG WON'T CHEAT FOR YOU, BECAUSE WE'LL KILL HIM IF HE DOES...
...AND HE WON'T CHEAT FOR ME, BECAUSE HE HOPES YOU'LL WIN.
WELL, SAVOR BATONNET?
CARE TO COOK FOR YOUR LIFE?
WHERE'S THE KITCHEN?

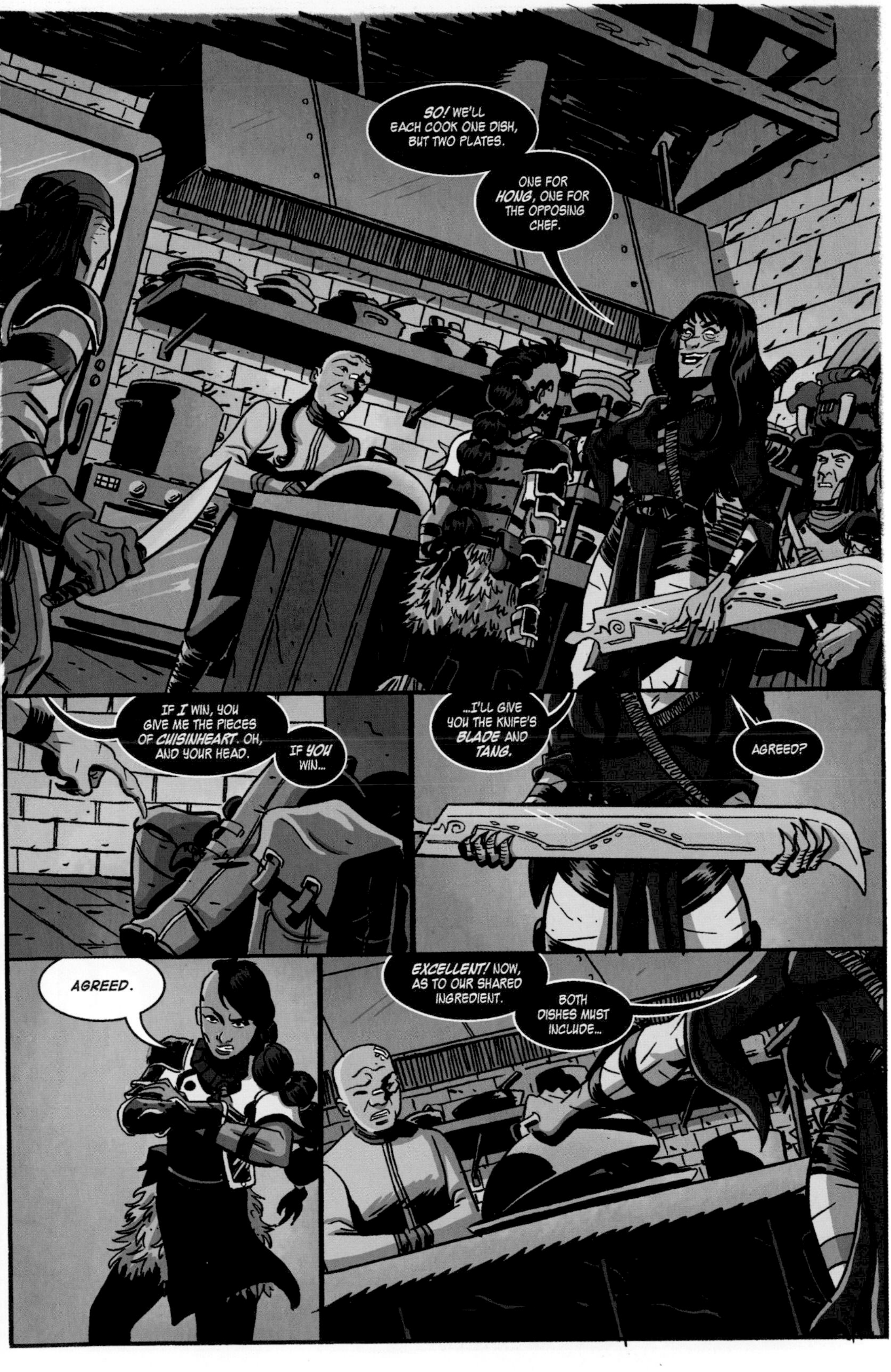
SO! WE'LL EACH COOK ONE DISH, BUT TWO PLATES.
ONE FOR HONG, ONE FOR THE OPPOSING CHEF.
IF I WIN, YOU GIVE ME THE PIECES OF CUISINHEART. OH, AND YOUR HEAD.
IF YOU WIN...
...I'LL GIVE YOU THE KNIFE'S BLADE AND TANG.
AGREED?
AGREED.
EXCELLENT! NOW, AS TO OUR SHARED INGREDIENT.
BOTH DISHES MUST INCLUDE...

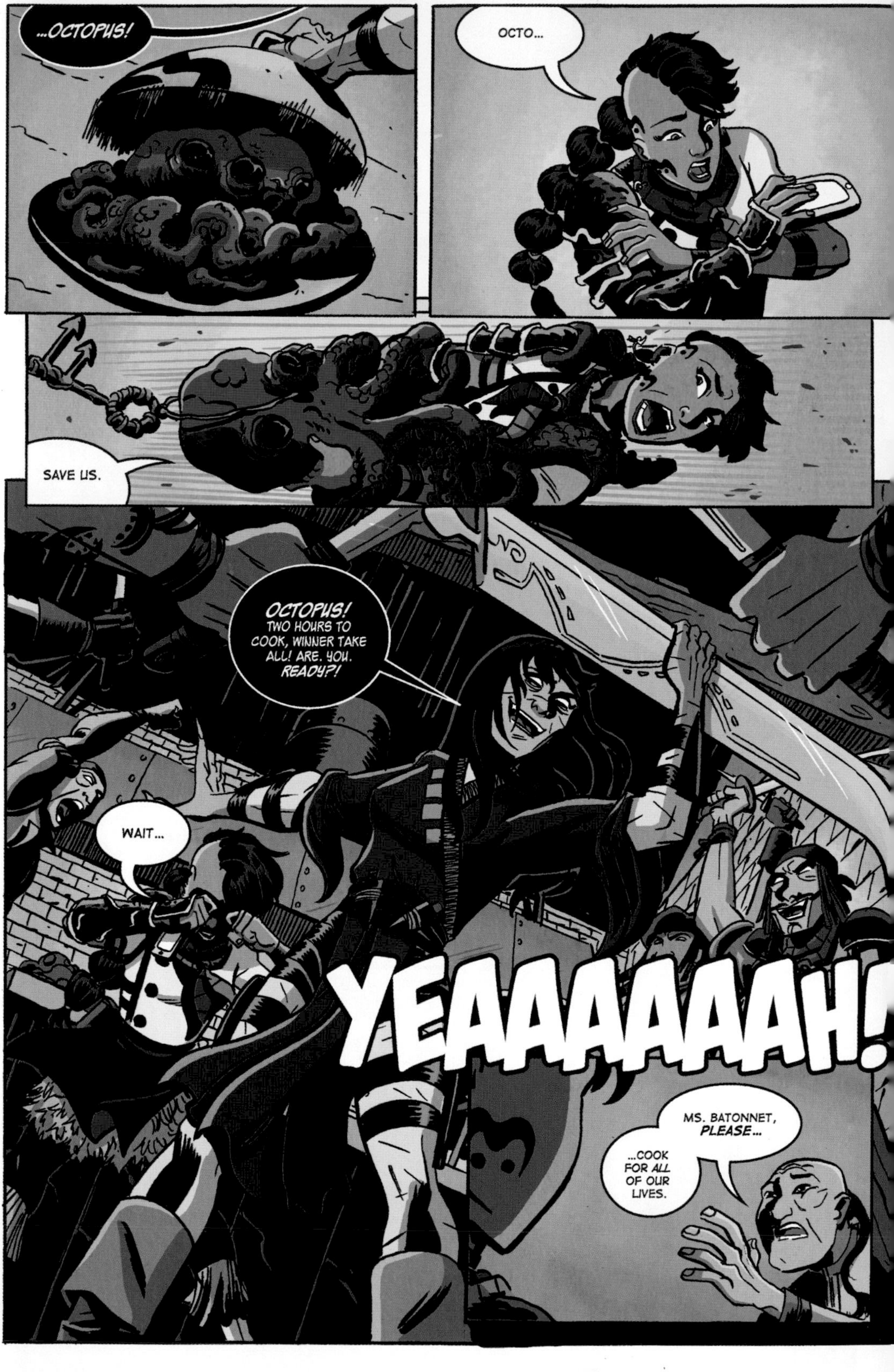
...OCTOPUS!
OCTO...
SAVE US.
OCTOPUS! TWO HOURS TO COOK, WINNER TAKE ALL! ARE. YOU. READY?!
WAIT...
YEAAAAAAAH!
MS. BATONNET, PLEASE...
...COOK FOR ALL OF OUR LIVES.

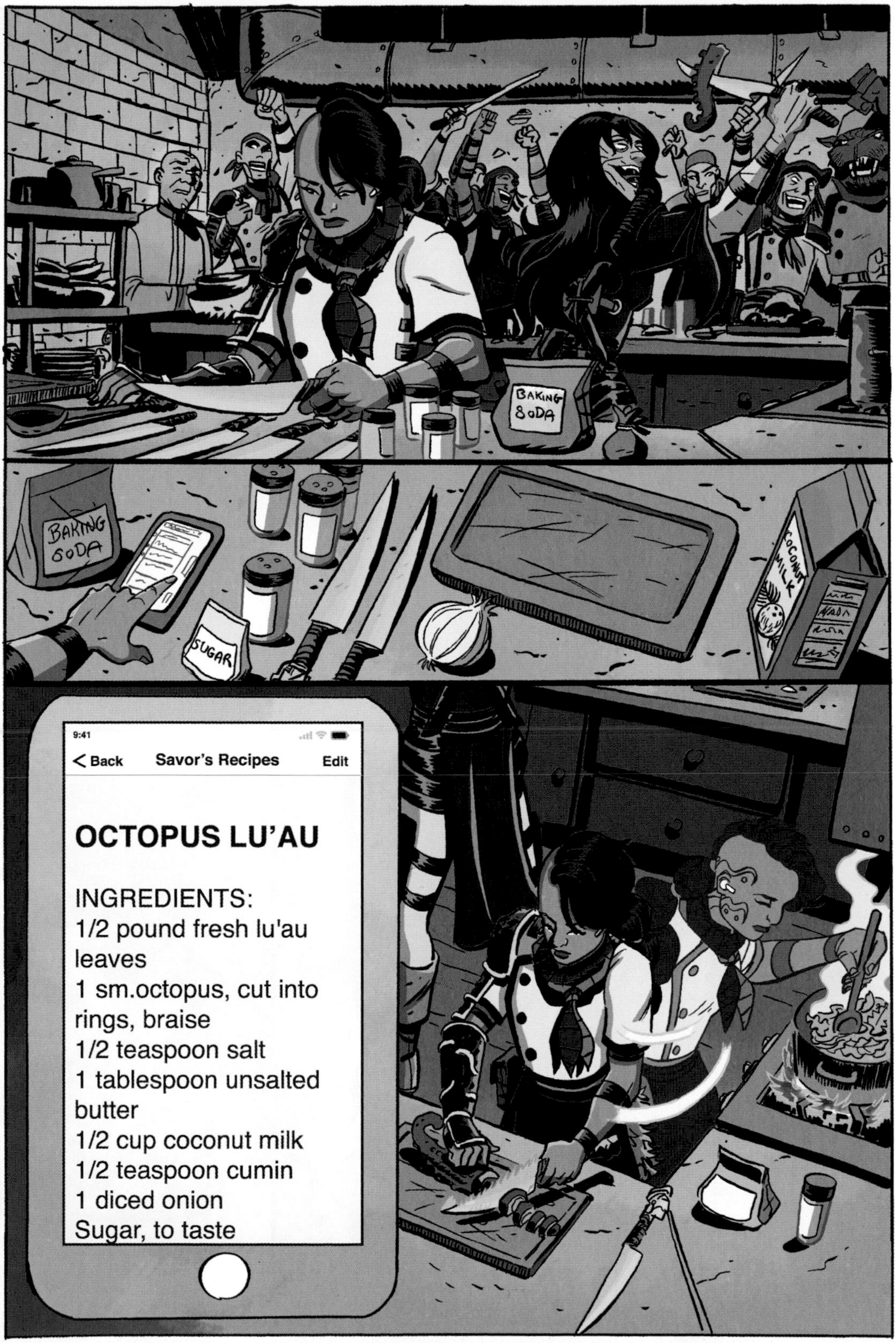
BAKING SODA
BAKING SODA
SUGAR
COCONUT MILK
9:41
< Back
Savor's Recipes
Edit
OCTOPUS LU'AU
INGREDIENTS:
1/2 pound fresh lu'au leaves
1 sm.octopus, cut into rings, braise
1/2 teaspoon salt
1 tablespoon unsalted butter
1/2 cup coconut milk
1/2 teaspoon cumin
1 diced onion
Sugar, to taste

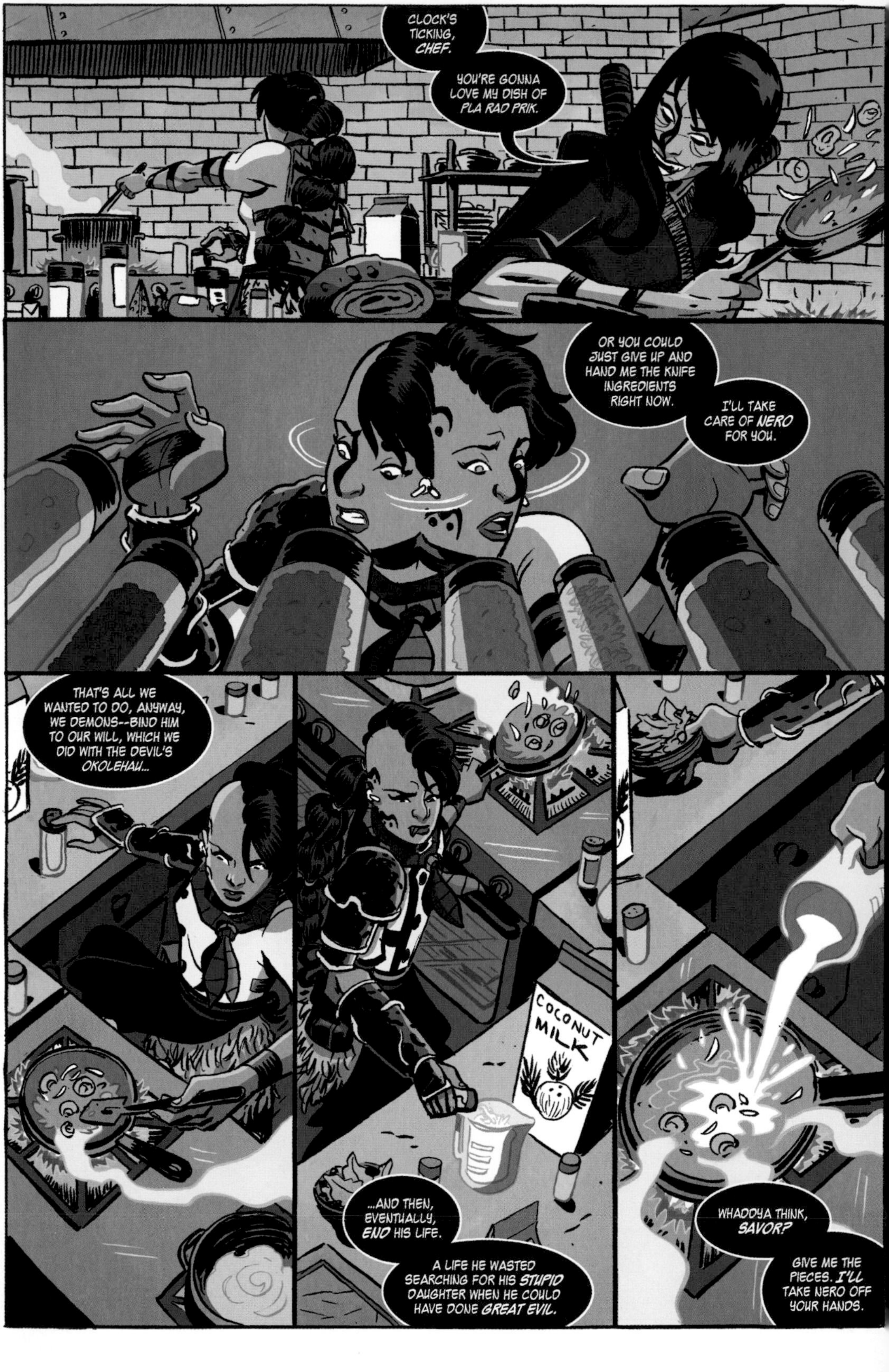

CLOCK'S TICKING, CHEF.
YOU'RE GONNA LOVE MY DISH OF PLA RAD PRIK.
OR YOU COULD JUST GIVE UP AND HAND ME THE KNIFE INGREDIENTS RIGHT NOW.
I'LL TAKE CARE OF NERO FOR YOU.
THAT'S ALL WE WANTED TO DO, ANYWAY, WE DEMONS--BIND HIM TO OUR WILL, WHICH WE DID WITH THE DEVIL'S OKOLEHAU...
COCONUT MILK
...AND THEN, EVENTUALLY, END HIS LIFE.
A LIFE HE WASTED SEARCHING FOR HIS STUPID DAUGHTER WHEN HE COULD HAVE DONE GREAT EVIL.
WHADDYA THINK, SAVOR?
GIVE ME THE PIECES. I'LL TAKE NERO OFF YOUR HANDS.

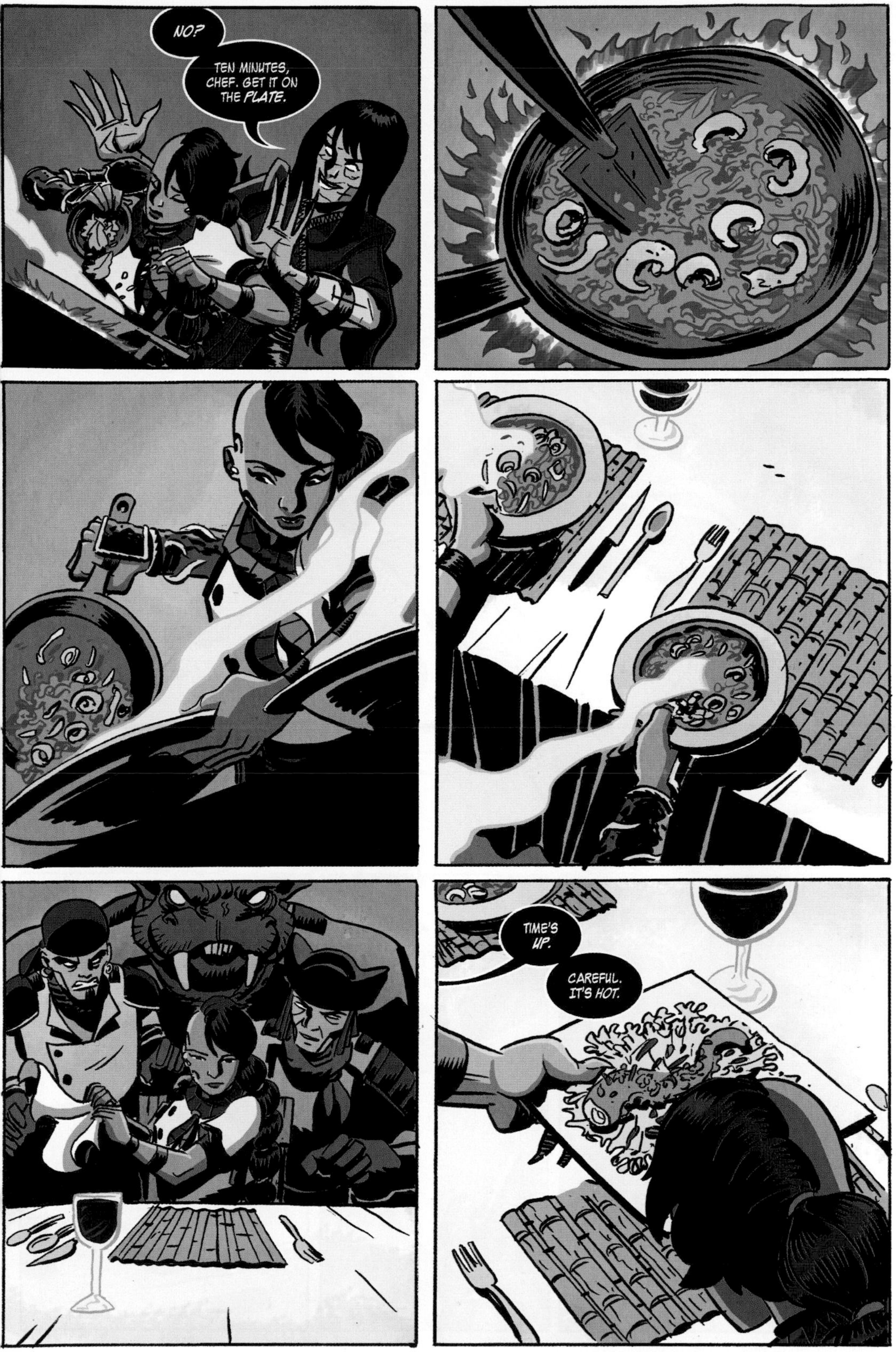
NO?
TEN MINUTES, CHEF. GET IT ON THE *PLATE.*
TIME'S *UP.*
CAREFUL. IT'S *HOT.*

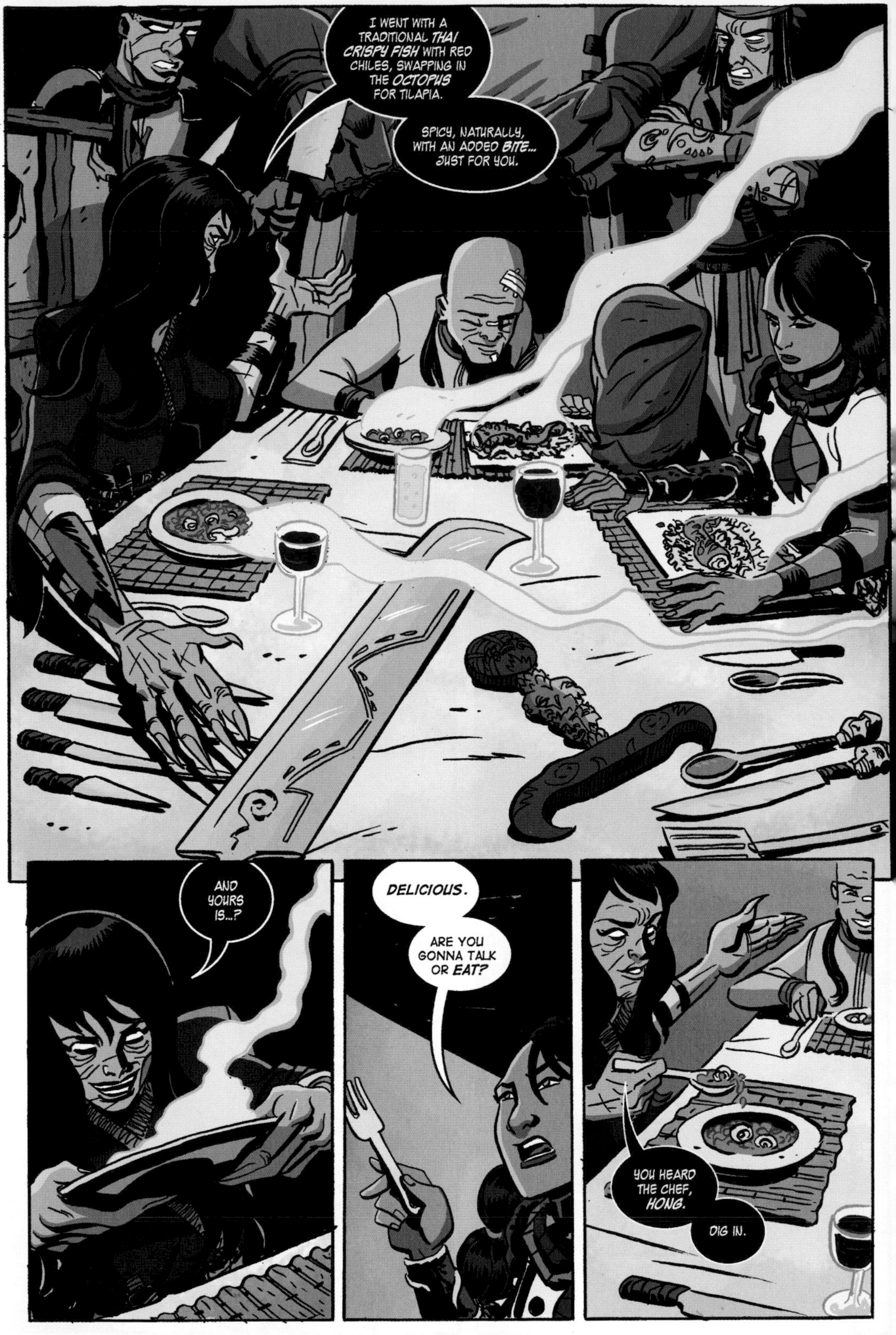
I WENT WITH A TRADITIONAL *THAI CRISPY FISH* WITH RED CHILES, SWAPPING IN THE *OCTOPUS* FOR TILAPIA.
SPICY, NATURALLY, WITH AN ADDED *BITE*... JUST FOR YOU.
AND YOURS IS...?
DELICIOUS.
ARE YOU GONNA TALK OR *EAT?*
YOU HEARD THE CHEF, *HONG.*
DIG IN.

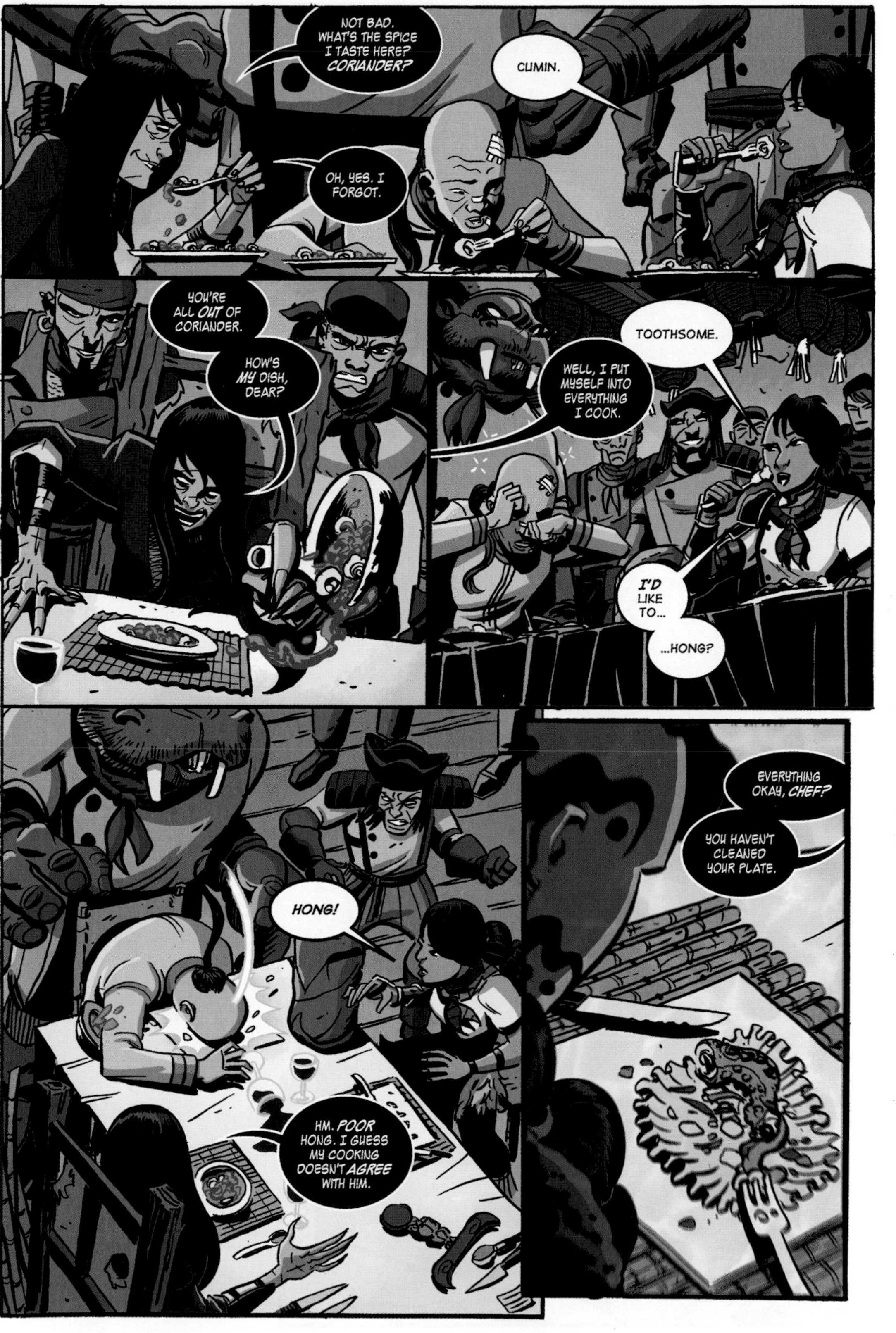
NOT BAD. WHAT'S THE SPICE I TASTE HERE? CORIANDER?
CUMIN.
OH, YES. I FORGOT.
YOU'RE ALL OUT OF CORIANDER.
HOW'S MY DISH, DEAR?
TOOTHSOME.
WELL, I PUT MYSELF INTO EVERYTHING I COOK.
I'D LIKE TO...
...HONG?
HONG!
HM. POOR HONG. I GUESS MY COOKING DOESN'T AGREE WITH HIM.
EVERYTHING OKAY, CHEF?
YOU HAVEN'T CLEANED YOUR PLATE.

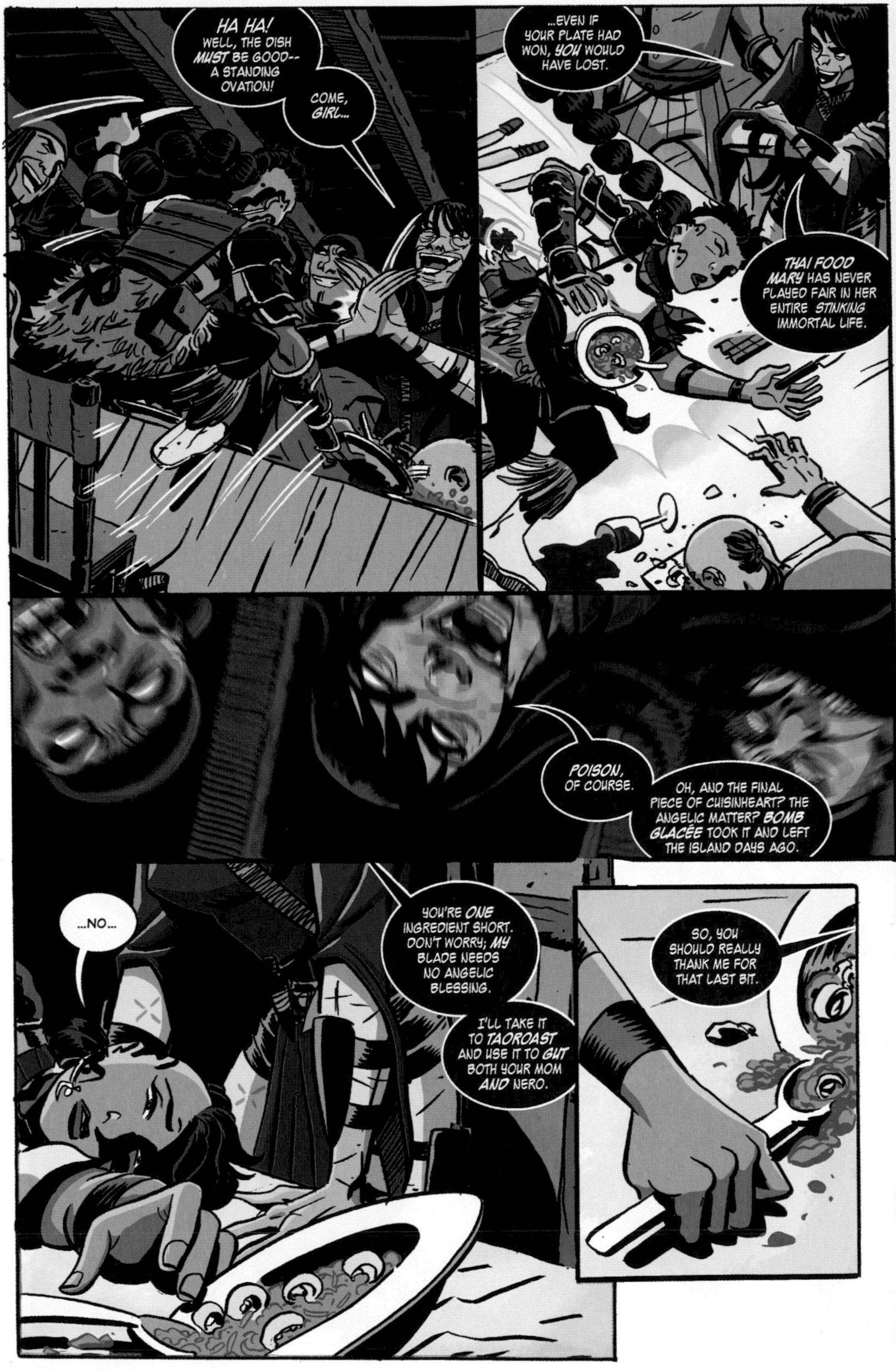
HA HA! WELL, THE DISH MUST BE GOOD-- A STANDING OVATION!
COME, GIRL...
...EVEN IF YOUR PLATE HAD WON, YOU WOULD HAVE LOST.
THAI FOOD MARY HAS NEVER PLAYED FAIR IN HER ENTIRE STINKING IMMORTAL LIFE.
POISON, OF COURSE.
OH, AND THE FINAL PIECE OF CUISINHEART? THE ANGELIC MATTER? BOMB GLACÉE TOOK IT AND LEFT THE ISLAND DAYS AGO.
...NO...
YOU'RE ONE INGREDIENT SHORT. DON'T WORRY; MY BLADE NEEDS NO ANGELIC BLESSING.
I'LL TAKE IT TO TAOROAST AND USE IT TO GUT BOTH YOUR MOM AND NERO.
SO, YOU SHOULD REALLY THANK ME FOR THAT LAST BIT.

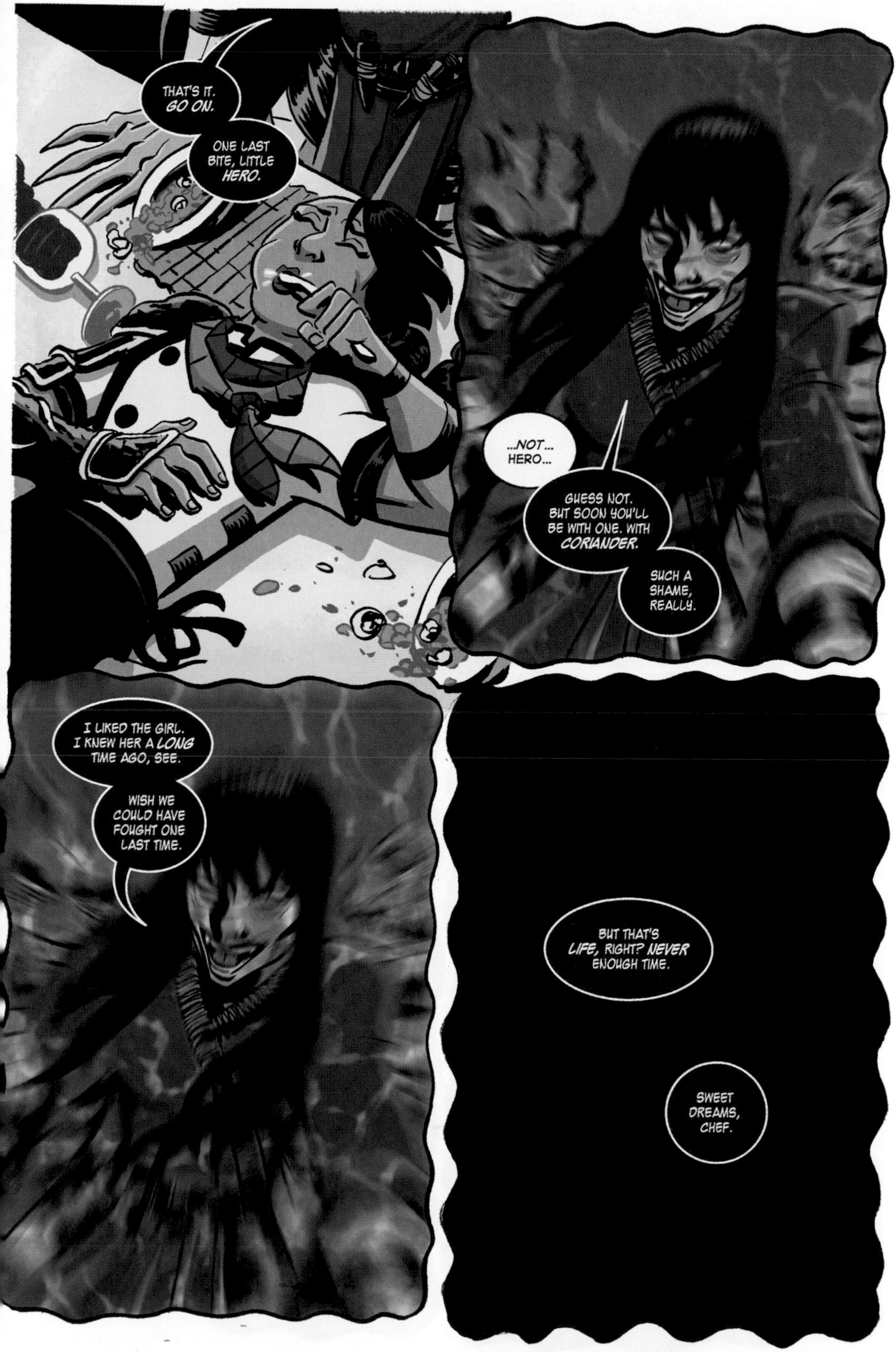
THAT'S IT. GO ON.
ONE LAST BITE, LITTLE HERO.
...NOT... HERO...
GUESS NOT. BUT SOON YOU'LL BE WITH ONE. WITH CORIANDER.
SUCH A SHAME, REALLY.
I LIKED THE GIRL. I KNEW HER A LONG TIME AGO, SEE.
WISH WE COULD HAVE FOUGHT ONE LAST TIME.
BUT THAT'S LIFE, RIGHT? NEVER ENOUGH TIME.
SWEET DREAMS, CHEF.

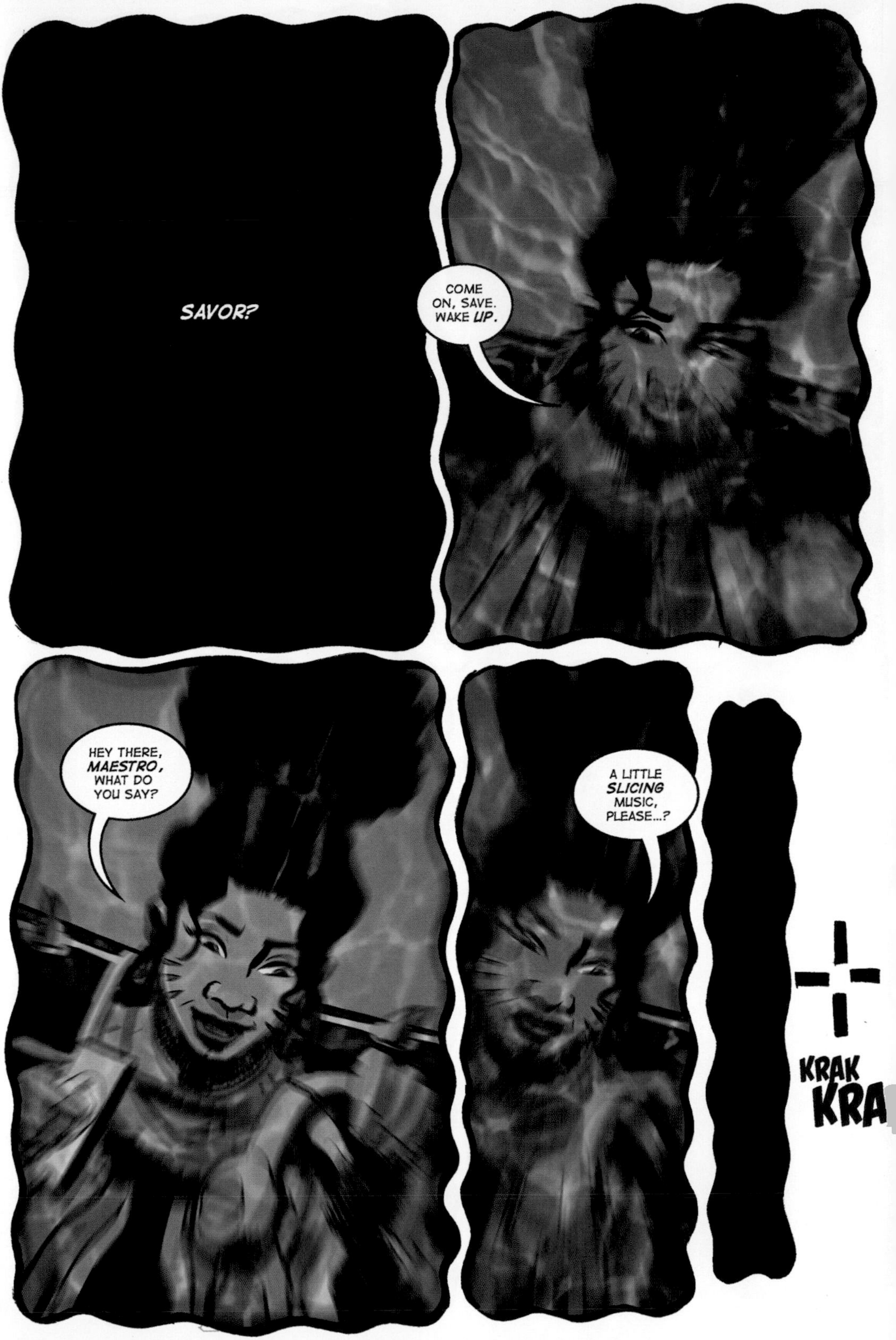
SAVOR?
COME ON, SAVE. WAKE UP.
HEY THERE, MAESTRO, WHAT DO YOU SAY?
A LITTLE SLICING MUSIC, PLEASE...?
KRAK
KRA

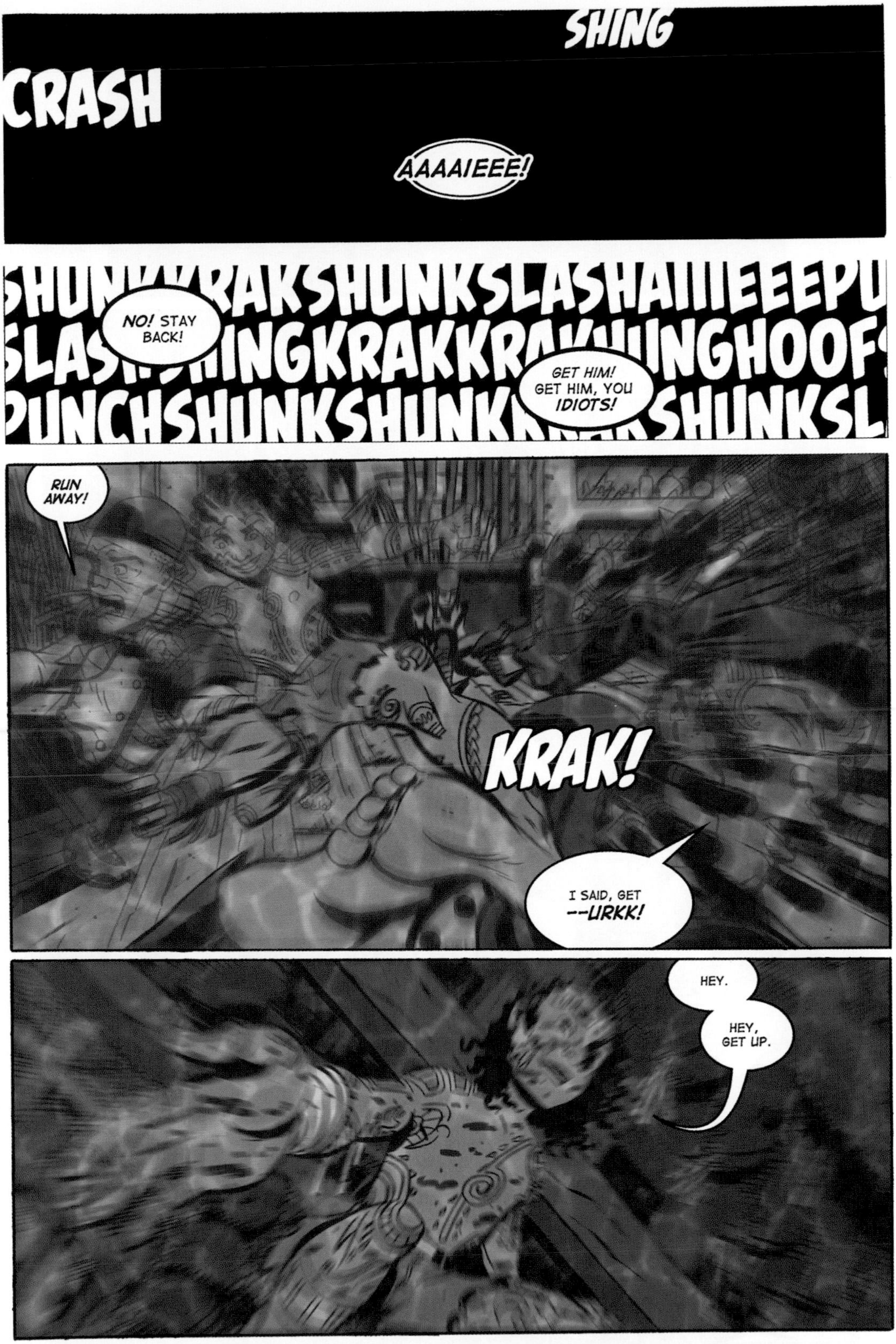
SHING
CRASH
AAAAIEEE!
NO! STAY BACK!
GET HIM! GET HIM, YOU IDIOTS!
RUN AWAY!
KRAK!
I SAID, GET --URKK!
HEY.
HEY, GET UP.

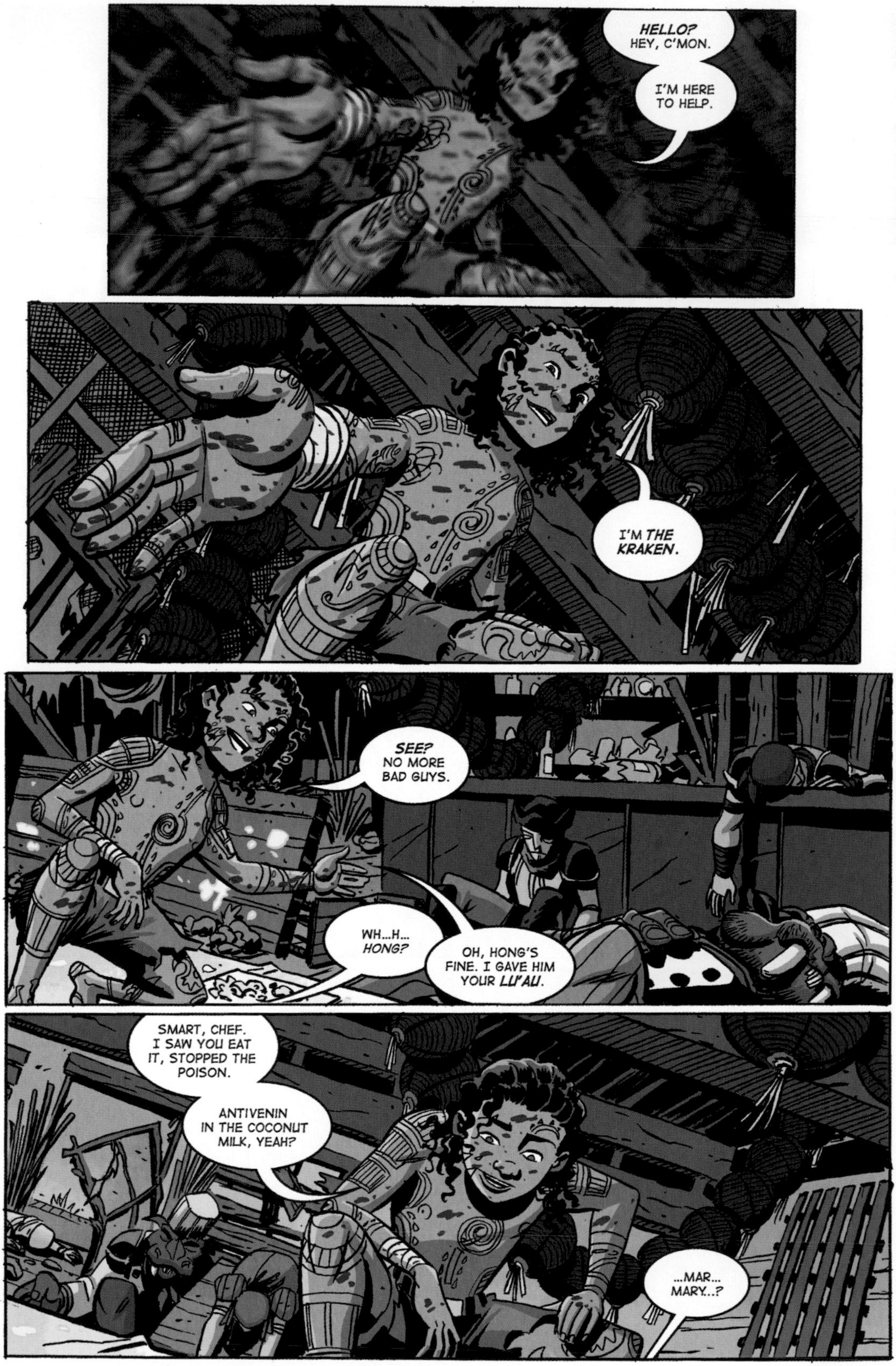
HELLO? HEY, C'MON.
I'M HERE TO HELP.
I'M THE KRAKEN.
SEE? NO MORE BAD GUYS.
WH...H... HONG?
OH, HONG'S FINE. I GAVE HIM YOUR LU'AU.
SMART, CHEF. I SAW YOU EAT IT, STOPPED THE POISON.
ANTIVENIN IN THE COCONUT MILK, YEAH?
...MAR... MARY...?

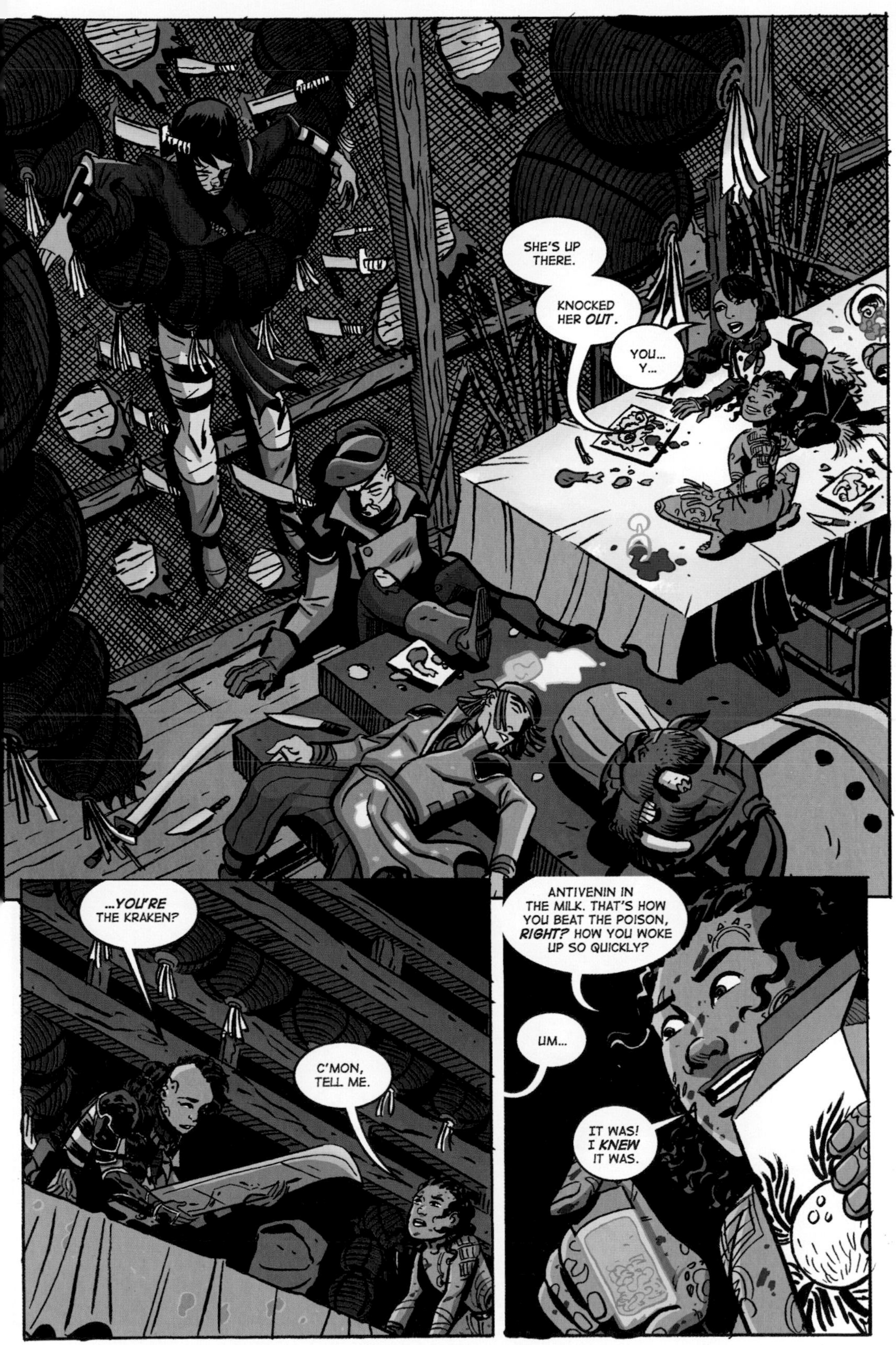
SHE'S UP THERE.
KNOCKED HER OUT.
YOU... Y...
...YOU'RE THE KRAKEN?
C'MON, TELL ME.
ANTIVENIN IN THE MILK. THAT'S HOW YOU BEAT THE POISON, RIGHT? HOW YOU WOKE UP SO QUICKLY?
UM...
IT WAS! I KNEW IT WAS.

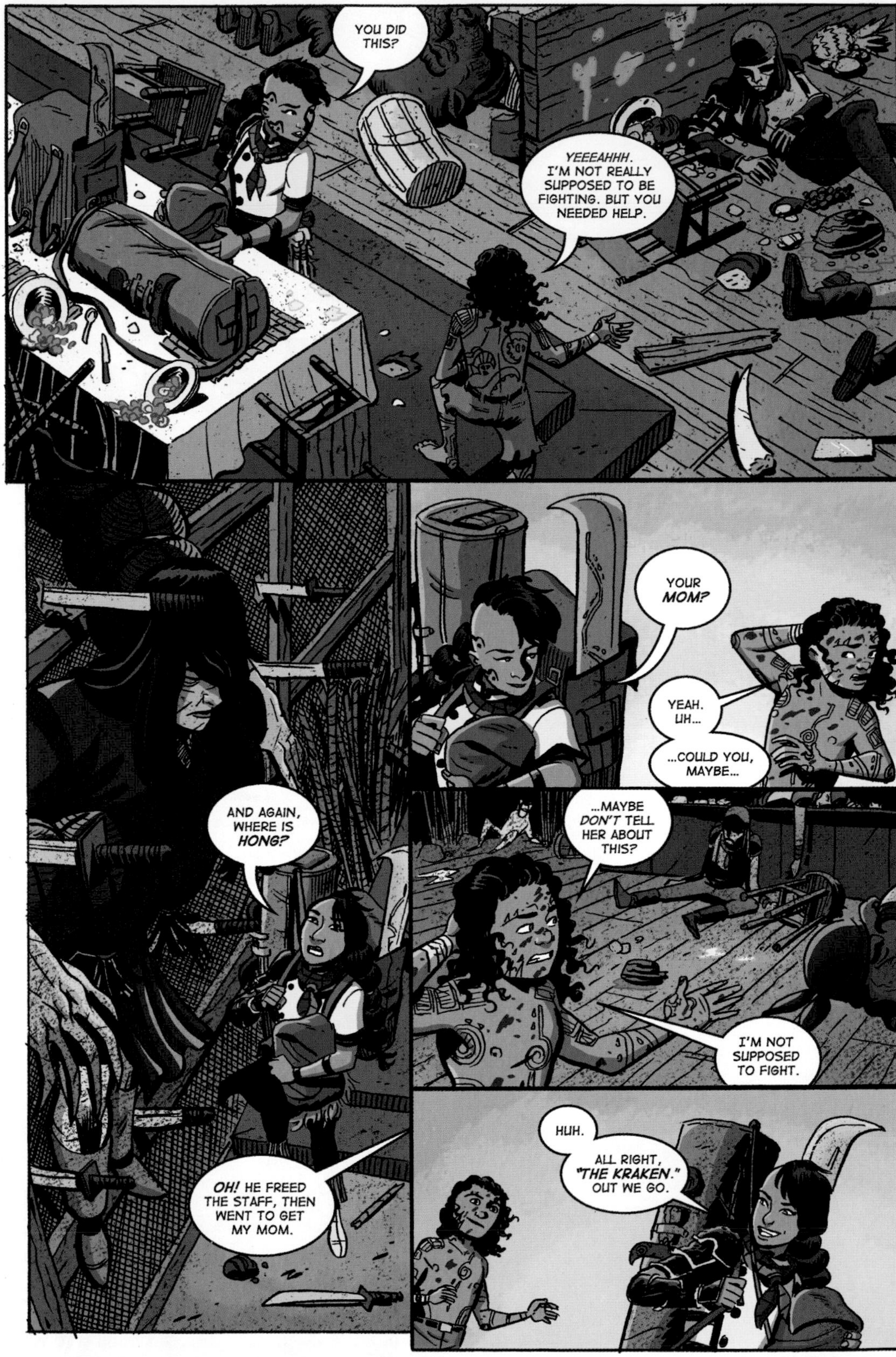
YOU DID THIS?
YEEEAHHH. I'M NOT REALLY SUPPOSED TO BE FIGHTING. BUT YOU NEEDED HELP.
AND AGAIN, WHERE IS ***HONG?***
OH! HE FREED THE STAFF, THEN WENT TO GET MY MOM.
YOUR ***MOM?***
YEAH. UH...
...COULD YOU, MAYBE...
...MAYBE *DON'T* TELL HER ABOUT THIS?
I'M NOT SUPPOSED TO FIGHT.
HUH.
ALL RIGHT, ***"THE KRAKEN."*** OUT WE GO.

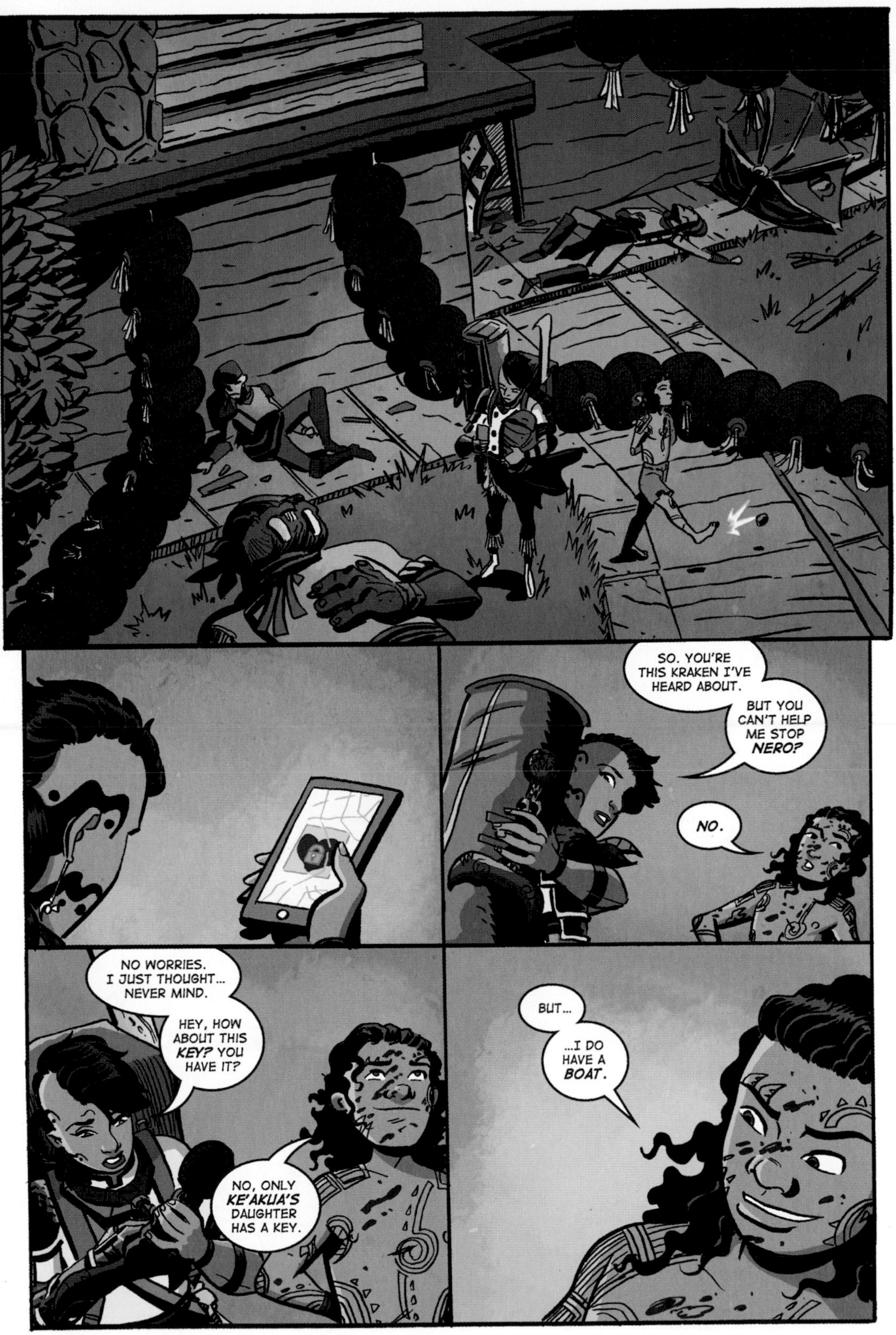
SO. YOU'RE THIS KRAKEN I'VE HEARD ABOUT.
BUT YOU CAN'T HELP ME STOP *NERO?*
NO.
NO WORRIES. I JUST THOUGHT... NEVER MIND.
HEY, HOW ABOUT THIS *KEY?* YOU HAVE IT?
NO, ONLY *KE'AKUA'S* DAUGHTER HAS A KEY.
BUT...
...I DO HAVE A *BOAT*.

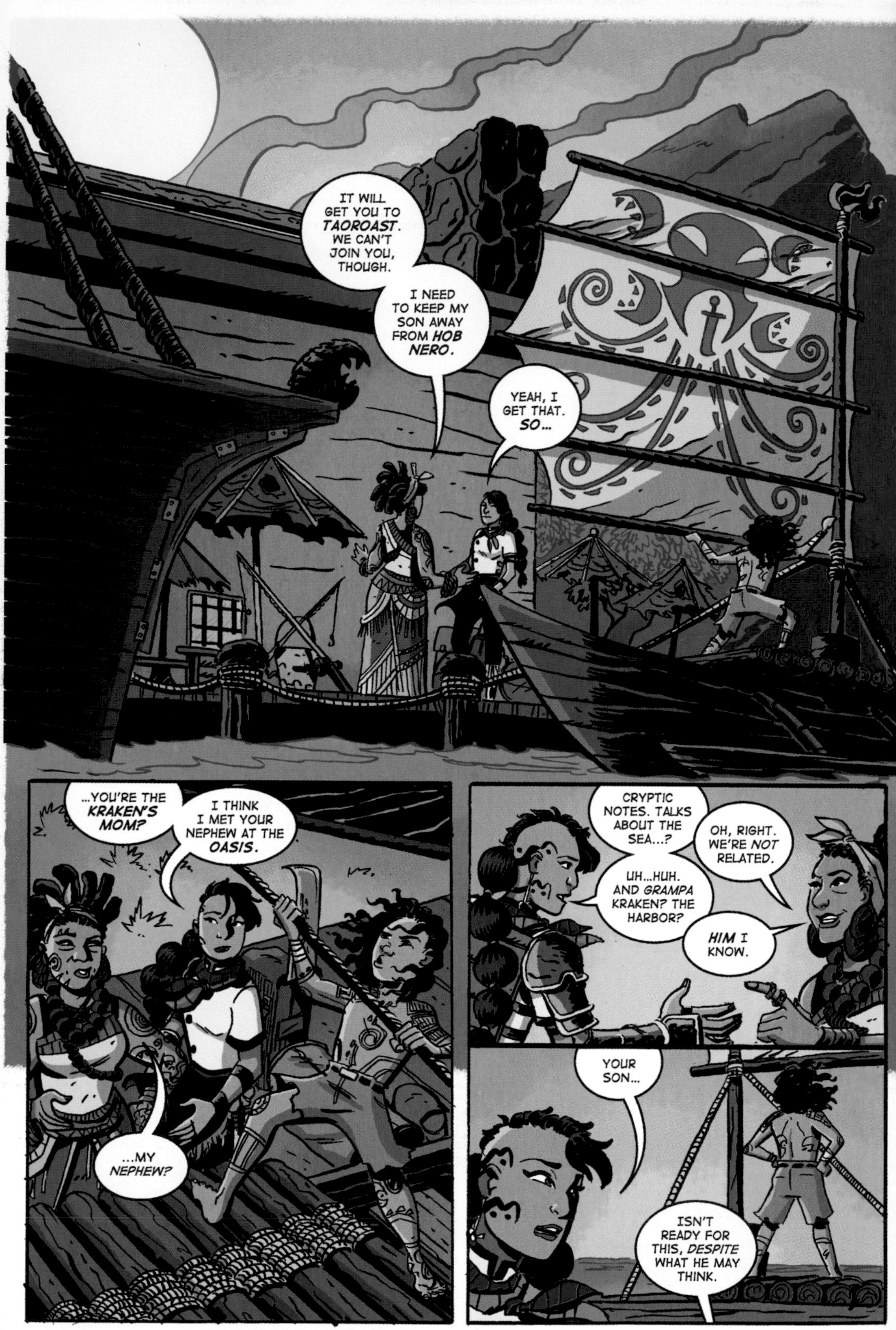
IT WILL GET YOU TO *TAOROAST*. WE CAN'T JOIN YOU, THOUGH.
I NEED TO KEEP MY SON AWAY FROM ***HOB NERO***.
YEAH, I GET THAT. ***SO...***
...YOU'RE THE ***KRAKEN'S MOM?***
I THINK I MET YOUR NEPHEW AT THE ***OASIS***.
...MY *NEPHEW?*
CRYPTIC NOTES. TALKS ABOUT THE SEA...?
OH, RIGHT. WE'RE *NOT* RELATED.
UH...HUH. AND *GRAMPA* KRAKEN? THE HARBOR?
HIM I KNOW.
YOUR SON...
ISN'T READY FOR THIS, *DESPITE* WHAT HE MAY THINK.

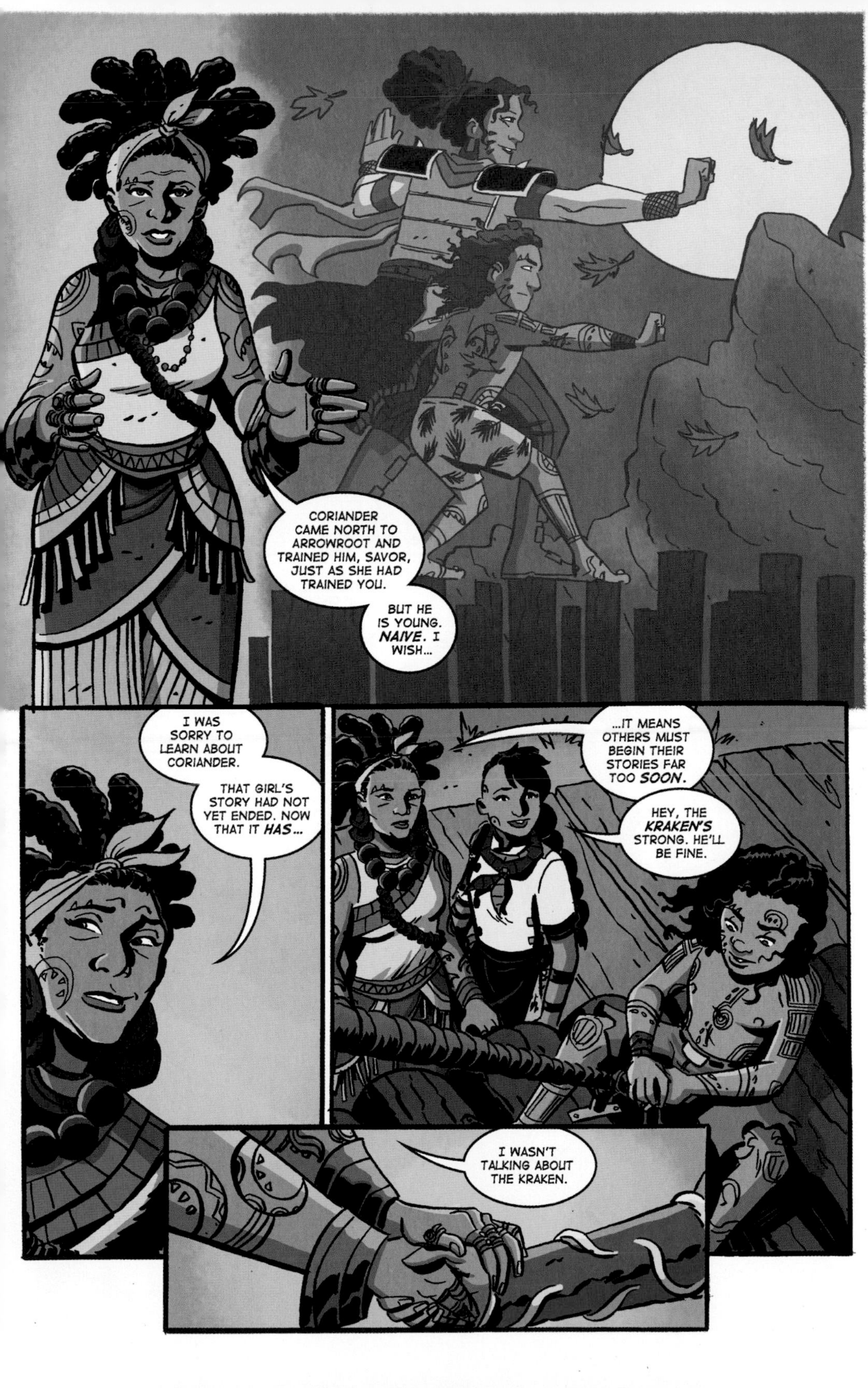
CORIANDER CAME NORTH TO ARROWROOT AND TRAINED HIM, SAVOR, JUST AS SHE HAD TRAINED YOU.
BUT HE IS YOUNG. NAIVE. I WISH...
I WAS SORRY TO LEARN ABOUT CORIANDER.
THAT GIRL'S STORY HAD NOT YET ENDED. NOW THAT IT HAS...
...IT MEANS OTHERS MUST BEGIN THEIR STORIES FAR TOO SOON.
HEY, THE KRAKEN'S STRONG. HE'LL BE FINE.
I WASN'T TALKING ABOUT THE KRAKEN.

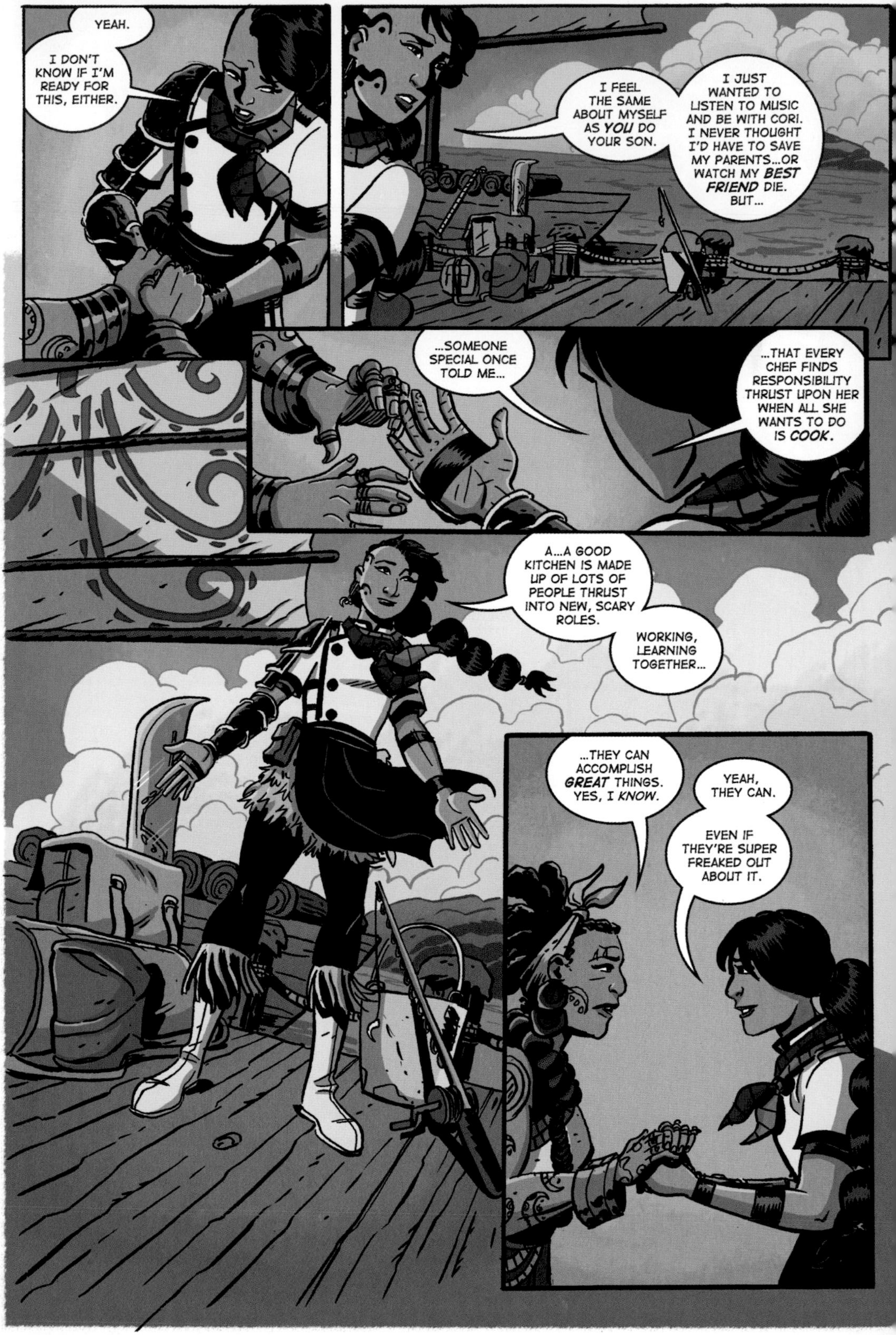
YEAH.
I DON'T KNOW IF I'M READY FOR THIS, EITHER.
I FEEL THE SAME ABOUT MYSELF AS YOU DO YOUR SON.
I JUST WANTED TO LISTEN TO MUSIC AND BE WITH CORI. I NEVER THOUGHT I'D HAVE TO SAVE MY PARENTS...OR WATCH MY BEST FRIEND DIE. BUT...
...SOMEONE SPECIAL ONCE TOLD ME...
...THAT EVERY CHEF FINDS RESPONSIBILITY THRUST UPON HER WHEN ALL SHE WANTS TO DO IS COOK.
A...A GOOD KITCHEN IS MADE UP OF LOTS OF PEOPLE THRUST INTO NEW, SCARY ROLES.
WORKING, LEARNING TOGETHER...
...THEY CAN ACCOMPLISH GREAT THINGS. YES, I KNOW.
YEAH, THEY CAN.
EVEN IF THEY'RE SUPER FREAKED OUT ABOUT IT.

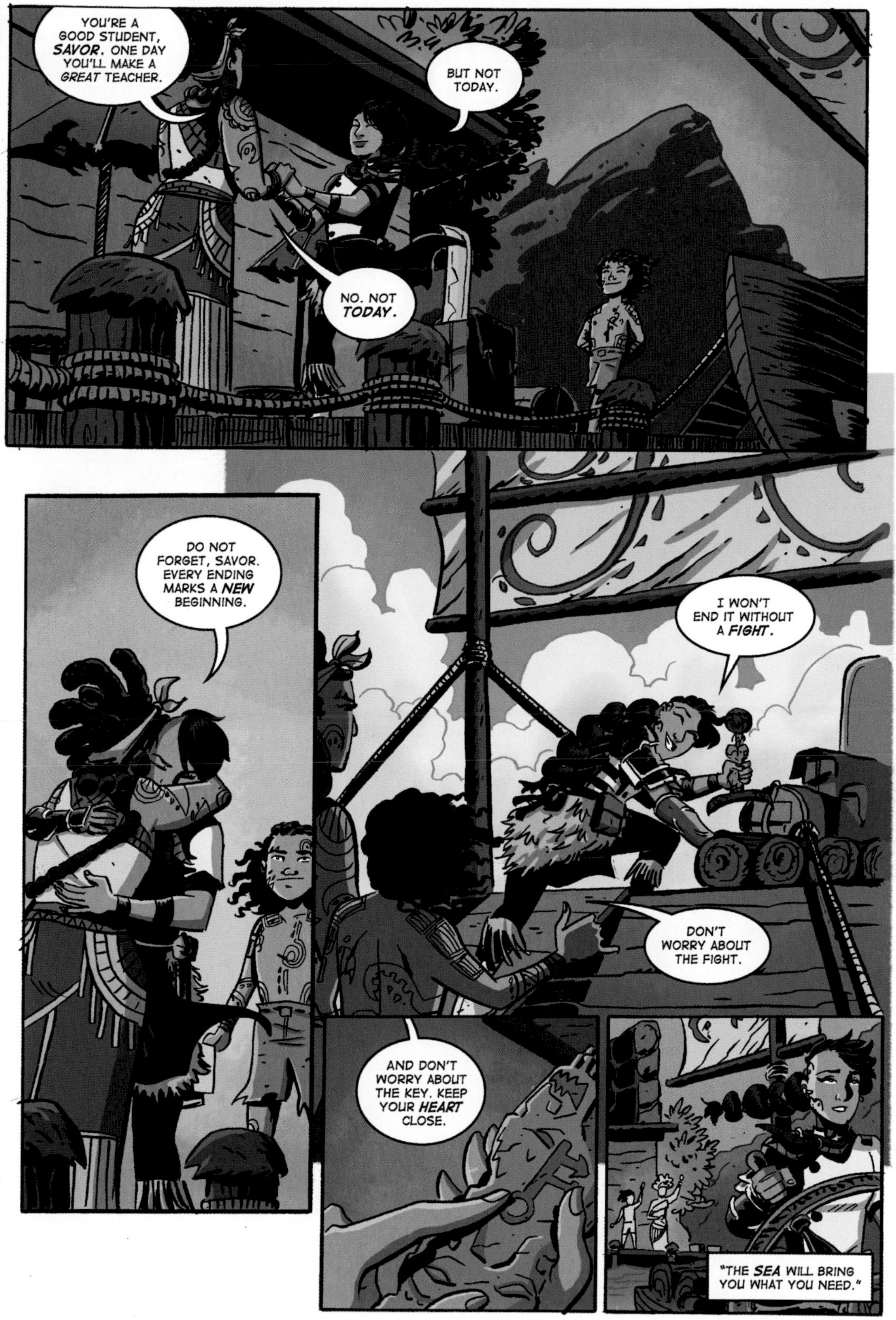
YOU'RE A GOOD STUDENT, SAVOR. ONE DAY YOU'LL MAKE A GREAT TEACHER.
BUT NOT TODAY.
NO. NOT TODAY.
DO NOT FORGET, SAVOR. EVERY ENDING MARKS A NEW BEGINNING.
I WON'T END IT WITHOUT A FIGHT.
DON'T WORRY ABOUT THE FIGHT.
AND DON'T WORRY ABOUT THE KEY. KEEP YOUR HEART CLOSE.
"THE SEA WILL BRING YOU WHAT YOU NEED."

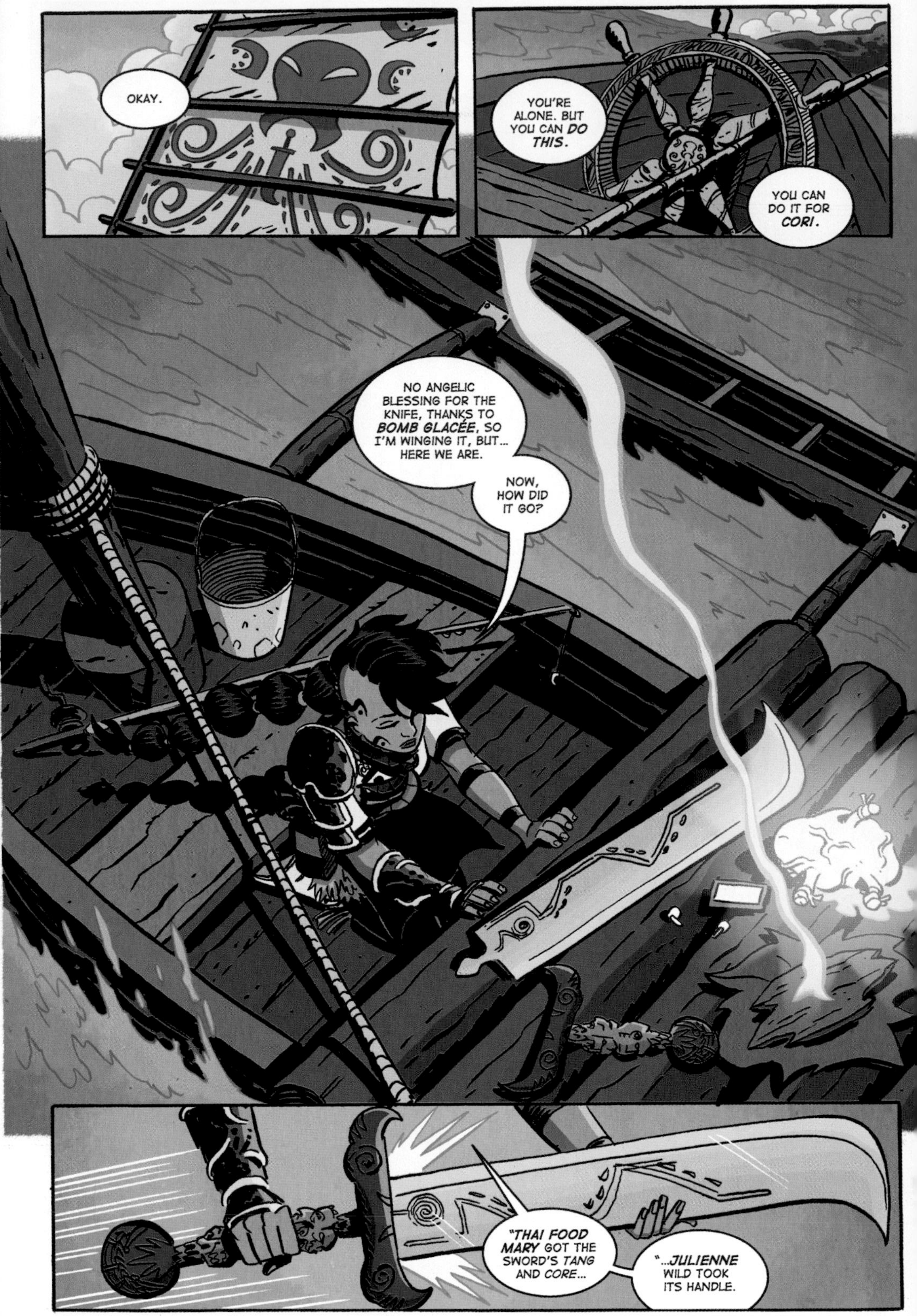
OKAY.
YOU'RE ALONE. BUT YOU CAN DO THIS.
YOU CAN DO IT FOR CORI.
NO ANGELIC BLESSING FOR THE KNIFE, THANKS TO BOMB GLACÉE, SO I'M WINGING IT, BUT... HERE WE ARE.
NOW, HOW DID IT GO?
"THAI FOOD MARY GOT THE SWORD'S TANG AND CORE...
"...JULIENNE WILD TOOK ITS HANDLE.

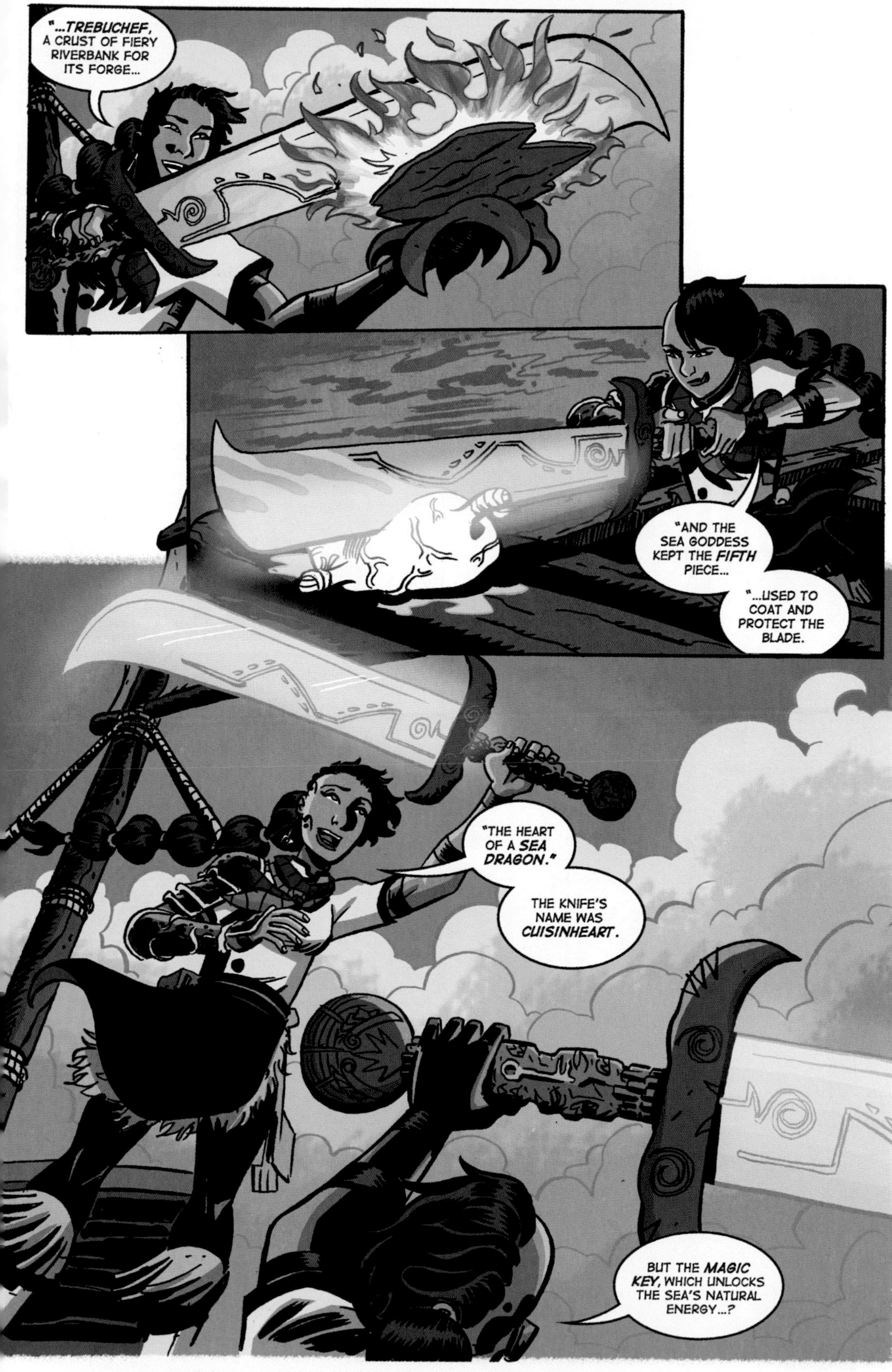
"...TREBUCHEF, A CRUST OF FIERY RIVERBANK FOR ITS FORGE...
"AND THE SEA GODDESS KEPT THE FIFTH PIECE...
"...USED TO COAT AND PROTECT THE BLADE.
"THE HEART OF A SEA DRAGON."
THE KNIFE'S NAME WAS CUISINHEART.
BUT THE MAGIC KEY, WHICH UNLOCKS THE SEA'S NATURAL ENERGY...?

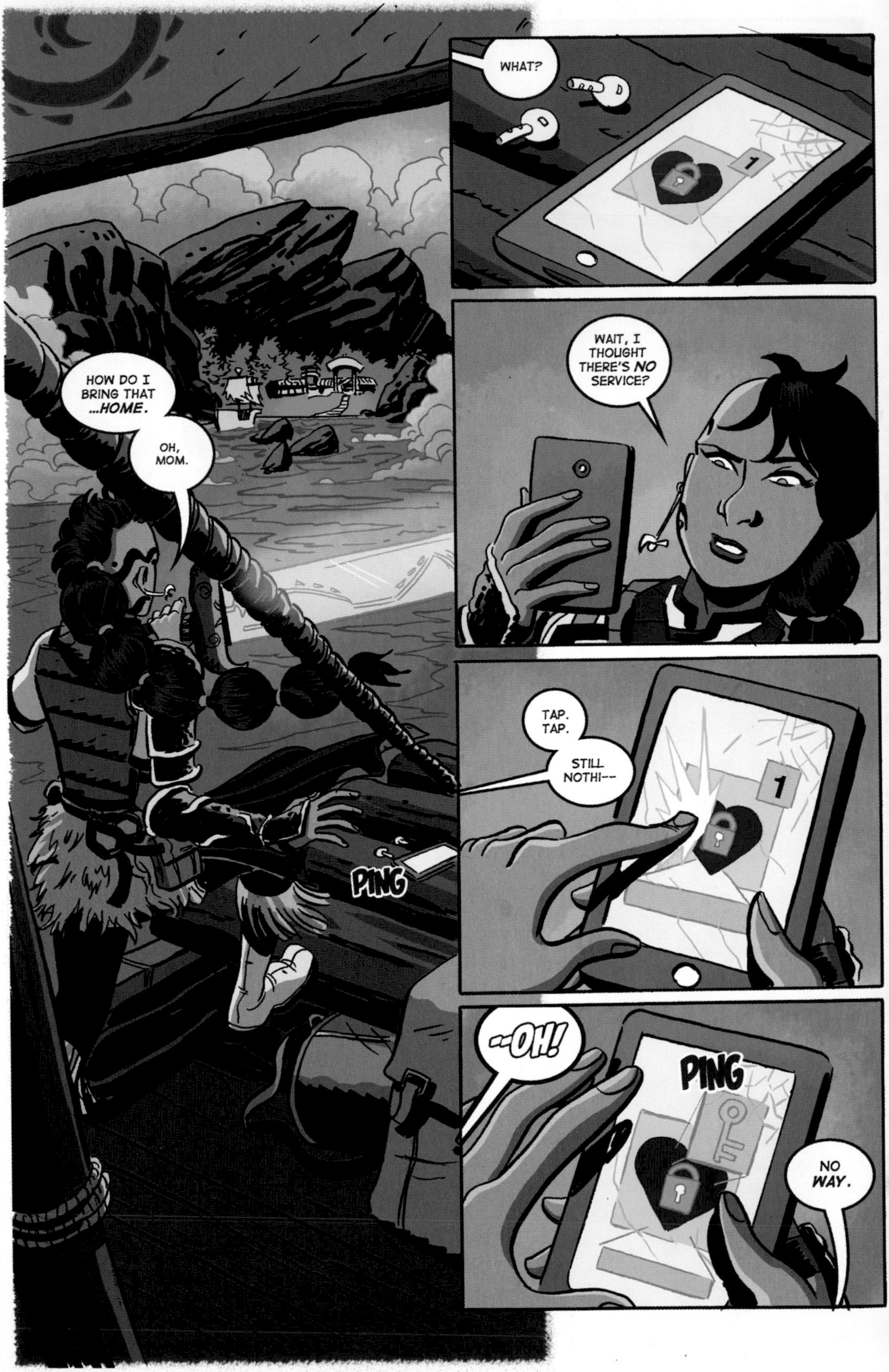
HOW DO I BRING THAT ...HOME.
OH, MOM.
PING
WHAT?
WAIT, I THOUGHT THERE'S NO SERVICE?
TAP. TAP.
STILL NOTHI--
--OH!
PING
NO WAY.

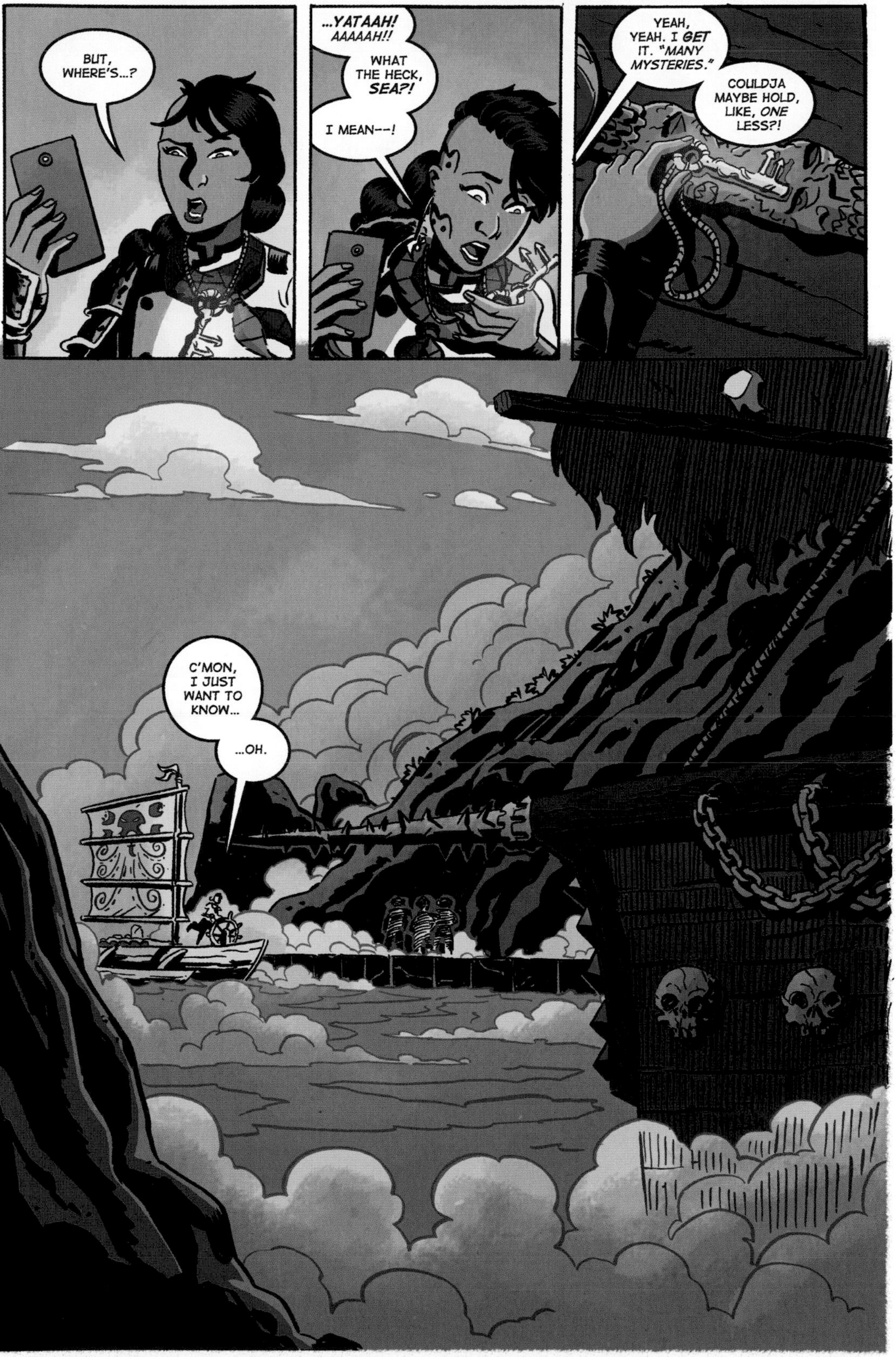
BUT, WHERE'S...?
...YATAAH! AAAAAH!!
WHAT THE HECK, SEA?!
I MEAN--!
YEAH, YEAH. I GET IT. "MANY MYSTERIES."
COULDJA MAYBE HOLD, LIKE, ONE LESS?!
C'MON, I JUST WANT TO KNOW...
...OH.

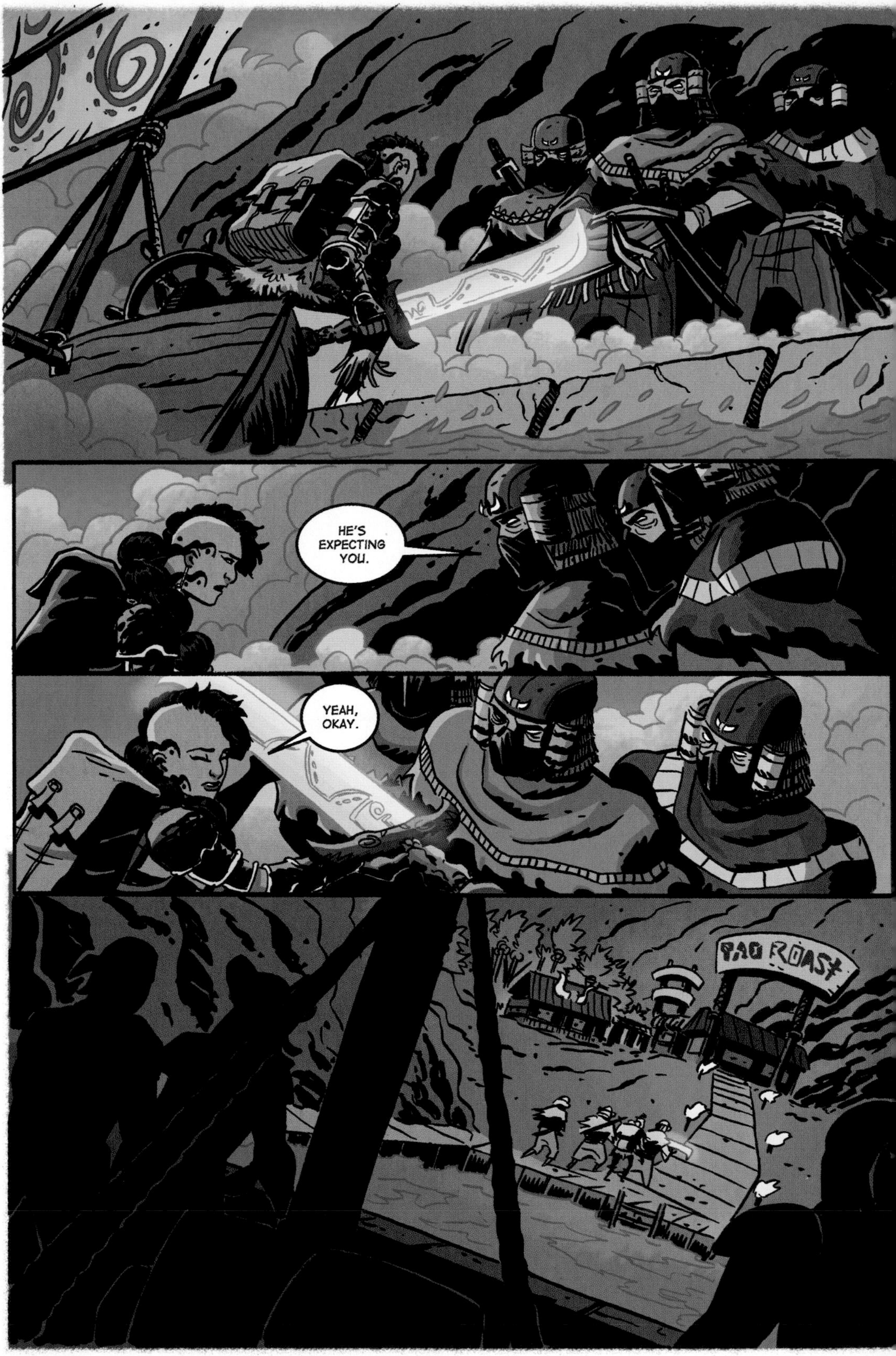
HE'S EXPECTING YOU.
YEAH, OKAY.
TAO ROAST

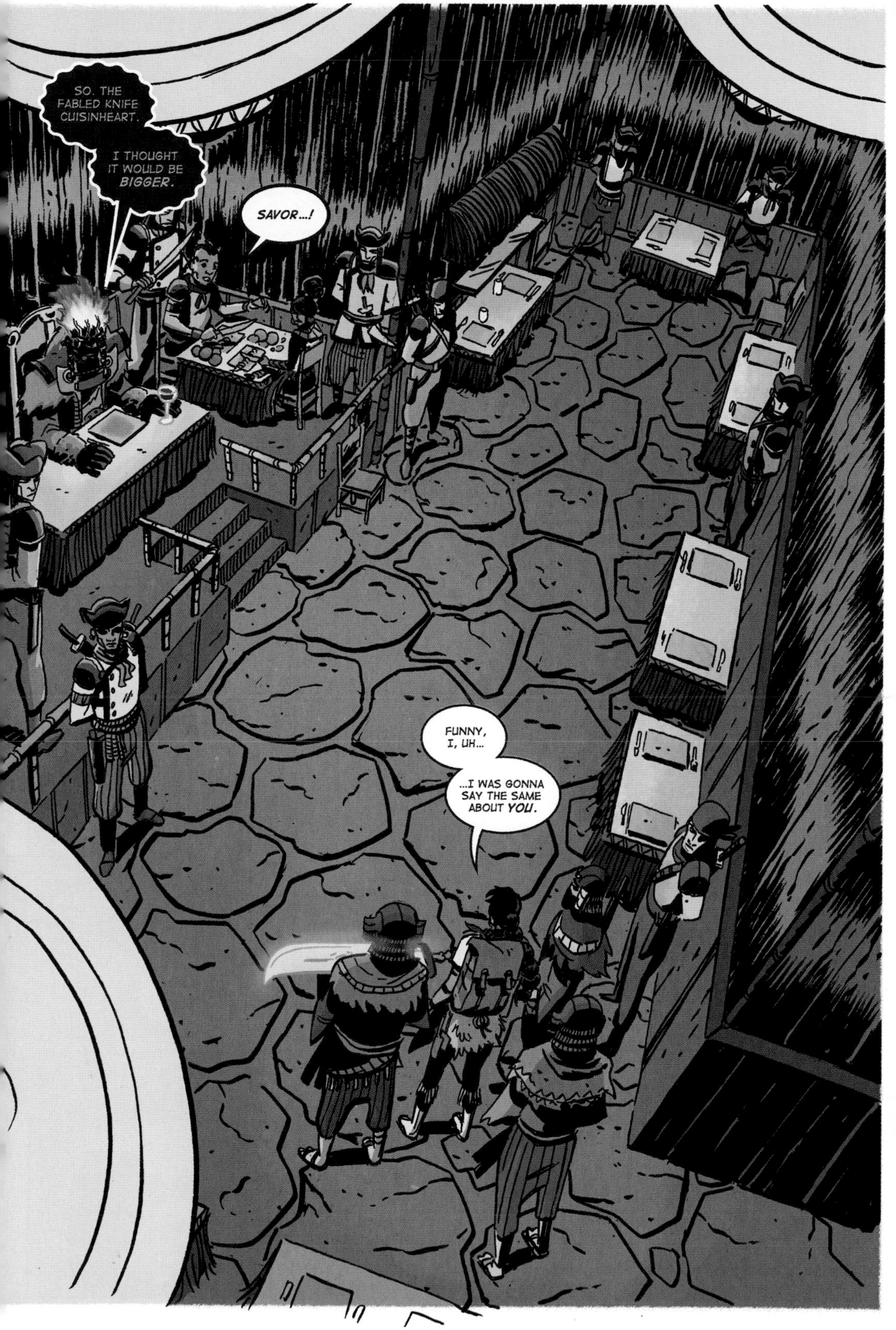
SO. THE FABLED KNIFE CUISINHEART.
I THOUGHT IT WOULD BE *BIGGER*.
SAVOR...!
FUNNY, I, UH...
...I WAS GONNA SAY THE SAME ABOUT *YOU*.

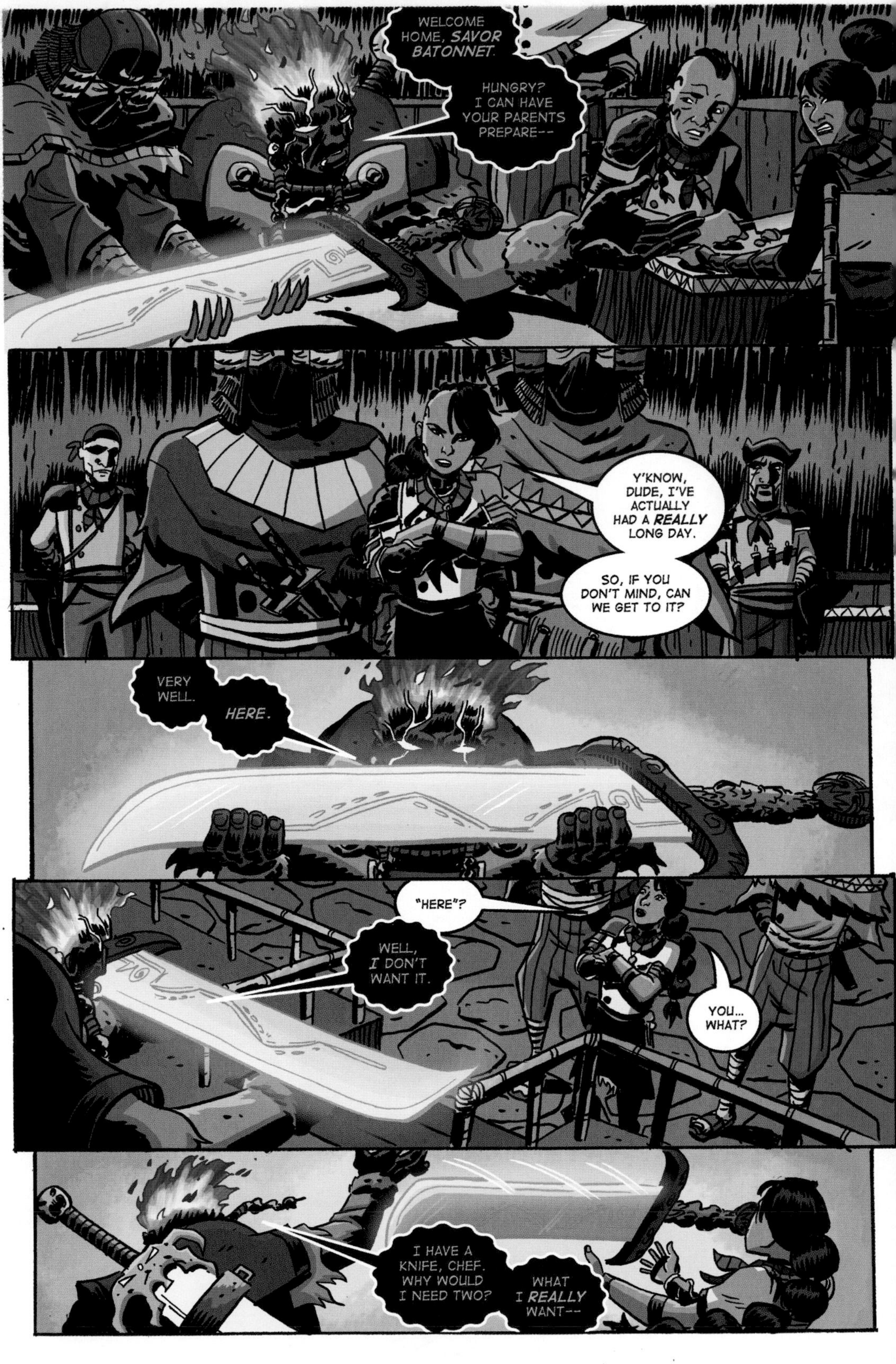
WELCOME HOME, SAVOR BATONNET.
HUNGRY? I CAN HAVE YOUR PARENTS PREPARE--
Y'KNOW, DUDE, I'VE ACTUALLY HAD A REALLY LONG DAY.
SO, IF YOU DON'T MIND, CAN WE GET TO IT?
VERY WELL.
HERE.
"HERE"?
WELL, I DON'T WANT IT.
YOU... WHAT?
I HAVE A KNIFE, CHEF. WHY WOULD I NEED TWO?
WHAT I REALLY WANT--

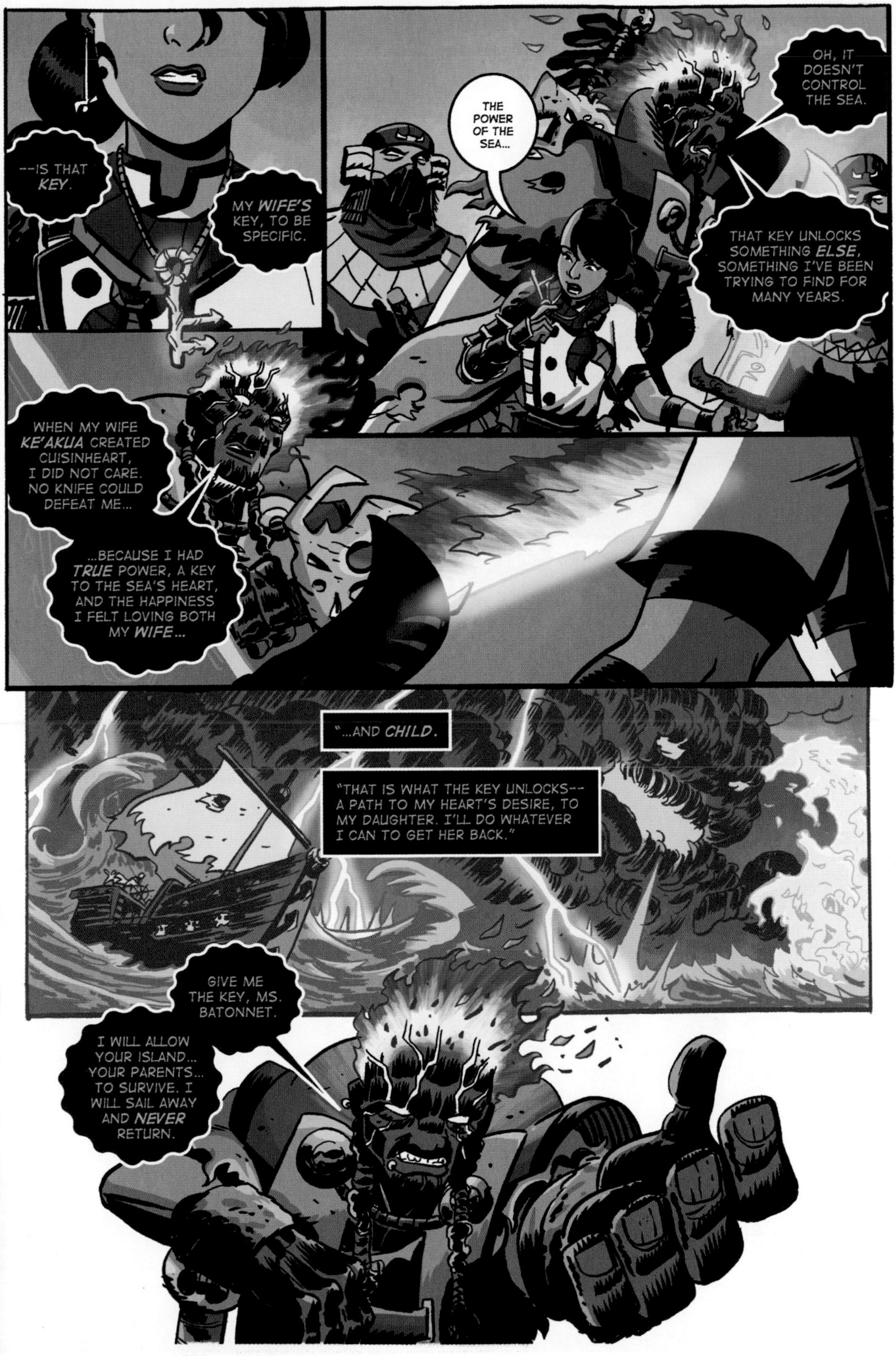

--IS THAT KEY.
MY WIFE'S KEY, TO BE SPECIFIC.
THE POWER OF THE SEA...
OH, IT DOESN'T CONTROL THE SEA.
THAT KEY UNLOCKS SOMETHING ELSE, SOMETHING I'VE BEEN TRYING TO FIND FOR MANY YEARS.
WHEN MY WIFE KE'AKUA CREATED CUISINHEART, I DID NOT CARE. NO KNIFE COULD DEFEAT ME...
...BECAUSE I HAD TRUE POWER, A KEY TO THE SEA'S HEART, AND THE HAPPINESS I FELT LOVING BOTH MY WIFE...
"...AND CHILD.
"THAT IS WHAT THE KEY UNLOCKS-- A PATH TO MY HEART'S DESIRE, TO MY DAUGHTER. I'LL DO WHATEVER I CAN TO GET HER BACK."
GIVE ME THE KEY, MS. BATONNET.
I WILL ALLOW YOUR ISLAND... YOUR PARENTS... TO SURVIVE. I WILL SAIL AWAY AND NEVER RETURN.

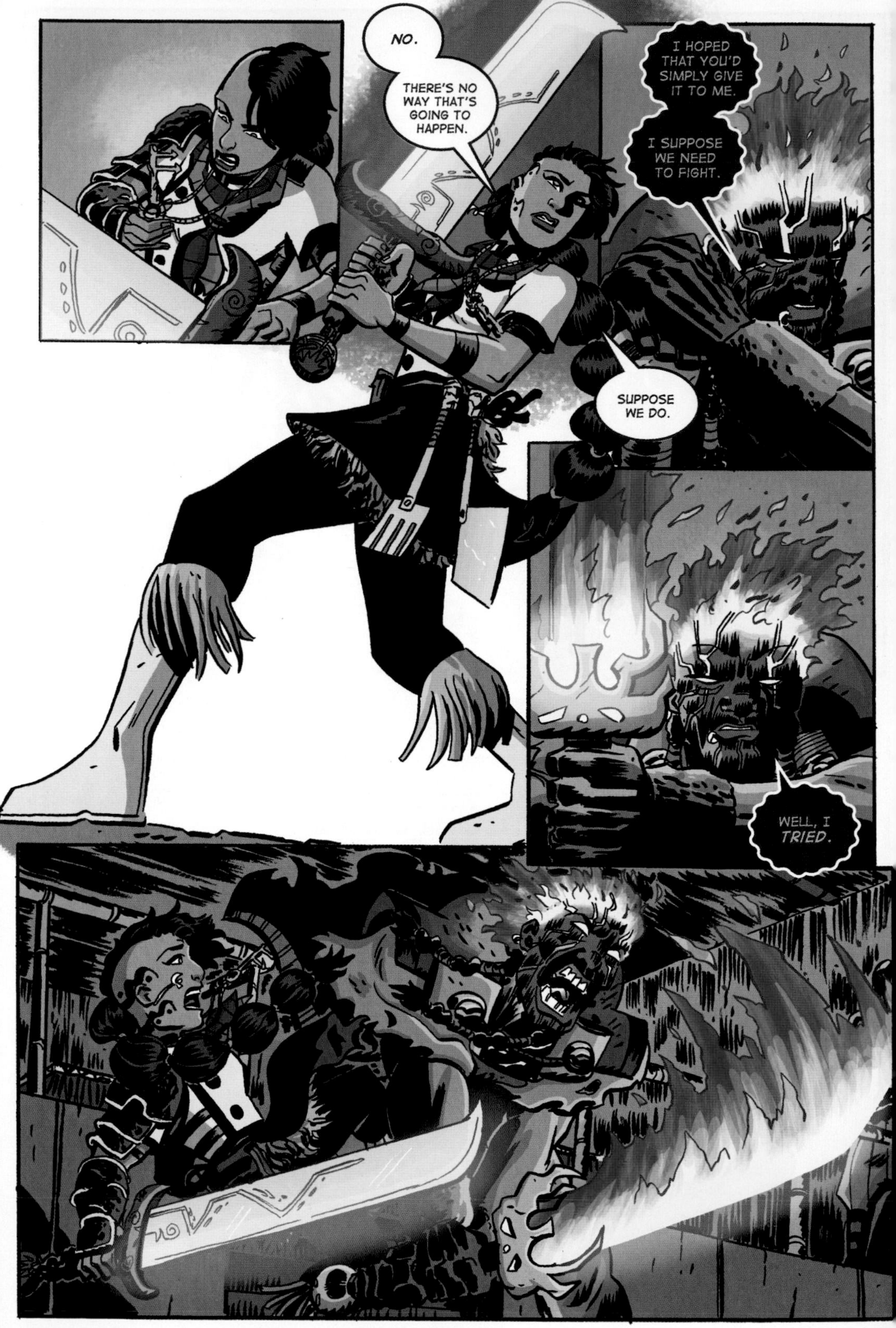
NO.
THERE'S NO WAY THAT'S GOING TO HAPPEN.
I HOPED THAT YOU'D SIMPLY GIVE IT TO ME.
I SUPPOSE WE NEED TO FIGHT.
SUPPOSE WE DO.
WELL, I TRIED.

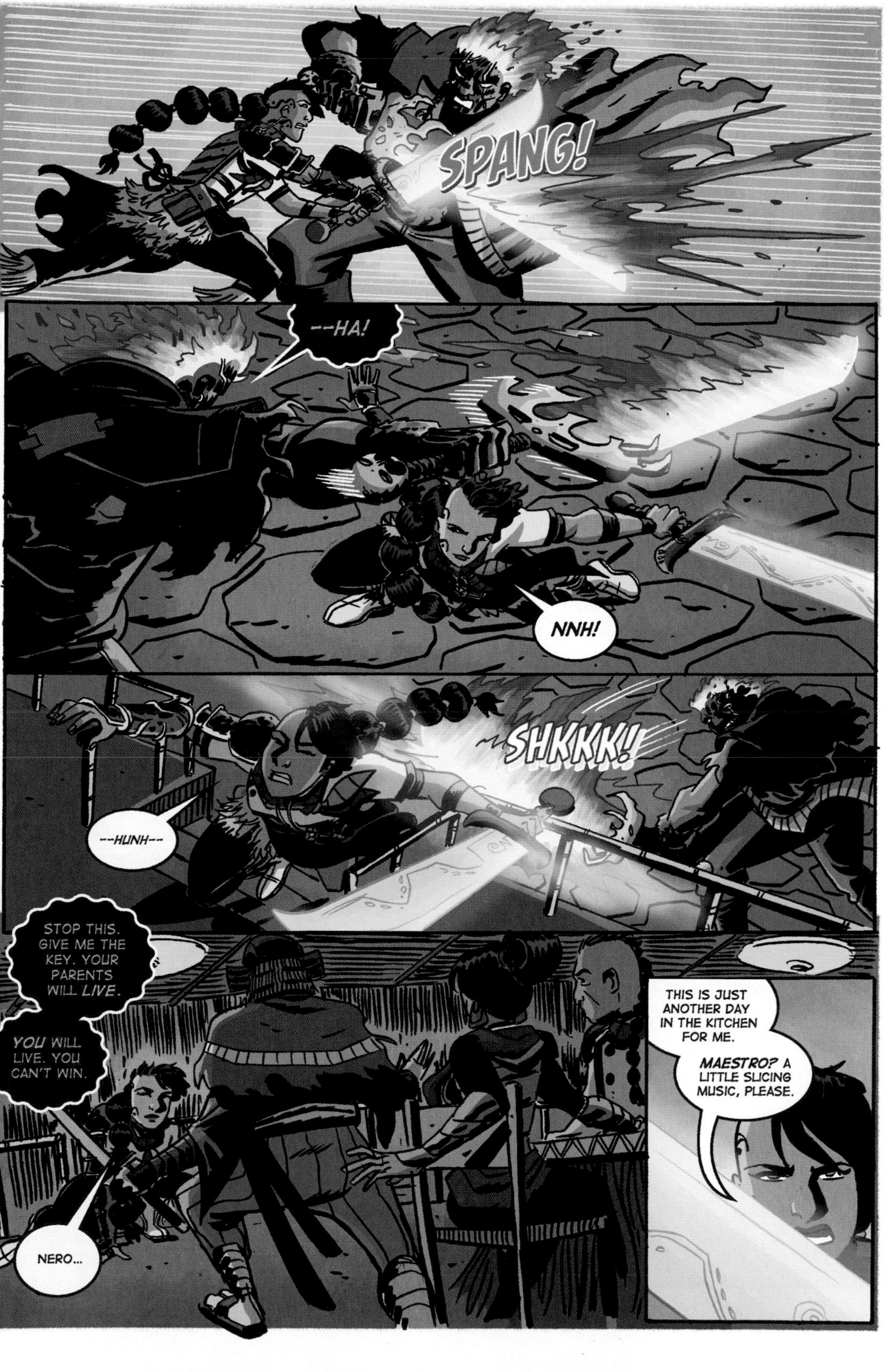
SPANG!
--HA!
NNH!
SHKKK!
--HUNH--
STOP THIS. GIVE ME THE KEY. YOUR PARENTS WILL *LIVE*.
YOU WILL LIVE. YOU CAN'T WIN.
NERO...
THIS IS JUST ANOTHER DAY IN THE KITCHEN FOR ME.
MAESTRO? A LITTLE SLICING MUSIC, PLEASE.

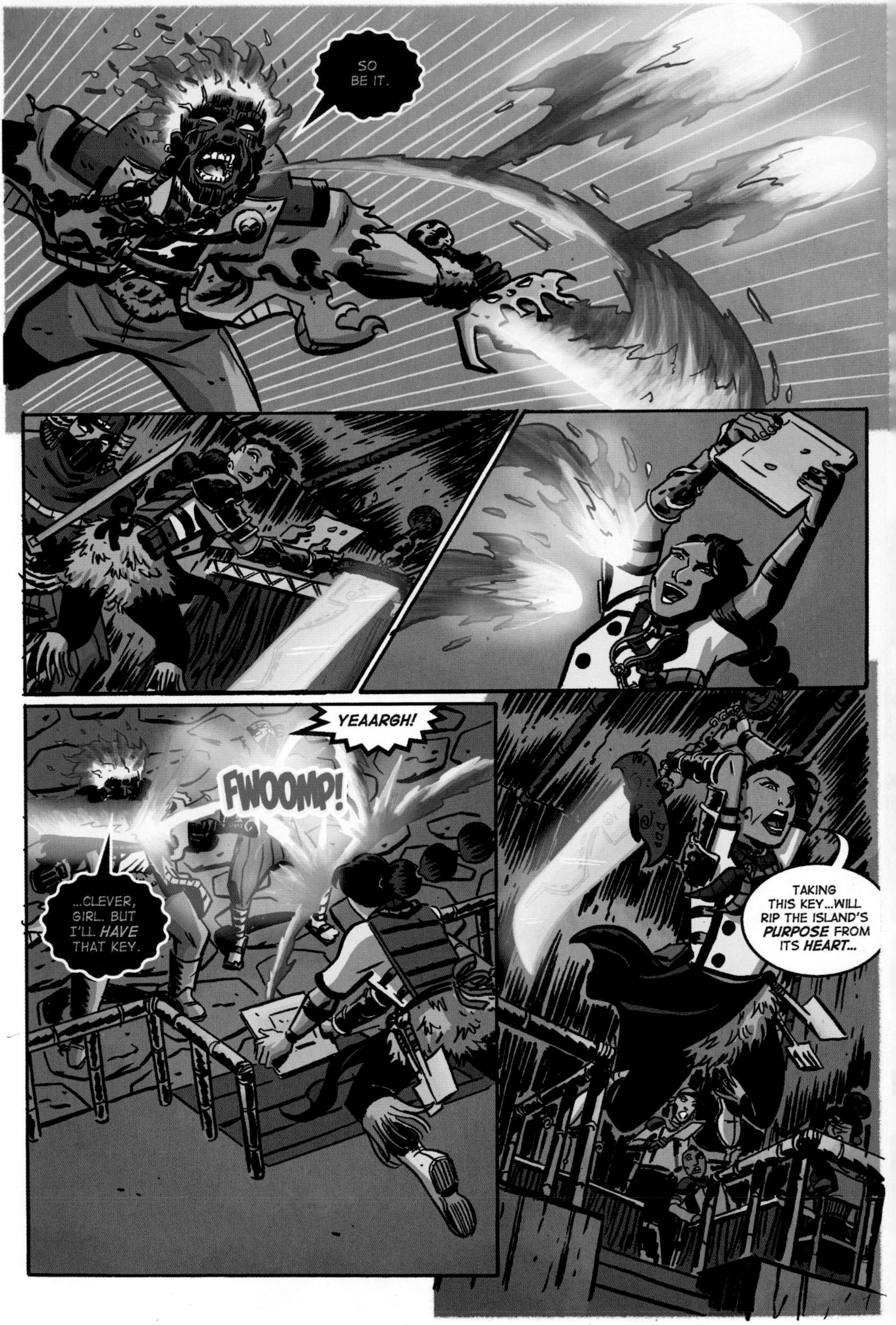
SO BE IT.
YEAARGH!
FWOOMP!
...CLEVER, GIRL. BUT I'LL *HAVE* THAT KEY.
TAKING THIS KEY...WILL RIP THE ISLAND'S *PURPOSE* FROM ITS *HEART*...

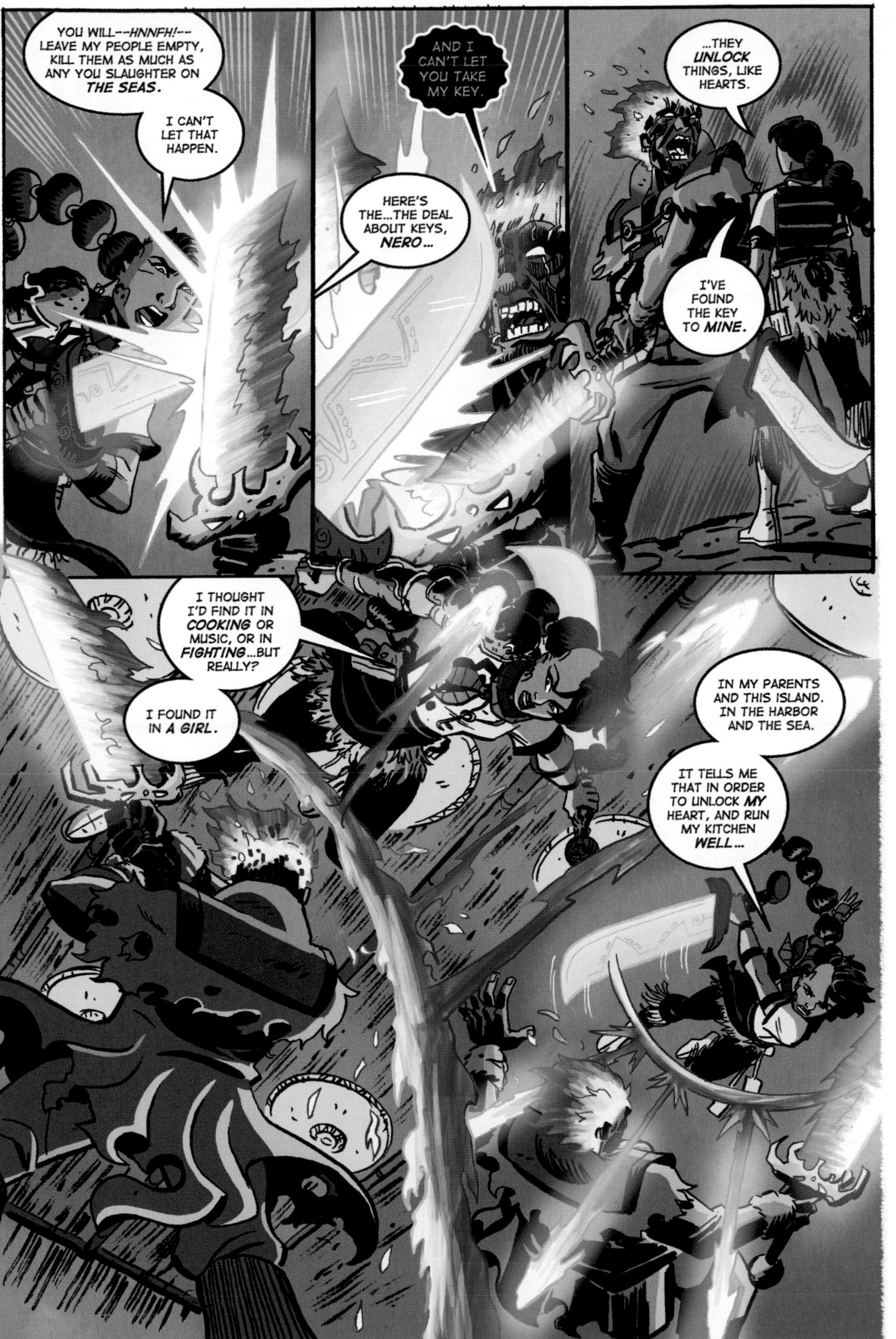
YOU WILL--HNNFH!--LEAVE MY PEOPLE EMPTY, KILL THEM AS MUCH AS ANY YOU SLAUGHTER ON THE SEAS.
I CAN'T LET THAT HAPPEN.
AND I CAN'T LET YOU TAKE MY KEY.
HERE'S THE...THE DEAL ABOUT KEYS, NERO...
...THEY UNLOCK THINGS, LIKE HEARTS.
I'VE FOUND THE KEY TO MINE.
I THOUGHT I'D FIND IT IN COOKING OR MUSIC, OR IN FIGHTING...BUT REALLY?
I FOUND IT IN A GIRL.
IN MY PARENTS AND THIS ISLAND. IN THE HARBOR AND THE SEA.
IT TELLS ME THAT IN ORDER TO UNLOCK MY HEART, AND RUN MY KITCHEN WELL...

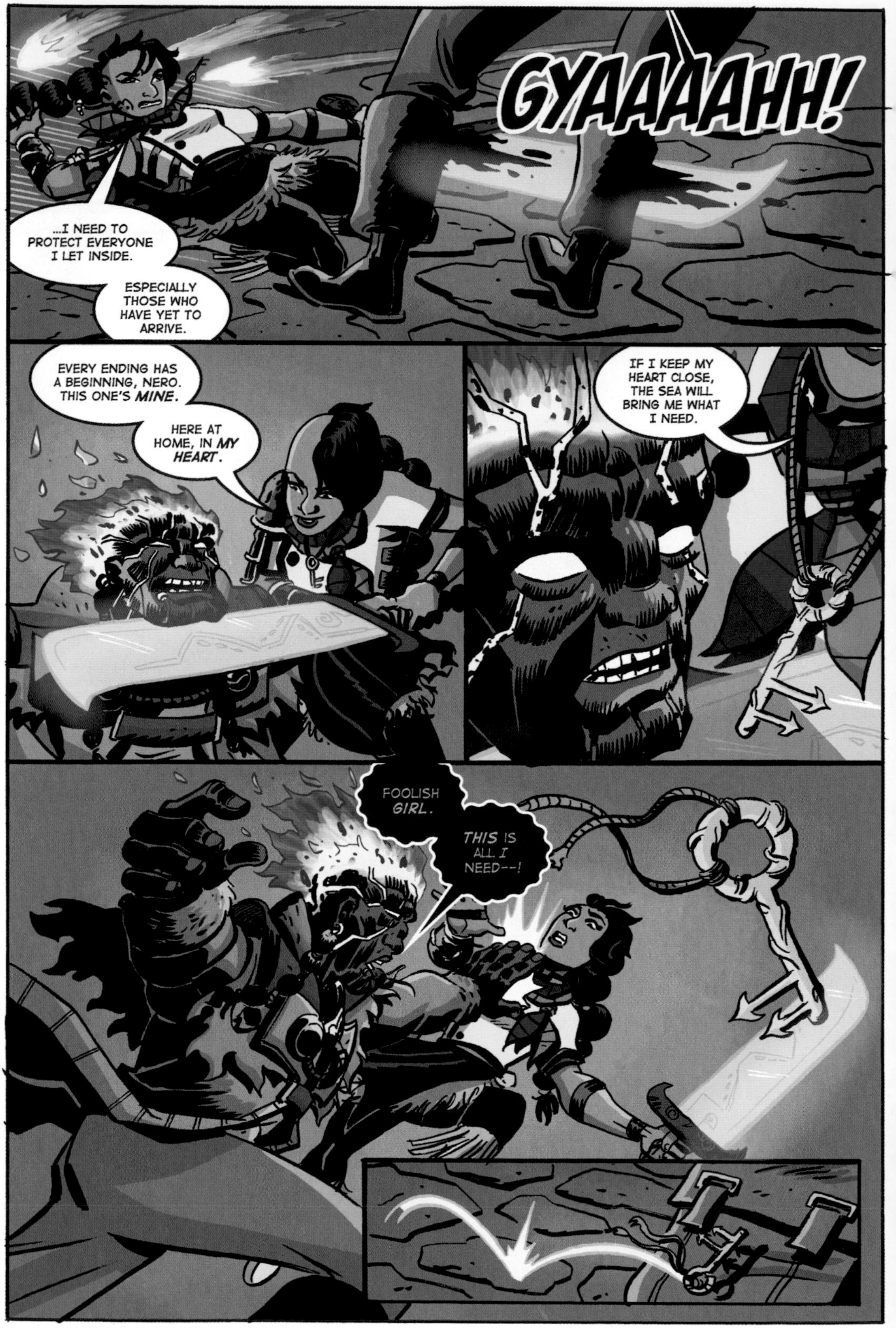
GYAAAAAHH!
...I NEED TO PROTECT EVERYONE I LET INSIDE.
ESPECIALLY THOSE WHO HAVE YET TO ARRIVE.
EVERY ENDING HAS A BEGINNING, NERO. THIS ONE'S *MINE*.
HERE AT HOME, IN *MY HEART*.
IF I KEEP MY HEART CLOSE, THE SEA WILL BRING ME WHAT I NEED.
FOOLISH *GIRL*.
THIS IS ALL. *I* NEED--!

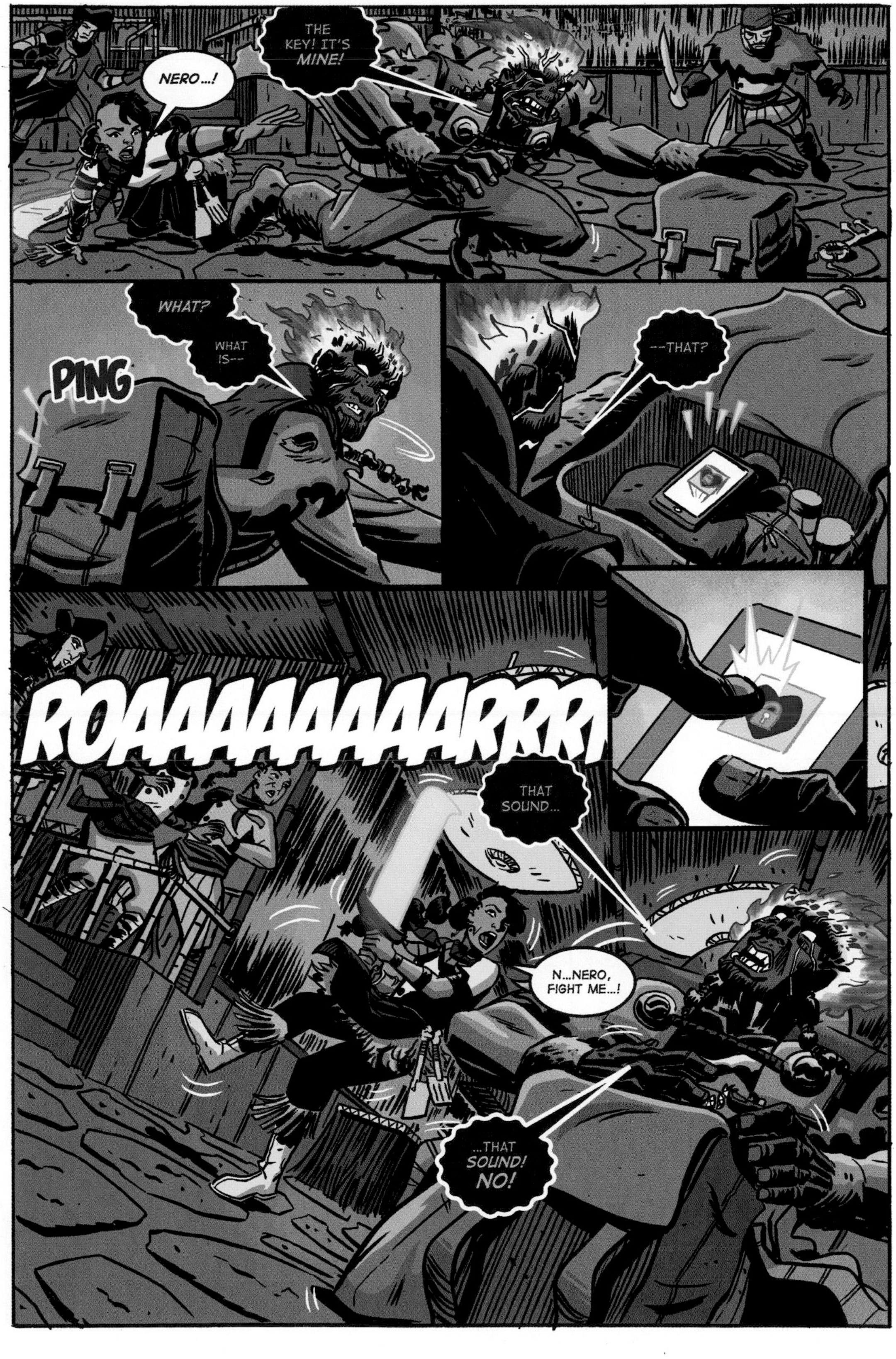
NERO...!
THE KEY! IT'S MINE!
PING
WHAT?
WHAT IS--
--THAT?
ROAAAAAAAAARRR
THAT SOUND...
N...NERO, FIGHT ME...!
...THAT SOUND! NO!

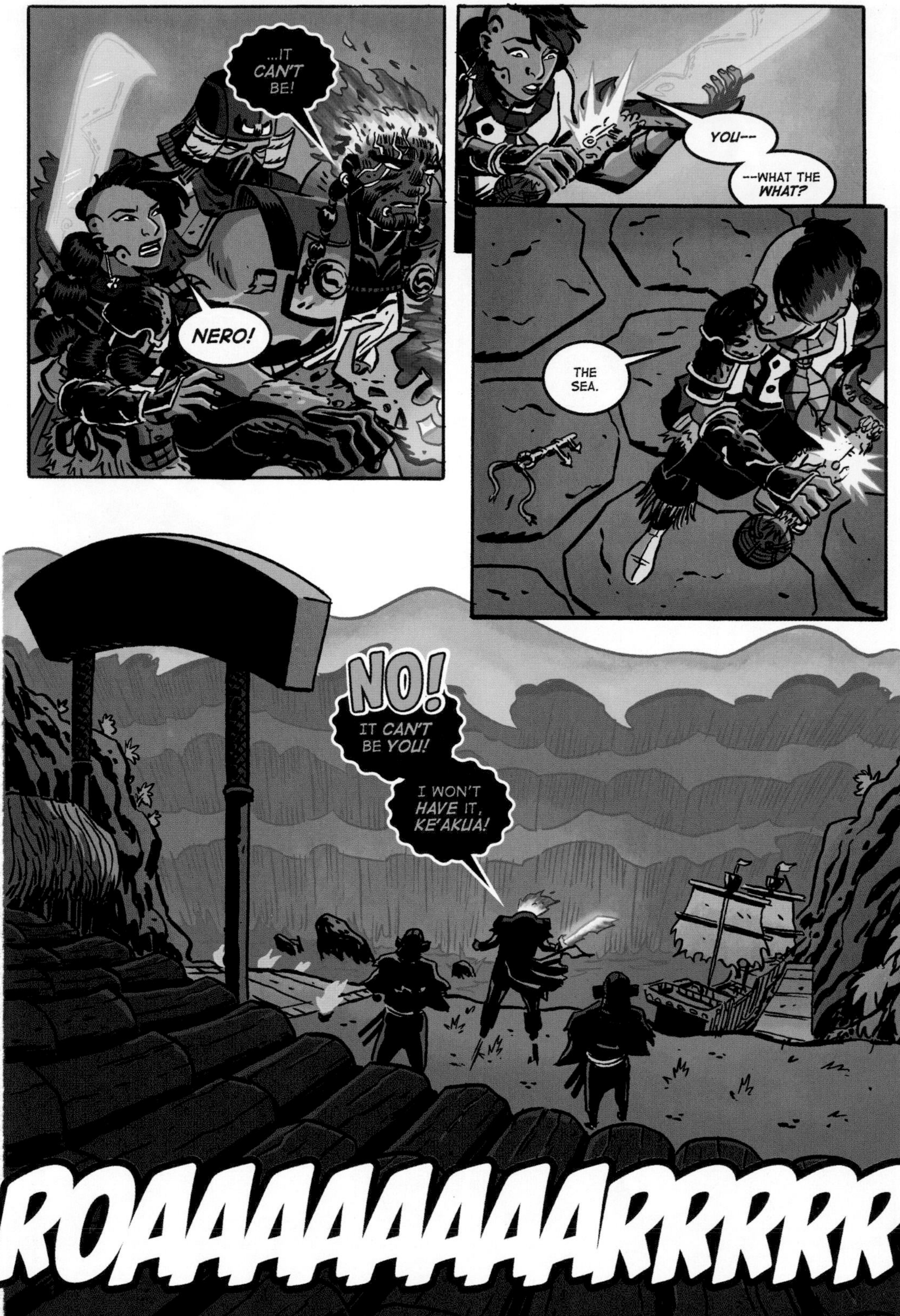
...IT CAN'T BE!
NERO!
YOU--
--WHAT THE WHAT?
THE SEA.
NO! IT CAN'T BE YOU!
I WON'T HAVE IT, KE'AKUA!
ROAAAAAAAAARRRRR

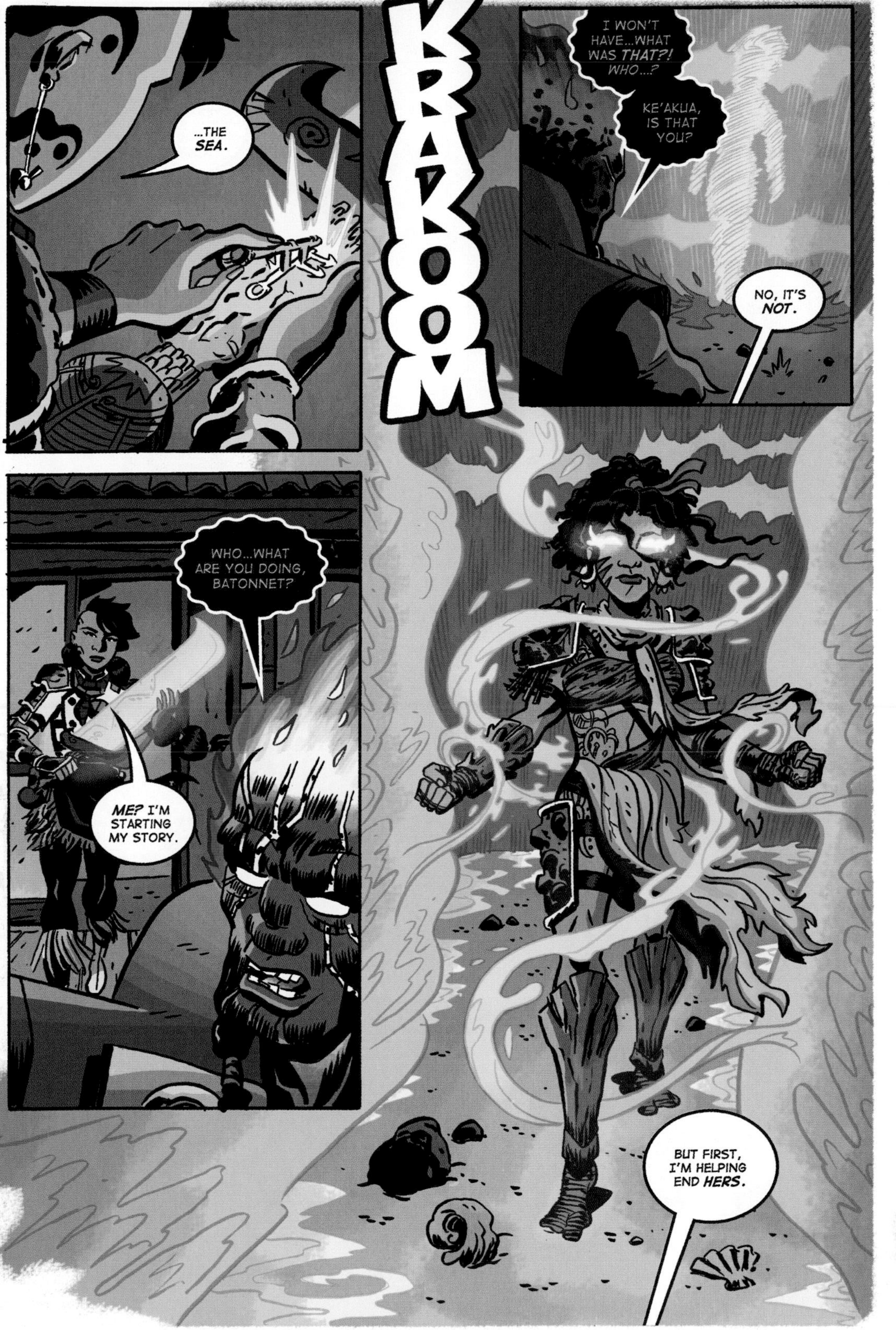
...THE SEA.
KRAKOOM
I WON'T HAVE...WHAT WAS THAT?! WHO...?
KE'AKUA, IS THAT YOU?
NO, IT'S NOT.
WHO...WHAT ARE YOU DOING, BATONNET?
ME? I'M STARTING MY STORY.
BUT FIRST, I'M HELPING END HERS.

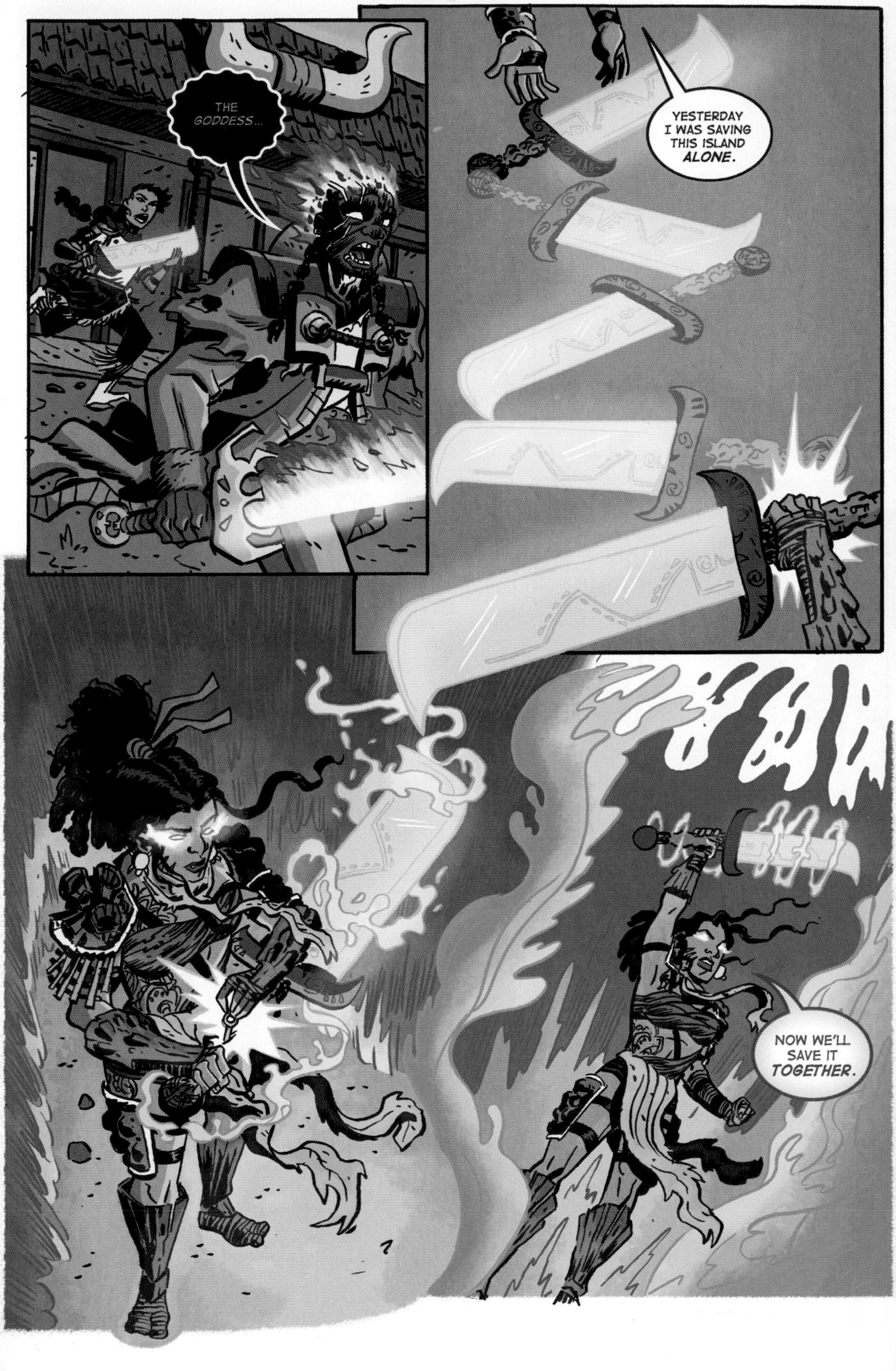
THE GODDESS...
YESTERDAY I WAS SAVING THIS ISLAND ALONE.
NOW WE'LL SAVE IT TOGETHER.

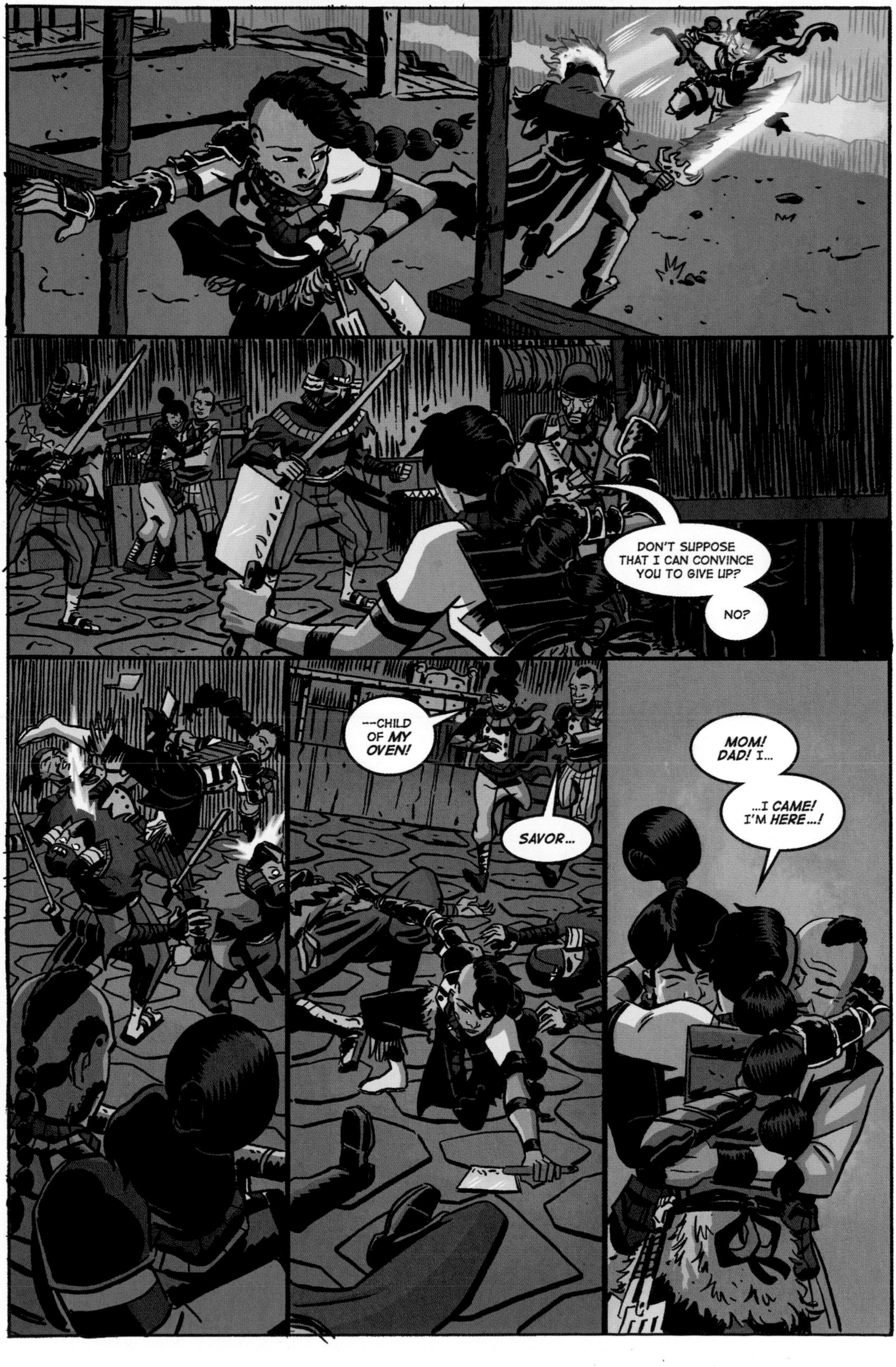
DON'T SUPPOSE THAT I CAN CONVINCE YOU TO GIVE UP?
NO?
--CHILD OF MY OVEN!
SAVOR...
MOM! DAD! I...
...I CAME! I'M HERE...!

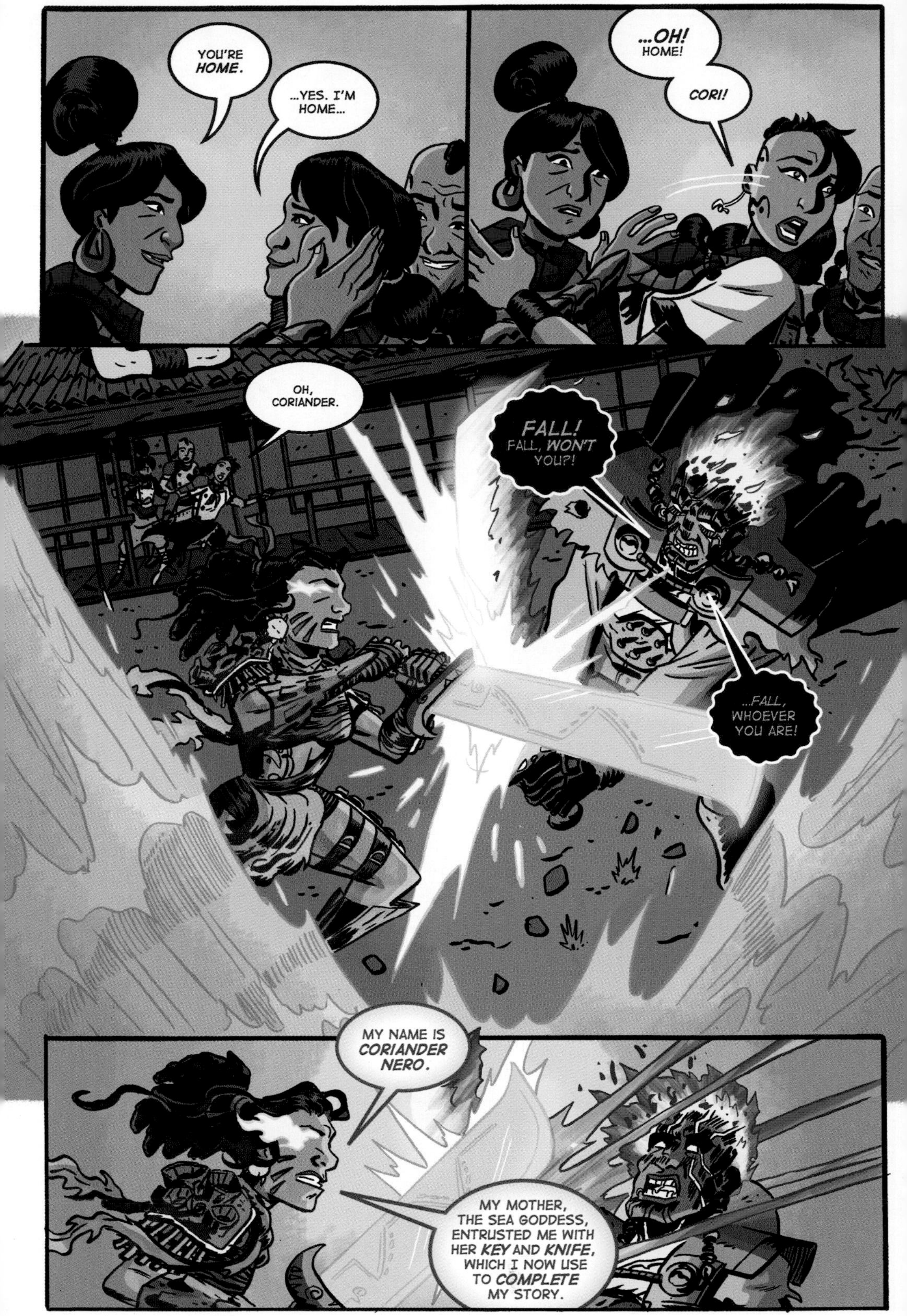

YOU'RE HOME.
...YES. I'M HOME...
...OH! HOME!
CORI!
OH, CORIANDER.
FALL! FALL, WON'T YOU?!
...FALL, WHOEVER YOU ARE!
MY NAME IS CORIANDER NERO.
MY MOTHER, THE SEA GODDESS, ENTRUSTED ME WITH HER KEY AND KNIFE, WHICH I NOW USE TO COMPLETE MY STORY.

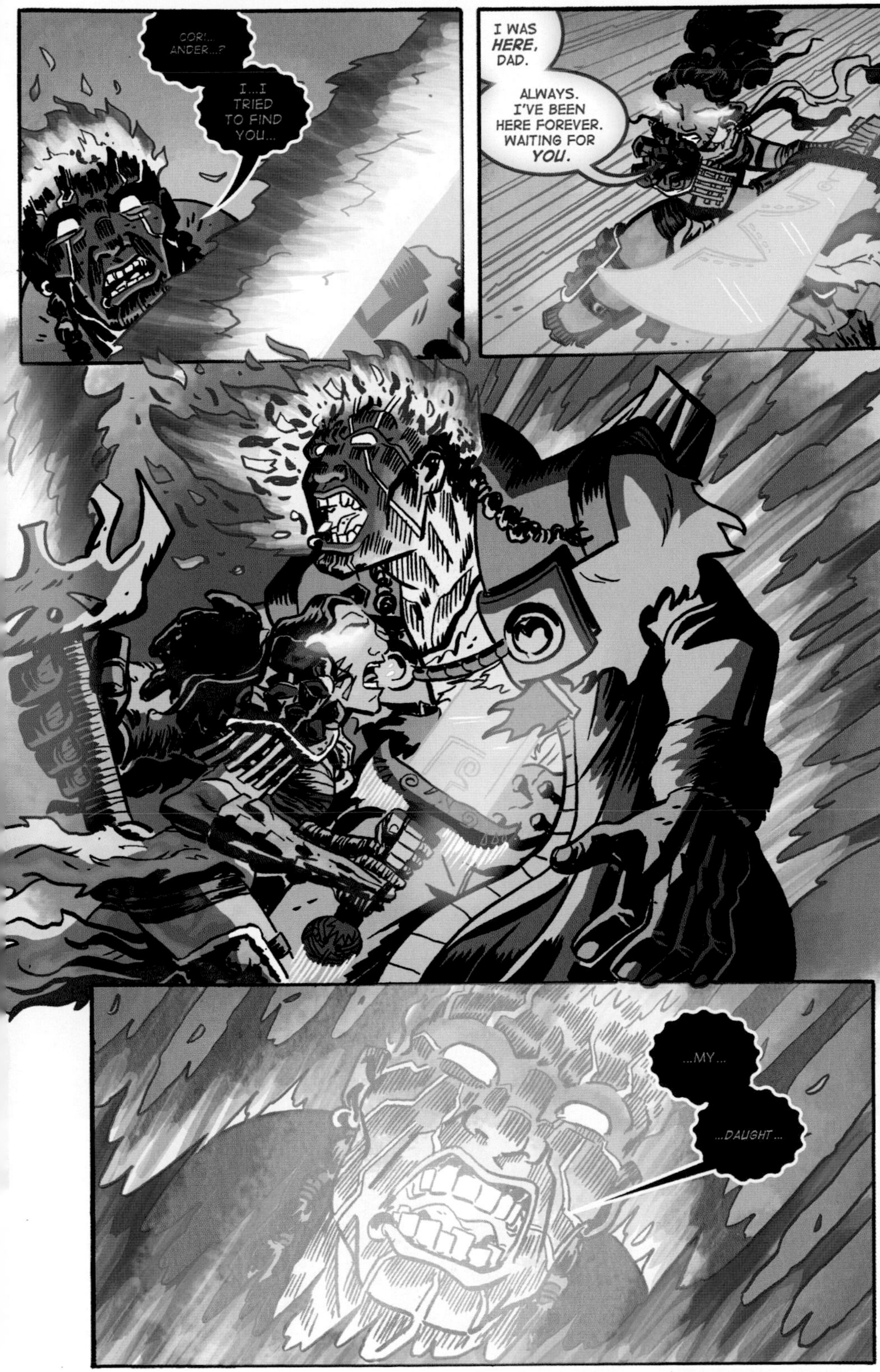
CORI... ANDER...?
I...I TRIED TO FIND YOU...
I WAS HERE, DAD.
ALWAYS. I'VE BEEN HERE FOREVER. WAITING FOR YOU.
...MY...
...DAUGHT...

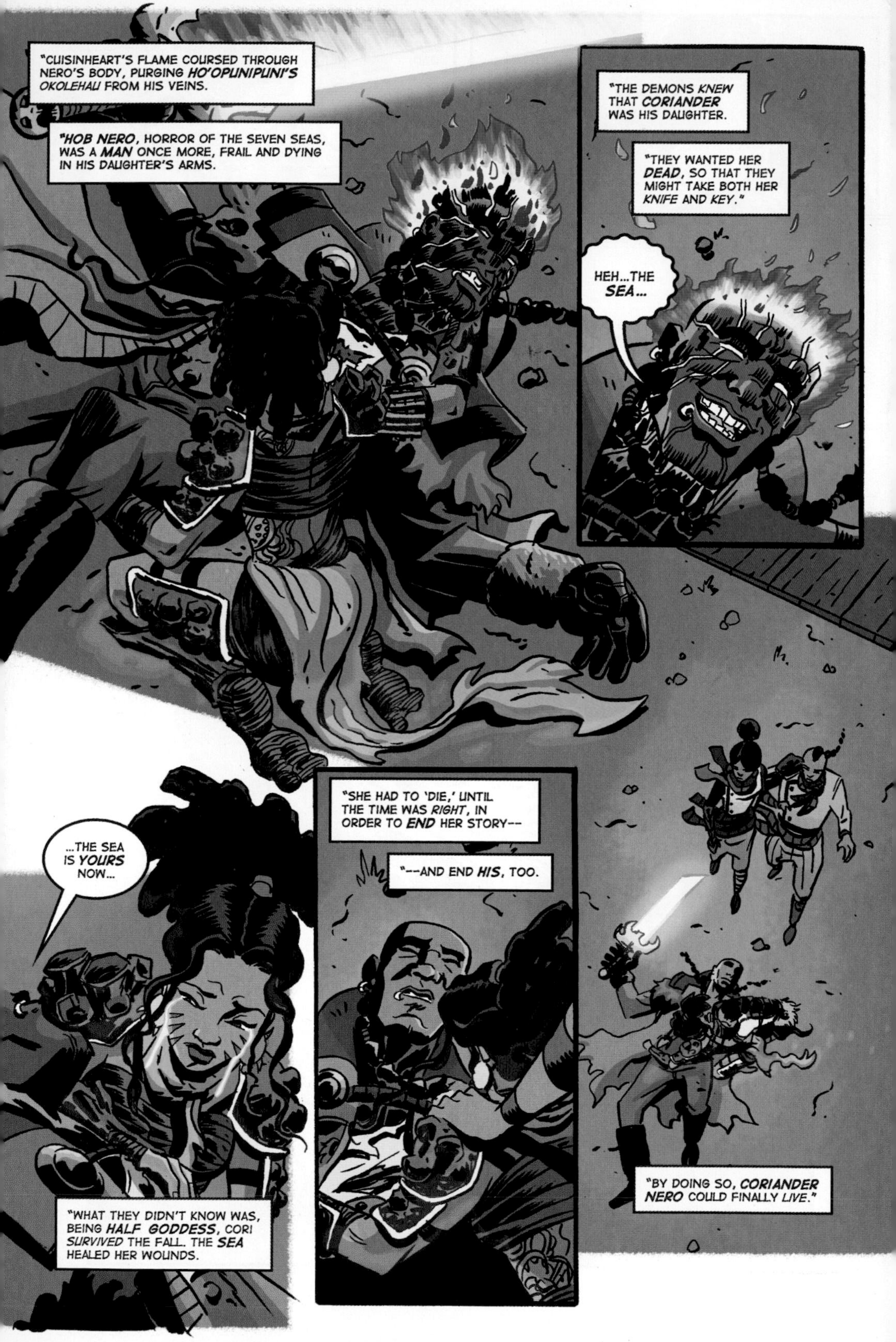
"CUISINHEART'S FLAME COURSED THROUGH NERO'S BODY, PURGING HO'OPUNIPUNI'S OKOLEHAU FROM HIS VEINS.
"HOB NERO, HORROR OF THE SEVEN SEAS, WAS A MAN ONCE MORE, FRAIL AND DYING IN HIS DAUGHTER'S ARMS.
"THE DEMONS KNEW THAT CORIANDER WAS HIS DAUGHTER.
"THEY WANTED HER DEAD, SO THAT THEY MIGHT TAKE BOTH HER KNIFE AND KEY."
HEH...THE SEA...
...THE SEA IS YOURS NOW...
"WHAT THEY DIDN'T KNOW WAS, BEING HALF GODDESS, CORI SURVIVED THE FALL. THE SEA HEALED HER WOUNDS.
"SHE HAD TO 'DIE,' UNTIL THE TIME WAS RIGHT, IN ORDER TO END HER STORY--
"--AND END HIS, TOO.
"BY DOING SO, CORIANDER NERO COULD FINALLY LIVE."

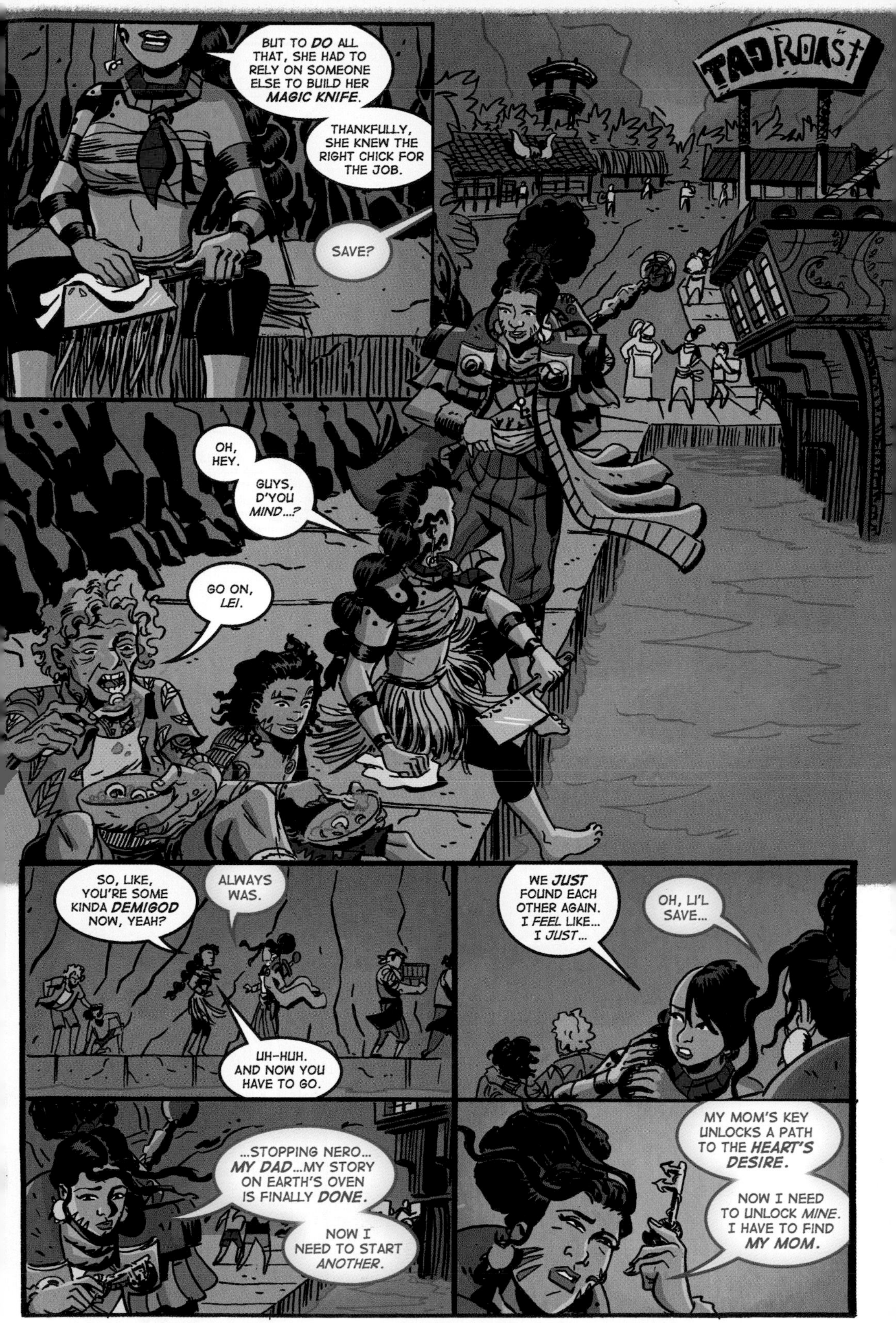

TAD ROAST
BUT TO DO ALL THAT, SHE HAD TO RELY ON SOMEONE ELSE TO BUILD HER MAGIC KNIFE.
THANKFULLY, SHE KNEW THE RIGHT CHICK FOR THE JOB.
SAVE?
OH, HEY.
GUYS, D'YOU MIND...?
GO ON, LEI.
SO, LIKE, YOU'RE SOME KINDA DEMIGOD NOW, YEAH?
ALWAYS WAS.
UH-HUH. AND NOW YOU HAVE TO GO.
WE JUST FOUND EACH OTHER AGAIN. I FEEL LIKE... I JUST...
OH, LI'L SAVE...
...STOPPING NERO... MY DAD...MY STORY ON EARTH'S OVEN IS FINALLY DONE.
NOW I NEED TO START ANOTHER.
MY MOM'S KEY UNLOCKS A PATH TO THE HEART'S DESIRE.
NOW I NEED TO UNLOCK MINE. I HAVE TO FIND MY MOM.

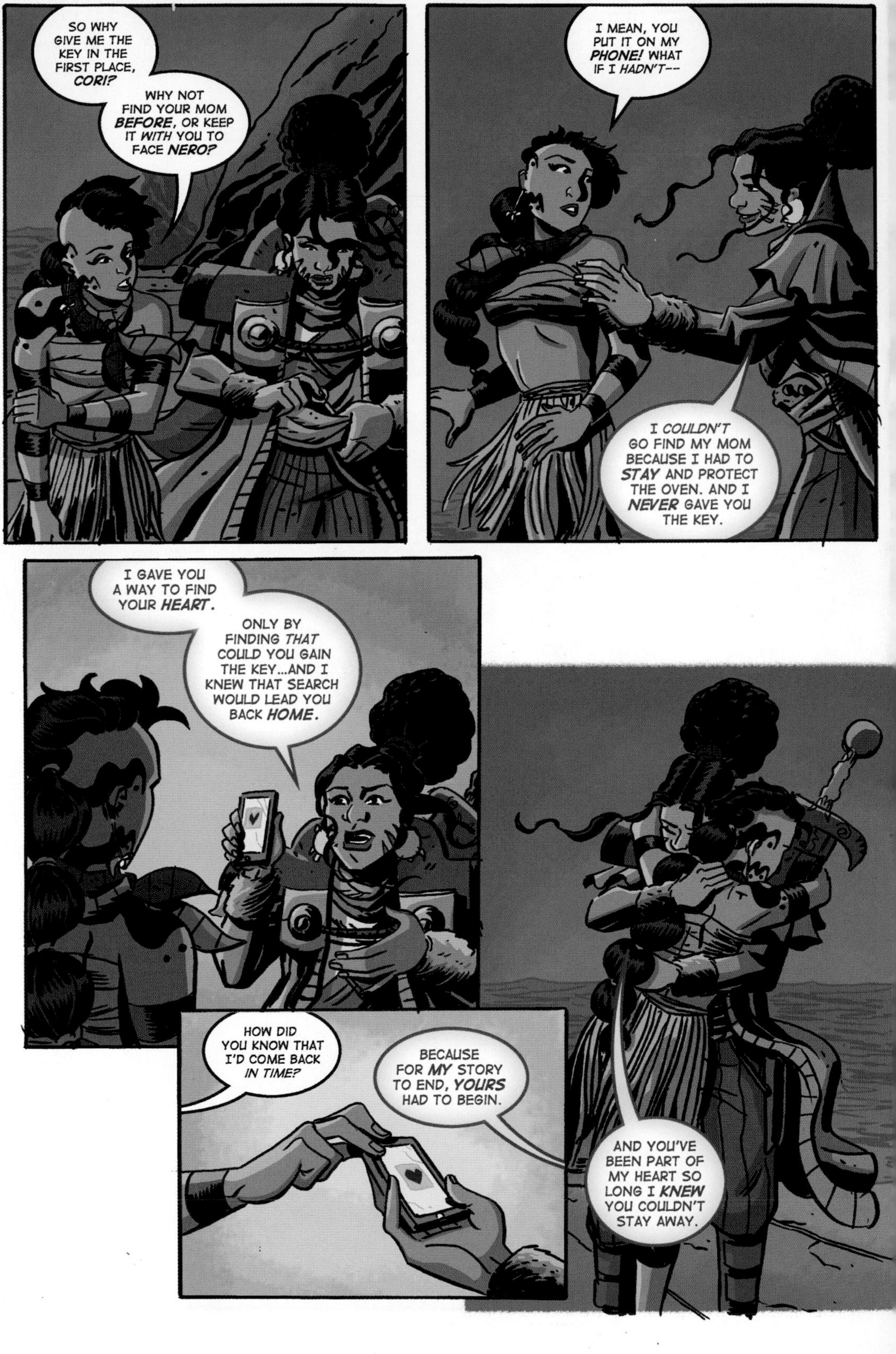
SO WHY GIVE ME THE KEY IN THE FIRST PLACE, CORI?
WHY NOT FIND YOUR MOM BEFORE, OR KEEP IT WITH YOU TO FACE NERO?
I MEAN, YOU PUT IT ON MY PHONE! WHAT IF I HADN'T--
I COULDN'T GO FIND MY MOM BECAUSE I HAD TO STAY AND PROTECT THE OVEN. AND I NEVER GAVE YOU THE KEY.
I GAVE YOU A WAY TO FIND YOUR HEART.
ONLY BY FINDING THAT COULD YOU GAIN THE KEY...AND I KNEW THAT SEARCH WOULD LEAD YOU BACK HOME.
HOW DID YOU KNOW THAT I'D COME BACK IN TIME?
BECAUSE FOR MY STORY TO END, YOURS HAD TO BEGIN.
AND YOU'VE BEEN PART OF MY HEART SO LONG I KNEW YOU COULDN'T STAY AWAY.

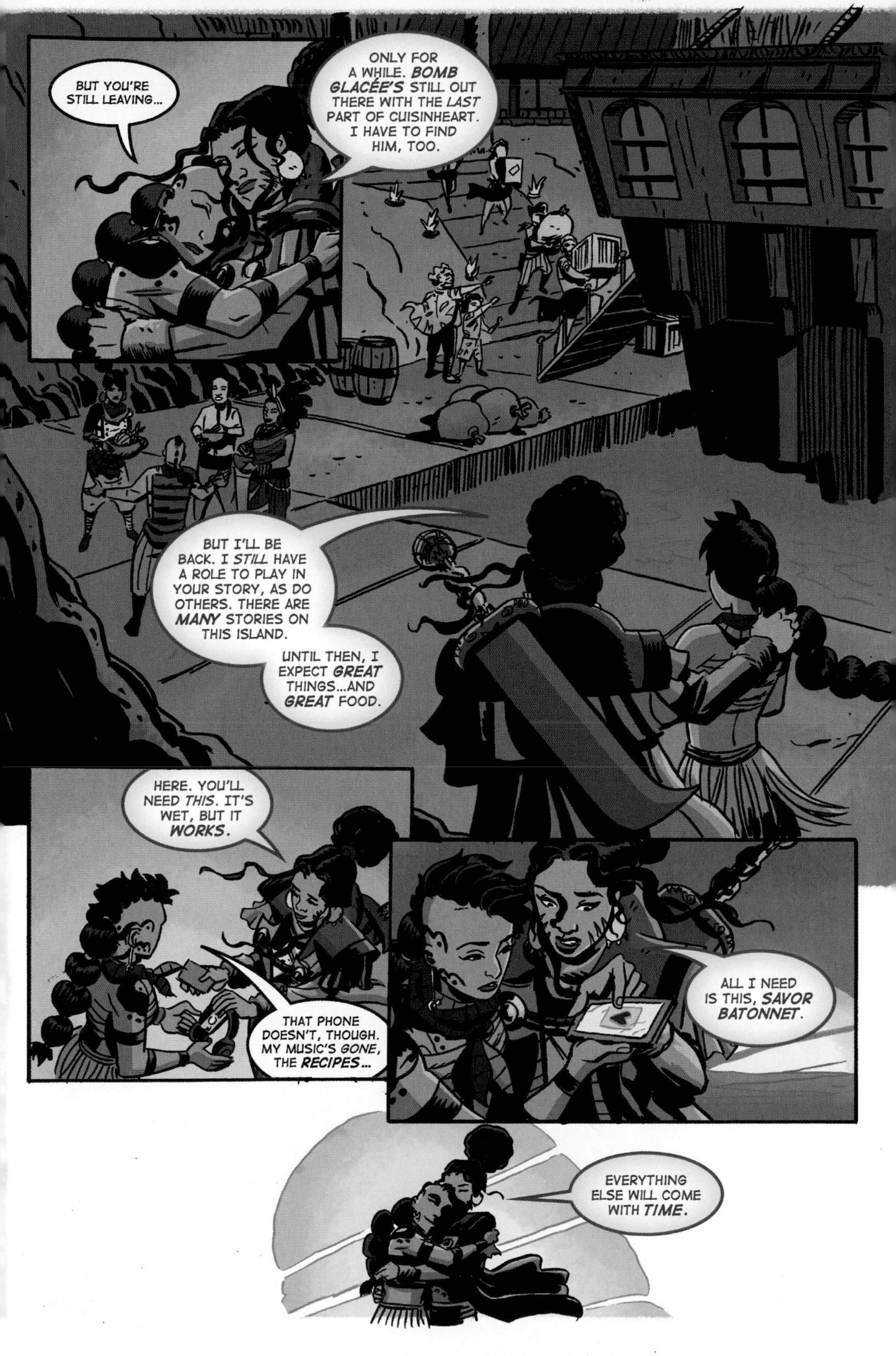
BUT YOU'RE STILL LEAVING...
ONLY FOR A WHILE. BOMB GLACÉE'S STILL OUT THERE WITH THE LAST PART OF CUISINHEART. I HAVE TO FIND HIM, TOO.
BUT I'LL BE BACK. I STILL HAVE A ROLE TO PLAY IN YOUR STORY, AS DO OTHERS. THERE ARE MANY STORIES ON THIS ISLAND.
UNTIL THEN, I EXPECT GREAT THINGS...AND GREAT FOOD.
HERE. YOU'LL NEED THIS. IT'S WET, BUT IT WORKS.
THAT PHONE DOESN'T, THOUGH. MY MUSIC'S GONE, THE RECIPES...
ALL I NEED IS THIS, SAVOR BATONNET.
EVERYTHING ELSE WILL COME WITH TIME.

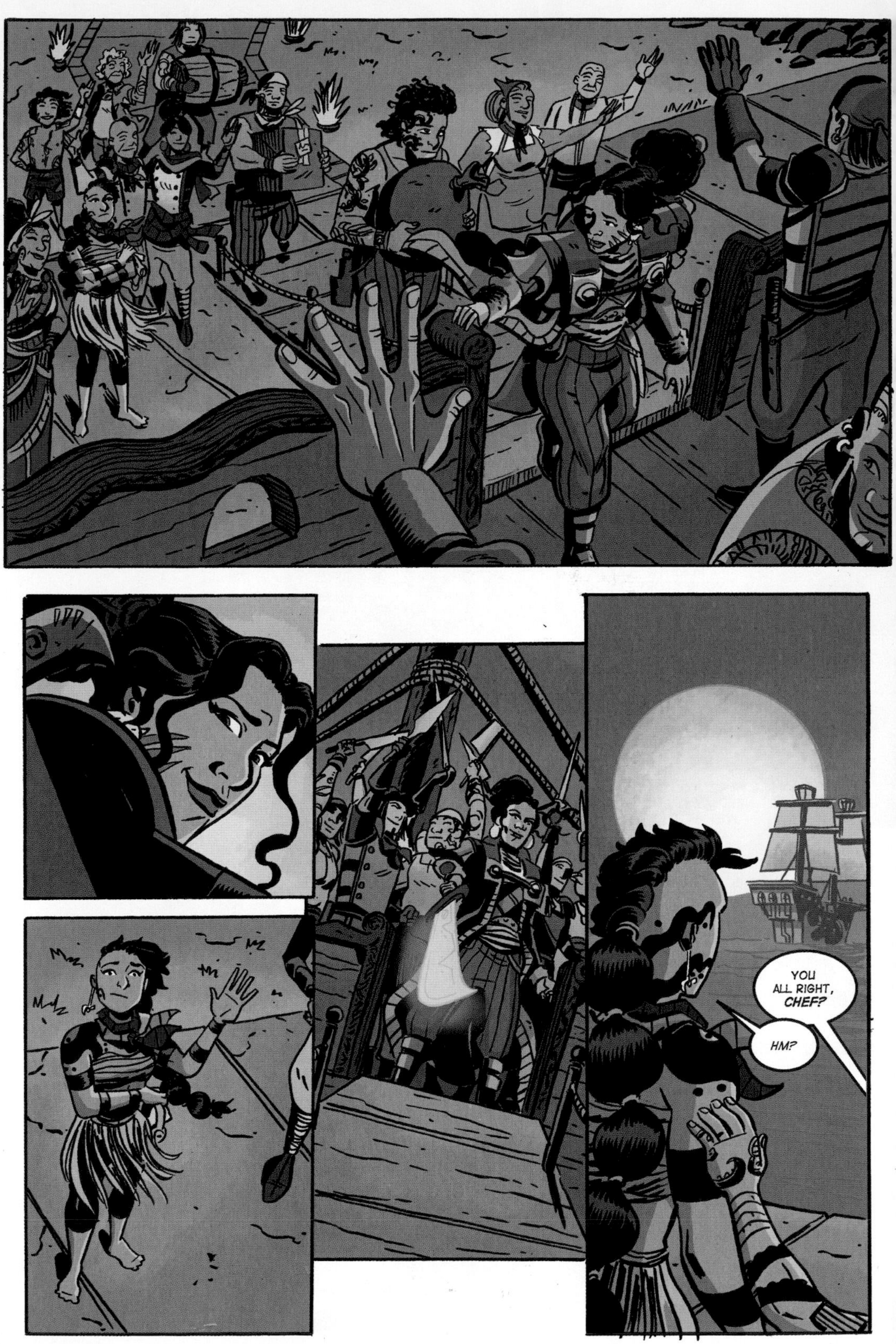
YOU ALL RIGHT, CHEF?
HM?

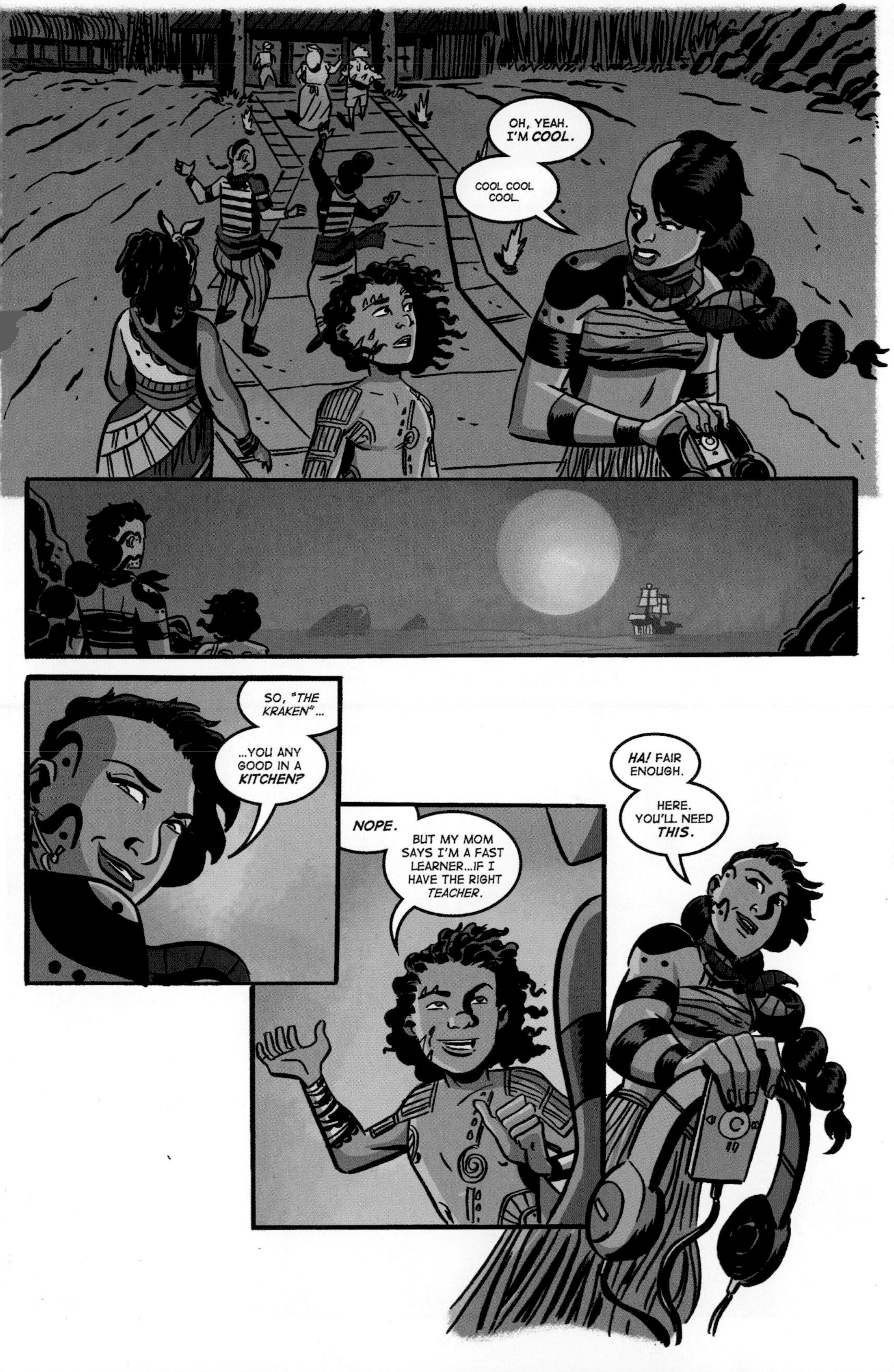
OH, YEAH. I'M COOL.
COOL COOL COOL.
SO, "THE KRAKEN"...
...YOU ANY GOOD IN A KITCHEN?
NOPE.
BUT MY MOM SAYS I'M A FAST LEARNER...IF I HAVE THE RIGHT TEACHER.
HA! FAIR ENOUGH.
HERE. YOU'LL NEED THIS.

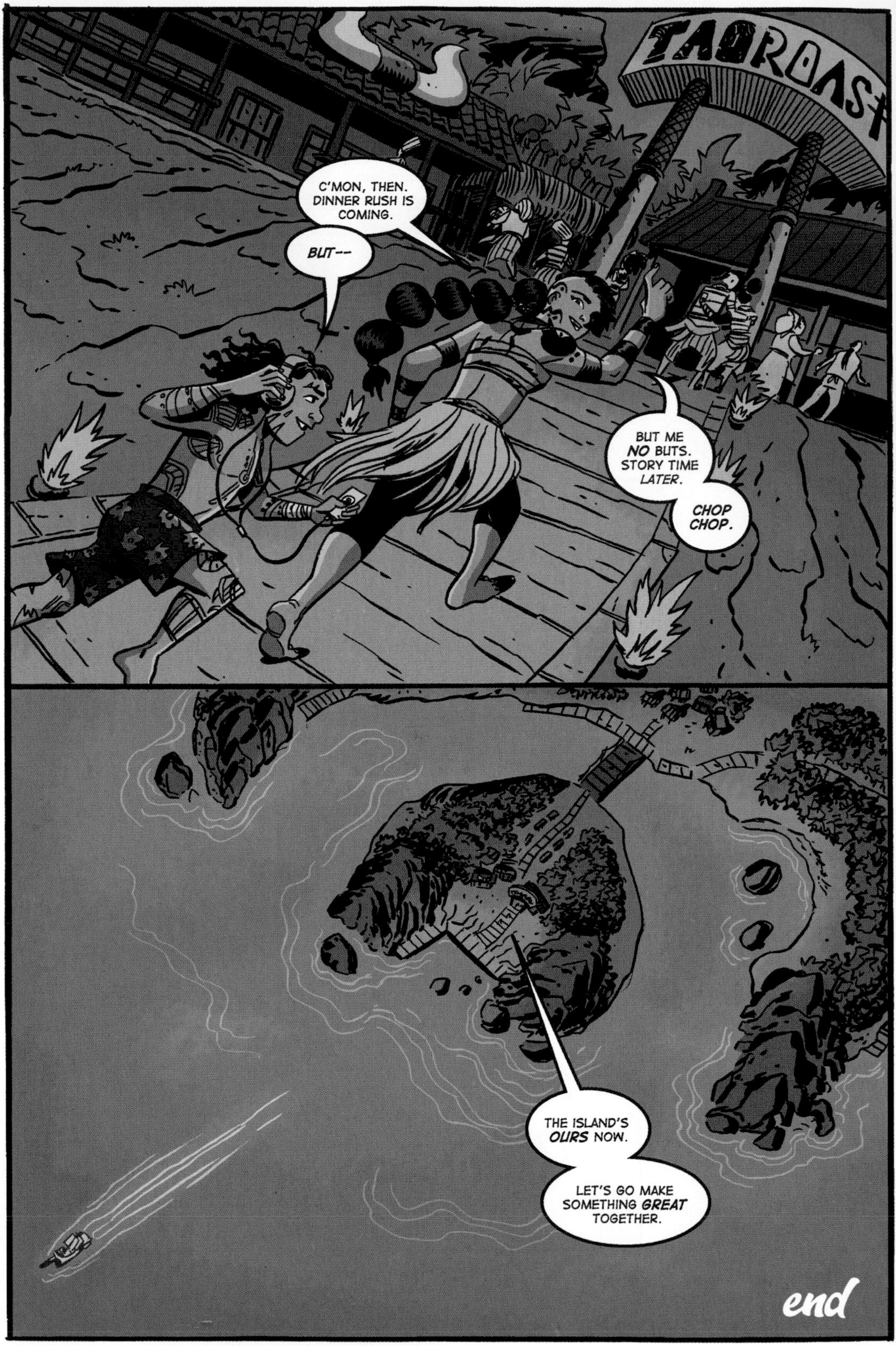
TAOROAS
C'MON, THEN. DINNER RUSH IS COMING.
BUT--
BUT ME NO BUTS. STORY TIME LATER.
CHOP CHOP.
THE ISLAND'S OURS NOW.
LET'S GO MAKE SOMETHING GREAT TOGETHER.
end

EARTH'S OVEN

Savor's Journey

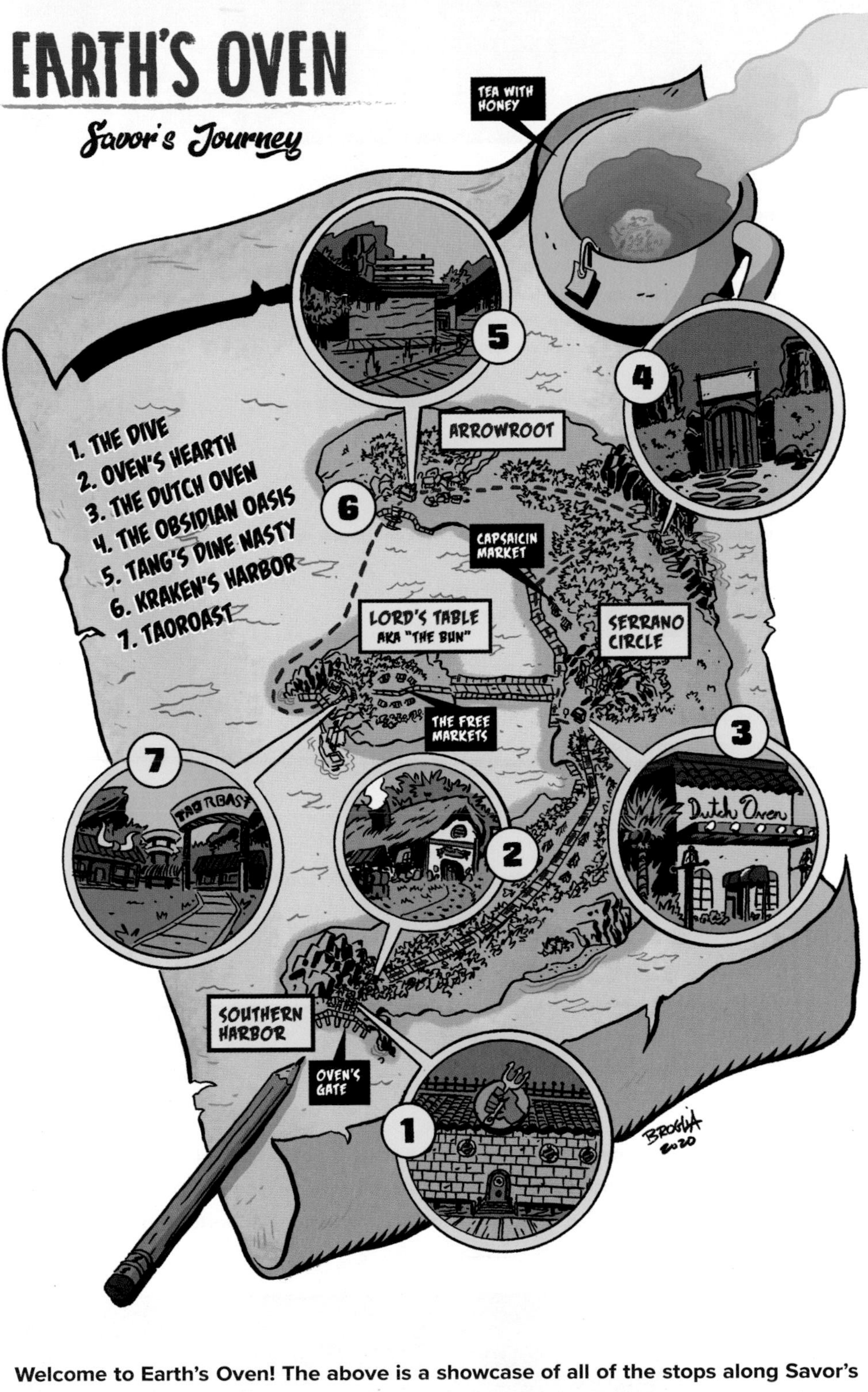
TEA WITH HONEY
1. THE DIVE
2. OVEN'S HEARTH
3. THE DUTCH OVEN
4. THE OBSIDIAN OASIS
5. TANG'S DINE NASTY
6. KRAKEN'S HARBOR
7. TAOROAST
5
4
ARROWROOT
6
CAPSAICIN MARKET
LORD'S TABLE AKA "THE BUN"
SERRANO CIRCLE
THE FREE MARKETS
3
7
2
Dutch Oven
SOUTHERN HARBOR
OVEN'S GATE
1
BROGLIA 2020

Welcome to Earth's Oven! The above is a showcase of all of the stops along Savor's journey to rescue her parents, as well as the island. Also, who doesn't love a good map?

Page 89 (5 PANELS)

PANEL ONE
Savor places a hand on the riverbank (in the obsidian sack) sitting on the table — She's on the left of the panel, Mary on the right across the table. Mary leans forward with Hong's rib-on-a-knife, dangling it as she eagerly sits forward to bait Savor.

SAVOR: What? Are you saying that you have Ke'akua's magic key?

MARY: If I am, what will you do for it?

PANEL TWO
Savor stares, no emotion, gauging the moment as pirates and demons look on.

PANEL THREE
Resigned, Savor begins to put in her ear buds.

SAVOR: You're totally gonna make me fight, aren't you?

PANEL FIVE
Mary stands, holding out one hand in an explanatory gesture as she casually gestures to her band of pirates with the rib-on-a-knife. Savor's outnumbered . . . Hong cowers.

MARY: Wait, wait . . . look around, chef. You'd never win.

MARY: But I agree. Instead of fighting, what would you say to a different test of skills?

SAVOR: Go on . . .

Here is one example of the process of a page, from script to finalized art! Each step of the process has input from the full creative team, and it's always a treat to see what Neil, John, or Frank have brought wonderfully to life!

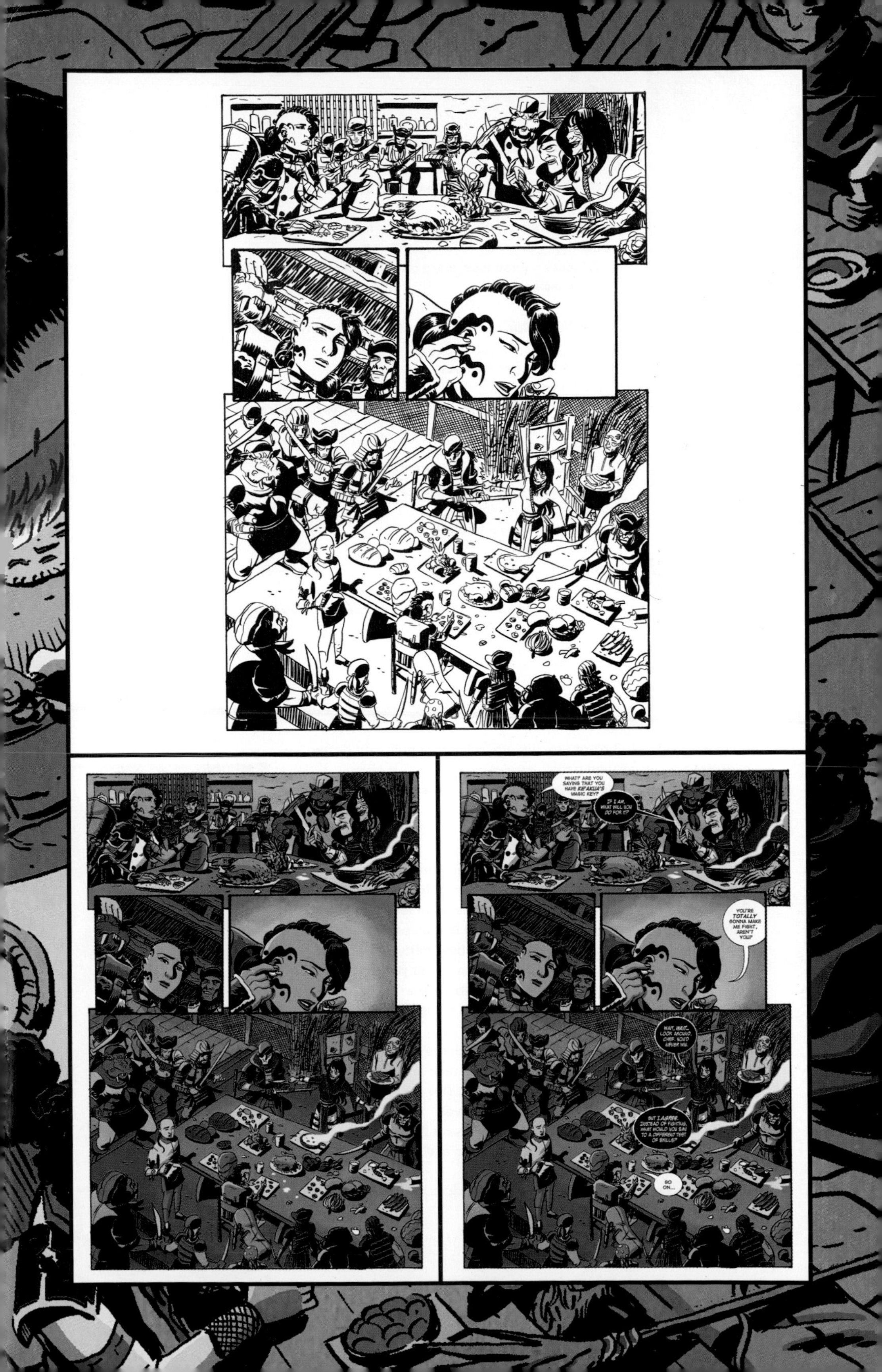
WHAT? ARE YOU SAYING THAT YOU HAVE KE'AKUA'S MAGIC KEY?
IF I AM, WHAT WILL YOU DO FOR IT?
YOU'RE TOTALLY GONNA MAKE ME FIGHT, AREN'T YOU?
WAIT, WAIT— LOOK AROUND, CHEF. YOU'D NEVER WIN.
BUT I AGREE. INSTEAD OF FIGHTING, WHAT WOULD YOU SAY TO A DIFFERENT TEST OF SKILLS?
GO ON...

Taoroast Laulau Slider

- Good on its own, but Mama Clara likes to include it in plate lunch *(like a bento; takeaway eating)*
- *Laulau* translates as "leaf leaf"—lu'au (taro) leaf on the inside, ti leaf outside
- Ti leaves = good luck; ward off evil spirits *(Boil and simmer an essence of ti to coat my knives?)*

Ingredients:

- 18–30 lu'au (taro) leaves
- 6 ti leaves
- 2 lbs ground beef (80/20) *(Most laulau contain butterfish, but Dad likes his beef!)*
- 1 egg
- 1 cup unseasoned bread crumbs
- 1 lb pork belly, cubed into 1/2-inch pieces
- 1/2 lb minced onion
- 1/2 lb cubed sweet potato
- 1 tbsp oregano
- Sea salt
- 6 Hawaiian slider rolls
- Optional: hot sauce *(Fill a misting bottle: use on your slider or to attack!)*

Directions:

For Beef:

1. Place the beef in a bowl with egg, bread crumbs, 1 tbsp salt, 1 tbsp oregano. Knead until thoroughly combined.
2. Take approx. 2–3 oz of the mixture, roll into a ball, and flatten slightly, forming a rough patty.
3. Set six patties aside on a plate or clean surface.

For Laulau:

1. Wash leaves, chop bottom stem of lu'au (taro) leaves into 1/2-inch pieces, set aside. Pat ti leaves dry and remove thickest center vein.
2. Cut 3–5 taro leaves in half. Create two stacks of leaves from the halves, placing each on flat surface, largest leaf on bottom.
3. In center of one stack of leaves, place a beef patty, a few cubes of pork belly, some of the onion, and some sweet potato. Add in several chopped taro leaf stems. Sprinkle liberally with sea salt.
4. Fold the taro leaves, wrapping fillings into a tight bundle. Repeat with rest of leaves and fillings.
5. Cut a ti leaf in half, then stack in a cross shape on a flat surface. Put a taro leaf bundle in the center of the stack and fully enclose with the ti leaves, tying the ends if possible. *(You can use twine. Also good as a garrote.)* Repeat with remaining leaves.
6. Steam six bundles in a slow cooker on low for 2–3 hours.
7. Unwrap ti leaf. Place taro leaf bundle onto a slider roll. *(optional: lightly spray with hot sauce.)*
8. Serve 2–3 sliders on a plate alongside pickles and either rice or yam fries.